PRAISE FOR THE KATE DANIELS NOVELS

MAGIC STRIKES

"This is one series that is on my 'absolutely must buy' list." —*Literary Escapism*

"A compelling urban fantasy filled with intrigue, magic, and action . . . Fans of Charlaine Harris and Kim Harrison will want to read *Magic Strikes*."—*Genre Go Round Reviews*

MAGIC BURNS

"Fans of Carrie Vaughn and Patricia Briggs will appreciate this fast-paced, action-packed urban fantasy full of magic, vampires, werebeasties, and things that go bump in the night." —*Monsters and Critics*

"With all her problems, secrets, and prowess both martial and magical, Kate is a great, kick-ass heroine, a tough girl with a heart, and her adventures . . . are definitely worth checking out." —*Locus*

"[*Magic Burns*] hooked me completely. With a fascinating, compelling plot, a witty, intelligent heroine, a demonic villain, and clever, wry humor throughout, this story has it all." —*Fresh Fiction*

"A new take on the urban fantasy genre, the world Kate inhabits is a blend of gritty magic and dangerous mystery." —*The Parkersburg Sentinel*

"The sexual tension Kate emits has me gritting my teeth." —*SFRevu*

continued...

"An excellent start to a brand-new series."

"Fans of *CSI* . . . *The X-Files*, and any other of a host of such subgenre offerings should be pleased."

"A perfectly paced supernatural mystery with bits of dark humor and—if you'll forgive the pun—a fair amount of bite."

"The strong story line coupled with a complex alternative history . . . will have readers hoping for more."

"*Magic Bites* is an enchanting paranormal whodunit that takes the supernatural into new, natural directions."

"[Andrews's] world building and characterizations are exceptional . . . *Magic Bites* is not to be overlooked."

"A unique world laced with a thick plot full of strife, betrayal, and mystery."

"The plot moves along at a pleasant clip, and the world building is interesting and well-done."

ON THE
EDGE

ILONA ANDREWS

ACE BOOKS, NEW YORK

THE BERKLEY PUBLISHING GROUP
Published by the Penguin Group
Penguin Group (USA) Inc.
375 Hudson Street, New York, New York 10014, USA
Penguin Group (Canada), 90 Eglinton Avenue East, Suite 700, Toronto, Ontario M4P 2Y3, Canada
(a division of Pearson Penguin Canada Inc.)
Penguin Books Ltd., 80 Strand, London WC2R 0RL, England
Penguin Group Ireland, 25 St. Stephen's Green, Dublin 2, Ireland (a division of Penguin Books Ltd.)
Penguin Group (Australia), 250 Camberwell Road, Camberwell, Victoria 3124, Australia
(a division of Pearson Australia Group Pty. Ltd.)
Penguin Books India Pvt. Ltd., 11 Community Centre, Panchsheel Park, New Delhi—110 017, India
Penguin Group (NZ), 67 Apollo Drive, Rosedale, North Shore 0632, New Zealand
(a division of Pearson New Zealand Ltd.)
Penguin Books (South Africa) (Pty.) Ltd., 24 Sturdee Avenue, Rosebank, Johannesburg 2196,
South Africa

Penguin Books Ltd., Registered Offices: 80 Strand, London WC2R 0RL, England

This is a work of fiction. Names, characters, places, and incidents either are the product of the authors' imaginations or are used fictitiously, and any resemblance to actual persons, living or dead, business establishments, events, or locales is entirely coincidental. The publisher does not have any control over and does not assume any responsibility for author or third-party websites or their content.

ON THE EDGE

An Ace Book / published by arrangement with the authors

PRINTING HISTORY
Ace mass-market edition / October 2009

Copyright © 2009 by Andrew Gordon and Ilona Gordon.
Excerpt from *Magic Bleeds* © by Andrew Gordon and Ilona Gordon.
Cover art by Victoria Vebell.
Cover design by Annette Fiore DeFex.
Interior text design by Kristin del Rosario.

ISBN: 978-0-441-01780-5

ACE
Ace Books are published by The Berkley Publishing Group,
a division of Penguin Group (USA) Inc.,
375 Hudson Street, New York, New York 10014.
ACE and the "A" design are trademarks of Penguin Group (USA) Inc.

PRINTED IN THE UNITED STATES OF AMERICA

10   9   8   7

To my husband.
I bet you didn't see that one coming.

Acknowledgments

This book wouldn't be possible without the efforts of Anne Sowards, my editor, who took a chance on an odd idea and whose guidance and insight once again turned a mess into a book, and without Nancy Yost, my agent, who always has my best interests at heart and saves me from myself. Thank you to both of you.

A great many people worked on this book. Thank you very much to Annette Fiore DeFex for the striking cover design; to Victoria Vebell for the stunning cover art; to Kristin del Rosario for the interior text design; to Joan Matthews for the copy edit (I have no idea how you put up with me); to production editor Michelle Kasper and assistant production editor Andromeda Macri, who oversaw the entire project; to Cameron Dufty, the editorial assistant, who fixed my emergencies; and to Ace's publicist, Rosanne Romanello, who tirelessly promoted the book. I'm deeply grateful to all of you.

Finally, thank you to all of you, the readers. Without you, none of this would be possible.

ONE

"ROSIE!" Grandpa's bellow shook the foundation of the house.

"Why me?" Rose wiped the dish-soap suds from her hands with a kitchen towel, swiped the crossbow from the hook, and stomped onto the porch.

"Roooosie!"

She kicked the screen door open. He towered in the yard, a huge, shaggy bear of a man, deranged eyes opened wide, tangled beard caked with blood and quivering grayish shreds. She leveled the crossbow at him. Drunk as hell again.

"What is it?"

"I want to go to the pub. I want a pint." His voice slipped into a whine. "Gimme some money!"

"No."

He hissed at her, swaying unsteadily on his feet. "Rosie! This is your last chance to give me a dollar!"

She sighed and shot him. The bolt bit between the eyes, and Grandpa toppled onto his back like a log. His legs drummed the ground.

Rose rested the butt of her crossbow on her hip. "All right, come out."

The two boys slipped from behind the huge oak spreading its branches over the yard. Both were filthy with reddish mud, sap, and the other unidentifiable substances an eight- and a ten-year-old could find in the Wood. A jagged scratch decorated Georgie's neck, and brown pine straw stuck out of his blond hair. Red welts marked the skin between Jack's knuckles. He saw her looking at his hands. His eyes got big, amber irises flaring yellow, and he hid his fists behind his back.

"How many times do I have to say it: don't touch the ward stones. Look at Grandpa Cletus! He's been eating dog brains again, and now he's drunk. It will take me half an hour to hose him off."

"We miss him," Georgie said.

She sighed. "I miss him, too. But he's no good to anybody drunk. Come on, you two, let's take him back to his shed. Help me get the legs."

Together they dragged Grandpa's inert form back to the shed at the edge of the clearing and dumped him on his sawdust. Rose uncoiled the metal chain from the corner, pulled it across the shed, locked the collar on Grandpa's neck, and peeled back his left eyelid to check the pupil. No red yet. Good shot—he would be out for hours.

Rose put her foot on his chest, grasped the bolt, and pulled it out with a sharp tug. She still remembered Grandpa Cletus as he was, a tall, dapper man, uncanny with his rapier, his voice flavored with a light Scottish brogue. Even as old as he was, he would still win against Dad one out of three times in a sword fight. Now he was this . . . this thing. She sighed. It hurt to look at him, but there was nothing to be done about it. As long as Georgie lived, so did Grandpa Cletus.

The boys brought the hose. She turned it on, set the sprayer on jet, and leveled the stream at Grandpa until all the blood and dog meat were gone. She had never quite figured out how "going down to the pub" equaled chasing stray dogs and eating their brains, but when Grandpa got out of his ward circle, no mutt was safe. By the time she was done washing him, the hole in his forehead had closed. When Georgie raised things from the dead, he didn't just give them life. He made them almost indestructible.

Rose stepped out of the shed, locked the door behind her, and dragged the hose back to the porch. Her skin prickled as she crossed the invisible boundary: the kids must've put the ward stones back. She squinted at the grass. There they were, a line of small, seemingly ordinary rocks, spaced three, four feet from each other. Each rock held a small magic charge. Together they created an enchanted barrier, strong enough to keep Grandpa in the shed if he broke the chain again.

Rose waved the boys to the side and raised the hose. "Your turn."

They flinched at the cold water. She washed them off methodically, from top to bottom. As the mud melted from Jack's feet, she saw a two-inch rip in his Skechers. Rose dropped the hose.

"Jack!"

He cringed.

"Those are forty-five-dollar shoes!"

"I'm sorry," he whispered.

"Tomorrow is the first school day! What were you doing?"

"He was climbing up the pines to get at the leech birds," Georgie said.

She glared. "Georgie! Thirty-minute time-out tonight for snitching."

Georgie bit his lip.

Rose stared at Jack. "Is that true? You were chasing the leech birds?"

"I can't help it. Their tails are so flittery . . ."

She wanted to smack him. It was true, he couldn't help it—it wasn't his fault he was born as a cat—but those were brand-new shoes she had bought him for school. Shoes for which she had painstakingly tweaked their budget, scrimping every penny, so he wouldn't have to wear Georgie's old beat-up sneakers, so he could look just as nice as all the other second graders. It just hurt.

Jack's face pinched into a rigid white mask—he was about to cry.

A small spark of power tugged on her. "Georgie, stop trying to resurrect the shoes. They were never alive in the first place."

The spark died.

An odd desperation claimed her, her pain shifting into a sort of numbness. Pressure built in her chest. She was so sick of it, sick of counting every dollar, sick of rationing everything, sick to death of it all. She had to go and get Jack a new pair of shoes. Not for Jack's sake, but for the sake of her own sanity. Rose had no clue how she would make up the money, but she knew she had to buy him a new pair of shoes right now, or she would explode.

"Jack, do you remember what will happen if a leech bird bites you?"

"I'll turn into one?"

"Yes. You have to stop chasing the birds."

He hung his head. "Am I punished?"

"Yes. I'm too mad to punish you right now. We'll talk about it when we get home. Go brush your teeth, comb your hair, put on dry clothes, and get the guns. We're going to Wal-Mart."

THE old Ford truck bounced on the bumps in the dirt road. The rifles clanged on the floor. Georgie put his feet down to steady them without being asked.

Rose sighed. Here, in the Edge, she could protect them well enough. But they were about to pass from the Edge into another world, and their magic would die in the crossing. The two hunting rifles on the floor would be their only defense. Rose felt a pang of guilt. If it wasn't for her, they wouldn't need the rifles. God, she didn't want to be jumped again. Not with her brothers in the car.

They lived between worlds: on one side lay the Weird and the other the Broken. Two dimensions, existing side by side, like mirror images of each other. In the place where the dimensions "touched," they intersected slightly, forming a narrow ribbon of land that belonged to both of them—the Edge. In the Weird, magic pooled deeply; in the Edge it was a shallow trickle. But in the Broken, no magic shielded them at all.

Rose eyed the Wood hugging the road, its massive trees crowding the narrow ribbon of packed dirt. She drove this way every day to her job in the Broken, but today the shadows between the gnarled trunks filled her with anxiety.

"Let's play the 'You Can't' game," she said to stave off the rising dread. "Georgie, you go first."

"He went first the last time!" Jack's eyes shone with amber. "Nyaha!"

"Yaha!"

"Georgie goes first," she repeated.

"Past the boundary, you can't raise dead things," Georgie said.

"Past the boundary, you can't grow fur and claws," Jack said.

They always played the game when driving through to the Broken. It was a good reminder to the boys of what they could and could not do, and it worked much better than any lecture. Very few people in the Broken knew of the Edge or the Weird, and it was safer for everyone involved to keep it that way. Experience had taught her that trying to explain the existence of magic to a person in the Broken would do no good. It wouldn't get you committed into a mental institution, but it did land you into the kooky idiot category and made people give you a wide berth during lunch hour.

For most people of the Broken, there was no Broken, no Edge, and no Weird. They lived in the United States of America, on the continent of North America, on the planet Earth—and that was that. For their part, most people in the Weird couldn't see the boundary either. It took a special kind of person to find it, and the kids needed to remember that.

Georgie touched her hand. It was her turn. "Past the boundary, you can't hide behind a ward stone." She glanced at them, but they kept going, oblivious to her fears.

The road lay deserted. Few Edgers drove up this way this time of the evening. Rose accelerated, eager to get the trip over with and be back to the safety of the house.

"Past the boundary, you can't find lost things," Georgie said.

"Past the boundary, you can't see in the dark." Jack grinned.

"Past the boundary, you can't flash," Rose said.

The flash was her greatest weapon. Most Edgers had their own specific talents: some prophesied, some cured toothaches, some raised the dead like Georgie. Some cursed like Rose and her grandmother. But flashing could be learned by anyone with a drop of magic. It wasn't a matter of talent but of practice. You took ahold of the magic inside you and channeled it from your body in a controlled burst that looked like a whip or a ribbon of lightning. If you had magic and patience, you could learn to flash, and the lighter the color of your flash, the hotter and more potent it was. A powerful bright flash was a terrible weapon. It could slice through a body like a hot knife through butter. Most Edgers never could get their flash bright enough to kill or injure anything with it. They were mongrels, living in a place of diluted magic, and most flashed red and dark orange. Some lucky few managed green or blue.

It was her flash that had started all of their trouble.

No, Rose reflected, they'd had plenty of trouble before her. Draytons were always unlucky. Too smart and too twisted for their own good. Grandpa was a pirate and a rover. Dad was a gold digger. Grandma was stubborn like a goat and always thought she knew better than anyone else. Mom was a tramp. But all those problems didn't affect anyone but the individual Draytons. When Rose flashed white at the Graduation Fair, she focused the attention of countless Edge families squarely on their little clan. Even now, even with the rifles on the floor, she didn't regret it. She felt guilty about it, she wished things hadn't gone the way they did, but given a chance, she would do it again.

Ahead the road curved. Rose took the turn a bit too fast. The truck's springs creaked.

A man stood in the road, like a gray smudge against the encroaching twilight.

She slammed on the brakes. The Ford skidded in a screech on the hard, dry dirt of the road. She caught a glimpse of long pale hair and piercing green eyes staring straight at her.

The truck hurtled at him. She couldn't stop it.

The man leapt straight up. Feet in dark gray boots landed on the hood of the truck with a thud and vanished. The man vaulted over the roof to the side and disappeared into the trees.

The truck slid to a stop. Rose gulped the air. Her heart fluttered in her chest. Her fingertips tingled, and she tasted bitterness on her tongue.

She stabbed the seat belt release button, threw the door open, and jumped out onto the road. "Are you hurt?"

The Wood lay quiet.

"Hello?"

No answer. The man was gone.

"Rose, who was that?" Georgie's eyes were the size of small saucers.

"I don't know." Relief flooded her. She hadn't hit him. She got scared out of her wits, but she hadn't hit him. Everybody was fine. Nobody was hurt. Everybody was fine . . .

"Did you see the swords?" Jack asked.

"What swords?" All she'd seen were the blond hair, green eyes, and some kind of cloak. She couldn't even recall his face—just a pale smudge.

"He had a sword," Georgie said. "On his back."

"Two swords," Jack corrected. "One on the back and one on his belt."

Some of the older locals liked to play with swords, but none of them had long blond hair. And none of them had eyes like that. Most people facing a truck head-on would be scared. He stared her down as if she had insulted him by nearly running him over. Like he was some sort of king of the road.

Strangers were never good in the Edge. It wasn't wise to linger.

Jack sniffed the air, wrinkling his nose the way he did when he looked for a scent trail. "Let's find him."

"Let's not."

"Rose . . ."

"You're on thin ice already." She climbed into the truck and shut the door. "We're not chasing after some knucklehead who thinks he's too important to walk on the shoulder." She snorted, trying to get her heart rate under control.

Georgie opened his mouth.

"Not another word."

A couple of minutes later, they reached the boundary, the point where the Edge ended and the Broken began. Rose always recognized the precise moment when she passed into the Broken. First, anxiety stabbed right through her chest, followed by an instant of intense vertigo, and then pain. It was as if the shiver of magic, the warm spark that existed somewhere inside her, died during the crossing. The pain lasted only a blink, but she always dreaded it. It left her feeling incomplete. Broken. That's how the name for the magicless dimension had come about.

There was an identical boundary on the opposite end of the Edge, the one that guarded the passage to the Weird. She never tried to cross it. She wasn't sure her magic would be strong enough for her to survive.

They entered the Broken without any trouble. The Wood ended with the Edge. Mundane Georgia oaks and pines replaced the ancient dark trees. The dirt became pavement.

The narrow two-lane road brought them past the twin gas stations to the parkway. Rose checked the parkway for oncoming traffic, took a right, and headed toward the town of Pine Barren.

Above them an airplane thundered, fixing to land at the Savannah airport only a couple of miles away. The woods gave way to half-finished shopping plazas and construction equipment, scattered among heaps of red Georgia mud. Ponds and streams interrupted the landscape—with the coast only forty minutes away, every hole in the ground sooner or later filled up with water. They passed hotels, Comfort Inn, Knights Inn, Marriott, Embassy Suites, stopped at a light, crossed the overpass, and finally turned into a busy Wal-Mart parking lot.

Rose parked on the side and held the door open, letting the boys out. Jack's eyes had lost their amber sheen. Now they were plain dark hazel. She locked the truck, checked the door just in case—locked up tight—and headed to the brightly lit doors.

"Now remember," she said as they joined the herd of evening shoppers. "Shoes and that's it. I mean it."

TWO

NOBODY said anything until a pair of small black and blue shoes perched on Jack's feet. They weren't Skechers, but they looked similar enough. To get the real thing, she'd have to go to the mall in Savannah, and she had to save every drop of gas or she couldn't get to work. Rose crouched and mashed the top of the shoe with her finger, looking for Jack's toes. Ample room. He grew like a weed, and she always tried to buy shoes a little bigger than he needed. "Do they feel too big?"

Jack shook his head.

"Do you like them?"

Jack nodded.

"Okay," she said, glancing at the price tag. Twenty-seven ninety-nine. She would've bought them even if it said fifty.

The boys watched her very quietly, standing in the aisle like a pair of frightened rabbit kittens. Rose sighed. "Would you like to look at toys?"

"Look" being the operative word. The boys stared at the action figures, transfixed by armor and muscles of colored plastic. Rose lingered by the end shelf. The stranger on the road kept popping back into her head. He wasn't local; she was sure of it.

The Edge was narrow here, only about twelve miles across. They didn't even have a real town, just a handful of houses randomly sprinkled on the outskirts of the Wood and grandly termed East Laporte. She knew all the local Edgers by sight, and she'd never come across anyone like the king of the road before. Those eyes weren't something she would forget.

If he wasn't from East Laporte, then he was probably

from the Weird. People from the Broken favored guns, not swords.

Rose bit her lip. The Edgers like her passed freely between the worlds, but crossing from the Broken or the Weird into the Edge was a different matter for those not born to it.

First, most people from the Weird and the Broken couldn't see past their respective boundary. If someone from the Broken tried to follow her into the Edge, she would vanish from their sight when she crossed. One moment she'd be there, and then she'd be gone, and they would keep right on driving in their own world. Because they couldn't sense the boundary, for them the Edge simply wasn't there. It didn't exist, like a room behind a door that forever remained closed. On the other side, most people of the Weird couldn't sense their boundary either and missed it as well, going about their regular lives, never knowing about the odd place next door that led to an even odder world.

Of course, there were always exceptions to the rule. Some people in the Broken were born with a magic talent. It lay dormant until one day they stumbled onto an unfamiliar road and decided to take it to see where it led. Some people in the Weird managed to discover the other dimension as well. And that brought the second problem: crossing the boundaries hurt.

There was nothing to be done about that. People like her lived in the Edge, because it was the only place they could retain their magic, and they worked and studied in the Broken, because that's where they made their living. But while they experienced aches and discomfort and a brief stab of pain during the crossing, a person native to the Broken or the Edge would endure agony.

Still, a few determined enough did make it through. Caravans from the Weird stopped by East Laporte every three months or so. Like most Edgers, she sank every spare dollar into buying junk from the Broken. Pepsi. Panty hose. Fancy pens. When the caravans arrived, she would carry her loot out and sell it to the caravan master at a markup or trade for the goods from the Weird, mostly odd jewelry and exotic trinkets, and then unload those goods at a couple of dealers in the Broken. A little extra money.

The caravans didn't stay long. The worlds were greedy.

Too much time in the Broken, and you'd lose your magic. Too much time in the Weird, and the magic would infect you and the Broken wouldn't let you back in. The Edgers had some immunity—they could last in either world longer than other people, but even they eventually succumbed. Peter Padrake, one of the most famous people from the Weird to have crossed into the Broken, had lost his magic years ago. He couldn't even enter the Edge anymore.

What would cause a man from the Weird to risk pain and the loss of his magic by traveling to the Edge? He didn't come with any caravan—those weren't due for another couple of weeks. It had to be some sort of emergency. Perhaps he was here for her.

That thought made her stop. No, she decided. She'd been left alone for the last three years. Most likely he hadn't come from the Weird at all. The Edge was narrow but very long, as long as the worlds themselves. It ran into the ocean in the East, but in the West it stretched for thousands of miles. True, the Wood usually kept the visitors out, but they did get travelers once in a while. They said that in the West, the Edge widened. Rumor had it that a chunk of a large Western city sat right in the Edge. Perhaps he'd come from there. Yes, that must be it.

Who cared where he'd come from anyway?

Rose sighed and picked up a big jug of bubble fluid, equipped with four wands. Georgie liked bubbles. He could keep them very still in the air for almost twenty seconds. She had already plunked down the money for the shoes. In for a penny, in for a pound. After all, Georgie hadn't done anything wrong, and Jack kind of got rewarded for ripping his new shoes. Might as well get the bubbles. It was good practice for Georgie. It would help him learn to flash . . .

It dawned on her that Jack got new shoes and Georgie would only get some lousy bubbles. It wasn't fair. No matter what she did, she just couldn't win. Gahh, what would be the right thing to do? To buy the bubbles or to buy nothing but the shoes? She wished she had a manual or something, some kind of instruction sheet that would clearly spell out what a responsible parent did in this sort of situation. Her imagination painted Georgie twenty years later, sitting in leg irons before some Broken psychiatrist. "Well, you see, it all started with bubbles . . ."

In the aisle, Georgie said something, and a deeper male voice answered. An alarm went off in her head. Rose leaned over, peeking around the bubble display. A man stood next to the boys, talking. She put down the bubbles and marched over to the newcomer.

He stood with his back to her. It was a broad, muscled back, covered with a faded green T-shirt that was tight across the shoulders and loose around his waist. The T-shirt had seen better days. His jeans fared no better: old, worn-out, gray from permanent dirt embedded in the weave. His hair was dark and worn on the longer side, not quite reaching his shoulders.

He wasn't a local Edger, and Jack would've smelled him if he was fresh from the Edge or the Weird. Magic didn't work past the boundary, but Jack's sense of smell was still keener than normal, and people with magic in their blood gave off a specific scent. She never smelled it herself, but Jack maintained they smelled like pies, whatever that meant. And he was under strict orders to tell her immediately if they encountered an unfamiliar pie-smelling person in the Broken.

As she neared them, she heard the man's voice. ". . . yeah, but his arms don't move. He's stuck like that. You can't make him fight."

He didn't sound like a child molester, but child molesters never sounded like child molesters. They sounded like your law-abiding, churchgoing, nice next-door neighbor. And they were very good with children.

Georgie saw her. "Rose, he likes the guys, too."

"I see," she said. If they were back in the Edge, and if she had the knowledge to convert her power into an environmental effect, her voice would have frozen everything in a twenty-yard radius. "And does he usually hang out in the toy aisle talking to little boys?"

The man turned. He looked to be in his late twenties. He had a handsome face with a square jaw and sculptured cheekbones. No baby fat remained on his face. His cheeks were hollowed, his nose narrow and well cut. She scrutinized his deep-set hazel eyes. The eyes reassured her: they were honest and direct. Not a child molester, she decided. Probably just a nice guy talking to the kids in the toy aisle.

He reached up and pulled a pirate figure from the top shelf. "Now this one moves. You can pose him." He handed the toy to Georgie, and the boys bent over it. "Sorry," he told her. "Didn't mean to alarm you there."

"I wasn't alarmed." She toned down the menace a little.

"My mistake." He turned back to the toys.

She stood next to him, feeling slightly awkward. "Buying for yourself or your son?" she asked, to say something.

"Myself."

"Ah. Are you a collector? One of those Never-Remove-from-the-Box types?" *Oh, that's good,* she thought. *Instead of ending this conversation on a somewhat comfortable note, ask the stranger more questions and insult him while you're at it.*

He glanced at her. "No. I take them out and I play with them. I stage huge wars. I also divide them by weight class." There was a slight note of challenge in his voice.

"Do you have many guys?" Georgie asked.

"Four boxes."

Rub it in, Rose thought with sudden venom, and immediately checked herself. He had no way of knowing that she couldn't afford to buy them toys. He was simply answering the question. She needed to end this conversation, buy the damn shoes, and go home.

"I keep waiting for them to make a good Conan figure, but they never do," the man said. "I stopped holding my breath. Was hoping for Green Arrow today, but nobody carries him."

"Which one?"

He gave her a suspicious look. "Hard Traveling Heroes."

Rose nodded. Having two little brothers made her into an action figure expert. "By DC Direct? Parallel Universe down the street has him, but it will cost you thirty bucks." She felt like slapping herself. It had just popped right out.

His eyes widened. "Can you tell me where it is?"

"We'll show you," Georgie volunteered.

She glared at him.

"We can show him the comics, right, Rose?" Jack's eyes were huge. "Please."

Rose had to concentrate to keep from gritting her teeth.

"That's okay," the man said. "I'll find it. Thanks for letting me know it's there."

He looked at her like she was some sort of maniac. "No, we'll show you," Rose found herself saying. "It's just down the street, but it's hard to explain how to get to it. Come on, boys."

Five minutes later, the four of them were walking down along the Wal-Mart sidewalk.

"Thanks again," the man said. "I'm William."

"Rose," she said and left it at that.

The boys seemed smitten with William. Jack in particular seemed fixated. It made sense—he was too young even to remember Dad, and none of their male relatives were ever around long enough to make an impression. A lonely kid abandoned by his father, who had run off after some phantom treasure, Jack was desperate for some male attention.

"I have new shoes," Jack said.

William stopped and looked at his shoes. "Cool boots."

Jack smiled. It was a tiny hesitant smile. He didn't smile very often. If Rose could've gotten ahold of Dad at this moment, she would've laid him out on the asphalt with one punch.

Georgie took a deep breath, plainly not wanting to be outdone in the coolness department. She could almost feel the wheels turning in his blond head. She should've bought him those damn bubbles so he could've at least said he had something new, too.

Georgie blinked a couple of times and finally burst out with the only bit of news he could scrounge. "I got grounded for snitching."

"Really?" William said.

Rose tensed. If he mentioned leech birds, she'd have to come up with some sort of explanation. But Georgie only nodded. "Uh-huh."

"That probably wasn't good."

"No."

William glanced at her. "Does your sister ground you often?"

"No. She mostly does this." Georgie rolled his eyes in perfect imitation of her and muttered, "Why me?"

William looked at her.

"What made you think I'm their sister?"

He shrugged. "You look too young. Besides, not many kids would call their mother 'Rose.'"

They reached the end of the sidewalk. She took the boys by the hand, and together they crossed the street and headed across the grass to a small plaza. "So you're not from around here?"

"No. Moved here a couple of weeks ago from Florida," William said. "Jobs are a bit better here."

"What do you do?"

"I lay floors."

Rose nodded. The area was booming. Every time she drove by, construction crews had cleared more of the forest to make room for new subdivisions and shopping centers. A floor installer could make some serious money here. No wonder he could afford four boxes of toys.

PARALLEL Universe sat sandwiched between a coffeehouse and a UPS shipping store. It was remarkably clean and organized as comic shops went. In his previous life, Peter Padrake was Commodore Peter Padrake, the scourge of the Blood Sea and loyal privateer of Adrianglia, a country in the Weird. A decade ago he had crossed from the Weird into the Broken to retire, somehow managed to transform his life savings into good old U.S. currency, and opened Parallel Universe. Peter ran his comic shop the way he must've run his ship: the place was pristine, the comics categorized by publisher and title, each in a clean plastic sleeve, each clearly labeled with a price sticker. The price was final. Peter detested haggling.

He greeted her with a sour look. Rose knew it wasn't personal. She was trouble, and Peter detested trouble even more than haggling.

"It's here." Georgie tugged on William's sleeve. "Over there."

William followed Georgie and Jack to the back of the store.

She smiled at Peter. He did his best to impersonate a stone idol from Easter Island. She drifted away from his stare to the back of the store, looking at the graphic novels on the wall as she passed. She loved comics. She loved books, too. They were her window into the Broken, and they let her dream.

Girl Genius . . . She often wished she could have been like Agatha, building superweapons out of a rusty fork, old bubble gum, and a piece of string. Rose picked up a graphic novel sealed in plastic. Twenty bucks . . . Not in this lifetime. She looked up and saw William listen while Georgie read out the description of the action figure from the back of the box. He wasn't a bad-looking guy, she reflected. Patient, too. Most men would've shrugged Georgie off by now. Maybe he was a child molester, after all.

Now there was a messed-up thought. Why would every man who paid a bit of attention to two boys obviously starved for male company automatically be some sort of criminal?

William smiled at her. Rose carefully smiled back at him. Something wasn't quite right about William. She couldn't put her finger on it. It was time to collect her brothers and go.

Rose skirted a small display and ran into Jack. He stood in the aisle completely still, knees slightly bent, barely breathing, his eyes focused on a rack of books, looking just like a cat fixated on its prey. She glanced in the direction of his stare and saw a brightly colored comic book. Not a regular American one but a fatter, smaller manga volume. The cover showed a teenage girl in a sailor outfit and a boy with white hair wearing a red kimono. Red letters slashed across the page: *InuYasha*.

Rose took the comic book off the shelf. Jack's eyes followed it. "What?" she asked.

"Kitty ears," he whispered. "He has kitty ears."

Rose examined the cover and saw furry triangular ears in the mane of the boy's white hair. She flipped the book. "It says here he is a half-man, half-dog demon. So these aren't kitty ears."

Rose could tell by the desperate look on his face that he didn't care.

She glanced at Peter. "You stock manga now?"

Peter shrugged behind the counter. "Those are used. A fellow brought them in. Selling them as a set, three for ten. If I sell them, I might order some new copies in."

"Please," Jack whispered, his eyes huge.

"Absolutely not. You got shoes. Georgie didn't even get anything."

"Can I have it then?" Georgie popped out of thin air next to her.

"No." She could swing three bucks maybe, but not ten, and she could tell by Peter's face that he wouldn't be breaking the three volumes up.

"I'll buy these for them," William offered.

"No!" She took a step back. They were poor, but they weren't beggars.

"Look, seriously, I dragged you down here and made you show me the shop. I'm getting the Green Arrow anyway; an extra ten bucks won't make any difference." He glanced at Peter. "I'll pay for those."

"Absolutely not," she said, loading her voice with steel.

"Rose, please—" Georgie began in a singsong whine.

She cut him off. "You're a Drayton. We don't beg."

He clamped his mouth shut.

"Figure it out and stop wasting my time," Peter said.

William looked at him. It was a thousand yard stare that pinned Peter down like a dagger. It wasn't even aimed at her, but an urge to back away and leave gripped her. Peter Padrake moved his hand to the drawer where he kept his .45 and stood very still.

She picked up the books and put them on the counter. "Ten, you said?"

"Ten sixty nine with tax," Peter said, his gaze fixed on William.

Rose smiled. She had exactly ten seventy-five in her purse. Gas money. Rose pulled out her pocketbook, extracted the soft dollar bills and three quarters, handed them to Peter, got her change, and all with the same smile on her face, she gave the books to the kids and marched out of the store, boys in tow.

"Rose, wait." William followed her.

Just keep walking . . .

"Rose!"

She turned and looked at him. "Yes?"

He closed the distance between them. "If I hadn't said something, you wouldn't have bought the books. Let me make it up to you. Go out to dinner with me tomorrow. My treat."

She blinked.

"I don't know anybody," he said. "I'm sick of eating alone. And I feel bad about the store."

Rose hesitated.

He leaned a little to look her in the eyes. "I really want to see you again. Say yes."

It had been forever since she'd been on a date. Any kind of date. Four years.

Tomorrow was Wednesday, the first day of school. The kids would want to see Grandma to tell her all about it. She could swing a dinner. But there was something about William that put her off. He was handsome, and she wanted to like him. She just didn't. The stare he'd given Peter had been almost predatory. "You're not my type."

"How do you know? We haven't said more than twenty words to each other."

That was true. She didn't know anything about him. But it was far more prudent to turn him down and go back behind her ward stones. *To hide.* And with that thought, something inside Rose reared up, the way it had in the beginning of fifth grade, when Sarah Walton first called her the daughter of a whore. The same Drayton stubbornness that made her grandmother famous reared its head. No, she thought. They wouldn't make her cower behind the ward stones for the rest of her goddamn life.

But they wouldn't force her to do something she didn't want to do either. That would be equally weak.

"You're a nice guy, William. But I really can't. Tomorrow is the first day of school, and I need to be home."

He looked at her for a long moment and raised his arms, palms out. "Okay. Maybe we'll run into each other again sometime." He made it sound like a promise.

"Maybe," she said.

THREE

WEDNESDAY rolled around way too fast.

A white truck sped by her, its horn blaring. Rose didn't even spare a glance. The needle on her fuel gauge had rolled to the left of the yellow "E."

"Just make it to the Edge," she murmured. "That's all I ask."

The old Ford rumbled on, creaking. She kept the speed at thirty miles an hour to save the gas. In the distance, the sun set slowly, threatening the sky with red. She was so late.

She had to stay overtime—at the regular seven-bucks-an-hour rate as usual. The T-shirt printer had an emergency. Some disgruntled employee had sprayed the floor with the tacky liquid they used to keep the T-shirts in place while the designs were inked into them. By the time the owners realized what had happened and called Clean-n-Bright, the floor was a horrid mess of every type of dirt imaginable. Only one thing removed the tacky spray—turpentine. She and Latoya had spent the last two hours crawling on their hands and knees drenching the tile in it. Her fingers smelled like turpentine. It was everywhere, on her skin, in her hair, on her shoes . . . Her back ached. She needed to get home and take a shower. True, she was a cleaning lady, but that didn't mean she had to smell like one.

A small part of her regretted not accepting William's offer. He wasn't boyfriend material, but he could've been a friend. Someone outside the Edge to talk to. Water under the bridge, she told herself. She said no, and she'd live with it.

Ahead the familiar curve of Potter Road appeared from the greenery. Finally.

The truck sneezed.

"Come on, boy. You can do it."

The Ford sneezed again. She took her foot off the gas, guiding the old truck into a turn, and let it roll up the road into the trees. They were down to ten miles per hour now. A bit more gas. A bit more . . .

They crossed the boundary, and the magic flared within her, filling her with warmth. The engine died with a soft murmur, and Rose let the truck glide off the road into the tangled brush. The greenery snapped shut behind her. She parked, got out, locking the Ford, and patted the hot hood. "Thanks."

It was the first day of school, and she was out of gas. At least Grandma had agreed to pick the kids up at the end of the road and watch them until Rose got home from work. Usually they walked by themselves, but today had to be special. They'd be bursting at the seams with earth-shattering revelations about going back to school.

Rose started up the road. Around her the Wood crowded the dirt path: huge trees braided their dark twisted limbs, the ground between their trunks soft with centuries of autumn. Pale blue horsetail vines tinseled the branches. Twilight crouched among the trees. The blanket of kudzu that swallowed trees whole in the Broken stopped at the boundary, and here the Edge moss had taken over, hugging the tree trunks like a velvet sleeve and sending forth tiny flowers on thin stalks that looked like overturned lady shoes: bright purple, mint green, lavender, pink. The scents of a dozen herbs mixed into an earthy, slightly bitter spice in the air.

Sinister noises came from the gloomy depths of the Wood, and occasionally a glowing pair of eyes ignited in the canopy. Rose paid it little mind. The Wood was the Wood; most things around these parts knew who she was and let her be.

Two miles separated her from the turnoff to the house, and Rose fell into a familiar, comfortable stride. It lasted until the third turn of the road. She halted. This was the spot where the man with two swords had leaped onto her truck.

Rose looked at the dirt tracks. Now that had been something else. As far as she could remember, the truck hood came to a little above her waist. She rocked experimentally on her toes and jumped as high as she could. Not even close.

If she took a running start, she could maybe get one leg up on the hood. But he had leaped onto the moving truck, landed on his feet, and kept going like it was nothing.

A tiny high-pitched noise from above made her raise her head. To the left a tall tree spread its branches over the path, leaning to the road. About nine feet off the ground, just before the tree trunk forked in two, a skinny shape hugged the bark. Kenny Jo Ogletree.

Kenny stood pretty far down on her favorite people list, only a step above his mother, Leanne, who had been best friends with Sarah Walton during high school and whose chief achievement was scrawling WHORES BITCH on Rose's locker with a permanent marker. Grammar wasn't among Leanne's strengths, but bullying she had raised to an art form.

The apple didn't fall far from the tree—at nine, Kenny was a bully and a loudmouth. About a month ago he and Georgie ran into a misunderstanding over a softball game and had to have words. If it wasn't for Jack, Kenny would've beaten Georgie bloody, but all the kids were afraid of Jack. Jack fought like every fight was his last, and he didn't always stop when he won.

Kenny clutched at the tree, standing absolutely still. His hands had gone white-knuckled with desperation. Grime stained his shirt and threadbare khaki shorts, and a long scratch along his thigh slowly dripped blood onto his calf. Kenny stared at her. His eyes were glassy, the whites starkly pale. Whatever problems she had with Leanne paled when faced with a nine-year-old boy terrified out of his wits.

"Are you okay, Kenny?"

He just stared.

The bushes on her left rustled. It was a purposeful, predatory sort of rustling. Rose backed away slowly.

A shiver ran through the thin stems. The branches bent, dark triangular leaves parted, and a creature stepped onto the road. Four feet tall, it stood upright, its body a mess of rotting, putrescent tissue clumped together in a grotesque patchwork. Rose saw the scales of a forest snake on the left leg, reddish fox fur on the shoulder, matted gray squirrel fuzz on the chest, brown stripes of a pig on the lower stomach . . .

Part of its gut was missing, and a rotting mass of intestines glared through the hole just under a narrow flash of ribs.

Its face was horrible. Two pale baleful eyes stared at her from deep sockets. They brimmed with intense, focused hatred. Under them a wide mouth gaped, armed with sharp triangular teeth, sprouting from the jaws in several rows.

A ragged, whispery wheezing came from the creature, heavy and wet. A wold. A thing of hate and magic, a living curse that drew power from its creator's rage. Someone had cursed some land or a house nearby, and the Wood gave the curse a form and a purpose: to kill everything it came across.

In the tree, Kenny whimpered like a kitten.

The wold opened its mouth wider and stepped forward, menace radiating from it like a foul corona. It wanted to murder her, to take a piece of her flesh and make it its own.

Rose raised her right hand.

The wold hissed. Its twisted limbs opened wide, releasing yellow claws.

A light sheen of magic coated Rose's fingers. The magic vibrated in her, straining to break free.

The wold ran at her, its black maw gaping, teeth and claws ready to rend.

Rose flashed. Magic shot from her hand in a glowing whip of white and struck the creature in the chest. The wold's momentum carried it another step, but the icy white flame of the flash burned it, burrowing into its chest, seeking its malice-coated core. Dismembering it wouldn't be enough. She had to kill the curse itself.

Chunks of flesh rained from the wold. Rose advanced, keeping the whip of light fixed on the creature. Her arm throbbed with tension.

The wold fell apart, revealing a small mote of darkness churning with violent red and purple flashes. Rose squeezed her fist. The white whip clutched at the darkness. She strained, squeezing tighter, her nails biting into her palm. With a sound like a cracked walnut, the mote collapsed in on itself in a shower of white sparks and vanished.

Rose let out a deep breath, stepped over the carrion littering the path, and walked up to the tree. "Come on," she said, holding out her hands.

Kenny stood frozen. For a moment she thought she'd have to go get his mother, but suddenly he let go and slid down the trunk, scraping himself against bark and all but falling into her arms. She had to drop him on his feet—he was too heavy.

"It's gone," she said and hugged him. "Dead and done. Understand?"

He nodded.

"It won't come back. If you ever see another one like that, you run to my house as fast as you can. I'll kill it. Go home now."

He peeled down the road at a dead run, veering left, toward the Ogletree house.

Rose looked back at the carrion strewn in the dirt. Only a handful of families could claim a magic user strong enough to create a wold, and all of those capable were older people and supposedly knew better. A wold couldn't be stopped. It was the kind of weapon that killed everything it came across. She hadn't seen one for years. The last time one popped up, it took a full-blown posse to hunt it down with gasoline and torches.

Something had to have gone seriously wrong for one of the locals to curse a wold into life. Something dire was happening. Cold dread settled in the base of her neck. For a moment she considered following Kenny Jo to find out if Leanne knew anything about it, but decided against it. Shortly after high school, Sarah had married well and moved to a nice house in the Broken. Rumor said, Leanne wasn't welcome at Sarah's new dream home, and it made her only madder at life than she already was. She and Rose hadn't spoken to each other since high school. She seriously doubted Leanne would suddenly open up to her.

Rose started up the road at a brisk pace. The faster she got home, the sooner she'd make sure that the boys were safe.

Few things happened in East Laporte without Grandma Éléonore's knowledge. She would just have to ask her about it.

"MÉMÈRE?"

Éléonore glanced at Georgie's face. She never could get him to explain how he knew to call her that. She had never spoken a word of French to either of them. But Georgie started saying it when he was two, with a light Provençal overlay. She had a feeling he didn't know himself why he did it, but every time he said the word, it brought her back to dry, warm hills, where she sat in the sunshine next to her own *grand-mère*, nibbling on *fougasse* that left a faint orange taste on her tongue and watching the men down in the village play *la longue* with the grace of ballet dancers.

She smiled at him. "What is it?"

"Can we go outside?"

Two pairs of eyes blinked at her from angelic faces: Georgie's blue and Jack's amber. Hooligans, both of them. "Is it dark?"

"We won't go past the ward stones."

She rolled her eyes. "Oh, and you think I was born yesterday, no?"

"Pleeease." Georgie's eyes would've done any puppy proud. Behind him Jack nodded earnestly.

"All right." She gave in before her heart melted. Rose would be none too pleased if she found out, but what Rose didn't know, she couldn't fuss about. "I don't trust the two of you. I'm coming out on the porch."

They were out the door before she got up off her chair.

Éléonore took her teacup to the porch. The old rocking chair creaked under her weight. The boys dashed into the yard.

Beyond the lines of the ward stones, the Wood shivered with life. The sky had darkened to deep soothing purple, and the leaves of the upper branches stood out, nearly black against it, rustling gently in the cool whisper of the night breeze. Here and there the white spires of nightneedle bloomed between the trees. Their stems, no more than green shoots during the day, released a cascade of delicate, bell-shaped blossoms with the first touch of darkness, sending a mimosa perfume into the night. Éléonore breathed it in and smiled.

So peaceful . . .

Unease flared at the base of her neck and rolled down her spine in a viscous wintry rush. She felt the press of some-one's gaze pin her, as if she had a bull's-eye between her shoulder blades. Éléonore turned, scanning the ward line.

There. A dark spot hovered at the outer edge on her left. It stood on all fours, dense and impenetrable, like a hole cut in the fabric of the night to reveal primordial darkness. She could barely see it in the gloom, its silhouette more of a guess than a certainty.

Éléonore's fingers found the small wooden charm hanging from her neck. She gripped it tight and whispered, "Sight."

Magic pulsed from her in a flat horizontal fan, pulling the landscape and the creature to her eyes in a rush. She saw darkness and within it a narrow slit of the eye: pale, weakly luminescent gray without an iris or a pupil. She tried to reach past it and glimpsed a hint of a form, churning with unfamiliar violence. Her senses screamed in alarm. The eye jerked out of sight. She released the charm in time to catch a blur of darkness as the creature vanished into the underbrush without a sound.

The Wood was home to many things, but Éléonore had never seen one so disturbingly alien. She glanced to the kids on the lawn. Safe behind the protective stones. It will be fine, she told herself. The wards around Rose's house were strong and old. The spells had rooted deep into the soil. Besides, Rose would be coming up the road any minute now, and Éléonore pitied any beast that tried to stand between her and the boys.

It was probably just some odd creature the Wood had disgorged. The forest stretched west of East Laporte and all the way into the Weird. Perhaps some Weird beast had crossed the boundary into the Edge. Stranger things had happened. No need to tell Rose about it, Éléonore decided. The poor child was paranoid enough as it was.

ROSE made the final turn and paused at the edge of the lawn. Grandma Éléonore sat on the porch, sipping hot tea from a teacup. Some time ago Grandma had decided she was old enough to cultivate a hedge witch look. Her gray hair was teased into a semblance of a crazy matted mess randomly decorated with feathers, twigs, and charms. Her clothes would've given any deconstruction-oriented designer a run for his money: they were artfully ripped and layered, until she resembled a half-plucked chicken with bits and tatters of fabric fluttering about her as she moved.

The authenticity of her costume was slightly ruined by the fact that both her rags and her hair were very clean and smelled faintly of lavender, and by a decidedly unwitchy teacup with a fluffy gray kitten on it.

"Were the boys any trouble?" Rose asked, coming to sit next to her.

Grandma rolled her eyes. "Please. I'm a hundred and seven years old. I think I can handle two hooligans."

The magic kept most Edge families alive and well long past their Broken peers, and Grandma didn't look a day older than fifty-five. It wasn't her age that was the problem, Rose reflected. It was that the moment the boys made their puppy eyes at her, all the rules and discipline flew out the window.

Behind Grandma the boys chased each other on the grass: Jack, nimble and lightning quick, and Georgie, a pale golden-haired shadow. Paler than usual today. One of them was impersonating InuYasha, the half-demon boy from the comic book; the other was probably Lord Sesshomaru, InuYasha's older and stronger demon half-brother. But which was which, she couldn't tell from here.

Rose did not regret buying the comics. The boys had latched onto them, and the precious volumes now occupied the treasured spot of honor on the top shelf in their bedroom.

Georgie ran out of breath and sat on the grass, slumping forward. Rose caught a sigh. He looked about to be sick.

Grandma pursed her lips. "What was it this time?"

"A baby bird." He'd raised it this morning, before she dropped them off at the school bus stop.

Georgie coughed and bent over on the grass. Jack stopped in midstride. He looked at Georgie for a long moment, his face blank and lost, then trotted over and sat next to him.

"If George keeps this up, it will kill him." Grandma shook her head.

Rose sighed. When Georgie resurrected something, he sacrificed a bit of his vitality to give it life. The stronger his power grew, the weaker his body became, as if his mind was the flame of a candle that burned too bright, destroying the wax too fast. They tried explaining. They tried talking. They tried threats and punishments and pleading, but nothing helped. Georgie breathed life into things that made him sad with their passing and simply didn't know how to let them go.

"What a pair." Grandma sighed. "A cat with a death wish and his brother who's trying to keep half of the Wood alive." Her voice broke a bit. "How's Cletus?" she said, making an obvious effort to sound nonchalant and failing.

"Same," Rose said.

A shadow clouded Grandma's eyes. She frowned and poured Rose a cup of tea. "The boys told me about this William. What does he do?"

Traitors. "He's a floorer."

"He sells flowers?" Grandma's eyebrows crept up.

"No. You know how roofers work on roofs? Well, he works on floors."

"Are you sure he isn't a child molester? Because that's what they do, they sidle up to the woman in the family, woo her, and then next thing you know they've got their di—"

Rose gave her an indignant stare. "He isn't a child molester."

"How do you know?"

Rose spread her arms helplessly. "He has honest eyes?"

"Is he handsome?"

Rose frowned. "He's a fine figure of a man. Dark hair, dark eyes. Handsome, I suppose."

"If he looks that good, why didn't you let him court you?"

"It didn't feel right," she said shortly.

Grandma looked at her, her blue eyes vivid on her wrinkled tan face, like two violets on a freshly plowed field. "I see."

"I saw a wold today," Rose said to change the subject.

Grandma raised her eyebrows. "Oh? How big?"

Rose lifted her hand to show about four feet.

"My. He was a big one." A flicker of worry mudded the clear blue of Grandma's eyes.

Rose nodded. "It chased Kenny Jo up a tree."

"Kenny Jo deserves it. Did you kill it?"

They shared a small private smile. A couple of weeks after Rose had flashed white, Grandma had made a small wold for her to kill. Practice, she had said. It was more than that—

it was a test. Grandma wanted to see how hot she could flash. Rose had blown the wold to pieces in the first ten seconds. Grandma didn't speak for a full half a day after that. Grandpa had called it a record of some sort and predicted Apocalypse.

Rose nodded. "Who could make a wold?"

Grandma set her cup down with a sigh. "That's a powerful curse. I can. Lee Stearns. Jeremiah Lovedahl. Adele Moore. Emily Paw. Her aunt, Elsie, could, too, but the poor woman lost her wits, what, two decades ago?"

"I heard she has tea parties." Rose drank her tea.

Grandma nodded. "I've seen her do it. She brings teddy bears to the picnic table and pours them invisible tea out of a plastic tea set. Sometimes the bears even drink it. There was some real power there, but it's all gone to waste now."

Rose opened her mouth to tell her about a man who liked to jump on moving trucks and stopped. It was just an isolated incident. Nothing would come of it. Why worry her?

"Whoever has done it, I'll find out. And I'm sure Jeremiah and Adele will want to give them a piece of their mind." Grandma rose. "Well, I'd better be going. I'll make the trip to Adele's tomorrow and see what she knows. The hooligans finished their homework. Also, Georgie has a note from his teacher, something about stone books."

"Stone books?" Rose frowned.

"Yes. I think he needs one made of marble."

"Marble composition book," Rose guessed.

"Yes, that's the one."

Grandma headed for the door and stopped, framed in the doorway. "Maybe you should give this boy a chance. Life doesn't have to end after the Graduation Fair, you know. It goes on."

She left. Rose sighed and poured herself more tea.

Give the boy a chance.

Rose mulled it over. Maybe she should have given William a chance. Most people in her position might have. She hadn't dated in years.

And that was exactly the problem. She hadn't dated in years, and her judgment wasn't sound. A part of her wanted to be pretty and carefree. In her rare moments of desperation, she wanted a man to look at her like she meant the world to him, and failing that, she would settle for someone who thought she was beautiful and told her so. William would probably fit that bill. Part of her pointed out that something was better than nothing. But if she ended up with the wrong something, she'd regret it for the rest of her life. Once bitten, twice shy. Living in your dreams meant bitter disappointment when you woke up. She'd learned that lesson well.

The incident with William unsettled her. He'd unwittingly pulled all of her old wants and hopes out of the recesses of herself where she'd carefully stuffed them, and dragged the entire mess into bright light. Now she had to deal with it, and she resented him for it. Come to think of it, any handsome man who asked her out would've set off the same chain reaction. She didn't want to go out with William just because he was in the right place at the right time. And she hated feeling desperate.

Rose got up, gathered the cups and the kettle onto a platter, and carried them off to the kitchen. It wasn't always this way, she reflected. No, she was never the most popular girl in school, but she had her share of guys knocking on her door. Back then she dated the kind of boys even a Drayton girl didn't feel right bringing home. Like Brad Dillon. Brad had black hair, hot brown eyes, and carved biceps. And the best ass in the county. But that was before the Graduation Fair.

East Laporte was too small to have its own high school, and most kids went to school in the Broken. There was a tiny church school for people who didn't have the papers or the money to bribe the principal of the Broken high school, but aside from that, you were out of luck. For those who did attend the school in the Broken, high school meant four years of pretending to be a normal Broken person. Four years of having your nose rubbed in how poor you were and in all the things you could never do: college, traveling, having a nice house . . .

That's why the Graduation Fair was a huge deal. It happened on the thirtieth of May, once the Broken schools let the kids out for the summer. It was the time for graduating seniors to celebrate their freedom. Everyone attended. Even the bluebloods from the lands neighboring the Edge came once in a while, cloaked in the powerful magics of the Weird.

Food stalls sprang up along the field's edge, caravans from the Weird arrived to exchange their goods for the trinkets from the Broken, and bouncy gyms and inflatable water slides were set up for the little kids. Once everyone ate and traded, people gathered at Crow's field to watch the seniors show off their flash. There was nothing simpler and more complicated than a flash: a burst of magic, pure and direct. Like lightning. It showed a person's power. The brighter and more defined was the flash, the stronger was the magic user.

The Edger kids kept to themselves even in the schools of the Broken, and once you hit high school, that's all anyone would talk about between classes and during lunch: who flashed what color the previous year. The best Edgers flashed pastel blue or green. You just hoped you didn't come out there and puffed out dark red, the weakest color, to the jeers of the audience. Only the bluebloods, the aristocrats of the Weird, flashed white, and even among them, not everyone could deliver a controlled whip of power.

Rose rinsed out the cups and put them back into the cabinet. Middle school had been hell for her. Leanne and Sarah, the two queen bitches, picked on her the entire time, because her mom had slept with Sarah's dad, lured him away from Sarah's mother, and then dumped him. Sarah's parents split, and Rose paid the price. She was the daughter of a whore, and a beggar whore at that, a girl who was ugly, poor, and good at nothing.

She began practicing her flash in sixth grade. She worked at it with a fanatical devotion. She practiced for hours, in private, determined to show them all. When her mom died her junior year of high school, it only spurred Rose on. Flashing became an obsession. She practiced, and practiced, and practiced, until magic flowed from her, pliant and obedient.

When Rose walked onto that field at the Graduation Fair, her head held high, she knew she was ready. She had years of practice behind her. She would finally shove it in their faces. She opened her hands wide and flashed an arch of purest white, as defined as any of the best bluebloods could hope to offer.

In her childish triumphant dreams, Rose had imagined people cheering, pictured herself being hired by a blueblood house, receiving training, going off to adventure in the depths of the Weird. She had done something truly remarkable. Not even a burst of energy, but an arch, crisp and sharp like a blade of a scimitar that played in her hands like a willing pet. *Top that, you assholes.*

Morbid silence greeted her. Fear stabbed her chest, and she realized suddenly that she might have made a mistake. And then Dad was there at her side, and he pointed his gun at the audience, and he and Grandfather took her off the field quicker than she could think, packed her into Dad's Jeep, and drove to the house like wolves were snapping at their heels. That night Grandma didn't sleep she walked the grounds, reinforcing the ward stones with her blood.

In the morning, four messengers waited by those ward stones. Three had come from the Edger families, and one from a blueblood noble house. Only the blueblood man was allowed to enter. He sat in their kitchen, an older grizzled warrior with a sword on his waist, and laid it all out. Only bluebloods flashed white. That was an unshakable fact. In two hundred years, no Edger had delivered such a focused and bright flash. Coupled with her mother's reputation, that could mean only one thing: Rose wasn't her father's daughter.

At that conclusion, Grandpa had to be taken out of the kitchen to keep from skewering their "guest" with his rapier.

Rose denied it. It simply wasn't true: not only did she look like a Drayton, but she was born exactly nine months following her parents' honeymoon. Her mother had lost her virginity on her wedding night. The sleeping around didn't start until Rose was in her teens—it was the death of her mother's parents that had triggered it.

The man shook his head. It didn't matter, he explained. Even if she was legitimate, no one would believe her. Those of blue blood possessed the potential for great powers. No body in their right mind could ignore the possibility that Rose could be a descendant of a noble family, a descendant who could in turn pass that precious blood to her children.

Finally she understood. She had hoped to wow everyone. Instead she had marked herself to be used as a broodmare.

The blueblood outlined his terms: a large stipend to her family, a comfortable life for her. They weren't offering marriage, like the other three messengers from the Edge. After all, they were an aristocratic house, and having a mongrel in their bloodline would be beneath them. They simply expected her to produce a horde of bastards to be used as retainers for their house.

Her father told him to get out.

It's amazing how stupid you can be when you're young, Rose reflected. Two days later, she had snuck away to see Brad Dillon. He told her, "Don't worry, babe. It's us against them. We can take them all on." They made out, and then he wanted to go to a club in the city "to show them all" that she wasn't scared. He asked her to go out and start her truck. He'd lost his license for doing ninety in a forty-five zone and then punching a cop, and she had to play the chauffeur.

She never made it to the truck. He came out of the house behind her, brandishing a bat, smiled, and clubbed her over the head.

She vividly remembered his smile. It was a smug grin that said, "I'm so much smarter than you, bitch."

He didn't hit her quite hard enough. His plan was to knock her out and deliver her to the Simoen family. The Simoens were always opportunistic, grabbing at every chance to get a bigger piece of the pie. Later she found out that Frank Simoen, the family's patriarch, promised Brad ten grand to deliver Rose. Ten grand. A fortune for an Edger. They'd wanted to get her hitched to Rob Simoen, Frank's son, so Rob's babies would one day flash white as well.

And Brad had tried. But Rose had jerked back at the last moment, and the bat glanced off, breaking the skin on her forehead. She stood there, her skull humming with pain, blood running into her eyes, shell-shocked. When Brad Dillon had swung that bat a second time to finish the job, he found out just how hot her flash could be. She didn't want to hurt him, but she did. And as he writhed on the ground at her feet, she cried and cried, because in that moment she realized that her life would never be the same.

What followed was six months of hell. The Edge clans went after her with a vengeance, some to get her for themselves, others so they could sell her to the highest bidder. At first she hid, then she fought back. It's true, she had only one weapon, but against it there was no defense. Sooner or later she was bound to kill someone, and once she had fried a drifter hired to kidnap her, the Edgers realized that she couldn't be controlled and left her alone. Shortly after that, Grandpa died, and then Dad got the idea for his latest brilliant scheme and departed, running away like a thief during the night. All she had left was a note ranting about treasure and how, when he returned, all of them would be rich.

Four years had passed. All her dreams died a quiet death. She earned her living like most poor Edgers did: by working a job in the Broken for minimum wage, paid under the table. She cleaned offices and made enough to buy food and clothes and a few items to barter when the caravans from the Weird came looking to trade Pepsi, plastic, and clothes for enchanted goods. It was good honest work. It put food on the table. And it killed her a little to do it.

She looked outside where the boys sprawled in the grass looking at the evening sky. At least when her parents had her brothers, they had the presence of mind to have Georgie at a hospital down in town and pay a midwife from the Broken to make sure Jack was legal, too. Both boys had Broken birth certificates and social security numbers. But she had been born in the Edge. Her driver's license was a fake, and her parents had to fork out a small fortune to the principal of her high school because her social security number belonged to someone else.

At least the boys were legal. And she wouldn't abandon them the way Dad did. She would starve if she had to, but they would go to a school in the Broken. That was the great thing about the Broken: you could succeed there on brains and drive alone, no magic required. When the boys grew up, they would have more choices than she did.

Still, she wasn't ready to put her dreams to rest either. One day, she'd find a way to live her life to the fullest. She was sure of it. She just had no idea how she would manage it.

FOUR

THE wind-up clock screamed at ten till six. Rose got up and went about her regular morning ritual: making coffee, fixing lunches, putting on her Clean-n-Bright uniform. She barely had a chance to taste her first cup of coffee when Georgie wandered out of his room, sleepy eyed, his hair tousled. He ambled over to the window and yawned.

"Would you like some Mini-Wheats?" she asked.

He didn't answer.

"Georgie?"

Georgie stared out of the window. "Lord Sesshomaru."

The demon brother from their comic book? "I'm sorry?"

"Lord Sesshomaru," he repeated, pointing through the window.

Rose came to stand behind him and froze. A tall man stood at the edge of the driveway. A cape of gray wolf fur billowed about him, revealing reinforced-leather armor, lacquered gray to match his cape, and a long elegant sword at his waist. His hair was a dark, rich gold, and it framed his face in a glacial cascade that fell over his left shoulder without a trace of a curl. She'd seen that hair before, just before its owner leaped onto her truck.

The pommel of the second, much larger sword, protruded above the man's back. The man's gaze fastened on her. His eyes flashed with a white glow, like two stars. Tiny hairs rose on the back of her neck.

"That isn't Lord Sesshomaru," Rose whispered. "That's much, much worse."

"What?" Sleep fled from Georgie, and he stared at her with wide eyes.

"That's a blueblood. Get Jack and get the guns. Hurry!"

* * *

ROSE walked out on the porch, carrying a crossbow. Behind her, Jack lay at the left window with his rifle and Georgie lay at the right.

The blueblood towered like a spire of gray ice just outside the ring of stones. Tall, with broad shoulders and long legs, he seemed knitted from menace and magic. *It's the wolf cape,* Rose told herself. Made him look bigger and scarier than he was.

She stopped just before the ring of wards and looked at his face. Her heart skipped a beat. His features were carved with breathtaking precision, combining into an overwhelmingly masculine yet refined face. He had a tall forehead and a long straight nose. His mouth was wide, with hard narrow lips, his jaw square and bulky, yet crisply cut. It wasn't a face whose owner smiled often. His eyes under thick golden eyebrows froze the air in her lungs. Dark grass green, they smoldered with raw power. She suspected that if she stepped over the stones and touched his face, he'd spark.

Rose leaned her crossbow on her hip and took a deep breath. "You're trespassing, and you aren't welcome."

"You're rude. I find it unattractive in all people, women especially." His voice sent a light, velvet shiver down her spine. It matched him, deep and resonant. Now that the first impact of his impossible face had worn off, she saw a network of small scars near his left eye. He was real, all right. He bled and scarred just like the rest, and that meant he wouldn't find bullets in his chest amusing.

"Get off my land and be on your way," she said. "I have two rifles trained on you as we speak."

"Two rifles manned by children," he said.

Damn Georgie. He shouldn't have let himself be seen. "They won't hesitate to shoot you," she assured him.

"I can rip through your wards with one blast. Bullets make no difference to me," he said. A white sheen rolled over his irises and melted into their green depths.

Ice skittered down her spine on sharp claws. He could, she realized. This wasn't an idle threat. He wasn't the first blueblood she'd fended off, but none had talked or looked like him. People said that the true aristocrats, bred for generations deep within magic, were striking. If that was true, he must've come from the dead center of the Weird. "What is it you want?"

"What do you think I want?"

She gritted her teeth. "Let me make this completely clear: I won't sleep with you."

Surprise flickered in his eyes. Thick eyebrows crept up. "What? Why?"

Rose blinked, lost for words. He actually found it shocking that she didn't fall over herself to spread her legs.

"I'm waiting for an explanation."

Rose crossed her arms. "Let me guess. You're the fourth son of a blueblood family down on its luck: no title to tempt an heiress and no inheritance money to purchase a noble bride. You've heard about the mongrel Edger girl who flashes white and decided that since you can't have an heiress or a title, you can at least sire a brood of powerful babies, so you came to shop for a bride in the Edge. I have no time for people like you."

"Trust me, you've never met anyone like me." He made it sound like a threat.

"You mean an arrogant snob who'd force a woman into his bed without any regard for her feelings? Actually, I've met plenty. Been there, done that, bought a T-shirt."

He frowned. "What do shirts have to do with anything?"

"There's nothing for you here. Go away, or I'll make you gone."

He grimaced. "You're rude, vulgar, and you speak in an atrocious fashion. You'll take so much work before you can be presentable. And you actually feel that you're a suitable spouse for me?"

That hurt. "That's right. I'm rude and vulgar. A mongrel. That's why you should leave me in peace. Run along to your fancy ladies. I'm sure one of them will gladly fall on her back for you and be overjoyed to pop out a litter of bluebloods. I won't marry you, and I won't be your mistress. Leave us be."

"I have no intention of leaving until I get what I want." He stated it as a fact and fixed her with his gaze. Fear blocked her throat. There was no give in those eyes and no mercy. Only savage magic and iron will.

"If I wish it, you'll marry me. Shooting me, running me over with a vehicle, or trying to sour my disposition will do nothing to help your cause."

She raised her chin. "I'll fight you to the end," she promised. "You'll have to kill me." She jerked her crossbow up, sighting his chest.

"I have no intention to hurt you. Go ahead and fire," he said. "I won't count it against you—it will save me some breath."

She shot him.

It happened so fast, she barely saw it: a thin shield of purest white flashed in front of him, striking the bolt in midair. The metal and wood disintegrated. He looked down on her. "Your bullets and your bolts can't injure me."

Rose bit her lip, fighting a shiver. It took all of her will to continue glaring at his face.

The menace in his eyes eased a bit. "I understand why you insist on being unreasonable. This is to be expected, considering your upbringing. Still, we have a dilemma. I mean to have you as my bride. You mean to refuse me. A man's home is his refuge. I have no wish to share mine with a feral cat who spends all her time sharpening her claws and thinking of inventive ways to flay me when my guard slips. Nor do I want to fight you, especially not with the children here. They might be accidentally injured, and witnessing our violent clash wouldn't be good for them. There's a traditional way to resolve this. Challenge me."

"What?" Rose blinked.

"Give me three challenges," he said. "Three tasks. I'll excel at each one. When I succeed, you'll come to me willingly and you'll obey me."

"And if you fail?"

He permitted himself a half smile. "Don't concern yourself with that possibility. I won't."

"If you fail, you'll go away and never bother us again."

He shrugged. "Yes, that's how those things are usually worded."

Rose's mind sped through the possibilities. "And if I refuse?"

A white glow frosted the green irises. The magic swelled

around him, building. It buckled in his grasp, plain even through the two lines of wards. He was monstrously power- ful. She got the message loud and clear.

Rose bit her lip. She had no choice. She couldn't risk fighting him straight on, not with the boys here. He was very strong, and she wasn't a pushover. He was right—if they clashed, the boys might get hurt just from the collision of their magics. Besides, she wasn't sure she could win a direct confrontation. But challenges? She could do challenges. If you can't outfight an enemy, outsmart him, trick him, swin- dle him—do whatever it takes to win. That was the Edger way.

"Three tasks," she said, managing to sound upbeat. "Whatever I wish?"

"Within the realm of possible," he said. "I can't pluck the moon from the sky and hang it around your neck."

"I want you to swear to the terms," she said.

He sighed. "Very well."

He pulled a narrow knife from his belt and showed it to her. The rays of the rising sun gleamed, reflecting from the wicked metal profile of the blade. "I, Declan Riel Martel, ade Dominik, ade Logran, ade Rotibor, Earl of Camarine, Lord of Longshire, Svyator, and Veres, hereby swear to fulfill three tasks given to me within the next two weeks by . . ." He looked at her.

"Rose Drayton." He owned more titles than TitleMax. Maybe he could pawn some of them off, if he was short on cash. With his looks and pedigree, surely some Weird duch- ess or baroness would gladly marry him. What was he doing here, shattering her life?

". . . Rose Drayton, provided they are within human lim- its. I swear to cause no harm to Rose or her family and lay no claim upon her or her loved ones while I'm engaged in this challenge. Should I fail, I swear to leave Rose Drayton and her family in peace . . ."

"Alive and uninjured," Rose put in.

"Alive and uninjured. Should I succeed, I'll gain a right to claim Rose Drayton."

He sliced his palm. Magic lashed at Rose. She stumbled back. The ward stones rose a foot above the ground, trembling in empty air in a struggle to deflect the surge of his magic, and crashed back into their spots.

"Your turn." He held the knife out, handle first.

Rose hesitated. He did swear. The oath was binding. He couldn't cause her any harm. She stepped over the ward lines and reached for the knife. Her fingers closed over its carved bone handle, shaped like the head of a snarling cat. "I, Rose Drayton, promise to give . . ." God, she couldn't even remember his names, there were so many. ". . . you three tasks. If you successfully complete them, I promise to come with you . . ." She paused. What exactly followed? She had to word it in the best way possible.

He beat her to it. ". . . and be pleasant and agreeable."

"That will take a miracle." She had expected him to add "and sleep with me." The way he put it left her some wiggle room.

"You're right," he said somewhat mournfully. "We did agree on human limits."

"And be pleasant and agreeable," she bit off before he changed it and backed her into a corner. "I so swear."

"Hopeless. The clumsiest oath I've ever heard. You've had no education at all, have you?"

She sliced her palm. Magic burst from her in an exhilarating rush, surprising in its intensity. The stones rose, shivering once more, and fell. She might not have his education, but she had plenty of power and a brain. She would handle him.

He nodded matter-of-factly. "You're mine."

She felt sick to her stomach. "We'll start on the weekend," she said, drawing herself to her full height. "Two days from now. During the week, I have to work."

He turned and walked away without a word.

Rose stared after him. He was the sword that had just sliced her life in half.

The screen door banged open. She turned to see both boys on the porch. Jack glared after the blueblood. His eyes were angry. "You shouldn't have promised, Rose!"

"I didn't have a choice." She strode back to the porch. "He is very, very strong."

"What if he takes you away from us?"

"He won't." Rose looked after the retreating gray figure. "He's a noble. He's used to people falling over themselves to cater to him. But we're not his servants. We're Edgers. He might be stronger, but we're smarter. We just need to stump him with a challenge. Don't worry. I'll think of something."

"Can we hide in the Broken if we lose?" Georgie asked.

She sighed. "That was very smart, Georgie, but no. We can't. First, my promise is binding. If I break it, it will come back to me in a very bad way, and I'm not sure being in the Broken would keep it from catching me. Second, some people from the Weird can enter the Broken for a few days without consequences. Even if we ran, there's a chance that he would find us . . ."

And he was a lot stronger, too. Just the breadth of his shoulders alone showed the kind of strength she had no hope of countering. She had a feeling that if she shot him, he'd spit the bullet out, sling her over his shoulder, and drag her all the way into the Weird.

What she really needed to do was to stay home to make sure she could pick the kids up from the bus stop and watch over them. But they had to eat, and missing a day of work wasn't an option. Her job, as bad as it was, was precious. Only businesses with ties to the Edge hired Edgers—the rest wanted a social security number and a driver's license, and hers wouldn't stand up to scrutiny. There were places unaware of the Edge that hired illegal aliens, but competition for those jobs was fierce, and they mostly wanted muscle for manual labor. She could be fired in a blink of an eye, and there would be a line of Edgers ready to take her place.

"It doesn't matter," Rose said firmly. "We won't run. This is our home. We're going to do what Edgers do best: we'll fight dirty. But we don't have to do anything about him till this weekend. For now, we just have to watch ourselves and think. Grandma can't pick you up today. She's off checking on something with Adele Moore deep in the Wood. And I have to catch a ride with Latoya, because our truck is out of gas. When you get off the bus, I want you to come straight home. Do you understand? Don't talk to anyone, don't linger, come straight home, get inside, lock the door, and don't open it to anybody. Especially him." She nodded in the direction the blueblood had gone. She fixed them with her stare. "Repeat it back to me."

"Come straight home," Georgie said.

"No lingering," Jack said.

"Get inside and lock the door," Georgie said.

"Don't let the blueblood in," Jack finished.

Rose nodded. It would have to do.

ELSIE Moore hummed softly to herself. It was near eleven o'clock. Time for the brunch. It was going to be a very special brunch, too: she wore her pretty blue dress and had her favorite baby blue silk ribbon in her hair. The sun still shone bright, the weather was pleasant, the garden flowers pretty, and the row of stuffed animals gazed at her with adoration in their plastic eyes.

Elsie smiled prettily, taking her seat at the green plastic table. "Mr. Pitt, Mr. Brosnan, Mr. Clooney, Mr. Bean, how do you do? Shall we have some tea and biscuits? It's always a pleasure to see you, Mr. Bana."

The bears looked suitably impressed with her excellent manners. As they should be—she was a lady.

She picked up the tiny plastic teakettle with little pink roses on the side and held it over Mr. Brosnan's cup. The soft fuzzy paws reached for it.

She tsked. "Mr. Brosnan, I am shocked at your manners. You must wait until I've served the tea to all the gentlemen."

The bear dropped his paws, looking ashamed at being chastised.

A nasty feeling crept down her back, as if someone had poured cold goose fat onto her skin. She gritted her teeth, trying to ignore it. This was going to be a *lovely* tea.

The feeling intensified. The sickening slimy magic stuck to her, trying to worm its way through her skin into her bony back, and deeper. It was trying to get inside.

Elsie dropped the teakettle and turned around.

It stood on the edge of the lawn, a thing knitted from shadows and darkness. It didn't like the light and stuck to the shadows cast by the shrubs, blending into the gloom, so the only thing she could see clearly were its eyes: two slits of uniform, slightly luminescent gray, like slanted holes into a skull stuffed with rain clouds.

She threw a teacup at it. "Go away!"

The thing didn't move. A second pair of eyes opened above the first, the same dirty gray. The top pair looked at the teacup rolling harmlessly in the grass. The bottom pair stared straight at Elsie.

The dreadful feeling along her back grew stronger. The cold slime slid its way around her neck and down. A faint prickling singed her chest and back, as if a dozen tiny needle-feet tested the durability of her skin.

Elsie screeched and swiped at the cups, grabbing the little plastic pieces in a frenzy and hurling them one after the other at the baleful eyes.

"Grandma?" Amy emerged from the house, wiping her hands on the corner of her apron. She ran over on pudgy legs. "What's the matter?"

Elsie pointed with her shuddering fingers at the dark thing. Amy brushed her curly blond hair from her face and squinted at the shrubs. "What?"

"It's trying to get me! It ruined everything!"

"The bush? The bush ruined everything?"

"Not the bush, the thing!" Elsie pointed straight at the creature.

Amy bent to look in the direction of her finger. "Grandma, there's nothing there but an old crape myrtle shrub."

Elsie slapped her cheek. "Stupid girl!"

Amy drew herself to her full height. "Now *that* was uncalled for. Into the house with you. Looks like you need a pill."

"No!"

"Yes."

Elsie tried to scratch, but Amy was stronger and outweighed her by a hundred pounds. She was lifted to her feet and guided firmly inside the house. She twisted her head and saw the dark thing slink to the table. She shrieked, but Amy just wrestled her forward.

A huge maw split open beneath the four eyes, revealing jaws seeded with wicked teeth. Elsie could do nothing but scream as the monster bit into Mr. Bana, ripping the small body of fur and stuffing in half.

* * *

ROSE heaved a large service vacuum into the back of the Clean-n-Bright service van. Latoya and Teresa were still inside Kaplan Insurance. Latoya was chatting up Eric Kaplan, while Teresa finished the bathroom. Eric was a handsome fellow, and he did a very good impression of a happy-go-lucky, none-too-bright type of guy. Latoya thought she could wrap him around her finger. Rose had her doubts. It was Eric's job to get people to like him and buy his insurance, and judging by the swanky office, he was rather good at it. He had succeeded where his uncle Emerson had failed. Unfortunately, his uncle Emerson also ran Clean-n-Bright, which made him her boss, and he wasn't half as pleasant as his nephew.

Rose leaned against the van. Worry sat in the pit of her stomach like a big heavy clump of lead. Dread had plagued her all morning, and she just couldn't get rid of it. Usually she could figure out the cause of her anxiety—money worries, more often than not—but today she just worried in general. It wasn't enough she'd run into a wold; now there was a blueblood to deal with.

She'd mentioned the wold to Latoya and Teresa, who made shocked noises, and then Teresa reported she'd run into Maggie Brewster the other day. Maggie, a gentle cross-eyed girl, had the foresight. According to Teresa, Maggie said something bad was coming. She couldn't say what exactly—Teresa didn't think she knew—but she could tell that feeling it scared Maggie out of her wits.

Maggie had been wrong before. She had predicted a hurricane last October and was convinced they'd all be blown away. Instead they got clear skies and June weather.

But Maggie had been right before, too. And that worried Rose. She felt as if an invisible storm was gathering and she was on the edge of it.

Rose shut the van door and jumped. William stood right next to her.

"Hi," he said.

She gulped. "God, you scared me."

"Sorry. Didn't mean to startle you." He leaned against the van. "I was just driving by on my way to a job, saw you, and thought I'd say hi. How are you?"

"I'm good, thank you." Here he was, handsome and willing, yet she didn't feel anything romantic. Her heart didn't "flutter." The realization was kind of freeing. Rose smiled. She was right. She didn't need to go on a date with him.

"How did the first day of school go?" William asked.

"It went fine."

He grinned. "They didn't have to tie Jack to his chair? He doesn't look like he could sit still for longer than five minutes."

She laughed quietly. "He's a good kid."

"Both of them are good kids." He nodded. "Is there any way I can talk you into lunch?"

She shook her head, smiling. "I don't think it would be a good idea, Will."

"Why not? It's not like I'm going to maul you."

She looked into his eyes and caught a glimpse of the same thousand-yard stare he'd trained on Peter Padrake back in the comic shop. He hid it right away, but it was there, waiting inside him. Rose hesitated. This wasn't going to be easy. "Sometimes two people meet and there is a connection of sorts. An instant attraction. You look at somebody and wonder what it would be like. I don't wonder that about you. You're a nice handsome guy. And I want to like you in that way, honestly I do, but there's just nothing there."

He just kept smiling, his grin plastic on his face.

"I'm sorry," she said. "That's harsh, and I feel bad about it, but I don't want to lead you on."

"Rose Drayton."

The voice stopped her in mid-word. She turned on her heel, her hands clenching into fists. "Brad Dillon," she said, her voice dripping with venom.

Brad looked just like he used to look in high school, when they'd dated. He had picked up a couple of new tattoos and his nose was now pierced, but other than that, he was same old Brad. Still the same hot brown eyes and handsome face. Still looking like he wanted to punch somebody, the arrogant prick. She used to think that smirk was sexy. Now she wanted to slap it off his face.

Her gun was in her tote inside the van, and Brad wouldn't exactly let her get it. Without her gun, out here in the Broken,

Brad had an advantage. He was bigger and stronger, and Rose had seen him fight enough times to know she couldn't take him by herself. But she would make it expensive for him.

Brad fixed his gaze on William, sizing him up. "Don't know who you are and don't care. Just want to know what you're doing with my leftovers?"

Rose braced herself. In a second William would slug him, and when he did, Brad would come right back at him. William looked strong, but Brad was no pushover and he fought hard and dirty. She tensed, ready to jump right in.

William looked at Brad with a slightly bored expression.

"She's a lousy fuck," Brad said. "I feel sorry for you."

William said nothing.

Brad tried again. "I'd wear two rubbers if I were you. If you go bareback with that whore, your cock might fall off in the morning. You don't want what she's got."

William's stare gained a harsh edge, but Rose couldn't tell if he was pissed off or scared. "This thing you're trying to start isn't worth my time," William said. "Are you done?"

"No."

"Get on with it. I'd love to chat, but I'm getting kind of hungry."

Brad looked slightly confused. "Screw off, asshole."

William shrugged. "Anything else?"

Brad glared at the two of them. She tensed, expecting him to leap at them, swinging. He hovered on the edge of violence, muscles playing along his jaw. Come on, she thought. Bring it. She almost wished he would.

"Your new man's a pushover." Brad sneered.

He was backing down. Rose waved her hand, trying to hide relief. "Keep on walking, Brad."

Brad turned on his heel and stalked off. Must've decided the odds were against him.

William smiled, looking nice and pleasant, that same flat smile glued onto his lips. "Old boyfriend?" he asked.

She nodded. "Something like that."

"Back to what we were talking about," he said. "I appreciate that you leveled with me. But I think if you gave me a chance, I'd change your mind."

"I doubt it," she murmured.

The door of the office swung open, and Teresa emerged into the sunlight. Short, stocky, and dark, Teresa took one look at William and stopped, drinking him in.

"I have to go," Rose said.

"Till next time then." William took a step back and strode off.

Teresa raised her eyebrows at her. Rose shook her head and climbed into the van. She had enough trouble as it was. She needed to get through the day, get home, make sure the boys were okay, and think up some challenge for the blueblood. She felt bad about cutting William's wooing short, but it was best this way. It wouldn't go anywhere between them. Concentrate on important things, she told herself.

THE day slowly cooled down to evening. Jack slipped outside the door and sat on the porch. The old wood was warm under his legs, heated by the late afternoon sun. He squinted at it, a bright yellow coin in the sky. Shiny.

Rose said to stay inside, but inside was boring. He stayed inside the whole day, in school, and he was good and didn't fight with anybody, didn't even scratch Ayden when he tried to steal his eraser. He ate the nasty fried fish sticks without complaints, even though they tasted like dirt mixed with some kind of mystery meat. He didn't get any warnings or yellow tickets, and now he wanted to be outside. What's the point of going to school if you can't go outside after? Besides, it was only four, and Rose wouldn't be home until five-thirty or even six.

He sat silent, watching the woods with wide-open eyes. Listening. So many little sounds. A bird, somewhere far to the north, screaming at an intruder to its tree. Angry, feisty squirrels swearing at each other in their squirrel chatter. He watched them play chase up the blue spike pine. The skin between his knuckles itched, wanting to split under his claws, but he sat still—the pine's branches were too skinny. He couldn't climb them. He'd already tried twice, and they'd broken under him both times, leaving him scratched and smudged with sticky tar.

A big bug landed on the board next to him. It was dark blue and glossy. Jack held absolutely still.

The beetle waddled along the wooden plank on black chitinous legs. Jack tensed, following it with his gaze. Pretty, shiny bug.

Footsteps approached from inside the house. Georgie, about to ruin the fun.

The beetle's back split, releasing a light fan of shivering, gently unfurling wings. The bug waddled on across the porch. Jack crept after it, soundless and slick.

"Jack, we're supposed to stay inside," Georgie scolded through the screen door.

The bug stopped at the end of the wooden plank, as if considering the plunge to the green grass below.

"Go away!" Jack mumbled through his teeth.

The beetle's wings trembled again. The two halves of its back rose, like another pair of hard blue wings above its insect shoulders.

"Jack, get back inside! Rose said . . ."

The beetle's wings sped into a blur, and it launched itself into the air.

Jack pounced.

He cleared the porch in a single leap, snapping at the beetle with his fingers, and landed in the grass, empty-handed. Missed!

Georgie jumped out onto the porch. "Come back here!"

Jack chased after the beetle. It flew left, then veered right, a fat bright buzzing thing on a whirl of cream wings. He leaped, so high for a second he was flying, and caught the beetle between his palms. "Gotcha!"

Sharp legs pierced his skin. He laughed and peeked between his fingers.

"Jack!" Georgie's voice rang like broken glass.

A stench lashed his nose, bitter and harsh, followed by a creepy feeling that something cold and slimy had dripped on the back of his neck. He whirled.

A beast stood on the grass. Five feet tall, it balanced on four skinny legs, its body turned at an angle, its head facing Jack. Its chest was deep, and past it, its body slimmed down, each of its ribs clearly visible, before terminating in powerful hindquarters. It looked like a racing dog. At first glance, the beast's hide seemed almost black, but when the sun touched its spine, the thick skin stretched over the beast's back turned a dark smoky purple tinted with black and green, like a bad bruise. It had no fur, only a row of short, sharp spikes running down the backs of its legs and along its spine.

The beast's head was long, very long, but without any ears. Two pairs of long slanted eyes stared at Jack with dull, weakly glowing gray, like fog backlit by headlights.

In his adventures in the Wood, Jack had looked into the eyes of a dire wolf, a fox, a bear, and countless other things for which he had no name, but none of them had eyes like that. They were cruel eyes. Cruel and merciless like the eyes of a gator.

The wards would keep it away. The wards . . . Out of the corner of his eye Jack saw the lines of ward stones—several yards away.

Jack froze.

He was vaguely aware of Georgie on the porch. His brother took one small step back. The beast raised its front leg, with a huge paw made of long clawed fingers, and stepped forward.

"Don't move!" Jack breathed.

Georgie became still as a statue.

The beetle slid from Jack's open fingers and crawled up the back of his hand to take flight. Jack didn't move, didn't even blink. His every instinct screamed at him that to move was to die, and so he stood petrified, caught in his terror.

The beast opened its mouth. Its lips drew back, revealing black jaws filled with terrible bloodred fangs. The gaze of the four eyes pinned Jack in place.

Jack swallowed. The bracelet on his wrist grew hot, but he knew that if he took the bracelet off and changed shape, the beast would get him for sure. He had to get behind the wards. That was his only chance. If he ran, the beast would chase him. He knew by the way it was built, lean and long-legged, that it was fast. It would catch him and rend the meat off his bones.

He shifted slightly, sliding a mere inch back along the grass.

"Right," Georgie's trembling voice called.

Jack turned a little, terrified to take his gaze off the four eyes, and saw the second beast padding slowly along the ward line. The second beast caught him looking and stopped to show him a forest of narrow red fangs. It would catch him if he moved. There was no escape. He was cut off.

Jack's heart hammered in his chest, as if trying to break free. The loud beat of his pulse filled his ears, pounding in his head. The world turned crystal clear. Jack inhaled deeply, trying to keep from getting dizzy.

"Don't move," commanded a quiet voice.

Jack turned his head. A few yards away the blueblood stood at the edge of the lawn. The giddy relief that had filled Jack vanished. The blueblood was an enemy, too.

The man stepped forward. His fur cloak lay behind him in the grass. Smoothly he pulled a long, slender sword from the sheath at his waist. His eyes looked past Jack, at the two beasts.

"Back toward me very slowly," the blueblood said.

Jack remained put. The blueblood wanted Rose. He couldn't be trusted.

The beasts advanced.

"I won't hurt you," the man promised. "You must come closer. Now."

A scent drifted down from him, a light, spicy aroma of cloves.

The blueblood was human. The beasts were not.

Slowly, as if underwater, Jack took a step back.

The beasts stepped forward in unison.

"That's it," the blueblood said. Jack clenched on to that voice and took another slow step.

The beasts moved closer.

A third step.

He saw the muscles bunch on their legs and knew they were about to charge.

"Run!" the blueblood barked and sprinted to him.

Jack dashed. He flew across the grass like there were wings on his feet. Out of the corner of his eyes, he saw the dark shapes veering to flank him. They would catch him, they would . . .

A hand grasped his shoulder and pulled him forward, past the man into the grass. Jack rolled, coming to a crouch.

The left beast leapt into the air. The blueblood slashed with his sword, and two halves of a dark body fell into the grass, twitching. The blade shone again like a sliver of moonlight, and the second beast's head bounced off the lawn.

The blueblood raised his hand and sank a short burst of white into the left beast, first one half, then the other. Acrid smoke rose, scratching the back of Jack's throat. The beast's legs stopped quivering.

The blueblood put another shot of white into the head of the second beast, turned, and bent down. Jack felt himself scooped off the ground, and he clutched onto the man's neck. Enemy or friend, he didn't care. The blueblood was warm and human, and he had a big sword.

"You did well," the blueblood said.

Jack held on tighter. His body shook and shivered, as if he were freezing.

Georgie ran off the porch and halted at the ward line, looking white enough to be dead.

The blueblood carried Jack to the line of wards and nodded at Georgie. "Move the rocks."

Georgie hesitated only for a minute.

FRIDAY, Rose murmured to herself, striding up the road to the house. Tomorrow was Friday, payday. She'd get her three hundred bucks and put some gas into the damn truck. Kitty ears or not, she wouldn't go without gas again.

All afternoon she had been plagued by anxiety. It started the moment she watched the kids board the bus and kept building and building, until it blossomed into a full-blown dread. The kids were well equipped to handle two hours at home by themselves. They knew how to shoot both the rifle and a crossbow, and they were safe behind the wards. But the worry spurred her on, and a mile from the house, she shouldered her tote and broke into a jog. She turned onto their narrow dirt path and ran past the bushes and into the yard.

Three dark stains dotted the grass, smoking, spreading foul magic into the air. The smell hit her like a punch to the gut: the thick rotten stench of greasy roast burned over a fire and left to rot. Rose gagged and sprinted up the steps to the house. She tore the door open, cleared the living room, and burst into the kitchen.

The boys sat at the table, watching the blueblood noble at the stove. He held a frying pan in one hand and a kitchen towel in the other.

Rose barely noticed as her tote slipped off her shoulder and fell to the floor, the gun making a dull clang.

The four of them stared at each other.

The blueblood flipped a pancake with a short toss of the pan.

FIVE

"YOU let him in?"

The boys cringed.

"Inside? Into our house?"

Georgie ducked as if she had thrown something at him.

"I'll deal with you later." Rose fixed the blueblood with her gaze. "You—leave now."

He slid the pancake onto a three-inch-tall stack, dipped a spoon into the sugar bowl, sprinkled sugar onto the pancake, and looked at her brothers.

"The first rule of etiquette a boy learns when he's about to enter society is that civility is due to all women. No provocation, no matter how unjust and rudely delivered, can validate a man who fails to treat a woman with anything less than utmost courtesy."

The boys hung on his every word. He glanced in her direction.

"I have met some incredibly unpleasant women, and I have never failed in this duty. But I must admit: your sister may prove my undoing."

Rose pulled the magic to her. "Get out."

He shook his head with a critical look on his face.

She clenched her fist. "You have ten seconds to exit my house, or I'll fry you."

"If you try frying me, I'll be seriously put out," he said. "Besides, pancakes taste much better fried, given that they are sweet and fluffy and I'm full of gristle. Would you like one?" He held the platter out to her.

The magic vibrated in her, ready to be released.

Jack slid off his chair and stood in front of the blueblood, blocking her.

"Move!"

"He saved me from the beasts," Jack said quietly.

"What beasts?"

"The beasts outside. They attacked me."

"How do you know he didn't conjure the beasts in the first place?"

"To what purpose?" the blueblood asked.

"To get into the house!"

"And why, pray tell, would I want to do that?"

Rose halted. She wasn't sure why he would want to do that. If there was something he hoped to gain by entering the house, she couldn't think of it. "I don't know," she said. "But I don't trust you."

He nodded to the boys. "Start on the pancakes. Your sister and I need to have a talk." He moved toward her.

She raised her head. If he thought he could order her around in her own house, he was in for a hell of a surprise. "Fine. We'll talk outside." Where Jack couldn't shield him.

The blueblood nodded, sidestepped her with smooth grace, and held the front door open for her.

"Don't hurt him, Rose!" Georgie said.

Jack looked like a wet kitten: miserable.

Rose marched onto the porch, shut both the door and the screen door firmly behind her, and pointed to the path. "Road's that way."

He descended the steps. Without the cape, he didn't seem quite as massive. The light, supple leather of his black jerkin hugged his broad, muscular back, which slimmed to a narrow waist caught by a leather belt, and long runner's legs in gray pants and tall dark boots. His movements had a sure but light quality about them. He wasted no gesture, economical yet adroit, and as he walked across the grass to the smoking stains, she was reminded of her grandfather. Cletus had moved like that, with the agility of a natural fencer. But where her grandfather had been lean and relied on speed, the blueblood, while probably fast, looked very strong. She had a feeling that if he hadn't jumped onto her Ford, the old truck would have crumpled around him like an empty soda can.

The blueblood stopped by the stain and glanced at her.

She crossed her arms. He held out his hand, inviting her to join him. Fat chance.

"Please grace me with your presence," he said as if she were a lady at some ball and he was inviting her on a balcony for a private chat.

He was mocking her. She bristled. "I can see everything from here."

"Do you care for your brothers?"

"Of course I do."

"Then I fail to understand why you take their safety so lightly. Come here, please. Or should I carry you?"

She jumped off the porch and walked over. "I'd like to see you try."

"Don't tempt me." He knelt by the stain and held his hand above it. The power coalesced below his palm. He murmured something in a language she didn't understand. The magic flowed, following his words, and the smoke condensed into a shape.

An awful beast stared at her. It was tall and long, with the deep chest and hindquarters of a greyhound. Its head on a long neck was almost horse-like in shape, except for the four dull gray slits of the slanted eyes. The creature's paws were disproportionately large, their fingers long and armed with three-inch claws. The thought of those claws ripping into Jack made Rose gulp.

Obeying the wave of the blueblood's hand, the beast opened his mouth. Its head nearly split in half, its maw gaping wide, wider, showing rows of triangular teeth, bloodred and serrated, designed to shred meat.

"There were two of them," the blueblood said softly. "One came from the left and the other from behind the house. They stalked Jack and meant to kill him. I understand that your education is lacking and you don't trust me, so listen to your instincts instead: you know that this is an aberration. This isn't an animal, but something else entirely. Put your hand into it."

"What?"

"Touch it. You'll feel the residual traces of its magic. It won't harm you."

Cautiously Rose touched the smoke. Her fingers tingled

with magic, and she felt it, an awful sensation of touching something slimy and rotting, yet coarse, as if she'd stuck her hand into a putrid carcass and found it filled with sharp grains of sand. She recoiled.

That wasn't enough. She had to learn more.

Rose forced her fingers back into the smoke. The revolting sensation claimed her hand again, and she grimaced, looking away, but held her hand within the creature. Her fingers numbed, and then she sensed a distant echo of foul magic, pulsing like a live wire within the memory of the beast. It was an alien magic, impassive and cold like the blackness between the stars. Rose withdrew her hand and shook it, trying to fling the memory of the feeling from her fingers. He was right. This was no natural animal.

The blueblood collapsed the smoke shape and offered her his hand. "Touch me."

She stared at his palm. Calloused. Probably from swinging that bloody sword.

"I won't bite," he said. "Not until you're in my bed, anyway."

"Never happen." She put her hand into his. Magic slid into her fingers. He was letting her see his power. It shone within him, warm and white, like a distant star. The star dimmed and vanished, as if hidden by a cloak, and suddenly Rose found her fingers in the hand of a man, who was studying her with a knowing smirk. His skin was warm and rough, his grip firm, and her mind came right back to his "biting in bed" remark.

Rose jerked her hand out of his fingers. His point was clear: even she knew that to summon those beasts, he would've had to open himself to their greedy magic. It clung to her still, trying to worm its way inside. Anybody in prolonged contact with the beasts or their source would be permanently tainted. She had detected none of their miasma within the blueblood. He was clean.

The blueblood raised his hands, as if asking for her feedback.

"You've made your point," she admitted. "You didn't bring them here. You've made much of your education, so I take it you know what they are. What are they, and what do they want?"

He looked lost in thought for a moment. "I have no idea," he said. "I'm calling them 'hounds' for now."

Great. Fantastic.

"I know they wanted to kill Jack," he said. "I don't believe he was a particular target. They would've gone for anyone else in his place. Their magic is . . ."

"Clingy," she supplied.

The blueblood nodded. "It seeks to assimilate. It's dangerous."

"Thank you, Captain Obvious."

"That's why I'll stay with you tonight," he said.

Rose blinked. "What?"

"I didn't come all this way to have my future bride consumed by some aberration. You're ill equipped to deal with this threat. If your sensibilities won't permit my presence in your house, then I'll remain here." He pointed to the porch.

"No!"

"Yes." He turned his back to her, walked onto the porch, and sat on the steps.

"I want you to leave."

"I'm afraid it's not possible. See, I promised your brothers that I'll keep them safe tonight, and I won't go back on my word. It's your right not to invite me inside, but I would appreciate a blanket. That would be simple human charity."

Rose felt like stomping, except she didn't want to give him the satisfaction of knowing how much he irritated her. "This is unnecessary," she said. "We're safe behind the wards."

"I'm not so sure."

"Look, I appreciate your intentions, but I want you to leave. Now."

He ignored her.

Rose glanced at the house and saw two little faces behind the window screens. Great. What to do now? Blueblood or no, he had saved Jack. He had sworn not to harm them, and flashing a man who was doing nothing to attack her went against her every instinct.

He couldn't really be trying to protect them. That would be . . . noble. She almost guffawed at the pun.

Fatigue mugged her like a wet blanket thrown over her

head. It had been a terrible day, and she had no energy to argue.

"Fine. You're welcome to the porch."

Rose went inside, pulling the door shut with a thud. The boys stared at her. "If he tries to come inside, shoot him," she said and headed for the shower.

SOMETIMES simple pleasures are best, and nothing compared with a shower after work. Having spent the entire day squirting cleaners and scrubbing office counters and walls, Rose now thoroughly scrubbed herself with Irish Spring and a fake sea sponge. It took her ten minutes to drown the day in shampoo and soap, and when she emerged, put on clean clothes, and brushed her wet hair, she felt almost human.

While she was in the shower, her fury at the blueblood's intrusion slowly melted into uncomfortable unease. The blueblood had saved Jack. He'd stayed with them because they were scared and even made them food, and then she'd treated him like dirt. She felt bad about it. This is stupid, Rose told herself. He was here to force her into marriage. All of this could be an act. She owed him no sympathy.

The creatures that had attacked Jack terrified her to the very depths of her being. Rose wished she could speak to Grandma, but with the evening rolling into night, the trip would have to wait until the morning. And Grandma Éléonore, although she would use a phone in a pinch, refused to keep one at her house.

In the kitchen, Jack brought her a pancake on a blue metal plate. "It's good," he told her. "He made them special. See, he put sugar on them."

Oh, for heaven's sake. "Tell me everything, from the beginning."

Ten minutes later, she pieced together the whole story. The blueblood had cut the beasts to pieces in a feat of incredible martial prowess demonstrated by Georgie with much vigorous waving of his fork, brought Jack inside, promised them that nothing bad was going to get them while they were in his care, and then proceeded to make pancakes. If he somehow staged this whole thing, which was still a possibility, it was masterfully done. The boys were now convinced that he could move heaven and earth. In their eyes, in the space of an hour, the blueblood went from the "shoot on sight" villain to a glorious hero of unmatched manliness.

"Did he eat?"

The boys shook their heads.

Great. Now she had a hungry "hero" on the porch without food or blanket. And her vague unease had blossomed into full-blown guilt. Completely crazy, she reflected as she pulled some sausage from the fridge and fried it. She should be shooting him in the head.

Rose divided the sausage onto four plates. "Eat your dinner."

She put a fork and a knife onto one of the plates. Georgie jumped off his chair, poured iced tea into a plastic cup, and handed it to her. Rose rolled her eyes and took the food and the tea over to the porch.

He sat in the same spot she had left him, staring at the sky colored with the first hint of sunset. The wind swiped stray hairs from his long blond mane. His huge sword lay next to him. Even at peace, he emanated menace.

Throw the plate at him and run, she told herself.

She set the plate next to him.

"Thank you," he said.

Now he thanked you and you go back inside.

Instead she leaned against the porch post. "Are you really going to spend the night on my porch?"

"Yes."

"I can perfectly take care of us myself. It's fixing to get dark. You should go back to wherever you're staying."

"I'm sure my tent will greatly miss me," he said.

"A tent?"

"Yes."

"You're sleeping in a tent? Why? Are you out of money?"

"On the contrary." He reached into his jerkin and produced a small leather wallet secured by a strap. He undid the strap, dipped his hand inside, and produced a gold coin. The sunset rays glinted on the metal surface.

A small fortune. She wondered how much it was worth. Would it feed them for two weeks? Three?

"So what's the problem?"

His face wore a perplexed expression. "I tried to seek lodging, but unfortunately most of your neighbors suffer from a critical lack of trust. They see me coming and lock their doors and shutter their windows, and no amount of yelling and wallet waving can persuade them to listen to reason."

Rose pictured him standing at the boundary of the Ogletree house in that enormous fur cape, with a giant sword sticking over his shoulder, roaring at the top of his lungs and then being upset that nobody came out, and laughed.

"I'm sure my predicament seems hilarious to you," he said dryly. "You live in an insane place populated by mad people without a shred of courtesy."

"Have you tried the McCalls down south? They could use the money."

He turned up his nose, oozing aristocratic haughtiness like it was cheap cologne. "I won't stay in a shack."

"Well, excuse me, Your Highness." She laughed harder.

"Some men in my situation would find your giggling offensive."

"I can't help it. It must be nerves." She shook with laughter. The fear that curled inside her in a small, cold chunk of ice melted. The blueblood wasn't harmless—far from it—but once she had laughed at someone, it was hard to go back to full-out terror.

"You could let me stay here. I would pay you, of course." He dropped the coin into the wallet. It made a metallic clink, announcing there were many more just like it.

"Oh, you're good," she said. "You want me to let you stay in our house?"

"Why not? I already promised to protect you, so I'm bound to this property by my own word, at least for tonight. You might just as well make some money from my misfortune."

"You're unbelievable." Rose shook her head. Why in the world did he want to get into her house so much? A small part of her wondered if he really was worried about the kids, but a much bigger part of her shook its head in cynical disbelief. He was a blueblood. He didn't give a damn about mongrel Edger boys.

"I'm simply pragmatic. You probably have a spare bed in that house, which, I hope, is clean and soft, and therefore much preferable to the hard wooden floor of this porch."

She actually considered it. He could bust her door down with one shove of his shoulder. In fact, he could probably go through a wall, if he set his mind to it. In terms of their safety, having him on the porch or in the house made absolutely no difference. The money would be most welcome. She could buy beef instead of chicken for once. An extra set of uniforms for Georgie. Lunchables for the kids. They always wanted them, but at $3.98 a pop, they were a rare treat.

"This would be a purely business arrangement, separate from our other agreement," she warned.

"Of course."

"I want you to swear that you won't attempt to molest me."

He looked her over very slowly. "If I chose to molest you, it wouldn't be an attempt. And you would be most enthusiastic about it."

Rose felt heat rise to her cheeks. "On second thought, I'm not sure that my house is big enough to contain you and your ego. Few places are. Promise or sleep outside."

"If you insist."

"I would prefer to hear the words."

He sighed. "I promise not to molest you, no matter how tempting."

"Or the children."

The smile vanished from his face. His eyebrows came together, and his eyes grew dark. "I'm a noble of the house Camarine. I don't molest children. I won't be insulted—"

"I don't care," she interrupted. "You can beat your chest with your fist in righteous indignation, or you can swear and sleep inside. Your choice."

"You're the most infuriating woman I have ever met. I swear not to molest the boys," he ground out.

Rose held out her hand, and he dropped a gold coin into her palm. A Weird doubloon. Even with the draconian fee Max Taylor charged for converting gold into dollars, the little coin was food for a month.

"I don't have change. Do you have something smaller?"

"Keep it," he growled.

"Suit yourself."

She opened the door with a mock bow and a big smile. "Please, Your Highness."

"My Lord Camarine will do."

"Whatever."

She ushered him inside. The boys had polished off the food and were washing their plates.

"Georgie, fetch his plate and drink from the porch, please. He will be staying in Dad's bedroom tonight—he paid for it. You're sleeping in my room on the floor."

The blueblood growled low in his throat.

In thirty seconds Rose and the blueblood sat at the table across from each other. Rose tried the pancakes. They were predictably cold, but still delicious, and she was ravenous. "God, these are good."

"Slowly."

Rose raised her gaze from her plate.

He sat very straight at the table, cutting the pancake with surgical precision.

"Eat slowly," the blueblood said. "Don't cut your food with the fork. Cut it with the knife, and make the pieces small enough so you can answer a question without having to swallow first."

Why me? "Right. Any other tips?"

Her sarcasm whistled right over his head. "Yes. Look at me and not at your plate. If you have to look at your plate, glance at it occasionally."

Rose put down her fork. "Lord Submarine . . ."

"Camarine."

"Whatever."

"You can call me Declan." He said it as if granting her knighthood. The nerve.

"Declan, then. How did you spend your day?"

He frowned.

"It's a simple question: How did you spend your day? What did you do prior to the fight and pancake making?"

"I rested from my journey," he said with a sudden regal air.

"You took a nap."

"Possibly."

"I spent my day scrubbing, vacuuming, and dusting ten offices in the Broken. I got there at seven thirty in the morning and left at six. My back hurts, I can still smell bleach on my fingers, and my feet feel as flat as these pancakes. Tomorrow, I have to go back to work, and I want to eat my food in peace and quiet. I have good table manners. They may not be good enough for you, but they're definitely good enough for the Edge, and they are the height of social graces for this house. So please keep your critique to yourself."

The look on his face was worth having him under her roof. As if he had gotten slapped.

She smiled at him. "Oh, and thank you for the pancakes. They are delicious."

SIX

ROSE awoke early. She had slept badly, in short bursts, waking up every hour or so to check on the kids. Twice she thought she heard something outside, and she went out onto the porch to investigate. She found nothing. Just the night, which, so mundane a day before, suddenly seemed sinister and full of danger.

When she did fall asleep, she dreamt of monsters, children screaming, and sliding out of control on wet mud that seemed never to end. By five, she gave up on sleeping and dragged herself upright to make coffee.

She passed by her father's bedroom. The door was closed. Last night she had given "Declan" a brief tour of the house, starting with the bathroom. He seemed to have matters well in hand. Rose wasn't surprised. The existence of the Broken wasn't exactly public knowledge in the Weird, but some nobility were aware of it, just like a few select Broken residents were aware of the existence of the Weird. He was probably high enough on the social ladder to be privy to secret information.

Tour finished, Rose gave Declan a spare toothbrush—his doubloon had paid for it and more—and a fresh towel, and made up Dad's bed with clean sheets and blankets. The kids told him good night, and he disappeared behind the door. She hadn't seen him in her midnight wanderings. Whatever phantom noises had troubled her failed to bother him.

Rose briefly considered knocking on the door but decided against it. She didn't have to leave, not yet, and she could use a calm moment with a cup of coffee before the kids rose.

She opened the windows to let fresh air in, boiled coffee in a small metal ewer her father called an *ibrik*, allowing the coffee to foam up twice before permanently taking it off the heat, poured herself a cup with a little bit of milk, and sat down at the table, fully intending to savor the drink. In front of her, wide windows offered the view of the lawn running into shrubs bordering the grass. Beyond them she saw the path curling into misty gloom between the trees. In the pre-dawn light, the leaves and the grass were dark and wet with dew. A chill filtered through the screen on the window. On mornings like this, she was grateful for a roof over her head and coffee. Rose brought the cup to her lips, blew gently, and touched the rim. Still too hot.

The creatures disturbed her. She'd never sensed anything so . . . so alien. All magic had a natural connection, even the vilest kind, but the beasts were disconnected from every-thing. They weren't undead; they weren't conjured, ani-mated, or transmuted. To do any of those things, one had to start with a natural element: rock, metal, living tissue, and that base left an imprint on the final creation. The beasts' magic had no ties to anything.

As much as it pained her to admit, she was deeply grate-ful that Declan happened to come along to save Jack. That, far more than the doubloon, had earned him a stay in her house. Her memory served up Declan, bursting with power, his eyes iced over with radiant white . . . He was something else. She'd thought of him several times last night, during her relay of catnaps and paranoid wakefulness. She still wanted to touch his face just to reassure herself that he was indeed flesh and bone.

Rose dragged her mind back to the problem of the boys. Without her truck, she had no way of getting the kids safely to and from the bus stop. Letting them walk by themselves was out of the question, not with those creatures around. She had to be at work by seven thirty and would likely stay there until five, if she was lucky, or six. The kids were released at three thirty in the afternoon, and the bus dropped them off at three forty-five. They couldn't walk up to the house by them-selves, not with those beasts around, and she didn't feel com-fortable making them wait that long by the main road. Grandma was likely still at Adele's. The old woman lived deep in the Wood, and whenever Grandma visited her, she usually lingered overnight.

The boys couldn't wait for two hours by the bus stop. The Broken had its predators as well. They would have to skip a day.

A movement on the path made her stretch her neck to get a better look. Declan emerged from the shadowy trail, running. She jerked upright, expecting pursuit. He ran to the lawn, leaned forward for a moment, shaking his head, and began to circle the house slowly in that telltale jogger way, walking off the burn in his lungs. Rose dropped back into her chair. Her pulse hammered. Prickly needles of adrenaline rush nipped at her arms. Damn him.

He probably didn't know the meaning of running from his attacker, arrogant ass that he was. Chew slowly, indeed.

She understood why he was the way he was. She'd read the *Encyclopedia of the Weird* and other books she bartered from the caravans. The nobles of the Weird enjoyed unmatched power. They ruled over their domains as individuals and over their countries as assemblies under the watch of a constitutional monarch. They were painstakingly bred, educated from birth, and brought up with the sense of belonging to the elite. Like purebred show dogs groomed for obedience training competitions. Their lives had strict rules. It was not really his fault for trying to impose them on everyone—he simply didn't know of any other way to be. But just because she understood where he was coming from didn't make him welcome.

Declan completed his circle and stopped right in front of the porch. He wore dark pants, a shirt with ripped-off sleeves that left his arms exposed, and light boots. Nice arms . . .

The way he had summoned an image of that beast yesterday; now that was impressive. She wanted so badly to learn how he did it, she'd almost asked. Almost. He'd laugh in her face. He already thought she was an ignorant, rude mongrel. No need to give him more ammunition.

The huge sword was still on his back. He shrugged it off and pulled off his shirt. Rose paused with the cup halfway to her lips.

His golden hair, damp with sweat, spilled down his back. Tall, big boned, layered with carved muscle, he was made with strength in mind, but the massive width of his shoulders and chest tapered to a flat stomach and narrow waist. His hips were lean, his legs long and powerful. Despite all his bulk, there was a honed sleekness about him—he was strong, supple, and quick, a man who spent all his life sharpening his body into a weapon. That's what they did, the nobles of the Weird. Their ultimate purpose was to lead armies into battle.

Declan turned very slightly. It was a tiny movement, but she caught it—he'd checked that he could be seen from the window. Ha! He was showing off for her benefit. Rose smiled into her cup. Blueblood or not, he was still a man.

Declan flexed a little, displaying a perfect chest to the grass, and stretched. Rose leaned her head to the side, following his movement as he turned, letting her stare trail the sharp line of his biceps to his muscled back, and over his chest to his flat, ridged stomach. They really did know how to make them in the Weird.

No hair on his chest or stomach. All of that muscle clothed in golden skin, slicked with sweat from running. Against the cold fog of the morning, he radiated heat as if lit from within by his own warm glow. He was beautiful. Even his iceberg eyes were captivating despite the menace.

She drank her coffee. He must've done something truly awful to have to look for a bride in the Edge. Maybe he was a rapist . . . No, she decided. She just didn't feel that creepy vibe from him. A killer maybe? Murdered the son of somebody important in a duel? That she could see.

He picked up his sword. Now what?

Declan held the blade above his head, pointing parallel to the grass. For a long moment he stood still, utterly focused, and then erupted into sharp strikes. He slashed and thrust, fluid muscles rolling under his skin, faster and faster, cutting down invisible opponents in a lethal dance born of melding the sword fight and art.

That was entirely more than a woman could take. Rose lowered her cup to the table, leaned her head on her elbow, and simply watched.

She harbored no illusions. The only value she had to him was in her ability to flash and bear children. If she agreed to become his bride or his mistress, she would live in the house of a cold frigid man who would probably despise her, among people who would be so busy looking down on her because of what she was, they would have no chance to find out who she was. Her brothers would be servants at best. It would be a terrible life. True, Declan was heartbreakingly beautiful and hypnotic to watch. But she would have even more fun when she watched that muscled back and that perfect ass recede as he walked down the path away from her house, never to return.

ELSIE sat in her room on the rocker, holding Mr. Clooney. Through the doorway she saw her granddaughter and her best friend, Leanne, talking in hushed voices. On the porch, Amy's daughter Mindy was trying to do the same with Kenny Jo, Leanne's oldest boy, but he wasn't answering.

The four-eyed creature sat in the doorway blocking Elsie's exit. She had spent the whole night drawing the ward glyphs on the floor with a Magic Marker. She would've drawn more, but the marker had run dry.

The creature leaned and nudged at the invisible wall of magic streaming from the glyphs. A spark shot from the twisted swirls and nipped the creature's chin. It sat back on its haunches and showed her its teeth: bloodred and nasty. It wanted to get her. She shook the teddy bear at it. It was the same one who killed Mr. Bana, she was sure.

"Thanks for coming," Amy said. "I don't know what got into her. She sat like that since yesterday noon. She won't come out, and I can't drag her out by myself."

"Older folks get like this sometimes." Leanne nodded in understanding.

Amy was tall and soft, with a round face and a round belly and round hair of little brownish curls. Leanne was about the same height, but skinny and wiry, with a sharp face. Like a blond ferret with boobs. All of the Meddlers' women bred that way. Elsie pursed her lips. Together they would drag her out. She'd tied herself to the rocker with her scarves, but she knew the restraints wouldn't stand up to them for long.

Two more creatures padded from the kitchen. One slunk by Amy, almost brushing her big butt. She shivered and glanced over her shoulder. The creature looked right at her. She shrugged and turned back to Leanne. Elsie sneered. Stupid girl.

The creature by the door smiled at her. Soon, its gray eyes promised. Soon.

"It's not that I want to manhandle her, but . . ." Amy leaned forward and said confidentially, "She's wet herself. I just don't want it to get around that I abuse my grandma and all that. You know how people are."

"You don't have to worry on my account," Leanne assured her.

The two creatures hooked their claws into the wall and began crawling up the side like two huge ugly lizards. Tiny flecks of plaster broke off and fell on the floor.

"No, I know. You don't gossip. I just . . . I sure do appreciate this. With Bob away hunting, I'm by myself here. I'd like to get it done before the younger kids are up. That's not something they need to see."

Leanne nodded. "Let's get it over with."

They headed to the door. The creature slunk out of the way, behind the couch. Leanne stopped in the doorway and stared at the floor covered with black lines. "Oh my."

"She's done it overnight. I don't even know what this is." Amy shook her head. "Last thing I need is some foulness to pop out of these glyphs. You know? I have kids in the house."

Leanne shook her head. "Sometimes the mind just gives out."

Amy crossed the room and stopped before Elsie. "Grandma. You've got to come out."

Elsie let go of Mr. Clooney and clutched the armrests of her rocker. They wouldn't be getting her out, not where the beasts could get her.

"If you're refusing to listen to reason, Leanne and I'll have to take you out by force."

Elsie dug her nails into the wood.

"Suit yourself." Amy sighed, leaned over, and tried to pull her free. "Oh, my Lord in Heaven, she tied herself to the chair. With her good scarves, too."

She went into a crouch to pull loose the knot by the chair legs, and Elsie raked her face. Blood swelled. Amy stared stunned, tears swelling in her eyes. "Grandma!"

Elsie raised her hands, her bony fingers curled like claws. "You leave me alone!"

Leanne struck at her left hand, pinning it down with both of hers. Elsie scratched at her, but Amy clamped her right wrist to the armrest. Elsie snapped, trying to bite, and Amy pressed her left hand onto her chest, pinning her to the chair. Elsie growled and gnashed her teeth, but couldn't reach Amy's arm.

They looked at each other.

"Now what?" Amy breathed. "I can't reach the knot, and if I let go, she'll claw us bloody."

"Kenny Jo!" Leanne called. "I'll get him to untie the knot, and then we move her just like this right into the shower. Kenny Jo!"

The screen door banged, and Kenny Jo crossed the living room and stepped into the bedroom. The glyphs shivered a little. Elsie buckled against Amy's hand. Kenny Jo wasn't a dud like Amy. "Run!" she yelled at him. "Run!"

"Ma?"

"I need you . . ."

The first creature padded from behind the couch and stared at Kenny's back. He turned and went white as a sheet. The creature stepped forward, rocking on its haunches. Kenny stumbled back. His mouth gaped open. He choked, struggling, gulped, and screamed, setting the glass on the windows ringing.

SEVEN

ROSE didn't remember her coffee until Declan was done with his workout. Her drink had gone cold. She got up to get a fresh cup just as he strode through the door. He dwarfed the kitchen, big, golden, and intimidating. At least his shirt was back on, which was definitely a good thing. "Coffee?" she asked.

He nodded. "Thank you."

She had hoped he'd take a shower, which would have gotten him out of the kitchen. She could've used a moment to cool off.

Up close, she caught his scent: a faint aroma of sandalwood and a very male musk emanating from his tawny, sweat-slicked skin. No, she told herself firmly and took a step out of his reach. He looked superb, he smelled like a drug, and if she went over and found out how he tasted, she would throw away her freedom, independence, and future with one kiss.

"I apologize for my attire," Declan said.

His attire was quite fine, thank you very much. In fact, she should probably go and get a big black trash bag and slide it over him. It would certainly make her life easier. "Not a problem. We don't have much use for ceremony and formal clothes in the Edge."

His gaze snagged on her Clean-n-Bright uniform. "Why are you wearing that?"

"It's my uniform. Everyone in my company wears it."

"It's hideous."

Rose felt her hackles rise. The neon green uniform was hideous, but she didn't appreciate him pointing it out. She opened her mouth.

"Yet despite it, you look lovely," he said.

"Flattery will get you nowhere," she told him.

"It's not flattery," he said coldly. "Flattery requires exaggeration. I'm merely stating a fact. You're a beautiful woman wearing an ugly sack of unnatural color."

Rose stared at him, not sure what to make of it. Was it a compliment or an insult? Unable to decide, she shrugged it off.

"It's customary to offer breakfast to boarders," he said.

"I hope you enjoy Mini-Wheats. That's all we have."

She pulled a box of cereal from the shelf and poured it into two bowls. "I wanted to thank you for saving Jack. And for staying with them and making pancakes."

"I did what any honorable man would do," he said.

"That said, I still refuse to go away with you." She added milk and pushed one of the bowls toward him.

"Duly noted." He hesitated as if deciding on something. "The boys are very brave."

"Thank you."

She sat across from him and looked at him. "Suppose, just for the sake of the argument, that you win the challenges. What are your intentions toward me? Am I going to be auctioned off to the highest bidder like a prized cow, or are you planning on keeping me for yourself?"

His eyes turned dark. "Did someone try to auction you off, Rose?"

"That's not important."

"On the contrary. The slave trade is forbidden in Adrianglia. If someone's selling people, I want to know about it."

She narrowed her eyes. "And what would you do about it?"

"I'd make them deeply regret it."

She had no doubt he could. "Why do you care?"

"It's my responsibility as a peer of the realm to make sure the laws of Adrianglia are upheld. I take it seriously."

"All that is good," she said, "but you still didn't answer my question. What are your intentions toward me?"

He leaned forward. Some of the hardness drained from his eyes. They turned deep and very green. "I intend to have you."

"In what sense of the word?"

A narrow smile tugged on the corners of his mouth. He looked utterly focused, like a cat about to pounce. "In every sense."

Rose choked on her coffee.

Georgie stumbled into the kitchen, rubbing his eyes. Instantly, Declan leaned back, his face casual.

There was a moment there when his eyes had lit up, and she thought he might have been pulling her leg. Almost as if he said that just to get a rise out of her. Could he be joking? Surely not. Not that she would put it past him to make fun at her expense, but he didn't seem capable of humor.

Rose added another bowl, poured the milk, and distributed the food. Georgie crawled into the chair next to Declan and poked at his Mini-Wheats with a spoon.

"Thank you for the meal," Declan said, picking up his own spoon.

"Thank you for the meal," Georgie echoed. Well, at least one good thing came from the blueblood being here: Georgie said thank you without being reminded.

Georgie looked at Declan, probably waiting for a clue to his next move. She understood why. Something about Declan telegraphed "man." It wasn't his face, although he was heart-stoppingly handsome, if grim. He had a great build and he carried himself well, but that wasn't quite it either. It wasn't his swords, or his cloak, or his leathers. It was something unidentifiable, something in his eyes or in the air he projected, something she couldn't quite pin down.

For lack of a better word, Declan radiated masculinity. The "depend on him in a dark alley" kind of masculinity. The "hit the bad guy with a chair before he shoots us" kind of masculinity. If they were attacked, he wouldn't hesitate to put himself between them and the danger, because that's what men did. The boys didn't stand a chance.

Under different circumstances, she might not have stood a chance either. But experience had taught her very well: bluebloods were to be feared and avoided. All that rock-steady manliness could be an elaborate act. She had to watch her every step.

Declan put a spoonful of cereal into his mouth. Georgie hesitated. Getting him to eat was an ordeal lately. He was hungry all the time but ate like a bird, a bite here, a bite there. And if he didn't eat enough, he got shaky.

Declan chewed, scooped more cereal into his spoon, put it into his mouth, and glanced at Georgie. Georgie fidgeted under the pressure of those green eyes, picked up his own spoon again, and started eating.

"Georgie, you're staying with Grandma today," she said.

"Why?"

"It's not safe to walk to the bus stop or back up from it."

Declan paused. "You're going to work? Shouldn't their safety be your first responsibility?"

"I know my responsibilities well, thank you very much. I don't work, we don't eat. It's that simple."

They chewed their food. She glanced at Declan. He ate quietly, enjoying his meal. He caught her looking.

"It's quite good, thank you."

He had to be used to much better. He was probably just being polite. "You're welcome," she murmured

Georgie stirred in his seat, glancing at her. "Jack said you smelled like William yesterday."

"Georgie!"

Too late. A predatory light sparked in Declan's eyes. The blueblood came to life like a shark sensing a drop of blood. "Who's William?"

"None of your business," Rose snapped.

"He's a guy. He likes action figures," Georgie said helpfully. "He asked Rose on a date, but she didn't go."

"Does your sister go on dates often?"

"Every week," Rose said.

"Never," Georgie declared at the same time. "It's because Brad Dillon tried to kidnap her on their last date."

She stared at him. How did he know that?

"Mémère told me. Brad hit her on the head with a club, and she fried him with her flash. Jack and I liked William okay. But Brad is a scumba—"

"George." Rose loaded her voice with steel. "Go brush your teeth and wake up your brother."

He slid off the chair and took off.

Declan leaned forward, his features iced over. "This William. What does he look like?"

"Shockingly handsome," Rose told him.

"That covers a lot of ground."

"You don't need to know what he looks like!"

"Of course I do. If I meet him, I'll have to discourage him from courting you. You don't want me to assault some random stranger, do you?"

She took her bowl to the sink.

"Rose," he called. "This is important. What does William look like?"

Rose rinsed out her bowl, glanced up to the window, and saw Leanne Ogletree on the path to her house, striding forward in a determined fashion. A worried expression pinched Leanne's face into a pale mask. If a big pink elephant with rainbow wings had appeared at the end of the path, Rose would've been less surprised. The words died on her lips. Now what?

Declan came to stand by her. "Who is that?"

"The former bane of my existence. Stay inside, please."

Rose braced herself and stepped out onto the porch.

Leanne walked up to the steps. She was a thin, narrow-hipped woman, who seemed to consist entirely of sharp angles: sharp elbows, prominent knees, defined face, and a stare, which, as Rose knew from experience, could slice like a knife. They hadn't spoken a word to each other for the last four years. Rose kept to herself, and Leanne wasn't a social butterfly either, not since Sarah Walton married and moved away. The few times they had run into each other in public, they'd silently conspired to ignore each other's presence.

It was damned hard to ignore somebody who was standing right there by the porch.

"Morning, Leanne." Rose kept her tone civil.

"Morning."

Leanne's face was pale, and in her blue eyes, Rose glimpsed a small echo of fear.

There were a dozen things Rose could say—about Sarah, who now refused to recognize Leanne; about Leanne's husband, Beau Ogletree, who had taken off to adventures unknown; about Leanne's dad, who just last Sunday got so hammered he puked his guts out right on the steps of the church, scandalizing all local Edger Christians forever. But

Leanne stood there, with that fear in her eyes, and Rose let it go.

"What's wrong?" she asked simply.

"It's Kenny Jo. We went to visit Amy Haire to help with her grandma Elsie. You know her."

"Elsie Moore? With the tea parties?"

"Yeah. She shut herself in her room and won't come out. She'd tied herself to her rocker, and when Amy and I tried to move her, she scratched Amy bloody. So I called Kenny Jo to come undo the knots while we held her down. He got into the room and started screaming. I tried to take him out of the room, but something ripped his clothes. It clawed the T-shirt right off of him and scratched his chest. Elsie says we can't see it because it's hiding and our magic isn't strong enough. But Kenny Jo sees it."

"Why come to me?" Rose asked.

"He was screaming your name." Leanne swallowed and said in a hoarse voice, "Look, I know I made your life hell in high school. But it's my kid in there. Please help me save my boy."

"You can't see anything outside of the room?"

Leanne shook her head. "I felt something. Cold and wet . . ."

"Like slime down your back?" Rose shivered, recalling the beast that attacked Jack.

"Yes. Like that."

"Wait here for me, please. I'll be only a minute."

ROSE hurried inside the house, dropped the attic's ladder, and climbed up, flicking on the light. For years the attic had served as the repository of all sorts of junk her father had found in his adventures, and now piles of bizarre objects greeted her: old books, broken weapons, twisted puzzles which, when solved, showed a way to some fabulous non-existent treasure, rolls of fake maps, dime-store antiques . . .

"Jack!" she called.

He scrambled up the ladder.

"I need the see-lantern. Hurry!"

He breathed in the stale scents of the attic, scrambled up

the pile of oddities, and plucked the lantern from the heap. It was an old, beat-up maritime lantern. Discoloration from years in salt water dappled its heavy metal base and ornate top. Rose shook it gently, holding it by the ring in its roof, and a tiny green light flared within the thick ribbed glass.

"Thank you!"

She climbed down, reciting instructions on the way. "Stay inside. Don't let anyone in or out. I'll be back shortly. If I'm not back by lunch, take the guns and go to Grandma's."

The boys looked at her.

"Okay?"

"Okay." Georgie nodded.

"Jack?"

"Okay."

"Good." She headed out of the house. "Declan?"

Dad's room was empty, the bed so neatly made, she almost did a double take. She hurried past it and saw him, in his full attire, cloak and everything, standing on the porch. Leanne gaped at him in stunned silence.

"I'm coming with you," he declared, punctuating the words with the white frost rolling over his green irises.

"Why?" Rose raced down the porch steps. Leanne took a moment to snap out of her Declan-induced trance and followed her.

"The creatures are dangerous," he said. "And you're a very stubborn woman. You might decide to get yourself killed just to spite me."

There was no way she could keep him from not coming with her. "Suit yourself."

She headed down the path, unreasonably irritated because a small part of her was thrilled to have a large, muscular man with a three-foot sword as her backup.

"Who is he?" Leanne murmured, catching up with her.

"A man who'll soon be leaving empty-handed," Rose said.

AMY'S house was a large, old affair that had started as an A-frame. Long ago it must've had a definite shape, but the Haires were famous for thinking they had carpentering skills, and over the years the house had grown several rooms. It looked like a sprawling mishmash now, sitting in the middle of a wide lawn and bordered by small flower beds, metal junk, and four old rusted cars, none of which had run in the last five or six years. The closer they came to the house, the faster Leanne moved. Rose clenched the lantern to her chest to keep it steady.

"What's the purpose of the lantern?" Declan asked. He had no trouble keeping up with them, not with those long legs.

"It's a see-lantern," she said.

"I realize it's a sea lantern."

"S-e-e, not s-e-a. Sight. It shows magic things to people who don't have enough magic to see them on their own." Neither she nor the boys ever had to use it, but her father had needed it once or twice and swore it worked. It would let Leanne see the danger, if there was any.

Declan frowned. "Everyone can see magic."

"Not in the Edge. Some of the people here have more of the Broken in them than of the Weird."

They ran up the steps. Leanne swung the door open. Rose paused and gently breathed into the triangular holes cut in the lantern's top. The pale green spark grew wider and spread, coloring the lamp glass pale emerald.

Declan snapped his fingers. "I see. It uses an Augustus spiral. The natural exhalation carries residual traces of personal magic, and the coil inside absorbs and amplifies them by cycling them through the loops and then emits the resulting Augustus wave as green light."

Envy bit at Rose. She had understood about two words of what he said, and she would've liked to know more. She lifted the lantern and peered inside.

The living room lay empty. Directly opposite her, across the living room floor, was a bedroom. The door stood wide open, and through the doorway Rose saw Kenny Jo standing alone, in a ripped T-shirt. The scratches on his chest looked shallow. To the right of Kenny, Elsie Moore waited, still tied to the rocker, just as Leanne had described. Amy sat between them on the bedroom floor, hugging her knees. All three of her children huddled around her, silent. The floorboards on which they sat were covered with arcane glyphs, written in black permanent marker.

A creature stuck its head out from behind the couch and peered at Rose with four slanted eyes filled with glowing gray smog. She knew what to expect from the ghostly image Declan had conjured, but seeing it in the flesh nearly made her vomit.

"Oh God!" Leanne gasped.

Amy cried out and immediately clamped her mouth shut, pulling the kids closer to her.

The beast was at least four feet tall. Its skin was dark purple mottled with sickly yellow and pale green, like an old bruise. The creature's mouth gaped open, exposing a forest of narrow deepwater teeth, scarlet red. A hound, Declan called it. The name fit.

A movement to the left made Rose turn. Another beast stared at her from behind the love seat. A third darted in the kitchen. She looked up, raising the lantern higher.

The ceiling teemed with hounds. They shifted along the boards like nightmarish dogs with horse faces and mouths full of dragon teeth.

God, there must be thirty of them in there. Rose gripped the lantern to keep her hand from shaking.

Most of the creatures clung to the wall above the door to the bedroom hiding the children, Amy, and Elsie. Their magic dripped down in a thick repulsive wave, over the wall, over the door, and down on the floor below. Rose couldn't see it, but she felt it, and it felt hungry.

Only now she noticed that the outer line of glyphs stopped six inches past the door, cut off abruptly as if erased. The flesh on her arms broke out in goose pimples.

"The hounds' magic is eating the glyphs. We have to get them out."

In the room, Amy clamped her hand across her mouth and sobbed. The children clutched onto her, all except Kenny Jo, who stood by himself, his eyes fixed on the floor. "I told you," he said with quiet triumph. "I told you."

"Okay," Rose murmured, thinking feverishly. "Okay. We go around back and we try a window." She knew it was a mistake as soon as she said it. Outside the hounds would mob them. There were simply too many.

"Won't work," Leanne whispered. "The window's only a foot wide."

On the ceiling, a scuffle ensued as the beasts realigned to face them.

"They see us." Leanne's voice snapped like a dry twig.

"It will be fine," Rose said firmly. Her mind was spinning a mile a minute, cycling through the possibilities, none of which were plausible.

The hound by the couch lowered its head and started toward her, four eyes fixed on her with predatory intensity.

"It wants you." Leanne backed away onto the porch. "It wants your magic."

Another beast dropped from the ceiling, flipping in the air and landing on all fours.

The magic at the door shaved another two inches off the lines of glyphs.

"Okay." Rose sucked in a breath. "We'll use me as bait. I'll draw them off, and you go and get the kids . . ."

The first beast was only ten feet away.

A hard hand gripped her shoulder and thrust her back behind Declan. In the instant of their touch, she glimpsed a tremendous power buckle and surge within him. His eyes blazed white.

"No, Declan!"

A phantom wind raised his hair. His eyes shone like two stars.

The creature leaped.

A half sphere of blinding white exploded from Declan, roaring like a tornado. Rose's breath caught in her throat.

The first hound perished in midair, swallowed by the light. The blast ripped through the furniture, hit the roof, and swept it away with a crunch of shattered wood. Declan snarled, straining. The white glow flared brighter, burned for a long breath, and vanished.

The roof and the far wall were gone. Rose stared at the sky.

Above them black dots peppered the clear blue, growing bigger and bigger . . . A shower of broken boards and charred beast carcasses rained on the floor with loud thuds. She blinked, and the next moment Declan's face blotted out the sky. "Are you hurt?"

His eyes showed sincere concern. She stepped back, stunned. "No."

"Good." Declan strode through the rain of refuse, unconcerned, crossed the floor to the room, and offered Amy his hand.

She stared at him in shock and slowly put her hand into his. He helped her to her feet. "You're safe now."

"Who are you . . . ?" Amy blinked.

"I am Lord Camarine."

Rose shook her head. All he was missing was the shiny white armor and unearthly light streaming down on him.

"Amy," Elsie Moore said in her crackling voice, her gaze fixed on Declan. "I want you to get me a new bear. A blond one."

EIGHT

BY the time they had calmed down the children and managed to pry Elsie from her chair and force her into the shower, it was well past seven. Rose realized that she wouldn't be making it to work anytime soon. Her uniform stank of greasy, burned flesh, and she had missed her ride with Latoya. She borrowed Amy's cell phone and called it in.

"You better get your ass in here." Latoya's voice gained a shrill quality. "Emerson's being a total dick today. He says either you get in now or he'll shred your check."

"What does he mean, shred my check?"

"It means he won't pay you for this week."

Rose stiffened. No gas money. Without the truck, she couldn't exchange Declan's doubloon for U.S. currency. They had enough groceries to last for three days, four if she was careful. She had no way to pay the electric bill, and it was due in five days. She had to get to work.

"I still have no gas, and it'll take me about a half an hour to clean up."

"Shit. I can't leave—I don't dare piss him off any more."

It hit her: the Broemmer account. Broemmer Hotel had fired Clean-n-Bright two weeks ago, because they caught Emerson overcharging them. Losing that account had dropped Emerson's business by almost a quarter, and he'd been biting at the bit to compensate for his losses somehow. She'd just singled herself out as the perfect scapegoat.

"Okay, wait, I got it," Latoya said. "We'll take an early lunch. Can you get to Burger King?"

Six miles. She could walk it. "Yes."

"Start walking. We'll head there for lunch and pick you up. Emerson won't even know when you got in."

A huge wave of relief rolled over her. "Thank you."

"That's what friends are for." Latoya hung up.

"I'm so sorry about all this," Amy said.

Rose forced a smile. "I was glad to help. I'm sorry about your house."

Amy paled a bit, glanced at the missing wall and busted roof, and forced a smile, too, plainly trying not to cry. "There was no help for it. At least we're all in one piece. Even Grandma."

Rose looked for Elsie Moore and found her in the yard at a picnic table. Elsie wore a fresh dress. She had braided her thinning hair and was flirting outrageously with Declan.

"How did it start?" Rose asked.

"She was having one of her parties, and something had chewed up a teddy bear. One of those things, I guess. Then she wouldn't come out of the room." Amy hesitated. "What are they?"

Rose shook her head. "Nothing I've ever seen before. Maybe she knows."

Amy sighed. "If she does, you're welcome to try getting it out of her. She won't tell me anything. She just calls me stupid."

Rose headed to the table. Elsie gave her the evil eye. Rose ignored it. "Hi there, Grandma Elsie," she said brightly.

Elsie pursued her lips and glanced at Declan. "We're having a special time," she said. "Go away."

"Oh, well, in that case, I'll just ask you a couple of questions and be on my way." *The sooner you answer them, the faster I'll go away.*

Elsie got the message. "Hurry up, then."

Rose crouched by her. "Do you know what those things are?"

"Evil."

"What sort of evil?"

Elsie shook her head.

"Have you ever seen one before? Do you know where they came from?"

"They were after my bears," Elsie volunteered. "So I cursed them."

Pieces clicked together in Rose's brain. "You made a wold?"

Elsie nodded. "But it couldn't kill them."

Amy, who had wandered over to the table, gasped. "You made a wold? Jesus!"

"It's dead," Rose told her. "It was after Kenny Jo, and I killed it."

"You've done lost your mind!" Amy stared at her grandmother. "Sending a wold out into the neighborhood? Who knows what it could've killed!"

Elsie pursed her lips.

"Honestly!" Amy put her hands on her hips. "What's next? Are you going to blight East Laporte?"

Rose sighed. That was the end of that. She wouldn't get anything out of Elsie now. She got up to her feet and glanced at Declan, standing to the side while Amy continued to chew her grandmother out.

"Thank you," Rose said. "You didn't have to help us, and you did. I'm grateful."

Declan's face thawed a little. "You're welcome."

Rose walked away. If Elsie didn't know what those things were, perhaps Grandma would. Unfortunately, all the evidence was here. To the left, in the woodshed, an overturned wheelbarrow sat by the log pile. Rose went into the shed, wrestled the wheelbarrow upright, and dragged it to the house. The nearest charred carcass lay only a few feet away. She put the wheelbarrow down and went to pick it up.

She couldn't even lift it, let alone carry it. Rose grasped its disgusting legs—the feet looked almost like ape hands—and put her back into it. The carcass slid across the floor. She dragged it to the wheelbarrow.

Leanne emerged from around the corner. Rose stopped. Leanne walked over. Without a word, she grasped the creature. Magic pulsed in her, and she picked the corpse up and slid it into the wheelbarrow and walked away.

That same talent—five seconds of incredible strength—had made Leanne the school's terror. She could only do it once every twenty minutes or so, but once was usually enough to do the job. Rose never thought she'd see it work for her. *I guess there's first time for everything.*

They'd never be bosom buddies, Rose reflected, pushing the wheelbarrow up the path to her house. But at least when

Leanne decided to stab her in the back, she might hesitate for a second or two.

The house looked undisturbed. Rose maneuvered the wheelbarrow behind Grandpa's shed. He slammed at the walls and hissed, but she just grunted at him. Later she'd wheel the hound corpse to Grandmother's for identification, but now she had to get her spare uniform on and start walking. She ran up the stairs to the porch and knocked on the door.

Georgie opened. "Get ready," she told him, running to the shower. "I'm taking you to Grandma's, and then I'll have to go to work."

GEORGIE sat on the porch steps. His overnight bag lay next to him. He always took the overnight bag just in case. Inside was a book about a boy who lived on the edge of the woods, an *InuYasha* comic book, spare socks, underwear, a T-shirt, and pants. And his toothbrush. Inside, Jack was banging things, looking for his sneakers. Georgie closed his eyes and pictured Jack's shoes. He felt a slight tug to the left and turned toward it. Not too far. A little more to the left . . . About fifteen feet. He opened his eyes and found himself looking at the kitchen window. Yep. The shoes were under the kitchen table. Jack must've pulled them off while he was eating dinner last night and forgotten about them.

He could go inside and tell Jack where his shoes were. Rose said to get ready quick. She had the *look* on her face. Georgie knew the look well. When she came out of the shower and saw that Jack didn't have his shoes, she wouldn't be happy. He could save Jack from getting in trouble, but those were new shoes, the *second* pair of new shoes. They cost a lot of money, and Jack had to learn to take care of them.

It was odd with Jack, Georgie reflected. Sometimes he'd find a piece of green bottle glass and carry it around with him everywhere for days, like it was some great treasure. But something like shoes or clothes, he didn't care about. They were poor. Rose tried to hide it, but Georgie knew they didn't have money. Jack needed to learn not to be wasteful.

Georgie turned his face to the sun and squinted, feeling

the warmth on his face. He didn't mind going to Grandma's, and he didn't mind skipping school. Oh no, he didn't mind that at all. Georgie smiled a private smile to himself. School was boring and tedious, and he didn't care for it. He studied and made good grades, because it made Rose happy. Sometimes she talked about him getting a good job in the Broken, if his grades were high enough. Georgie didn't want a job in the Broken. The Broken had no magic.

Staying at home also meant he might get to keep an eye on Declan. It was his job to keep an eye on things. That's what Dad said before he left. He was only six back then, but he remembered. Dad put his hand on his shoulder and said, "You mind the family, Georgie. Keep an eye on your sister and brother for me." He wasn't a baby. He knew Dad didn't really mean it, but he did it all the same because somebody had to do it.

He wasn't sure about Declan. Rose said all bluebloods couldn't be trusted. Rose was often right. When she said someone couldn't be trusted, they usually turned out to be a scumbag. Georgie ducked his head and looked around. He knew he hadn't said the cuss word out loud, but it never hurt to make sure nobody heard him.

So Declan was a bad guy. But Declan had saved Jack. And he didn't seem mean. There were many kinds of mean: mean like Kenny Jo, who was always angry about something. Mostly, Kenny was angry about his dad leaving him. Georgie understood being angry about that, but still, his own dad left, and nobody saw him going around picking fights with people.

Then there was mean like Olie, who was too stupid to know when he was being mean. Olie killed a puppy once because it bit him, smashed her head with a rock. The puppy hadn't known any better. She was just playing. Olie cried afterward, because he felt bad. Georgie heaved another sigh. It took him two days to put the puppy's head back together with his magic, and when he'd raised her, she still didn't look quite right. He'd concentrated on fixing her so hard, he got sick, and then Rose cried.

And then there was mean like Brad Dillon. Brad was cold and vicious. There was something wrong with him.

But Declan had no meanness. Jack thought his swords

were awesome. Georgie agreed about the swords, but he'd watched Declan make a ghost of the beasts that had attacked Jack, and in his opinion, that was even better. Georgie held his hand out, closed his eyes, and pretended to call up the beast. Except if he could do it, he'd do it even cooler. Maybe have some dark smoke swirling about him. And his eyes would be shiny. And maybe he'd say some mysterious incantation. Or not. Maybe it would be cooler if he said nothing. And if he had a sword, it would be long and slender. Like Grandpa's blades.

A drop of cold, slippery magic touched the back of his neck and slid down along his spine as if something rotten had splattered him with its nasty juice. Georgie gagged. His eyes snapped open.

A beast stood in front of the house on the path. The color of an old bruise, it stared at him with four slanted gray eyes.

Georgie froze. Jack taught him to never run from animals that could catch him. If he ran, the beast would chase. He didn't know if it could get through the wards to catch him, but he didn't want to find out.

The beast put one paw forward—it was a long ugly paw. Most animals had toes, but this one had fingers tipped with wicked red claws. The paw touched the ward, testing it. A stream of nasty magic slithered toward Georgie. He sensed its hunger: sticky, cold, starved, it wanted to wrap itself around him and suck out his magic. He swallowed. His heart beat so fast, it was trying to jump out of his chest. *Don't run. Don't run.*

Behind the beast, where the path curved, Declan stepped out of the bushes. Georgie glanced at his face. Declan nodded wordlessly, coming up behind the beast on soft feet, silent like a fox creeping through the Wood. Georgie stared at the beast. *Don't look at Declan. Don't give him away.*

The beast opened its mouth and showed Georgie his teeth: big, sharp, and red like blood. Its magic waited, hungry, ready to pounce on him and gobble him as soon as he moved.

Declan pulled a huge sword from the sheath on his back.

Georgie stared directly into the beast's eyes. Cold sweat broke out on his forehead.

Declan struck. The sword sliced though the air in a shiny metal arch and cut the body in two.

Wow.

"You okay?" A bolt of white flashed from his hand into the dead beast.

Georgie remembered to breathe and swallowed. Nausea tugged at his stomach. Desperately trying not to hurl, he dragged himself up, picked up a ward stone, letting Declan in, and once the blueblood stepped over the line, he dropped the stone back in place and went to slump back on the porch steps.

Declan came to sit next to him. "Lean forward," he ordered. "Put your head down, between your knees. That's it. The sickness will ease up in a minute."

Georgie bent forward, his head low. Slowly the nausea receded.

"That was smart," Declan said. "Staring the hound down."

"I didn't want it to know you were there."

Declan nodded. "Thank you. I appreciate it."

The beast's magic shivered. Georgie sat up. Next to him Declan put his hand on his sword.

A foul gray liquid spilled from the hound's carcass. The flesh and bone melted, turning into pale goo. The magic curved around it, twisting like cotton candy on a stick. Dark vapor streamed from the surface. The puddle shrank, and the vapor grew darker and solidified into a tall man. A long cloak with a hood hid him, pooling about his feet and turning into smoke at the edges.

Georgie sucked in a sharp breath. The man's magic pressed on him, trapping him like a huge heavy slab of rock. Fear skittered down his arms, leaving goose pimples.

"He can't hurt you in this form," Declan's quiet voice said next to him. "His magic might slither in, but it will be weak. Show no fear. Don't give him the satisfaction."

The vapor man turned to them. "Ah. I wondered who shot off a military-grade flash wave in this forsaken place. Just had to see for myself. I had a glimmer of hope it was my dear brother, but I see it's just you." His voice was soft and gentle, but for some reason it chilled Georgie all the way to his bones.

"What's with the cloak?" Declan said.

The man ignored him. "And who would you be?" The darkness of the hood swallowed the man's face, but Georgie knew the man's eyes fixed on him, pressing down on him like a great weight. Magic snaked from the man in long, translucent tendrils of dark smoke. They licked the ward and slithered through it.

Georgie stared with wide eyes as the magic crept closer. It was hungry . . . So very hungry.

Declan flashed. A screen of white shot from him, stinging the tendrils. The dark magic recoiled.

"Keep your claws off the kid," the blueblood growled.

Georgie breathed a little.

"Mmmmmm." A low deep sound rumbled in the phantom man's throat. "As brash as ever, Declan." The magic swirled around him, each translucent tentacle encircled by a thin vein of dark purple. The puddle rolled forward, and the man advanced.

Georgie sat frozen. Declan was right there, and he didn't move. He just sat there, looking slightly bored.

The puddle touched the ward and stopped.

"Interesting," the man murmured. He raised his arms, elbows close to his body, hands up. The sleeves of the robe fell back, revealing long, slender fingers stained with a mottled patina of purple and yellow. Just like the hounds' hides, only pale. "Let us see," he said softly, stretching "see" into a snakelike whisper.

The magic shot from him in an explosion of darkness and clamped on to the ward, biting at it, trying to pull it apart. The tentacles flailed and jerked, but the ward held. The man glanced down, and the magic tendrils struck at the closest ward stone. They clamped on to it and twisted, trying to jerk it up.

The man arched his back, straining. His dark magic pried the rock loose. The puddle at his feet shrank faster.

Georgie's heart beat so fast inside his chest he thought it might explode.

The ward stone rose two inches. A pale network of translucent reddish magic stretched from it, burrowing down into the ground, as if the stone had roots.

The man's rigid body shook with strain. The stone gained another inch of height, pulling more red roots out of the ground on both sides with a creaking sound. He clawed at the air. The ward stone shivered and crashed down into place.

Declan laughed, but it was harsh and cold, and Georgie wasn't sure what was more frightening, the dark man or the way Declan bared his teeth.

"They know how to root their wards," Declan said.

The man flicked the sleeves of his robe back over his hands, first left, then right. "No matter," he said. "I'll still kill them all."

"Not while I'm here, Casshorn."

The man turned to Georgie, and once again, he felt as if the man's gaze pierced him and clenched his heart in a cold fist.

"Boy . . ." Casshorn said. "I shall make you a deal. Remove the stones. Let me in. I'll let you and your family leave. You can trade your lives for Declan's. After all, he can't be anything to you. You probably met him only a day or two ago."

Georgie swallowed. His thoughts broke to pieces and ran in all directions, and no matter how hard he tried, he couldn't catch any of them.

"It seems like a hard choice," the man said. A kind tone overlaid his words, but it was shallow, and beneath it Georgie sensed ruthless hunger. "But upon closer examination, it really isn't. You have a mother. She loves you. She feeds you, and clothes you, and brushes your hair. And you love her, am I correct? There is nothing stronger than the bond between a mother and her child. Your mother would do anything to keep you safe. Now I give you a chance to do something for her. You can save her life. That's a wonderful trade, boy. The life of your mother for the life of a stranger. That's a good, honorable trade." He motioned with his right arm. "Come to me."

Georgie finally managed to pin down a thought. "No."

"Will you really let your mother die?" The man rocked back.

"I have no mother," Georgie said. "And you're lying. You would kill everyone."

"From the mouths of babes . . ." Declan said.

Casshorn sighed. "It is a shame. I was looking forward to watching you strike the boy down, Declan. Witnessing you do things you hate is highly entertaining. No matter. Soon, I'll watch you fight my wolf, which should prove quite a spectacle." Casshorn turned to Georgie. "Are you sure you don't want to move the stones, boy? I promise, I would make it quick, if not painless, for you."

"Leave him be," Declan said.

"I can't," Casshorn said, his voice slightly puzzled. "You see, he is so very full of magic. It awakens a most peculiar sensation in me. A kind of longing. I think it's hunger. They say that human meat has a peculiar taste. I've been developing a craving for it of late. It's odd. I've never been guilty of gluttony, but once I kill you, Declan, I think I'll gorge myself on your flesh."

Georgie shuddered. Declan simply stared.

Rose's voice floated through the kitchen window. "I found them! Honestly, Jack, is it too much trouble to take care of your shoes?"

"A girl," Casshorn said. "Of course. Is she delicious like the child?"

Declan said nothing.

"I see. There is another child inside, isn't there? You do understand you can't protect them? I'll pick them off one by one, when you're not looking. And then I'll feed. Especially on the girl. Such a lovely voice. I bet she's succulent. Juicy." Casshorn shivered. "It was a mistake to come here alone, Declan. You aren't enough to stop me, and the locals are too weak to help you. They scurry to and fro like garbage rats atop their little garbage heap between the worlds, but in the end they will all die. I know why my brother sent you—he hopes to avoid the scandal. I know why you've agreed to come alone—you're still hoping to save the wolf from the executioner's axe. None of it will make an iota of difference. As usual, you're too late . . ."

"You're raving," Declan told him.

"Am I? I must be." Casshorn sighed again in resignation. "It's time to go, I suppose. I leave you with this parting thought: you may think you can put yourself between the girl and my hounds in the Edge, but what will you do when she goes into the Broken, where my wolf prowls? He will slit her throat and paint himself red. You remember how much he enjoys murder . . ."

The puddle beneath Casshorn had dried up completely. He began to fade from the bottom up. "This is just lovely," he said. "And here I was thinking I would get bored." He dipped his fingers into his hood and held them out as if blowing a kiss. "Until later, children."

He vanished. The last shreds of magic dissolved into the air. Nothing remained of the beast or the puddle.

Georgie swallowed. His whole body had gone numb, and now little needles pricked his fingers and feet. "Who was that?"

"A sick man overdue for his cure," Declan said, looking at his sword. "For him, there is only one kind."

"He's evil," Georgie said softly.

"Yes, he is."

"Is he really going to eat me?"

Declan looked like he hurt himself. "He'll try. He won't succeed. I'll stop him."

Georgie hugged himself. "Why would he want to eat anybody?"

"He's ill," Declan said. "He wanted power, and now he has it, and it's twisting him."

"Is he going to kill Rose?"

"I promise you I'll take care of Rose," Declan said. "Nothing will happen to her or you, as long as I'm around. Rose doesn't trust me, and she and I will have to settle this between ourselves. But you and your brother mustn't fear me. If you're in danger, find me and I'll help. You don't have to handle it on your own. I'll protect you. Do you understand?"

Georgie nodded. He understood, and he felt deep down that Declan meant it. Still, Declan wasn't to be trusted.

"I'd appreciate it if you didn't tell your sister about this. No need to worry her."

Georgie nodded to keep him happy. Declan got up and headed down the road, back in the direction from which he had come. In a few breaths he disappeared behind the bend. A moment later Rose burst out the door, Jack behind her.

Georgie jumped to his feet. "I have to tell you something."

"Not right now!"

"But Rose!"

"Not right now, Georgie. It can wait until I get back. Come on."

Rose and Jack took off down the road, and Georgie had no choice but to follow.

NINE

ROSE waited inside Burger King. It was twenty past eleven, and the lunch crowd had yet to gather. She'd made it just in time—two minutes after she'd walked through the door, the Clean-n-Bright van, carrying Latoya, Teresa, and a couple of other women, rolled into the parking lot. They sat down to eat, and she sat down to think.

Rose shifted, trying to get comfortable in the concrete-hard chair. She had no appetite. Visions of terrifying bruise purple creatures kept flittering across her mind. She'd left the boys with Grandma, and Éléonore was no lightweight. Still, the anxiety ate at Rose. She regretted coming to work, but Emerson left her without a choice. She couldn't afford to have her check shredded.

Latoya swept by, carrying her tray. She was tall and looked taller, her body sharp and narrow-boned, all angles and long limbs. Her hair was thick and lustrous, falling down in curvy waves she'd bleached to platinum blond. The blond had worn off, and Latoya's waves had gained a slightly greenish tint. People called her Mophead, although never to her face. You messed with Latoya at your own peril,

"You want some food?"

"No." In a rush Rose had forgotten to make a lunch, and she had no money.

"Girl, you've got to eat!"

Rose shook her head. "I'm not hungry. Really."

Latoya turned to the counter, where tiny Juniper Kozlowski manned the register in her manager's uniform. "She won't eat, June."

Juniper bristled. "You come to my place, you have to eat, Rose."

"Thanks, I'm not hungry."

Latoya grimaced. "At least come sit with us."

"If I sit with you, you'll try to feed me." Rose smiled.

"Well, you have to eat!" Latoya grunted. "Look, don't worry about Emerson. He's an ass, but you're one of his best cleaners."

"I'm not worried," Rose lied. "Thank you for picking me up."

Latoya shook her head and sat at the bigger table to the left, with the rest of the Clean-n-Bright crew.

Rose looked out the window. She wasn't in the habit of feeling sorry for herself, but she had to admit that lately life just kept kicking her. First, the blueblood, then the hounds, and now, once her shift ended and she went back, she would have to fight Emerson for the money she had earned.

Of all these concerns, the blueblood and the beasts were most dire. The creatures did resemble hounds, lean demonic dogs from some awful nightmare. And they wanted magic. Their power fed on it. Was there some sort of purpose to their attacks? If they assaulted people at random, drawn to magic, then the four of them, the boys, Grandma, and she, would be their prime targets. The Draytons were among the most magical of the Edge families. Nothing that a blueblood like Declan would be impressed with, she was sure, but by Edger standards, they stood out. How would she protect the boys?

Rose felt a spike of panic and squished it down. First things first. She'd take the carcass of the dead hound to Grandma once her shift was over. Then they would go from there.

And then there was Declan. She had no clue how she would challenge him. What couldn't he do? What did the fairy-tale girls do in this situation? She strained, trying to remember. Most of the stories involved sorting rice from wheat and weaving gold cloth from straw. She wasn't sure if he could weave gold from straw but she wouldn't be surprised if he managed it somehow. No, it had to be something else. Something she knew for sure would work. Some challenge with a trick to it.

Declan's face surfaced in her memory. What an arrogant ass. She glanced at her uniform. So what if it was an ugly sack of unnatural color?

He'd said she was beautiful.

A man did tell her she was beautiful, wonderful, kind, and smart before. He even told her that he loved her and offered her a safe haven for the boys. And she believed him, right until the point she found out he planned to sell her off.

Declan was an enemy. A very odd kind of enemy, who saved small kids from monsters, tore roofs off houses with his flash explosions, and concerned himself with her safety. She had to keep reminding herself that he was the enemy, because the impact his presence had on her was staggering. It must be his size. Or maybe his sword. Or the unbelievable power of his flash. Or maybe all of the above . . .

Or the fact that he was incredibly handsome, and she had to keep iron control of herself to stop thinking about him. As far as she knew, he couldn't read her mind, but getting rid of him would prove much harder if he knew what went through her head this morning while he waved his sword around. She had to be adult about this: yes, he was hot and she was vulnerable. She got it out of her system this morning, and that would be the end of that.

His flash was something else. Most people tried to flash by holding their hand as a weapon and pushing the magic out of it. Unconsciously, they shaped the flash with subtle pressure into a form similar to their arm—a long ribbon—and it never occurred to them that it could take any other shape. But he'd managed a perfect half sphere. Rose still practiced with her flash every day if she could help it. It had become second nature to her, and she caught herself doing it without thinking, the way some people tapped their foot or fidgeted. But she'd never tried a half sphere before.

She'd figured out how Declan had done it a moment before he'd let it loose: he'd held the magic inside him, ratcheting the pressure higher and higher, and then dropped his guard on the front of his body completely and let it rip. The flash simply burst out of him, sweeping everything on its way. It was beautiful.

Rose had done it twice on her way to the boundary. Hers was much smaller in magnitude, a mere whisper compared to his roar, because she still had to walk and work afterward. But she knew she could do it, and when she poured enough power into it, her flash wave would be devastating.

Oh, she couldn't wait to show him. That would knock some of that blueblood haughtiness down a peg. She just needed a good opportunity.

He couldn't find lodging in the Edge. That was too funny. When did he learn to make pancakes? Maybe it was part of their blueblood tutoring: eight o'clock—swordplay, nine o'clock—archery, ten o'clock—pancake making . . .

Latoya said something from her table.

"Huh?"

"I said, what's his name?"

Rose frowned. "Whose name?"

"The guy you're mooning over."

"I'm not mooning!"

Latoya glanced at Teresa. The older woman nodded. "Mooning. Definitely."

Rose rolled her eyes and turned to the window. She wasn't mooning. She was planning strategy. Declan had to have a weak point. Somewhere. Everybody had a weak point.

He was arrogant. That was something. And he didn't know the Edge. She had to give him some sort of challenge that involved knowing the terrain, something that appeared deceptively easy, so easy he didn't try very hard until it was too late . . .

A man slid into the opposite chair. He had wide shoulders and green eyes, and he wore a Carolina Panthers ball cap on his head.

Rose stared in complete astonishment. A pair of worn-out jeans and a green sweatshirt toned him down a bit, but not nearly enough. She was aware of the shocked silence at the table next to her.

"What are you doing here?" she hissed.

"Perhaps I missed the sight of your lovely body," he said.

"What?"

Declan leaned closer. "My promise not to ravish you doesn't extend to this fine establishment, does it? As I recall, it's only valid under your roof. How could I pass on such an opportunity?"

"If you touch me, I'll hit you with this chair," she ground out.

"I had no idea you enjoyed rough courtship," he said with

a straight face. "It was never my particular favorite, but I'll do my best to play along, provided I'll get you in the end."

Rose opened her mouth, but nothing came out.

"Would you like me to be quiet?" he asked.

"Yes!"

"If you kiss me, I promise to be quiet for a very long time."

The thought of him bending down and kissing her zinged through her brain, and she clenched her hands together under the table, grimly determined to hide it. "You have no sense at all, do you?"

"You're quite easy to rile up." He leaned back. "Your brother is right. You don't date."

In her mind she picked up the chair and hit him over the head with it. "What are you doing here?"

"I thought I might have a word with your employer," Declan said. "Amy mentioned that he decided not to pay you."

Amy shouldn't listen to other people's phone calls. "You'll do no such thing. How did you find me?"

"I followed you. You walk quickly, but I'm used to marching."

"You can't be out here. This is the Broken!"

"I'm aware of that," he said. "Crossing into it felt like my guts were being ripped out."

"You could've died."

He shrugged. "I doubt it. It hurt, but the pain passed."

She once saw a caravan master from the Weird try to cross into the Broken. He'd gotten upset over the prices and decided he'd go and get the Broken goods for himself, cutting out the Edger middlemen. Two steps into the nine-foot-wide boundary he went into convulsions. The Edgers let him hurt for about a minute or two and then came to get him. He didn't complain about the prices anymore after that. Declan's crossing must've been agony. She didn't quite know what to make of it.

"Where did you get the clothes?"

"Leanne gave them to me. She insisted, actually. She said my appearance might cause a, how did she put it, 'fainting epidemic.'"

Dear God.

Behind Declan the door swung open, and Brad Dillon sauntered into the Burger King. "Well, lookit here. Rose Drayton and her faggot boyfriend. We meet again." Brad's voice rang through the Burger King, and Rose found herself the focal point of ten stares. At the counter Juniper went white with fury.

Rose glared. First, Declan, now Brad. She just couldn't catch a break.

Brad slouched in the aisle, hand in the pockets of his jeans. "Wait. You're not the same guy, are you? You get around, Rose."

Declan glanced at him and looked back to her. "Who is he?"

"Nobody," Rose ground out, looking at Brad. "Are you following me now?"

"I saw your friend from across the street and couldn't help myself."

They'd had run-ins before, but he'd never followed up like this. For one, she knew where to find him—he still lived in his trailer in the Edge, where she was the strongest. For another, she never rose to the bait. But now he'd met William, decided he was easy pickings, and wandered over to harass him. Except Declan wasn't William.

"Piss off, Brad!" Latoya called from her table.

"Shut the fuck up, Mophead, before I come over there and make you swallow your teeth."

Declan's green eyes fixed on Rose. Brad couldn't see his face, but she could. It was merciless and so iced over it was nearly cruel. "This is Brad?"

Rose was too mad to answer.

"Do you want to keep talking to him?" Declan asked.

"No."

The blueblood rose. "Excuse me for a moment." He nodded to Brad. "Let's go chat."

Brad pulled his hands out of his pockets. "I'm always up for a chat."

They left the Burger King, heading to the left, Declan moving in unhurried strides and Brad ambling to the right of him. Rose stared after them, stunned. Now what?

At the counter Juniper waved her thin arms. "Rose, drive-through window! Come on!"

Rose jumped up and ran behind the counter, following Juniper to the back, Latoya at her heels. She ducked between the fryer and the wall and ran into a patch of freshly mopped tile.

"Careful, wet, wet!" Juniper yelled.

Rose's feet slid on the floor. She crashed into some boxes and scrambled to the window. The two men stood in back, past the drive-through lane. Juniper flipped the switch, and Rose heard Declan's voice, distorted by static.

"You want to talk, now's a good time," Declan said.

"Fu—"

The punch was so quick, Rose barely saw it. Brad stumbled back, clutching at his gut, shook his head, and lunged at Declan. "Sonova—"

Declan's fist caught him in the left side with a solid crunch. Brad stumbled to the side, wincing.

"Ouch," Latoya squeaked.

Brad whipped about. "I'll—"

Declan rammed his fist into Brad's solar plexus. Brad bent over. Spit dripped from his mouth in a long sticky strand. He clenched and vomited a gush of foamy liquid onto the asphalt.

"Eww. In my goddamn parking lot, too." Juniper skewed her face.

"That last one hurt a bit," Declan said. "Take it easy. You have time."

Brad made some hoarse noises and stumbled a few steps, still bent over. About ten seconds later, he finally straightened and wiped his mouth with the back of his hand.

"Ready?" Declan asked.

Brad raised his fists. "Motherfu—"

The punch took him off his feet. He curled on the ground, cradling his gut.

Declan leaned over him. "Done?"

Brad nodded, his face twisted.

"Okay. Anytime you want to speak to Rose, you let me know and we'll do this again. Understand?"

Brad nodded again.

Declan rose and headed to the entrance.

Rose ran back in a mad dash, sliding on the slick floor. By the time Declan reached the door, she was barring the doorway. "Let's go out for some fresh air."

"As you wish."

Brad chose that moment to stagger out from behind the Burger King, holding a cell phone to his ear. At the sight of them, his eyes went wide and he ducked behind the building.

A moment of vicious satisfaction claimed her, but Rose had no time to savor it. She grabbed Declan's arm and pulled him down the narrow sidewalk, away from Brad before he saw him and decided to finish what he started. "What are you doing?"

"Walking with you."

"You can't just come in and destroy my life!" She took a deep breath and forced herself to calm down. He was trying to help, and he'd done a lot for her. "I've known Brad for years. He has done people a lot of favors, the kind one doesn't forget. What happened between us happened long ago, and he was punished for it already. You just started a new war. He'll be gunning to get at me now."

"He's most welcome to try it," Declan said with a grim finality that promised painful things in Brad's future.

"You just don't understand. Just like with Amy's roof."

"What about Amy's roof?"

It's not that he was stupid. Quite the opposite: Declan was probably one of the smartest men she'd ever met. He simply had no idea how life worked in a small Edger town. It probably made no sense to someone not born here.

She stopped and met his gaze. "Declan, I appreciate what you're trying to do, but I don't need you to fight my battles. It would be wonderful if life was simple and your beating up Brad solved all my problems, but in reality, it will only bring me more trouble. Thank you, but please go away."

Declan's eyes studied her. "Very well, my lady."

He turned and walked off.

Rose watched him go and headed back to the restaurant. Brad's humiliation would come back to haunt her. She knew it would, but it was so worth it. She recalled him crawling on the asphalt and practically skipped.

Latoya thrust the Burger King's door open. "Your new boyfriend is a psycho killer!"

"No, he isn't. And he's not my—"

"I'm telling you he's a Navy SEAL or something. Or one of the commando ranger guys. You know the kind who survive in the woods by eating bugs and take down the whole camp of terrorists with a handgun and a small rock."

Rose shook her head.

"And he's a looker, too," Teresa added. "Just like the other guy."

Latoya's eyes lit up. "What other guy?"

EMERSON'S voice ricocheted from the walls of his small office, filling Rose's head with ringing. "You think you can just miss the morning, and I won't know about it?"

Rose held her temper in check and faced Emerson. A slight man of average height, he was balding and doe-eyed. Emerson came from an old local family. His grandfather sold insurance, his father had expanded the business, his younger brother still ran it, but Emerson had failed to make his mark. He was arrogant, condescending, and lost his temper easily, which made him a terrible salesman. When people bought insurance, they wanted to be reassured, and the only thing Emerson reassured them of was his own inflated ego.

He had called in a snarling rage about two hours after they left Burger King and demanded Latoya bring her back to his office at the end of the shift. Apparently so he could cause permanent damage to her hearing.

"What do you have to say for yourself?"

"There was some trouble at Amy Haire's house . . ."

"I don't give a fuck." He stared at her for a long moment, his nostrils flaring. "I'm not paying you for this week."

"Emerson!"

"What? Are you going to tell me it's illegal and I can't do it? Well, guess what. I just did."

Rose clenched her teeth. Emerson was always an ass, but this was going too far. "I haven't missed a day of work in two years!"

Emerson laughed. "You know what, I changed my mind. You're fired."

"Fired? What for?"

"For absenteeism. You want to complain? You go right ahead. Who the fuck will listen to you? You're an illegal, and I can do whatever the hell I want with you."

Her face grew hot. He opened his mouth to rant some more, saw the look in her eyes, and clamped his jaw shut.

"You do whatever lets you sleep at night, Emerson," she said evenly. "But don't ever come to the Edge when I can find out about it."

She turned, left the office, and kept walking through the hallway to the outside. Latoya was nowhere in sight, frightened off by Emerson's hysterics. Such was the Edge way: every family for themselves. Friend or not, Latoya wasn't about to let her own job go down in flames.

Rose paused on the curb, staring at Emerson's red Honda SUV with a vanity plate that read BOSSMAN. Bossman. What a joke.

She was numb. It hadn't hit her yet, she decided. It would eventually, and then she'd probably hide and cry somewhere.

Rose shouldered her bag and started walking.

TEN

TWO hours later, Rose sank onto the porch steps, her phone next to her. Her feet ached. She used the time it took her to cover four miles from the Clean-n-Bright office to her house to search for a new job. She had exhausted every lead and called in every favor. Nobody was hiring. Nobody expected to hire anytime soon.

Rose experienced her first pang of fear. She had no way to provide for the children.

She had always worked. Ever since Dad left and even before that, she had always provided for them. They weren't rich, but the kids never went hungry. What could she do now? She had no reserve. What little jewelry Mom had was long gone—it went into the truck. First, the transmission went, then the muffler, then the belts . . . There was always something wrong with it, something requiring another injection of cash.

The junk in the attic would bring them nothing. She had tried to sell it before, at a swap meet and at a yard sale, but hardly anyone bought a thing. She'd made a total of seven dollars and twelve cents.

There was a spot in town in front of a small fried chicken joint, where a truck stopped every morning to pick up laborers. They were paid cash. She drove past them on her way to work: men, mostly Latino, chatting in Spanish. Before she had this job, she even tried waiting with them, but the truck driver explained to her that they didn't want women. They wanted men, who could clear away the brush and do construction.

The only reason Emerson had hired her in the first place was because he and her father had been buddies when they were young. But now with Dad gone . . .

She still had the doubloon. By now the news of her firing would have spread, and Max Taylor would know she was desperate. He'd charge her an arm and a leg to convert the doubloon into cash. Her chances might be better with Peter at Parallel Universe. He charged a steeper fee, but he never haggled and never tried to pull a fast one. The doubloon would bring in enough money for a couple of weeks. She'd just have to borrow the money for gas, drive out there, and hope she could work it out with one of them.

And then what?

Maybe she could just leave. Take the kids, use what money she made off Declan's gold, and just go. The Edge was narrow but long: it wrapped the junction of the two worlds like a ribbon. There were other settlements, bigger than East Laporte. There had to be jobs there. But at least here she had the house. Anywhere else, she'd have to pay rent . . .

The sound of approaching footsteps tore her from her thoughts. A long-legged, lanky man strode down the path. The sun played on his reddish hair. She would've known that red anywhere. Rob Simoen. His father had hired Brad to kidnap her all those years ago, so she could marry Rob and make a brood of powerful babies for the Simoens.

Rob came up and stopped at the ward stones. He had a bit of power. He flashed green, which wasn't too shabby for an Edger. He was older than she by three years and well off. He was also a first-rate asshole.

"Hi, Rose," he said.

She just looked at him.

"I heard you've lost your job."

Well, that was fast. "Came to gloat?"

He smiled. "Yeah, a bit. Did you hear? We at Simoen Chevrolet just got ourselves a new cleaning crew. Our offices will be all clean and bright."

Rose blinked as the picture snapped together in her head. "Your dad paid off Emerson to fire me."

"Something like that."

She frowned. "It's been four years. Why do you even care what I do?"

"Word is, you got a boyfriend, who's good with his fists.

Actions have consequences, Rose. You see, Brad works for us. Odd jobs, mostly. We like to look after our people."

"How nice of you." She'd known Brad's beating would come to haunt her, but she'd no idea it would be this fast. They hit her where it hurt the most. Magic clung to her. Too bad Rob was too smart to start something.

"Getting Brad beat up wasn't a good move."

"I didn't get him beat up. Brad managed that all by his lonesome. So what does he do for you anyway? Brad isn't much good aside from his fists . . ." Rose didn't even try to keep her mouth from curving. "You use him as enforcer, don't you? To collect and repo your cars. I saw him calling on his cell right after he got his ass handed to him. Was that to you? Tell me, was his voice slurring a little? Because the last I saw him, your precious enforcer was curled up on the pavement in his own vomit, looking for his mommy. He must've jumped on that phone the second he could talk." She laughed. "Oh, that didn't look good for your dad, did it?"

The sugary expression slid from Rob's face. "Never you mind. Let's talk about you. How exactly are you going to feed those bastard brothers of yours?"

"None of your business."

"You know . . ." Rob frowned, pretending to be immersed in thought. "I've always fancied you."

Declan emerged from the brush and started toward Rob in a very determined fashion. He must have followed her this entire time. She wouldn't put it past him. He probably thought this was his chance to get into her good graces—his Icy Lordship, all poised for the rescue. She glanced at his face, and alarm shot through her. She always thought that seeing murder in someone's eyes was a figure of speech, but when she looked at Declan, she saw it crystal clear.

She crossed her arms and looked above Rob's head at Declan. "It's a bad idea."

Declan kept coming. He didn't walk, he stalked, huge and lethal and very angry.

"Oh no," Rob said. "It's a great idea. I'll make you a deal: you suck me off, and I'll see about getting you your old job back."

Oh, you sad, slimy bastard.

Muscles played along Declan's jaw. He would kill Rob if he got his hands on him.

"If you do this, I'll never speak to you again," she promised him.

Declan halted for a moment.

"Oh, I like it when you get mad," Rob said. "The way I look at it, my dad promised you to me four years ago, but I never got to have you. Like a Christmas present I never got to unwrap. I figure, I'm long overdue."

She had seconds to get rid of Rob. Rose faked a sigh. "You're right, Rob. I do need a job, and nobody seems to be hiring. I guess I've been chased into a corner."

"I'm glad you see it my way."

Declan resumed his march.

Rose smiled. "The thing about being in the corner is that now I've got nothing to lose. And I have this powerful urge, Rob. A very powerful urge to hurt somebody."

It took him a second. "You're getting ahead of yourself there, bitch."

"I think I'll start with you," she said. "You know, when I flashed Brad, he pissed all over himself. I think I'd like to see you wet your pants, Rob. And then I think I'll go over to your family home and see if your daddy wets his pants as good as you do."

"You wouldn't dare."

"What do I have to lose, you dimwit?" She laughed and began to rise from the steps.

Rob's mouth hung open. He turned and saw Declan, looming in his path. Rob went white as a sheet.

Rose resorted to the last weapon in her arsenal. "Declan, *please* don't hurt him."

Declan leaned an inch toward Rob. His voice was a low snarl. "Run."

Rob dashed down the path. He was never a good runner, but he cleared the stretch to the road at record speed.

"You shouldn't have stopped me." Declan stared after him. He looked like he was about to change his mind. No matter how fast Rob ran, Declan would catch him.

"I could've hurt Rob. First, I could've shot him." She reached into her tote and showed him her gun. "Second, I could've fried him with my flash. I didn't hurt him. I could've, but I didn't."

His eyes narrowed. "Why? Do you have feelings for him?"

"No! At least not the kind of feelings you're asking about."

"Then why?"

"It's kind of complicated. I'll explain it if you promise not to go off hunting Rob."

He mulled it over. "Very well." His tone made it plain that he was doing her a favor.

Rose did her best to disguise letting out a breath and sat in the grass on her side of the ward line. He sat cross-legged and looked at her. He was still wearing the jeans and the sweatshirt. The jeans hid most of his boots, and from his feet up to his neck, he should've looked like a man from the Broken. Should've but didn't. He held himself like a man who never rode in a crowded bus. His shoulders were too wide, his posture too forceful, and if he were to step into one of the busy malls of the Broken, people would probably trip over themselves to give him his space.

His hair added to the effect, but his eyes and his face were worst of all. Even when he was calm, like now, his eyes made you catch your breath. They were the eyes of a noble from the Weird, who expected to be obeyed and would enforce his orders without a moment's hesitation. Instead of looking like a native of the Broken, Declan ended up looking like a blueblood who had dressed up in otherworldly garb for Halloween.

And she had to explain the complex rules of the Edge to him. How would she ever find the words?

"In the Broken, when a man assaults a woman, the police are called," she said. "They review the evidence, and if there is enough of it, the man is taken into custody, charged with a crime, tried, and if found guilty, put away into a prison. What happens in the Weird?"

"In Adrianglia, a similar process," Declan said. "Sheriffs examine the evidence and take the guilty party into custody. If they fail to apprehend him, they call the headhunters, and if they fail, they call the Marshal. Someone like me."

She would definitely prefer the headhunters. It sounded ominous, but not as bad as he. "It's your job to apprehend criminals?"

"Only some. You have to do something remarkable to gain my attention. Please continue."

"Do you know what happens in the Edge?"

"I expect you'll enlighten me," he said.

"Nothing." She checked his face to see if it sank in, but it might have been a mask for all the good it did her. "In the Edge, there are no police, no marshals, sheriffs, or any kind of protection. There is no impartial third party. Instead, the entire community of East Laporte sits there and watches to see what will happen. Because there are so few of us, everyone knows everybody else and everything we do has consequences."

She took a deep breath. "If a woman gets assaulted, it's between her family and the family of her attacker. They might come to an agreement of some sort on restitution or punishment. Or they might spend the next few decades lying in wait with their guns trying to splatter each others' brains all over the local greenery. Nobody likes a feud. Feuds are messy: many families are related, and when a feud flares, all of East Laporte can go up in flames. Innocent people get hurt, and the trade suffers. A lot of us make a good chunk of our money from trading with the caravans from the Weird and then selling what we bartered in the Broken. If the caravans know there's a feud, they'll skip the town and visit someone else."

He nodded.

"We try not to feud. We try to be reasonable. That means that punishment has to fit the crime. Let's say a man tried to kidnap me. I would be within my rights to kill him, and I've done it before."

Declan gave her a probing look. "You've killed a person?"

"Twice. But only in self-defense. My father and grandfather did some killing to protect me, too. Nobody can get mad about that. Sure, relatives of people whom we killed hate us and will take pains to ruin my life if they get a chance, but public opinion is on my side. I was attacked, and anybody in my place would defend themselves. That's reasonable, right?"

"For the sake of argument, I suppose so."

"Now let's take Brad. I was only a kid. I thought I loved him. I came to him in the most difficult time of my life, hoping that he would be my shelter. My rock in the storm. And he tried to knock me out with a club and sell me to Rob's dad. I hate him. I hate him so much that when he's near, my hands curl into fists and I don't even know it. When you beat him bloody today, it was glorious."

The hard line of his mouth relaxed slightly. "Glorious?" he said.

She nodded. "I'll cherish the memory of him rolling around in his own puke for the rest of my life. But it cost me my job."

"I've heard," he said. "It wasn't my intent to make you lose your employment."

Rose waved her hand. "No need to be so modest. You planned it all out brilliantly—getting me fired, cutting off my only source of income, all the while positioning yourself as my hero and savior."

Declan's eyebrows came together. "That *is* brilliant. I wish I would've thought of it. Alas, I was simply being charitable to a fellow human being. Brad needed to talk. All I could do was lend him a willing ear."

Declan the Good Samaritan. She grinned. "You also generously lent him your fist."

"Well, you didn't expect me to slap him with an open hand. One simply doesn't," Declan smiled back. It was a genuine smile, and it transformed his face. Instead of a blueblood, in the space of a moment he became a man, a living breathing man, irresistibly handsome, and funny, and someone she wished she knew. The effect was shocking.

Rose looked at her feet, trying to hide her eyes before he saw her reaction. Which was the real Declan? That was the question.

"Back to Brad," she said. "When he hit me with a bat, I flashed at him. It was a low flash, and it didn't kill him, but it hurt him very badly. I still hear him screaming in my sleep. As far as the Edge is concerned, that particular crime has been punished. Now you've opened a new can of worms."

"But it was a glorious can," he reminded her.

She laughed in spite of herself and looked up at him. "Quite. Brad got his ass handed to him, and the Simoen family retaliated by making my job disappear. I don't blame you for it. Nobody could've predicted that my job would evaporate. But at the end of the day, I still have no way to feed my family."

"I'm sorry," he said.

"Thank you."

"It's like a complex mathematical equation," Declan said. "The balance must always remain at zero."

"It doesn't always. People get away with all sorts of things. But we do like to balance the books. People will give you a chance to settle things yourself, but if you go killing and maiming people left and right, pretty soon the entire town will pool its resources and take you down no matter how powerful you are. Let's go back to Rob. He's a worm, and propositioning me was a low thing to do. It was humiliating. I humiliated him in return. We're even, and what's best is Rob thinks that nobody knows about this but the three of us. He'll remember it and you, and he'll try to kick me if he gets an opportunity, but it's not like he was beaten in public and became the laughingstock of the Edge. If you go after him and pummel him into pulp, he'll have to retaliate. The Simoen family is large and wealthy. My family is very small. I shouldn't probably be telling you this, but all I have are my brothers and my grandmother."

"I deduced that," he said. "I know that you love your brothers and wouldn't rely on them for protection unless you had no choice."

"I think you understand now," she said. "I can't compete with the Simoens. My flash is very hot. But if you beat up Rob, I might never get a chance to use it. The Simoens might just shoot me from some tree and nobody would blame them."

"That's wrong," he said.

She shrugged. "It's the way things are done here. I appreciate you making an effort to understand. I know that it must be very odd to you, seeing as the bluebloods are the ultimate authority in the Weird."

"That's not strictly accurate. The law is the ultimate authority. We're simply better trained and educated to enforce it than most other people, but we're as bound by it as any other citizen."

"What does the law say about forcing a woman into marriage?" she asked.

"The law applies only to the citizens of the Weird, and you aren't one."

Ouch. Always on the outside looking in. Rose got up and brushed off her jeans. "Well, it's good then that you'll lose and head back home empty-handed."

"I won't lose," he said. "But from now on, I'll attempt to keep the social rules of the Edge in mind."

She blinked, surprised. Declan had more twists and turns than Rough Butt Creek, which ran through East Laporte. First, he saved Jack. She could rationalize that—after all, if he intended to marry her, it was in his best interest not to stand idle while her brother was torn to pieces. But then he rescued Amy and her children, and followed her into the Broken, and now he conceded he was out of his depth, something she thought would've shattered his icy bearing. "Why did you save Amy?" she asked him.

"Why wouldn't I? She was in trouble, and it was in my power to help her. That's what any reasonable person would do. Why did you? You were ready to be bait to save a child of Leanne, who, by her own admission, tormented you in childhood."

"That's different."

He leaned forward, interested. "How?"

Rose searched for words. She hadn't really given any thought to why she had done it. She had reacted on instinct. "He's just a boy," she said finally.

"And if it was Leanne in that room, trapped? Would you still have gone to save her?"

"Yes." How exactly did he turn the tables on her? She should be the one asking questions.

"Why?"

She pursed her lips. "Because nothing Leanne had done to me would be as awful as being torn apart alive by those creatures."

"It was brave of you," Declan said.

She didn't care what he thought, she told herself. His opinion didn't really matter.

"Let me stay with you," he said.

"Not in a million years." Declan, the blueblood, was dangerous. Declan, the human being, was ten times more so. "You really should stop trying to get into my bed, Declan. It won't happen."

"If I was trying to get into your bed, I'd do something along these lines."

In her short dating life, Rose had been hit with a few "come hither" stares, but Declan left them all in the dust. He focused on her to the exclusion of all else, not really staring, but gazing in fascination, as if he were pulling her onto a tightrope above a chasm and didn't care if they both plunged to their deaths as long as she came to him. It pierced her defenses, and Rose blushed, suddenly awkward and hyperaware as if she were a teenager catching a boy looking at her and realizing for the first time that she was a woman.

"Rose," he said, as if tasting her name in his mouth. "Let me in."

She simply shook her head. It was all she could do.

"Shall I strip and try to entice you with my manly body?"

And just like that the spell was broken and she laughed. "It won't work, but if you do want to make a spectacle of yourself, who am I to stop you, Your Excellency?"

Declan sighed. "'Your Excellency' is the proper form of address for an ambassador or a bishop of the Zoroastrian or Catholic faith, as they style themselves as ambassadors of their God's will. I'm neither a bishop nor an ambassador. When it comes to societal niceties, you're hopeless. But have no fear—I'll arrange for lessons. Lots and lots of etiquette lessons. Luckily, I have both money to hire the best teachers and patience to wait until you learn."

She bristled, and instantly his face snapped into that blueblood stone-hard expression.

"I'll get your things," she told him and turned.

"You work very hard, and you're too proud to take charity," he said. "I find it admirable. But there's a fine line between proud and unwise. As you pointed out, you're a single woman in charge of two boys. You're unemployed with no prospects of obtaining a new position, you're facing a danger of unknown magical origin, and you're ill equipped to deal with it. I need a place to stay. I'm willing to employ you as my hostess and will defend you and your brothers against this danger or any other for the duration of my stay. I have already sworn not to harm you and your family. You get money and a capable adult male under your roof, while I get a room and three meals a day. To turn me away is both foolish and irresponsible, and you're neither."

She stopped. He was right. "What do you get out of it?"

"As I've mentioned, I intensely dislike sleeping in a tent. But more importantly, I've made the trip into the Edge, and should I come back empty-handed, with wild stories of some phantom hounds that killed my bride-to-be, I'd be a laughingstock. I can't afford to lose you now. If you persist in this unwise course, I'll pitch my tent right here, in the spot where I stand, and I'll do my best to defend you regardless. However, my defense will be much less effective."

Of course. A purely mercenary reason. She had expected nothing else.

The children had to eat. Her grocery supplies consisted of three packs of Ramen noodles, six drumsticks, some rice, a few potatoes, half a container of bread crumbs, and a pound and a half of ground beef in the freezer. And he would protect them. They both knew she would accept his offer. Rose grasped at straws, trying to find some way not to feel as if the choice had been stripped away from her, but found none. Suddenly she was simply weary. "That's the other thing I don't quite understand about you. You're an earl. You have money. You're not ugly."

"I'm quite handsome, actually," he said.

Handsome was for ordinary mortals. She rolled her eyes. "And so modest, too. Why are you here trying to get me to marry you?"

"I'll tell you, if you let me in."

"How much are you willing to pay?" she asked.

"Our standard rate. A doubloon a day."

It was generous. More than generous—some families would put him up for a week for a single coin.

"Half a doubloon a day," she said.

"No, you see, the idea behind bargaining is that you ask for a larger amount."

Apparently, he understood sarcasm just fine. He just chose not to notice it, when it failed to suit him. "I know that you in the Weird think that all Edgers are swindlers. We aren't. I won't take more than what's fair, because I don't want to feel indebted to you. For your half-doubloon, you'll get the use of the bedroom and three decent meals a day, and your laundry done, should you need it. You'll get nothing else. I'm letting you under my roof, and I expect you to behave with respect toward me and my brothers. Should you breach this agreement, you'll immediately leave. Should I breach it, I'll refund all related money. Am I making myself clear?"

"Perfectly. Should I swear a blood oath?"

"No. Your word's sufficient."

He rose, picking up his sword. "You have it."

Rose removed the ward stones. He stepped inside.

"Suppose I offered you a carte blanche," he said.

"What does that mean?"

"You leave with me. I'll support you in a respectable style. I'll pay for the education of the boys. In return we'll share a bedroom."

"Respectable style?" She chewed on those words. Here was a contradiction if she ever saw one.

"Two, three hundred doubloons a month. Enough for a modest but comfortable life. Obviously, I would take care of your rent, tuition for the children, and extraordinary expenses."

"Obviously." She shook her head.

"Is that a yes or a no?"

She simply looked at him.

"I take it by your frigid countenance that it's a no," he said. "And more, you believe me to be an idiot for offering it to you."

"Even if you're not lying, even if you intend to do everything exactly the way you suggest, you asked me to become your whore. I don't have anything against women who chose that sort of life. But I'm not, nor will I ever be, one of those women. If you were to offer me a job, the type of job where I didn't have to earn the roof above my head by spreading my legs, I would consider it. But I don't really trust you farther than I can throw you, and since you're large and muscular, that wouldn't be very far. And I'm not positive it would be a good idea to depend on you for my livelihood anyway. I don't want your money, Declan. I'm not a beggar or a free-loader."

He was studying her, and she wondered if he really had meant the offer or if it was some sort of a test. Either way, he had her answer, and she meant every word.

"My money would let you leave this place."

"This place is my home. Would you do it if you were me?"

"No," he said immediately.

"Why do you think I would?"

A hint of a mordant smile tugged on the corners of his mouth. "I didn't think you would."

"Then why did you offer?"

"I wanted to know what you would say. I'm trying to learn more about you."

She spread her arms. "What you see is what you get."

His eyes sparked with green. "Is that a promise?"

God damn him. "I meant that I have no big secrets. Unlike you. Why are you shopping for a bride in the Edge?"

"I'll be thirty in a month. The covenant of our title requires me to marry before I turn thirty, or I won't inherit the domain."

"That's a bit ridiculous."

He nodded. "On that we're in complete agreement."

"So what prevented you from getting married in the Weird?"

"I'm afraid my reputation among my peers has been somewhat tarnished." He walked up the porch and held the door open for her.

"Why?"

"It became known that I had a rather fertile imagination, when it came to private activities."

She stared at him. "What sort of private activities?"

This time he did smile, and it turned his face wicked. "Disrobe, and I'll be happy to demonstrate."

ELEVEN

IT took Rose a good half hour to get rid of Declan. She'd keyed the ward to him, and finally he'd left to get the rest of his supplies. She waited for about five minutes, grabbed the wheelbarrow, and drove the body of the dead hound to Grandma's. If they could figure out what it was or where it had come from, they could find a way to fight it.

The wheel stuck on some random rock. The acrid stench rising from the carcass would've made even Grandpa Cletus vomit. Rose thought she would be used to it by now, but no, after a third of a mile, she could still smell the dead bugger.

Rose cursed at the wheelbarrow, gritted her teeth, and forced it through the trellis shrouded in tiny pink roses into her grandmother's yard. She took a deep breath and pushed it back behind the house, out of sight, and threw a tarp over it just in case.

Grandma Éléonore was in the kitchen, drinking tea. "I heard you lost your job," she said the second Rose stepped into the kitchen.

Oh, for the love of God . . .

"And I hear you have a fellow staying with you. According to Marlene, who heard it from Geraldine Asper, who heard it directly from Elsie Moore, he's some sort of a looker."

"He's just a boarder." Rose went to the sink and scrubbed her hands with soap. The last thing she needed now was a lecture on the terrible dangers of letting bluebloods into the house. "Just a bit of money to tide us over."

She hoped and prayed that once the looker fetched his possessions, he'd stay at the house and not go searching for her. Having him turn up on Grandma's doorstep would mean nothing but trouble.

"According to the hooligans, this boarder has a huge sword."

Rose rolled her eyes to the ceiling. "What else did they tell you?"

"Not much. They've been very closemouthed about it. Not at all like them. Is he handsome?"

"He is."

"It isn't William, is it?"

"No," Rose sighed, dropping into a chair and reaching for the spare cup.

Above them the ceiling shook with quick thumps. The kids were playing in the attic again. "What did you learn at Adele's?"

"Oh, this and that. Lots of gossip. Paula's expecting twins. They aren't her husband's, and when he finds out, there'll be hell to pay. Some other things." Grandma looked away.

"What else?"

Grandma heaved a sigh. "Dogs have been disappearing. Seth Hines has gone into the Broken. Took his wife and son with him and left pretty much everything behind. His sister got ahold of him, but he won't talk. She got very little out of him. He'd told her they'd been attacked by something, some strange creatures. Oh, and he claims a blueblood rescued them. Because that's just what we need, nobles from the Weird."

Yes, they definitely didn't need any more of those. Rose wiped her hands on a towel. It had to be Declan, of course. Who else? "I think I've got one of those creatures in a wheelbarrow at the back porch."

Grandma Éléonore rose. "Let's see it."

They stepped out onto the back porch. Rose drew the tarp aside. Éléonore brushed the tips of her fingers across the creature's hide, leaned close, until her nose almost touched it, sniffed the charred hide, and straightened.

"What is it?" Rose asked.

Éléonore's forehead wrinkled. "I don't know," she said softly. "Let's brew some tea and find out."

* * *

GRANDMA Éléonore picked up a piece of white chalk and drew a compass rose on the surface of the table with brisk practiced movements. Georgie stood by the table, transfixed. Jack scooted on his chair, holding his hands together, as if in prayer.

Rose placed a fat candle at tramontane, the "north" point, and lit it. The tiny blade of the flame danced on the wick. A cube of ice graced levante, the "east." Rose added a chunk of granite at the ostro, "south," and looked at Jack.

"Now?" he asked.

"Now."

Jack opened his hands and dropped a fat green caterpillar onto the table. Rose nudged it onto ponente, the "west," and spat on it. The caterpillar squirmed, but remained put, pinned by the small charge of magic.

This was the old familiar Edge magic. Not flashy or scientific, but the simple earthy kind that worked. Declan would sneer at it, just like all of his lofty friends would sneer at her if she ever left with him. That was fine. She had nothing to prove to him and no intention to give up her freedom. No matter how he looked at her.

Grandma Éléonore snapped a small ziplock bag open and dropped a sliver of the beast's flesh into the center of the rose. The stench nipped at the inside of Rose's nostrils. She grimaced and turned away to gulp some untainted air.

"Why does it stink so bad?" Jack clamped his nose shut.

"We don't know." Grandma Éléonore motioned them to the table. "Hold hands."

They stood around the table, holding hands.

"Concentrate on the flesh." Grandma Éléonore took a deep breath and began to chant.

"All that is from all that was, return to your root, obey my words. All that is from all that was, return to your root, obey my words . . ."

The magic streamed from them, locking onto the odorous chunk. A thin puddle of water spread from under the ice cube, forming a perfect circle. The hunk of granite shuddered, little flecks of quartz glistening. The flame of the candle grew to two inches. The caterpillar writhed.

The flesh in the center refused to move.

They tried it again ten minutes later.

Nothing.

"It's like it's not of this earth," Rose murmured.

"There are other things we can do." Grandma Éléonore pursed her lips.

They could and they did. Four hours later, Rose could barely lift her head. Grandma Éléonore picked up a rolling pin, looked at the chunk of flesh—their third, the first two had been consumed by various spells—and hit it with the rolling pin.

Rose frowned. "What for?"

"To make me feel better."

Her cell phone rang. Rose jumped six inches in the air.

"Who's calling you?"

"I don't know!" She pulled the phone open. Maybe it was a job offer. "Hello?"

"Hi, Rose," a male voice said on the other end.

"Hi. Hold on a minute." She covered the phone with her hand and mouthed "William" at Grandma.

"Go." Grandma Éléonore nodded to the back porch.

"I'll just be a minute," Rose promised.

She went out the back porch, across the grass to the old wooden swing hanging from the massive limb of a gnarled oak. The night had fallen, the darkness cool and spiced with the delicate, slightly bitter scent of Poor Man's Orchids dripping from the vines winding about the tree and the faint mimosa perfume of nightneedle flowers. The house windows cast off weak light onto the darkness-drenched lawn.

"How did you get my number?" She scooted onto the swing.

"One of your friends gave it to me. The one with green hair."

Latoya. "How do you know her?"

"I came by your work. I thought maybe I could take you to dinner. They said you were fired."

She heard real concern in his voice. "Yes, I was."

"Sorry to hear that. How are the boys taking it?"

"They don't know yet."

"So you need a job? I could ask around . . ."

But of course, they wouldn't hire her. Not with her stellar Edge paperwork. Still, it was so thoughtful of him to offer. "That's very nice of you, but I'm doing okay for now."

A faint edge appeared in William's voice. "I heard there was a man involved."

Latoya and her big mouth. By now the whole Edge knew she was let go because of a man. Not that she gave a damn about what they thought or said about her. "I wasn't fired because of him. You see, Emerson, my boss, and my father, they used to be friends. I don't even know why I'm telling you this . . ."

"Probably because you need someone to talk to. I'm here, and I've got time."

She sighed and pushed against the ground out of habit, starting the swing swaying back and forth. The chain protested quietly.

"What is that creaking?" he asked.

How in the world did he hear it through the phone? "I'm sitting on an old swing."

"Ah. So what about this Emerson?"

"Like I said, he and my father used to be friends. Then my father left. He went on to . . . to adventure. Emerson stayed behind, married, got a job in the family business, and tried to live a quiet life. I think, though, he always wanted to go off with my father, but never got brave enough to break free. In the last year, Emerson's life fell apart. He didn't do so well as an insurance salesman, and his dad made him run Cleann-Bright instead. His wife left him. He has money problems, and he's skimming off the top of the business. It's all crashing down around his ears. I think every time he saw me, he thought of my dad living the good life somewhere. He would've fired me anyway, sooner or later."

"He sounds like a real prize, this Emerson."

"He's just an unhappy, angry man. I don't have to put up with him anymore, and I'm glad. It's in the past now."

"You know, you could've told me about this other guy," William said softly. "I'm not afraid of a little competition."

She hesitated. "William, I thought we had settled this." *Please, don't make me hurt your feelings again.*

He laughed quietly. It was an odd laugh, deep and bitter.

"Don't worry. I remember where we stand. Since you told me something private about yourself, I'll tell you something private about me. I never had a family like you do, Rose. That's why I like you so much. You're kind and smart, and pretty, and you take care of your brothers. Nobody ever took care of me like that. I think I always wanted to find someone like you to settle down with. To have a real family. I don't know if I would be good at it, but I'd like to try. I would keep you and the kids safe. Nobody would ever hurt you. Sorry, but I can't just let you get away without a fight."

A heavy weight settled on her chest. There was sincerity in his voice that was impossible to fake. He just laid it all out for her.

"William," she said as gently as she could. "I'm sorry that you're alone. But I don't think I—I don't think we, me and the boys, are the right family for you. I know that you think of me as Rose, the big sister to the boys, but I'm my own person. I want to be happy, just like everyone else. When a man joins our family like that, it will be because I love him. I don't think I would ever fall in love with you. There is no spark between us, and you know it as well as I do."

She listened to the long silence.

"You're an odd woman, Rose," he said finally. "Most women would enjoy all the attention."

"I have enough attention as it is," she murmured.

"From that man who got you fired?"

Rose sighed. "He's an arrogant ass who thinks I'm lower than dirt. If I could get rid of him, I would."

"I could run him off for you."

"No, I think it's best I handle it myself. I—"

She raised her eyes and saw Declan standing two feet away, his sword on his back.

"Rose?" William asked. "Hello?"

Declan's eyes blazed like two white stars. He held out his hand. "Give me the phone, Rose."

"Who's that?" William asked. His voice lost all warmth.

"Let me speak to him." Declan reached for the phone.

"I have to go," she told William. "Talk to you later." She snapped the phone closed.

"Damn it," Declan snarled. "I told you to give me the phone!"

She jumped off the swing. "How long have you been standing there?"

"Long enough. Was that William?"

She ignored him and headed to the house.

"Answer me," he demanded.

"I don't have to," she said, struggling to keep her calm. "You have no right to order me around." Rose marched to the back porch.

"You stubborn fool, you have no idea who you're dealing with."

"I have a very good idea." She stopped and looked at him. "Let's get this one thing completely clear. You don't own me. I'm not your slave or your servant, and I don't give a damn what color your blood is, how old your family is, or how much money and power you have. I let you stay in my house because you pay me and I'm backed into a corner. Don't think for a moment that I'll let you give me orders and run my life."

She turned on her heel and went into the house. Declan was only a step behind.

Grandmother sat at the kitchen table. Her face was very pale. Her gaze fixed on Declan, as if he were a murderous maniac. Rose didn't blame her. His eyes were completely frosted over and his face promised a storm.

"Where are the boys?" Rose asked, noticing Declan's cloak, draped over a chair. So he'd come here first, and then tracked her down to the back.

"Asleep," Grandma said, her voice carefully neutral.

"No need to wake them, then. Declan and I'll go up to the house. I'll come back for the boys in the morning."

Declan swiped his cloak, hanging it on his left arm, bowed, and gently picked up Grandma's hand, brushing his lips across her knuckles. *"Je vous remercie avec tout mon coeur pour votre accueil si chaleureux et de votre gentillesse. Bonne nuit, Madame Éléonore."*

"Je vous en prie. Au revoir." Grandma's voice was clipped with tension.

Rose bristled. Her knowledge of French was minimal, but

she caught "thank you" and "your kindness." Declan stepped to the outside door and held it open for her.

"Rose, you can stay here," Grandma said quickly.

"I'll be fine." Rose forced a smile and left the house.

She waited until they cleared the lawn and started down the path to her house, before she spun to him. "What did you say to her?"

"I said, 'Thank you very much for your cordial reception and your kindness. Good night, Mrs. Éléonore.'"

"What were you doing in my grandmother's house?"

His voice was acid. "Looking for you. You were gone for a long time. I thought you might be in danger, and I tracked you down. It wasn't exactly difficult—your wheelbarrow left very clear tracks."

She glared at him. "You terrified my grandmother."

"I was the very soul of courtesy."

"Yes, that's why she's sitting in the kitchen with a deer-in-the-headlights look on her face. Don't come here. Ever. My grandmother has nothing to do with any of this."

He stepped closer to her. "Now, you listen to me. There are things going on here that you aren't equipped to deal with, and whether you like it or not, I've chosen to protect you from them. If that means I have to enter your grandmother's house or follow you into the Broken, then you'll just have to deal with it, because even if the lot of you pile all of your magic together, you can't stop me."

The magic buckled inside her, spurred by her anger. The night gained a pale shimmer, and she realized her flash had leaked into her eyes, making them glow. "I wouldn't be so sure," she ground out.

His eyebrows came together in disbelief, and then his own eyes blazed white. They glared at each other.

"No more stalling, Rose. You've lost your job. You have all the time in the world now. You've promised the first challenge tomorrow. Deliver."

"You'll have your challenge."

"I look forward to it."

"Fine."

"Fine."

They didn't speak all the way home.

TWELVE

JACK sauntered into the house, following Rose and Georgie. Rose headed into the kitchen, Georgie went into their room, and Jack ambled a bit in the living room, deciding what to do. If he went back outside, he'd have to stay inside the ward lines. He could go to the kitchen and steal something to eat . . .

Jack passed by the door to Declan's room and froze. The blueblood sat on the bed. In front of him on a rough canvas lay knives. Many, many sharp knives. The sun filtered into the room through the window, and the light played on the smooth surfaces of the blades.

Declan picked up a knife and drew a soft cloth over it. A spicy scent spread through the air. Cloves.

Jack liked the way Declan smelled. Like pumpkin pie spice, mixed with leather, and sweat. It wasn't a girly type of smell.

Declan raised his hand and motioned for him to enter. Jack snuck in, making no sounds, and stopped by the bed. He didn't say anything, just watched the cloth slide up and down the blades with a very soft sound: *whoosh, whoosh, whoosh* . . .

"Do you like school?" Declan asked.

"No."

"Why not?"

"They make us sit still for a long time."

"Is it hard for you?"

Jack shrugged his shoulders. "Rose says if I want to be a good predator, I have to learn to be patient and do it. She says patient predators don't go hungry as much."

"And you want to be a good predator?"

Jack nodded.

Declan took another rag, dabbed some oil on it, and threw it to him. Jack snatched the rag out of the air, fast, before Declan could change his mind. He looked at the blades and looked at Declan. The blueblood nodded.

Jack's hand hovered over a large, flashy dagger. No, too big. Big meant slow. He was a small cat, and he was strong for his size. There were things that were a lot bigger and stronger, but few things were faster.

"Trailing point knife," Declan said as Jack held his hand over the narrow blade with an upward curving back edge. "The curve makes the blade longer. It's light and quick. Good for slashing."

Jack moved his hand to the knife to the right, with a back edge that swooped down in a concave curve to a razor-sharp point.

"Yatagan clip. The back edge curves down. Some people leave the back edge false, so it's dull. I like mine sharp. It's a fast knife. Good for tight quarters and quick stabbing."

Jack stared at them, torn. Slashing like claws or stabbing like teeth? Finally he picked up the yatagan clip and gently drew the cloth along the blade. His teeth did more damage than his claws. Jack drew the cloth along the blade. *Whoosh.* He smiled.

"Do you know what 'anemic' means?" Declan asked.

Jack shook his head.

"It's a kind of disease that happens when your body lacks blood or iron. People who have it become tired quickly. They're usually pale and weak. Have you ever heard Rose mention it when she talks about Georgie?

"Georgie isn't anemic," Jack said. "He would be okay except for Grandpa. Grandpa and all the animals are making him sick."

"Grandpa?" Declan raised his eyebrows.

"We keep him in the shed out back," Jack said helpfully. "So he doesn't eat dog brains."

Declan gave him an odd look. "Charming Edge custom, keeping elderly relatives locked up."

"Because of Grandpa, Georgie can't fight that good. I protect him in school, but he'll go into middle school when he's twelve and I won't. I don't know what to do about that yet."

Declan gave him another odd look. "Is the schoolwork hard?"

Jack shook his head. "Boring. We do word lists. You have to memorize the way words are spelled and pretend to read them back. I don't have to. I already know how to read. Rose taught me."

"What about math?" Declan asked.

Jack shrugged. "I can add things together. I already know how many angles are in a triangle. It's called tri-angle. I'm not stupid." He held on to the knife a bit too long, but made himself put it down and looked at the trailing point blade. Declan nodded.

Jack took the knife into his fingers. He liked the way it felt, light and comfortable. "Lunch's awful," he volunteered. "They give you fish sticks. They taste like cardboard. Georgie says they're made from mystery meat. Nobody eats them."

"Have you ever eaten cardboard?"

Jack nodded. "I chewed it."

"Why?"

"I wanted to know if it's good to eat."

Jack put the knife down with reluctance.

"What kind of animal do you change into?" Declan asked.

Jack narrowed his eyes into sly slits. "I'm not supposed to tell you."

"Why not?"

"Because Rose told me not to talk to anybody about it."

Declan leaned forward and fixed him with his eyes. Jack tensed. If Declan were a changeling, he'd be a wolf, Jack decided. A large white wolf. Very smart and with big teeth.

"Do you always do what Rose says?"

Ooooh. That was a trick question. If he said he did, Declan would think he was a mama's boy. If he said he didn't, he'd have to tell him that he was a cat. Jack thought about it. "No. But I always know I'm supposed to."

"I see," Declan said.

Jack decided he had to explain, just so there wouldn't be any doubt that he wasn't a mama's boy. "My mom died. My dad left to hunt for treasure. I don't remember him. He was a good dad, I think, but he might have been not that smart, because when Grandma talks about him, she calls him 'that stupid man' sometimes. She can do that because he's her son, so I don't get mad."

"Aha," Declan said.

"So until my dad comes back, I'm Rose's cub. So I have to do what she says."

"Makes sense," Declan said.

"You like Rose?" Jack said.

"Yes, I do."

"Why?"

"Because she's smart, kind, and pretty. She stands up to me. That's hard to do."

Jack nodded. That made sense. Declan was hard to stand up to. He was tall and big and he had a sword. "Rose is prickly."

"She is certainly that."

"She's nice, too," Jack said. "She takes care of me and Georgie. And if you ask her really nice, she'll make you a pie even if she's tired from work."

"And she's funny," Declan said confidentially. "But I'd appreciate it if you didn't tell her that. If she knew I thought she was funny, she might not take me seriously. Women are like that."

Jack nodded. He could keep a manly secret, and it wasn't something that Rose had to know. "If you win the challenges, you'll take Rose away."

"That's the agreement," Declan said.

"Can we come?"

"Yes."

"Breakfast!" Rose called.

Jack started for the door and turned. His eyes flashed with amber fire. "I won't help you win," he said.

Declan grinned. "I wouldn't have it any other way."

ROSE crouched by him. Jack wished he were bigger. He disliked it when people crouched to talk to him, but he knew Rose did it so she could look at his eyes.

"Focus, Jack."

He nodded.

"You don't chase the leech birds. You don't stop to catch a bunny. You run as fast as you can, and when you get tired, you hide as well as you can. Do you understand me?"

He nodded again.

"Repeat it."

"Run and hide. No leech birds."

Rose bit her lip. "It's very important. I know that Declan saved you and he's nice to you, but he won't be nice to me if I have to go away with him."

"He said we could come."

Rose stopped. "Where?"

"With him and you."

Rose hugged him. "Jack, of course he would say that. He would say anything to get the two of you on his side. You can't trust him."

Jack squirmed until she let him go.

Rose sighed and took hold of his bracelet. "Are you ready?"

He nodded.

"Run and hide."

"Run and hide," he repeated.

Rose slipped his wrist out of the bracelet. The room swayed. The floor buckled and punched him in the face.

ROSE stepped onto the porch. Declan waited for her in the yard, his handsome face serene.

"You wanted a challenge."

Declan nodded. "I'm a-flutter with anticipation."

A-flutter. Right. Rose held the screen door open and let Jack onto the porch. He padded out on disproportionately big round paws and blinked at the sun with huge amber eyes. Thick fur, spotted with rosettes of rust and deep brown that seemed almost hunter green, clothed him in a dense coat. Jack wrinkled his muzzle, shaking his white whiskers. The long chocolate tufts of fur at the tips of his large ears trembled.

He looked adorable, like a poufy, stout kitten on long

legs, slightly larger than a big house cat, but she knew those big, soft paws hid razor-sharp claws. Even at eight, Jack was deadly. In lean times, when they didn't have meat, he went out hunting and more often than not came back with a turkey or a hare, sometimes slightly chewed up. Jack knew the Wood like the back of his hand. And when he didn't want to be found, even an experienced hunter couldn't discover his hiding place. She had to resort to magic to find him.

"Here is your first challenge." Rose smiled. She crouched and petted Jack on the head. He rubbed against her knee. She whispered, "Go!"

Steel muscles tensed under the fur. Jack leaped off the porch, sailing through the air as if he had wings. He landed in the grass and bolted, his rosettes blending into a blur. A blink and he vanished in the trees.

Declan looked after him. "What is he?"

"Edge lynx." Rose straightened. "You have until morning to catch him. If he returns here free by sunrise, you forfeit."

Declan nodded, picked up a sack lying at his feet, and headed into the forest.

RUN and hide.

Run.

Run.

Run.

A hare scent trail. Tasty. Have to keep running.

Jack leapt over the log and kept going, flying over the forest floor. Heat spread through his muscles. The scents of the Wood bathed his face. He kept going, faster and faster, leaping from one moss-covered trunk to the next. Above him, leech birds circled with guttural cries somewhere high above the canopy.

Run and hide. No leech birds.

He dashed to and fro, confusing his scent trail just in case, leaped and ran deeper and deeper into the Wood, until finally he grew tired and scrambled up the trunk of a huge pine into the dense blanket of needles and lay on a branch, panting.

Birds chirping, little tiny fat birds. Tasty.

A squirrel poked its way out of the hole in the tree.

Jack lay still for a long time. Long enough to make him sleepy. He yawned, closed his eyes, and sank into a warm, happy nap.

A long twisting sound echoed through the Wood, jerking him awake. It wasn't like any noise he had ever heard. Like a long wail. It pricked his ears, and he rose to a half crouch.

It was a trap.

He lay back down.

It was a trap, because Declan was smart.

What made that sound? What if it wasn't Declan? Jack rose again and lay back down. Run and hide. He ran and he hid.

He waited for the sound to come again. He waited and waited, but the Wood was full of little animal noises and no wails.

It didn't hurt to look. He would be very, very careful. Very careful.

Jack slunk up the tree branches, higher and higher, digging his claws into the fragrant bark, until he reached the top of the pine towering above the foliage. The sun shone from high above—he had slept for several hours.

In the distance a tiny star sparkled among the greenery.

Jack crouched in surprise.

The star winked at him, a little shiny spot. Oh, he wanted to see it. First the sound, then the star. Curious.

The spot of light trembled and swayed back and forth, glinting.

He had to see it up close. Just to find out what it was. He would be careful. Nobody would know.

Jack slid down and set out through the branches.

He moved quietly and slowly, like a shadow on soft paws, leaving no sign of his passing, taking his time. Up and down the branches, through the tangles of wild whiteberry, through the sea of dense feathery ferns, up the mossy fallen tree, onward and onward, until he came to the edge of a clearing and melted into the darkness between the branches.

In the clearing a long lean sapling bent nearly to the ground, held by a rope. The rope was attached to a piece of wood, and that piece of wood was thrust into a stick driven into the ground. A spring snare. Jack had seen those before.

The piece of wood was a trigger bar. There would be bait attached to the trigger bar by a rope. Jack slunk through the shadows, circling the snare. Sure enough, a taut rope was attached to the trigger bar and on the end of that rope hung a star. Jack lay down and squinted against the glare. Not a star but the knife, the wicked, sharp, pretty knife he had cleaned in Declan's room.

Oooooooooooooh.

Jack forgot to breathe.

The knife rotated on the rope, glinting in the sun. Sharp. Shiny.

He had to have the knife.

Jack lay still, listening, waiting. Traces of Declan's scent hung above the clearing, but the blueblood was long gone.

The moment he touched the knife, the rope would yank the trigger, and the sapling would jerk straight, pulling a hidden loop. The loop would catch him and send him flying through the air.

Jack swallowed. This had to be done very carefully.

"SHOULDN'T you be out looking for my brother instead of sitting here eating lunch?" Rose passed the potatoes to Declan.

"You're supposed to want me to fail, remember?" Declan snagged two additional Edge burgers off the platter. He seemed to really like them. They weren't anything special. She'd seasoned the ground beef with garlic, salt, pepper, and a pinch of swamp spice, added an equal amount of cooked rice, shaped the mix into oblong patties, rolled them in bread crumbs, and fried them. The rice made the meat go twice as long, and nobody could taste it.

Declan ate like a horse. If he did manage to catch Jack, which she seriously doubted, Rose vowed to go down to Max Taylor's and exchange the two doubloons now in her possession for some money. She would need more groceries to feed him.

Having him in her kitchen was like trying to serve lunch to a deadly tiger. Declan was too large, his shoulders too broad, his eyes too predatory. His face was inscrutable. She wished she could search his head and find out what really went on in there.

He caught her looking and hit her with a direct stare. His gaze lingered on her face.

On the other hand, it probably was best she didn't know what he was thinking.

Declan sliced a piece of the burger, put it into his mouth, and chewed with an expression of complete happiness. "My wife will never have to cook," he said.

"Why?" Georgie asked, imitating Declan's surgical precision with his own knife and fork.

"Because I employ a cook. But I want you to promise me, Rose . . ." He put another piece of the burger into his mouth and paused.

"You really should cut your food into pieces small enough so you don't have to swallow before you can talk," she said. *Take that, Mr. Manners.*

"I wasn't busy chewing. I was savoring the taste. It might surprise you, but when I find something delicious, I take my time to enjoy it."

His gaze caught hers just in case she missed his innuendo.

"You don't say," she said dryly.

He ate another bite. "Promise me that when we marry, you'll occasionally make these. As a special treat."

"You're impossible," she told him and slid the platter of burgers closer to him in spite of herself.

Georgie poked his burger with his fork and leaned over to Declan. "Her fried chicken is better," he said.

"Georgie!" She glared at him in outrage. "Whose side are you on? You're not supposed to tell him my fried chicken is good."

Georgie blinked in confusion. "What am I supposed to say?"

"You're supposed to tell him I'm a horrible cook, so he'll go away and leave us alone."

Declan made an odd noise that sounded somewhat like a strangled cough.

Georgie glanced at Declan. "He'll never believe me. He likes your burgers."

"You have to convince him. Be charming. Use your Edger wiles."

Georgie furrowed his eyebrows in thought and looked at Declan. "Don't eat her fried chicken. It tastes good, but she puts rat poison in it."

The inscrutable mask on Declan's face shattered. He leaned forward and laughed.

KNIFE. Knife, knife, knife.

Jack crawled through the grass like a fluffy caterpillar. He'd circled the clearing three times, studying the lure from all angles, until he finally determined the size of the loop. It lay in wait in the grass, ready to snag him the moment the knife was touched.

But the loop was long and narrow. He could jump over it. He knew he could.

Jack crouched in the grass, tight and ready from the ends of his white whiskers to the tip of his short tail. Jump, bite the knife, and spring the trap.

Sure, the lure would've caught any other beast, but Jack wasn't a dumb beast. He was smart.

Jack exploded into flight. He sailed over the loop, air rushing past him, everything crystal clear and slow around him. The handle of the knife loomed before him. He bit it, the feel of its treated wood handle like honey in his mouth, and flew by, free and clear. The sapling sprang upright. The loop whistled past him. Safe!

A green net rushed at him from below. He tried to veer in midflight, but it caught him and clamped him tight. He scrambled in its soft folds, slicing at it with his claws. The knife slid from his mouth and fell through the mesh to the ground. A meow of despair broke from Jack. He bounced a couple of times in the knot of the net, suspended high above the ground like a kitten in a sack, and then the net was still.

THIRTEEN

A whispery rustling of leaves made Jack open his eyes. He unsheathed his claws and hissed.

Declan emerged from the undergrowth. He moved quietly and his eyes were different now: focused and dark. Hunter's eyes. Jack tensed.

The blueblood approached the net and then stopped, looking up.

"Are you hurt?"

Jack hissed and spat, growling fighting noises.

"I'll take that as a no." Declan bent down, picked up the knife, wiped the handle on his sleeve, and sat on a mossy log.

"There is a great difference between a knife and a sword."

He unsheathed the smaller sword he carried at his waist. The afternoon sun caught it, turning the blade into a beautiful long claw bright with reflected light.

"Swords are long and cumbersome. They are made to kill your opponent in battle from a distance." He glanced at Jack with his scary green eyes. "Swords are not for you."

He sheathed the sword and picked up the knife. "Knives are quick. Efficient. Quiet. There's no such thing as a knife battle. When a knifemaster pulls out his blade, he doesn't want to fight off his opponent. He means to kill him."

Declan leapt off the log and struck at the empty air so quickly he became a blur.

"Rogues carry knives."

The knife sliced and stabbed unseen opponents in a shimmering dance of steel. Jack watched, mesmerized. So quick.

"Thieves. Spies. Assassins. They carry knives."

Declan tossed the blade into the air, caught it by the tip, and flipped the knife so the handle landed into his palm. "A knifemaster armed with a blade like this can go through a room full of soldiers. I've seen it happen."

Jack wanted the knife so badly, even his tail itched for it.

Declan examined the blade. "A fighting knife like this can't be stolen. But you could earn it."

Jack pricked his ears.

"If you prove to me that you can be quick, efficient, and quiet." Declan sat back on the log. "Two miles north from here, there is a trail of the beasts that chased you. They run fast along the ground and they can climb, but they're slow in the trees. A forest cat can easily outrun them in the branches. If such a cat were to track them, quietly and patiently and find their lair . . ."

Jack growled and spat. He would fight them, he would . . .

"No fighting," Declan said. "Sleek, stealthy, and silent. Like a knife sliding into a man in the darkness. Track the beasts. Find their lair. Don't be seen. If you do this and show me where they are, you'll earn the knife."

He smiled. "But that's an adventure for tomorrow. Right now we have to decide what to do with you. I caught you fair and square. Are you going to come quietly like a wise and patient predator, or will I have to carry you in the net, like a wild beast?"

ROSE sat in the attic, the enormous dusty *Encyclopedia of the Weird* spread open on her lap. The book was two feet tall, about a foot thick, and heavy as hell, and her thighs were sweaty and rapidly going numb in her jeans.

She had gone through the *Bestiary* but found nothing that had to do with the hounds. The *Encyclopedia* was her next best bet.

She turned the big page and adjusted her posture a bit. Her butt was going numb, too.

Adrianglia, Formal Forms of Address. She scanned down the ranks . . . *Earl. Earl of "Domain Name." Lord "Name."* She yawned and flipped back a page.

Earl—derivative of the Northland *jarl*. Equivalent to *Count* in Gaulic Empire. Landed noble above viscount but below marquis.

What was his name . . . Earl Carmine? Carmaine? Camarine. Yes, that was it. She turned the pages to the index and found *Earl Camarine*.

Earl Camarine: noble ruling Earldom of Camarine. Traditional domain of the Duke of the Southern Provinces. Most frequently used as a courtesy title.

"Courtesy title." She wasn't sure exactly what that meant, but she got the gist of it. For all of his la-di-da manners, Declan wasn't even a real earl. Rose snickered.

"Rose!" Georgie's high-pitched voice shattered her thoughts.

"Coming!" She pushed the book off her lap and went down the ladder, dusting off her jeans. "Georgie, did you go outside?" She marched onto the porch. "Didn't I tell you to stay inside?"

Declan stood in the yard. In his arms curled Jack. His eyes were shut. He growled softly in his sleep and kneaded Declan's arm with his claws. Declan didn't even wince. "I think he's tuckered out. Where do you want him?"

The world reared and kicked her in the teeth. She took a moment to recover, and when she spoke, her voice was almost normal. "I'll take him."

Declan gently deposited Jack into her arms. "I'm sure it would hurt his feelings, but he makes a handsome kit."

"You should've seen him when he was a baby," Rose said through her shock. "Nothing but fuzz and ear tufts. Every minute was like a *National Geographic* Kodak moment."

She took Jack inside and gently put him in his bed.

In an hour she served dinner. Jack slept through it. Afterward Georgie curled up to reread *InuYasha*, yet again, and Rose brewed a cup of tea and escaped onto the porch. Her solitude didn't last.

Declan sat next to her on the steps. "Disappointed?"

His voice held no mocking, and she shrugged. "Yes. How did you do it?"

"I set four traps and baited the most obvious one with a knife he drooled over in my room."

What did she expect? After all, Jack was only eight. It was a huge burden to put on him. She shouldn't have done it in the first place. When she had pictured Declan tracking Jack through the woods, the idea of him setting traps and lures had never entered her mind. "Boys and knives," Rose murmured. "Irresistible attraction."

"We never grow out of it."

He certainly didn't, considering how many swords and knives he dragged around with him. Dad's entire room was full of blades.

In the soft light of the afternoon, Declan's features gained a new tint. His eyes looked into the distance. He seemed to be wrestling with his thoughts. The harsh line of his mouth relaxed. His gaze lost its aggression. Sitting like this, he seemed almost approachable. The urge to touch him returned. It was natural, she told herself. He was so handsome, and she had no life. But just because she felt the irrational desire to kiss him didn't mean she had to follow through with it.

The last time he let the blueblood persona slip, he was reasonable. Maybe if she told him a little more about them, he would understand and leave them in peace.

"You seem to like Jack," she said carefully, testing the waters.

"He tried his best," he said. "Tell me, why didn't he change shapes when the hounds were after him on the lawn? The survival instinct should've driven him to become a lynx in the face of danger."

Rose looked into her cup. "It might be different in the Weird, but when changelings shift in the Edge, it's almost like a seizure. They fall down and convulse. It's frightening, and it can last up to a minute. If he had changed shapes, the creatures would've torn him apart before he had a chance to finish. It took us a long time to teach him not to go cat every time he got scared. Did you see the bracelet he wears?"

"Yes."

"I taught him that so long as the bracelet stays on, he knows not to change shapes. It's not actually magic, or anything. Just conditioning."

"That must've taken a lot of work." His voice betrayed respect.

"It did."

Declan hesitated, mulling something over. Something was clearly eating at him.

"In the Weird, the changeling children are segregated and taken to special schools until they become adults," he said finally.

She glanced at him. "You exile children?"

Declan grimaced. "It's not exactly like that. There are specialized trainers, who oversee their education . . ." He fell silent. "Yes," he said with a measure of resignation. "We exile changeling children. It's common wisdom that it's better for them."

"I can see how people would think that."

His thick eyebrows crept up. "I didn't expect you to agree with that."

"Some changelings are born human. Jack was born a kitten. We knew something was wrong when he was in the womb, because my mother felt claws, and when Grandma did her spells, all the tests kept pointing to the forest. We couldn't take my mother to the hospital, because my parents were afraid Jack would die without magic, and my dad had to pay a huge bribe to the midwife from the Broken, so we could get him the proper documents. When Jack was born, he wouldn't nurse. My mother would pump her breast milk, and we had to feed it to him out of a bottle. It took him three days to change into a human, and when he finally did, he was still blind for almost a month. He looked odd as a baby. I thought he was deformed."

She swallowed the last of her tea. "Even now, with Jack, it's . . . it's hard. He has moments when he stops understanding what's being said. He hears the words and knows what they mean, but they just don't penetrate. He doesn't always comprehend why people react the way they do. And he fights like a maniac. Older kids are terrified of him. Every time my phone rings and it's the school, I get panicky, because I always think he must've hurt someone. So yes, I can see how some people might find it too much. Ordinary human kids are hard enough as it is. Don't get me wrong, I would never give Jack up. Never. They'd have to pry him from my dead fingers. But I always wonder, what if I'm doing things wrong?"

"He's one of the most socialized changelings I have ever seen," Declan said. "He goes to a regular school. He plays. He's smart and can be reasoned with, and he shows empathy for other people. He talked about protecting George. I don't think you understand how remarkable that is."

She glanced at him. "He's just a little boy, Declan. You talk like he isn't human."

Declan's face looked haunted. "I have a friend," he said. "We were soldiers together."

Not only was he a blueblood, but he was also a soldier. An officer, no doubt. No wonder he thought ordering people around was the only way to communicate. "How long were you in the military?"

"Ten years," Declan said.

"That's a long time," she said.

"I thought it was better suited to me than being a peer," he said.

"Why?" she wondered.

"I wasn't responsible for anyone but myself," he said. "It was simple that way."

So not an officer then. "Were you happy?"

"I was content," Declan said. "I was good at killing, and I was praised and rewarded for doing it well. It felt like the right place for me at the time."

"I thought you were all about balls and etiquette and womanizing," she needled him.

The look she got back was deadly serious. "You have an odd view of the life of a peer. Mostly it's work. Lots and lots of work and lots of responsibility. At that time in my life, I didn't want it. I still don't, but now I have no choice."

His voice was bitter and hollow. Rose looked away, not sure what to do with herself. "Tell me about your friend."

"He's a changeling," Declan said. "A predator like Jack. There are few paths a changeling can take in our society, especially if they aren't born into a family of means. My friend was born poor. He was abandoned by his mother at birth and given to the Citadel, Adrianglia's premier military school. Changelings born into wealthy families are taught a certain way so one day they can reenter society."

"And your friend wasn't?" she guessed.

Declan shook his head. "He was a ward of the realm, and the realm never meant for him to live with other people. They made him into a killer. He was raised to have no emotions, only strict control and strict punishment when he failed. He told me that he grew up in a bare room, twelve feet by ten feet, which he shared with another boy. He was allowed no personal possessions except his clothes, a toothbrush, a comb, and a towel."

"That's awful," she said. "You can't lock children up like that. Any children. Jack has to be able to run in the Wood, to play. Without it, he would—"

"Go insane," Declan finished. "Or learn to survive and carry a lot of hate."

"How could your friend become a soldier after this? He had to have been"—she searched for a right word and couldn't find it—"not okay."

"He fit right in," Declan said. "We were in the Red Legion. We did the necessary things people don't want to know about."

"Black ops?" she asked. What do you know, Latoya proved right—he was one of those bug-eating, wilderness-surviving, take-out-terrorists-with-a-pinecone-and-bubble-gum types.

"Black sounds about right. We went where nobody else could go, and we were very good at killing everything we found there. We weren't bound by treaties or conventions. In that type of unit, few things are certain. You rely on yourself and, if you're lucky, on a man or woman next to you. I watched out for my friend, and he watched out for me. He saved my life a few times, and I repaid the favor. Neither of us counted who owed what to whom. I would've died for him if needed."

"Why?"

"Because he would've done the same for me," Declan said.

"Who did you fight?"

Declan shrugged. "The Kingdom of Gaul. The Spanish Empire. The FOGL."

"What is the FOGL?"

Declan dragged his hand across his face as if trying to peel the memories off. "It's a religious sect. Forces of Great Lucifer. Their prime directive is to establish dominion over the entire world, and they go about it in pretty terrible ways. Adrianglia is full of refugees, from past conflicts and present. Some of them commit heinous crimes and require extraordinary measures to be neutralized. During one of these missions, things went wrong and my friend made the mistake of behaving like a human."

"What happened?"

"There was a dam. A small band of criminals held it and its workers for ransom. They had attached a device to the dam supports and threatened to set off an explosion and drown the town below it. The dam was very old, almost labyrinthine, and everyone who knew its layout was inside, being held hostage. My friend went in because he was a changeling. He could rely on his sense of smell, and our superiors counted on his logic prevailing if he had to make a morally difficult choice. He was told that if the situation put the lives of the hostages against the security of the dam, he was to place greater importance on keeping the dam intact. If the dam had failed, the potential loss of life would be much greater than the deaths of the six people trapped inside.

"He tracked down the hostages, but the criminals had quarreled, and one of them set off the charges. My friend had a choice: he could go after the charges or he could save the hostages. He had what he called an attack of humanity and rescued the hostages. The dam burst, flooding the town. The flood didn't result in any deaths, but the financial damages were staggering. He was court-martialed."

"Why? For saving people?"

"For disobeying an order. He was sentenced to death."

"But nobody was hurt!"

"It didn't matter." Declan's face was merciless. "You see,

they wanted to kill him not because he disobeyed the order but because he was a changeling who was judged unstable. They had turned him into a lethal killer, and they were happy to use him as long as he did exactly as told. But now they could no longer predict his actions."

"They were going to put him down like an animal? What kind of country would do that?"

"He was a ward of the realm, and the realm was afraid of what he might do next. They didn't want the responsibility of keeping the public safe from him."

"Did you try to help him?"

"Yes. I left the military and assumed the title, because my status as a peer would give my words greater weight. I petitioned, I lobbied, I argued that if an ordinary soldier were in his place, he wouldn't have received the death penalty."

He'd abandoned his career to rescue his friend, and he said it without any bravado, like it was the obvious logical thing to do, not even deserving a second thought. Ten years of his life, and he'd turned his back on it for the sake of another person. Not many people would do that. She wasn't sure she could've done it. That was admirable.

Rose bit her lip. "Did you save him?"

"No. I failed."

He'd said it with such bitterness. His eyes had turned distant and mournful, as if dusted with ash. She wanted to reach out and touch him. To somehow make it better.

"At the last moment, Casshorn, the brother of the Duke of the Southern Provinces, adopted my friend, assuming complete responsibility for his actions. Because Casshorn was childless, and a high peer, he claimed the bloodline privilege. Basically, my friend was his only heir, and as such, the realm couldn't kill him. Casshorn paid an exorbitant sum for his release."

"That was very kind," Rose said.

Declan gave her a flat look.

"What did I say?"

"Casshorn is a brigand. He's a slimy stain upon the honor of the Duke's house. He didn't adopt my friend out of kindness. He adopted him because that was the only way he could've saved him from execution. See, my friend is lethal with a blade, and he hates—"

A clammy touch of foul magic brushed her. Rose froze. She didn't really believe they had killed all the beasts, but she had hoped. Apparently, she was wrong.

"Keep talking," Declan said. "I doubt the creature understands what's being said, but it's likely sensitive to the tone of our voices."

"Where is it?" she asked lightly.

"On the left, near a small shed. Let's get up and stroll a bit."

He rose and offered her his hand. She took it mechanically, before realizing she had done it, and they walked side by side, wandering toward the road. Her hand rested in Declan's calloused fingers, as if they were a couple of teenagers going steady. He was building his magic for one hell of a flash, his whole body wound tight, full of barely contained violence. It was like walking next to a tiger who decided that he liked you: Declan held her hand lightly, but he wasn't about to let her get away.

He squeezed her fingers. In that moment Rose felt a connection between them, an alarmingly intimate bond. She glanced at him to reassure herself she was imagining this and saw the same thought mirrored on his face: he had her hand and he liked it.

She turned away.

"A little closer." Declan applied subtle pressure to her arm, but didn't let go of her hand.

The creature crouched in the myrtle by the shed. To see it out like this, unafraid in full daylight, was eerie.

Declan's voice was steady. "When I say duck, you—"

"No."

"What do you mean, no?"

"I don't want you to kill it. You'll do your big kaboom thing and blow my shed to smithereens." And Grandpa Cletus with it. She didn't even want to think what it would do to Georgie.

He glanced at her, indignant. "I don't go kaboom."

"Tell it to Amy's roof."

"That kaboom is the reason all of us are still breathing."

The creature watched them, making no move to advance.

"I'm not saying it wasn't necessary. But that was her house. She isn't a noble swimming in money. She can't just wave her hand and get another roof. You didn't even warn her first. People need to have a moment to prepare for that kind of shock."

Declan halted, and so did she. They stood entirely too close. Her back was to the creature. Its magic dripped onto her skin, squirming along her spine in a slippery trickle.

Declan locked his teeth. It made his jaw even squarer. "That hound is less than two feet away from the shed. There's no way I can strike at it and not singe the shed. It's physically impossible. And I've left my swords inside."

"That's why you should let me take care of this."

"How, pray tell, will you manage that?"

"Like this." She spun around and whipped a blindingly white line of magic at the beast. The flash snapped, slicing the beast's head off its neck like a giant razor blade. The headless torso froze in a half crouch for a long moment and toppled over. The oppressive magic vanished.

Declan stared at her, openmouthed.

Rose smiled.

Declan released her fingers and strode to the headless body. "Hmm," he said.

"Hmm back at you," she told him and went to check the brush for signs of other beasts. She didn't feel any, but it didn't mean they weren't there.

They searched the bushes, but no other beasts were in attendance.

"Where do they keep coming from?" Rose wondered. "And why?"

"Why is simple. They hunger for the magic."

"I guess I better get a shovel. We should bury that damn thing."

"Who taught you to flash?" He said it like he expected her to lie.

"Nobody taught me. I practiced for years. Several hours a day. I still do, when I have time."

Declan's face reflected disbelief.

"Don't look so surprised," she told him. "I'm the Edger

girl who flashes white, remember? The reason for your trip to this horrible, awful place where you have to mingle with unwashed commoners."

"I knew you could flash white. I didn't know how precise you are."

"You're precise. You knocked aside my bolt."

"Yes, but I didn't aim for the bolt specifically. I just sent a wide pulse of magic from the front of my body, like a shield. It would've knocked away one bolt or ten."

"Oh. Well, thank you for the tip! Now I know how you did it."

They looked at each other.

"Just how precise are you?" he asked.

She gave him a sly Edger smile. "Do you have a doubloon on you?"

He reached into his pocket and produced a coin.

"I'll make you a deal. You throw it in the air, and if I hit it with my flash, it's mine."

Declan looked at the doubloon. It was slightly larger than a quarter from the Broken. He tossed it high above his head. The doubloon spun in the air, catching the sunlight, shining like a bright spark . . . and fell into the grass stung by a thin white whip of her flash.

Declan swore.

She grinned, plucked the still-hot coin from the grass, blew on it, and showed it to him, taunting him a little. "Groceries for two weeks. A pleasure doing business with you."

"I've only met one person who could do that," he said. "She was a flash-sniper in our unit. How can you do this with no proper training?"

"Did you study flashing?" she asked.

"Yes."

"Why?"

"Because it's the best weapon available, and I wanted to be good at it. And everybody in my family was good with it. I was a noble, and I had to uphold the honor of our name."

"I had a much better motivation than you," she said. "When I was thirteen, my mother's parents died in a house fire. Grandpa Danilo always smoked like a chimney. The whole house was covered with cigarette butts, and one night he'd smoked one too many. Nobody got out alive, not even my grandparents' cat. Their death broke my mother. She just kind of died right then, but her body kept on living. She started sleeping around and didn't stop. She'd have anybody who'd have her. Married, blind, crippled, crazy, she didn't care. She said it made her feel alive."

"I'm sorry," he said. "It must've been very painful for you."

"It wasn't fun. People called my mother a slut to my face. Leanne, who lent you the clothes? She used to chase me around the school, chanting 'whore's bitch.' She'd written it on my locker once in big letters. You were the son of a nobleman, handsome, wealthy, probably well liked. Poor little rich boy. I was the daughter of a whore, penniless, ugly, and despised. I had a lot of motivation to flash well. I wanted to ram my flash down the world's throat to show everyone that I was worth something."

"How did it work out for you?"

"Not so well," she admitted. "But now playing with my flash is a habit. I taught myself a lot of fun tricks."

"Aha." Declan pointed to the tree. "Double slicer."

The magic slashed from him in two even streams, running low through the grass, and collided in a brilliant explosion at the tree. He had used a mere fraction of his power, just to show her the move. Declan had better control than she had thought.

"Don't be upset if you can't do it right away," he said. "It takes a bit of pra—"

He clamped his mouth shut with a click as she sent two identical streams of magic into the tree.

"Oh my . . ." she murmured innocently.

"Ball lightning." A sphere of magic ignited over his shoulder and smashed into the tree in a shower of sparks.

She hadn't seen that one before, but she had practiced making spirals for years—mostly because she thought they looked neat—and a sphere was just a folded spiral. The trick would be to snap it with a spin, the way he had done. She concentrated and watched in satisfaction as a white ball formed over her shoulder. It was a bit lopsided and it didn't spin as well as his, but she was able to send it flying into the bark.

Declan shook his head. "Unbelievable."

"It's killing you that you can't stump me, isn't it?" Rose grinned. She never got to show off. To have him here as her audience was satisfying beyond words. She'd managed to impress a blueblood from the Weird. An earl and ex-soldier. It didn't get better than that.

Declan planted his feet into the grass and concentrated. His eyes shone. A ghostly breeze stirred his hair. A crisp line of white burst from his back to rise two feet above his head. The top of the magic line curved down, stretching all the way to the grass in a white half arch, and began to circle him, drawing a perfect ring in the dirt.

Wow.

"Ataman's defense," he said, letting it die.

Rose tried it. She had no problems creating the straight upward line, but as she tried to bend it down, it struck at the grass under a sharp angle, not curved gently the way Declan's had.

Declan smiled.

"Let me see it again, please."

He reconstructed the arch. "It took me a year of constant practice to learn how to do this."

Rose watched the arch go around him. Turn. Turn. Turn. Like a whip. Turn. "Give me a few minutes."

"You have time." He sat in the grass.

"Are you just going to sit there and watch me?"

"Yes. Watching pretty peasant girls is what we poor little rich boys do best."

"Peasant?"

He shrugged. "You started the name-calling."

She snorted and went to work. It was harder than it looked, and for the first few minutes the sight of him on the grass distracted her. He looked like a painting with his strong body, long lean legs, and absurdly handsome face. There was humor in his green eyes, and when their gazes met by chance, he winked at her. She nearly singed herself with her own flash. But soon, she sank into the task, and Declan and the rest of the world faded.

Sometime later Declan stirred on the grass. "Do you want me to tell you how it's done?"

"No!"

He grinned.

She struggled with it for another half hour, until it dawned on her to put a spin into the line. At first it merely sagged, but the harder she pushed, the lower it curved, until finally her line of white arched down gracefully and spun about her, like an obedient pet.

She turned, thrilled, and saw him striding across the lawn to her. He paused and ducked under the spinning line of her flash. He was so close, they practically touched. She let the flash die.

"That's incredible," he said quietly.

"It's not that incredible," she said.

"It took me a year to learn it."

"I practiced a lot more than you."

"I can see that."

She glanced at his face, and all thoughts scattered from her head. She saw admiration and respect in his eyes, an acknowledgment one would give an equal. They looked at each other. Slowly his eyes darkened to deeper green. The way he looked at her made her want to take the half step to close the small distance between them, open her mouth, and let him kiss her. She could almost feel his lips on hers. Like playing with fire. Rose moistened her bottom lip, biting it a little to get rid of the phantom kiss, and saw Declan's gaze snag on her mouth.

Oh no. No, no, no. Bad idea.

He took a step forward, his hand reaching for her. Rose sidestepped.

"Thank you. It means a lot to me, coming from someone like you. I think we better dig a grave for that thing. The stench is killing me."

She headed to the back of the house for a shovel.

"Rose," he called. His voice was deep and touched with a hint of command. She pretended not to hear him and hid behind the shed.

She'd done precisely the same thing for which she had berated Georgie during lunch. Declan had won the first challenge, and if he did have any doubts about her abilities, she had shattered them. Now he knew that not only could she flash white, but she did it extraordinarily well. And the way he looked at her left her with no questions: Declan wanted her. She had to stump him on the second challenge, or in a few days she'd be packing her things and following him into the Weird.

FOURTEEN

THE first word that came to mind when one saw Max Taylor was "solid." About two hundred and fifty pounds, he had the build of a pro wrestler gone to fat. His bullet-shaped head was shaved bald, and his small gun gray eyes were the very definition of unfriendly as he stared at Rose's truck through his store's front window.

Rose slid her vehicle into the parking spot in front of Taylor's Metal Detectors. The yellow script in the window, bright and shiny in the morning light, promised to purchase rare coins and scrap gold for the best prices.

Georgie fidgeted in the backseat, uneasy. Yesterday's chicken episode reminded her that placing all her eggs in one basket wasn't the most prudent course of action. True, she wanted Georgie to earn good grades, and go to school in the Broken, and possibly get a decent paying job there, but in the end Georgie lived and breathed magic. He was an Edger. She had neglected the Edger part of his education, and it was time to correct that oversight.

"There are two people in Pine Barren who can fence precious metals," she said. "Gold, silver, jewelry, anything like that. One is Peter Padrake and the other is Max Taylor. Peter is very straightforward in how he deals. He'll charge you a flat forty-five percent fee. That means that for every hundred dollars, Peter takes forty-five and you keep fifty-five."

Georgie's smart eyes turned calculating. "So he takes almost half?"

"Yes. He won't try to cheat you, but he also won't haggle. Peter's comics store is doing well, and he has money. He doesn't have to hustle to make a living, so he can afford to let some deals go. That's why you must only go to Peter as a last resort. Always come here first." She glanced at Max through the windshield. "Max Taylor will try his best to dupe you. He'll claim your stuff is fake, and he'll try to give you some ridiculously small amount for it. He's a big man, and he'll get loud and try to intimidate you. He also keeps a gun in his desk, and he likes to take it out and wave it around during haggling. Now, I heard a rumor that the gun isn't even loaded, but we know what the golden rule for guns is, right?"

"Every gun is loaded," Georgie recited.

"That's right. We treat every gun as if it's loaded, with a round in the chamber and the safety off. We never point guns at other people, even when we think they're not loaded, unless we intend to shoot the person, yes?"

"Yes," Georgie agreed. "We hold the gun to the side and down, so we don't shoot our feet by accident, or barrel up."

"Very good." She nodded. "So the golden rule says, we must treat Max's gun as if it's loaded."

"Would he shoot us?" Georgie shifted in his seat.

"Not very likely," she assured him. "His store is a front. Nobody buys metal detectors. The only way he can stay in business is to make money off people like us. If he shoots someone, what would happen?"

"People would go to Peter instead," Georgie said.

"That's right. If we're smart, we can get Max to come down on the fee. Anything below a third is good. So, we're going to sit here in our truck for a bit more, as if we're deciding what to do, and then we'll go inside and haggle. No matter how loud or stupid Max gets, keep calm."

"Okay," Georgie promised.

Rose dug in her pocket and pulled out a rumpled piece of paper.

Jack joined me for the morning exercise. We'll be back before lunch.

Declan

She had awakened to find this piece of paper on the table. She was a light sleeper, but Declan moved like a wolf, and nobody could hear Jack when he didn't want to be heard. They had snuck out of the house like two thieves in the night.

Rose frowned at the note. When he was tiny, Jack used to run off into the woods. Left to his own devices, he'd be gone for days, and so Rose kept some of his fur and hair and claw and nail clippings so she could find him. She had done a quick scrying spell, but it had a short range, and Jack was nowhere within two miles from the house. That meant Declan had taken him into the wilderness of the Wood.

Her initial impulse was to run after them, but Rose stopped herself. First, she had no idea where they had gone. Second, her kitchen was empty—they literally had nothing to eat. The last of the cereal was gone. Georgie had finished it. He was still hungry, and she was hungry as well. Georgie couldn't go too long without a snack, not with the drain his magic placed on his body. She could spend a couple of hours searching for Jack, or she could go and get some money and buy food. So she had borrowed four dollars from Grandmother—it nearly killed her to do it—put a gallon of gas into the truck, and drove out to see Max Taylor.

It irritated her that she hadn't woken up in time to stop Declan. Logically, she had nothing to worry about. Declan had sworn not to harm the boys. Jack was a changeling just like Declan's friend, and the emotion she had glimpsed behind Declan's blueblood facade felt genuine to her. He had saved Jack once; it made no sense that he would put him into any sort of danger. Besides, the safest place in the Edge now was by Declan's side.

She kept herself from panicking through logic, but worry ate at her. Jack was gone. They'd probably gone deep into the Wood. Why? They didn't tell her, and there was nothing she could do about it, not without making some major magic happen.

Inside the store, Max started rearranging things on his desk. "See? He's getting antsy. Let's go."

Rose popped the doors open, and together she and Georgie stepped into the shop.

Max sat behind the glass counter. "What do you got?"

Rose showed him the doubloon. He reached for it, but she shook her head. "You can see it from right here."

Max squinted. "A hundred bucks," he said.

She closed her fist over the doubloon and nodded to Georgie. "Let's go to Peter."

"That damn pirate won't give you more," Max growled.

Rose gave him a withering look. "The coin is exactly one-half ounce of gold. Right now a half-ounce U.S. Gold Eagle is trading for four hundred and fifty-seven dollars and forty-seven cents and a half-ounce Maple Leaf is going for four hundred and sixty-four dollars and ninety-four cents."

"How did you know that?"

"I went to the library and looked it up on the Internet. Peter charges a flat forty-five percent, so I should get at least two hundred and fifty dollars for each of my coins."

Max's beady eyes shone. "Coins?"

"Coins. As in more than one."

"How many do you have?"

She shrugged. "Three for now. There will be more."

"Nine hundred and fourteen dollars for the whole thing," Max offered.

"That's a third. I don't think so. I might go as low as twelve hundred."

"Nine fifty."

"Eleven seventy-five."

"You won't get a better price . . ."

She shrugged. "I can always take it to a jeweler in the city. It's an hour's drive."

Max reached under the counter. By the time he'd pulled out a Glock and put it on the glass, Rose's gun pointed at his head.

"That's a .22," Max sneered. "It will bounce from wet laundry."

"I can shoot you three times before you squeeze off one shot. You think my bullets will bounce off Max's face, Georgie?"

George didn't miss a beat. "If they don't, we can take him into the Edge and I'll raise him."

Max blinked. Rose smiled at him.

"One thousand twenty-eight dollars and twenty-five cents!" Max said.

A twenty-five percent fee. "Done."

She didn't put away the gun until they peeled out of the parking lot.

"You did very well," she told Georgie.

Georgie smiled in the rearview mirror.

Tiny sharp needles prickled Rose's hands, a belated reaction to the adrenaline rush. It finally sank in—she had a month's worth of money.

"What would you like to eat?"

"Whatever I want?"

"Whatever you want."

"French fries," Georgie said. "And chicken nuggets. And then maybe shrimp."

Shrimp would have to wait till home, but nuggets and fries she could manage. Rose made a left into the McDonald's drive-through.

ROSE took her gaze off the road for a second to steal a glance at the white Wal-Mart bags in the passenger seat. She'd bought beef, and chicken, and shrimp for Georgie. She managed to snag a couple of packs of country-style pork ribs on sale. She'd gotten potatoes. And cheese. And the tomatoes she liked. And apples for Jack. And eggs, and butter, and milk, and cereal . . . The truck was full of bags. She was too paranoid to put them into the truck bed. Who knew what might happen? They could fall out or fly off.

She had enough groceries for a month, and all of her bills were paid. It was a most wonderful feeling. She would go home and spend an hour putting it all up, separating the meat into dinner-sized portions, wrapping it in plastic wrap, and putting it all into her freezer. Rose grinned. No worry about the food. For a month.

"Rose?" Georgie asked.

"Hmm?"

"Why don't you like Declan?"

Now there was a loaded question. She wanted to tell him the truth, without mincing her words, but both he and Jack were smitten with Declan. Looking at him from the boys' perspective, Declan was the very definition of cool. They were two boys raised by women. Enter Declan, who had swords and magic, who was strong and manly, and who stood up to her, something neither of them could do. It's little wonder they wanted to be like him.

For the thousandth time, she wished Dad hadn't run off.

"Do you like Declan?" she asked carefully.

"Yes."

"Why?" she asked.

"He's smart," Georgie said. "He knows a lot of things, and his magic is as good as yours. He said that his house has its own library, except you don't have to have a card to check the books out. You can just go and take one whenever you want."

Rose's heart clenched a little in her chest. "I see." She swallowed. Declan was working on the kids, more so than she had realized. He was working on her, too. She couldn't get him out of her head.

This would have to be phrased very carefully. Anything she said to George would find its way to Jack. She didn't want to destroy their fragile faith in the only cool guy they knew, and she definitely didn't want this situation to turn into "Big bad Rose drove the super-cool Declan away." But she didn't want to delude them either.

"We've had people from the Weird approach us before to get me to go away with them," she said, choosing her words as if she were walking a tightrope and the wrong one could pitch her to the side. "You probably don't remember because you were little."

"Like Declan?"

She doubted there was another Declan. The world wouldn't be able to stand more than one. "Not quite like him. A couple were retainers of the nobles and one was a lesser blueblood."

"What happened?"

"Well, the first retainer tried to bribe Dad and Grandpa with presents. And when he figured out he was wasting his time, he set our house on fire. He thought that if we had nothing left, I'd leave with him. That's why the wards are so far out from the house now and my bedroom has different walls. The second retainer had a lot of people with him, and they tried to blockade the house. Dad shot him in the head, and then they went away."

"What about the blueblood?"

Rose sighed. "Oh, he was a special kind of worm. He was very sweet and nice. And very handsome. He tried to 'court' me. He'd bow down, and recite poetry, and tell me I was beautiful. I almost believed him. And then the caravan from the Weird came into town and one of the traders, Yanice—you remember her, right?"

"She wears a veil," Georgie said.

"Yes. Yanice recognized him. He was a slaver and a wanted criminal. If I had gone with him, he would've auctioned me off like a cow. I wouldn't have a choice—I would be forced to go with whatever man bought me." She wouldn't have. She'd have fought to the end, and they would've had to kill her, but there was no need to frighten George.

"Declan isn't like that."

"We don't really know what Declan is like. All that we have to go on is what Declan tells us and how he acts. I know he seems like a cool guy." She fell silent, realizing she wanted very much to believe that he was a "cool guy." He seemed . . . it would be a shame if he turned out to be a scumbag. There was warmth underneath all that arrogance, and more, there was integrity. She sensed it very clearly. Declan had a moral code. She suspected that there were lines he wouldn't cross, but she didn't exactly know where those lines lay.

"We don't know what he'll be like once I agree to go with him," she said. "What if he takes me with him and leaves you here? He told Jack that he would take all of us with him, but really nothing would force him to keep his word. What if he does take us with him and then makes you into servants or drops you off at some orphanage?"

Or kills them and leaves their bodies on the side of the road. His promise not to harm expired once he won the challenges. Surely, he wouldn't. Not Declan. But again, she had no guarantees.

"Besides, if I go with Declan, I'll have to be his wife. And Declan doesn't love me."

"Why not?" George asked.

"Because I'm not a lady. I don't have good manners, I'm not educated, and I'm not demure and sweet. I say what I mean, and I'm not always nice. He probably thinks he can force me to be pleasant, but no matter what clothes I wear and how you mess with my hair, I'll still be me." Crude, vulgar, and disagreeable.

Rose sighed. "See, Declan is used to people obeying his orders. Back in the Weird, when he orders something, people fall over themselves to make it happen. I'm not like that. That's why we argue so much. We would drive each other insane, and if we fought, Declan would win. My magic is like a lightning strike. It's precise and contained, because I have good control. Declan's magic is like a hurricane. Terribly, terribly powerful. He blew the roof off Amy's house."

"Really?"

"Yes. His flash just exploded and killed a whole bunch of those hound beasts. Tore the roof right off."

She stopped herself. Last thing she needed was a new way to feed Georgie's hero worship. "Bottom line: we can't trust Declan. He's very strong, and we don't want to be at his mercy."

If she were born into a good Weird family, it might have been different, Rose thought, guiding the truck up to Grandma's house. She might have had tutors and clothes. Of natural colors. She would have been witty and carefree, and then Declan might have thought she was the coolest thing since sliced bread. He might have tried to win her. Now that would be an interesting exercise: the arrogant, icy, monstrously powerful Declan bowing and asking her to dance or making polite small talk with Grandma in French before asking for permission to take Rose for a stroll in the park. Oh, that would be hilarious.

She killed the smile that stretched her lips and let the fantasy die. Living in a dream never did her any good. She would never be a lady. She was born an Edger mongrel. Good for—how had he put it?—a carte blanche, but little else.

Yesterday when he stepped close to her and she looked into his eyes, she realized he wanted her. Not just her, the white-flashing-freak, but her as a woman. It wasn't a calculated move like that stare he had given her before. It was a completely spontaneous and honest declaration of attraction, and it was completely devastating. She had thought about it all evening, and then half of the night, and now again, she was thinking about it and couldn't let it go. The idea of being in Declan's bed filled her with a kind of happy terror. It wasn't an altogether unpleasant feeling, and she was furious with herself for it.

He was so out of place in her house that Rose never expected him, and when she ran into him while straightening up or cooking, her heart did a little skip. That skip was dangerous. Watching him, talking to him, was dangerous. She had been fooled before, and she couldn't afford to be fooled again. She needed to get her head on straight.

When she allowed herself to dream, being the object of a blueblood's lust didn't enter her fantasies. No, she dreamt of a regular guy, a nice guy with a steady job, someone who'd love her as much as she loved him and take care of her just like she would take care of him. Someone like William. Except her heart didn't make those little jumps when she saw William.

She pictured herself living in the Broken, with a regular guy, just like a regular family, going to a regular job . . . Dear God. She would slit her own throat out of boredom.

"I don't know what I want," she mumbled.

Five minutes later, she drove up to Grandma's, parked, and eyed the house. Grandma had to be dying to give her a piece of her mind regarding Declan. This morning Rose got away without a conversation by making excuses about Georgie needing to eat. Maybe if she got lucky, she could get away with her hide intact again.

"Come on, Georgie." He climbed out of the truck, and together they made their way up the steps and into the kitchen, which smelled like vanilla and cinnamon.

"Smells like cookies," Georgie said.

Grandma Éléonore smiled and handed him a plate of cookies. "There you go. Why don't you go to the porch, Georgie, and let me and Rose talk a bit."

Rose bit her lip. She knew what was coming and tried to beat a hasty retreat, just like this morning. "I brought back your four dollars," she announced, putting the money on the table. "I really can't stay. I have groceries in the truck and they might spoil . . ."

"Sit!" Grandma pointed to a chair.

Rose sat.

"Where is Jack?"

"With Declan."

"And you trust Declan enough to leave a child with him?"

Rose grimaced. "They snuck out this morning. By the time I woke up, they had gone beyond the scrying spell. Jack worships the ground Declan walks on, and he probably wanted to show off in the Wood. I'm not happy about it, and I'll chew him out when they get home, but I don't think Declan would hurt him or let him be harmed. He saved Jack once, and I don't believe he has it in him to injure a child."

"And what makes you think so?"

Rose shrugged. "It's a feeling I get from him."

"A feeling?" Grandma fixed her with an intense blue gaze. "I'll hear about the blueblood. All of it."

All of it took almost a half hour. The more Rose talked, the more the corners of Grandma's mouth sagged.

"Do you like him?" she asked when Rose fell silent.

"Why would you even ask me that? I—"

"Rose! Do you like him?"

"A little," Rose said. "Just a little."

Grandma sighed.

"Most of the time, I want to strangle him," Rose added to ease her fears.

For some odd reason, her attempt to reassure Grandma actually made things worse. Éléonore's face paled. *"Que Dieu nous aide."*

God help us . . . "What did I say? I don't like him enough to go away with him. He's arrogant and overbearing and—"

Grandma raised her hand, and Rose fell silent. Éléonore opened her mouth, closed it, and shook her head. "Anything I say will only make things worse," she murmured.

"What do you mean?"

Grandma sighed. "You have a flaw, Rose. You're daring. Just like my Cletus, just like your father. It's a Drayton trait, and it has brought us nothing but misery. You see a challenge, and you must go after it."

Rose blinked. She didn't chase challenges, at least not intentionally. At least she never thought she did.

"And this Declan, he's a terrible challenge," Grandma Éléonore continued. "Proud and powerful. And he looks . . . You know yourself how he looks. I know you'll turn yourself inside out, trying to win. Declan is the same way: he saw you out the window on the phone and went out the back door like he was about to storm a castle. He has decided you're his."

"I'll undecide it for him." Rose snorted. "He thinks he's already won. Well, I have a surprise or two coming."

"That's what I'm afraid of," Grandma murmured. "You must understand, he's a dangerous man. Very dangerous. I cursed him."

"You what?"

"I cursed him," Grandma repeated. "That evening when William called, he came through the door asking for you, and I didn't know who he was, so I cursed him."

Oh God. "What did you cast?"

"Rubber legs."

The Edgers had many talents. The ability to curse wasn't the rarest talent, but it was one of the strongest. The older you were, the stronger was your cursing. The elder Edgers had the cursing monopoly, and they didn't warm up to new-comers until they were past middle age, which for some Edger families hit around seventy or so.

For most curses, there was no cure. They had to be broken by the target or left to run their course. If the target did manage to break your curse, the magic lashed out back at you. While you tried to deal with the consequences, a very put-out cursee might arrive with his trusty shotgun, intending to use you for target practice. And if the curse did succeed, often the family of the afflicted would petition one of the older cursers for help to bring you down to size. Then you really had problems. An Edger had to be well along in years and have a good deal of respect before she could get away with cursing someone, or the retribution would be swift and brutal.

Rose had learned cursing when she was only six, by accident, just like everyone else. The family was out at a barbe-que, and a girl named Tina Watty had stolen her doll and thrown it on the grill. Rose wished Tina's hair would fall out. As soon as she said it, her magic gushed, and then they had to go home. The next time she saw Tina, her long blond hair was gone, and short stubble covered her head.

Everyone was allowed one curse, their first one, because that's how you learned you had the power. But after that, you learned to control yourself or there would be hell to pay. Luckily for her, Grandma was a curser as well, one of the best in East Laporte, and Rose got more education in the art of cursing than she would ever need. The only proper way to learn curses responsibly was to suffer through most of them. Grandmother knew a lot of curses, and Rose had wanted to learn badly. She'd tried rubber legs on for size when she was twelve.

Rubber legs was an excruciatingly painful curse. The victim felt her legs torn apart like string cheese. If she tried to take a step, she would inevitably plummet to the ground. The curse left no harmful effect and vanished after a half hour or so, but meanwhile a person could lose her mind.

And Grandma had cast it on Declan. It was a wonder he didn't slaughter the lot of them.

"Why would you curse him?"

Grandma shrugged. "He surprised me."

"What happened?"

"Your blueblood grunted a bit and shrugged it off. Just muscled on right through it. And that's when I hit him with the bottle of olive oil and missed. He dodged, took the bottle out of my hands, and told me in perfect French that while he appreciated my vigor when defending my family, if I attempted to hit him again, I would sorely regret it."

That sounded like Declan. "He's good at intimidation," Rose said.

Grandma nodded, her eyes opened wide. "Oh, I believed him. Besides, the curse had backlashed and I had to sit down. Do you know what I was going to do for a living before your rogue of a grandfather sailed into port with his ship and a dashing smile?"

"No."

"Our village supplied retainers for Count d'Artois of the Kingdom of Gaul in the Weird. My family, in particular, had served him for years. Trust me, I recognize blood when I see it. I don't know what Declan told you, but that boy has generations of blueblood ancestors to prop him up."

Rose waved her hands. "I don't think he is all that high on the peer ladder. Sometimes he forgets to act like a blueblood, and he's almost normal. Besides, I checked him in the *Encyclopedia*, and it says 'Earl Camarine' is a courtesy title. He probably got it for his military service in the Red Legion."

Grandma's mouth closed with a click.

"What did I say now?"

"Nothing," Grandma said. "Nothing at all. You're right, Jack is probably safe with him. Still, don't you think you better check on them?"

Rose glanced at the clock on the wall. Thirty minutes past noon. She was late, but the change in subject was awfully sudden. "There is something you're not telling me."

"Dear, I could fill this room with things I'm not telling you."

Grandma had that particular glint in her eyes that said arguing was useless. Rose shook her head and went to look for Georgie. She found him curled up on the daybed, asleep.

"Leave him with me," Grandma Éléonore said. "He needs the rest. I'll walk him back when he's awake."

Rose sighed, hugged her, and left.

She went down the steps, crossed the lawn, and went to her truck. A challenge chaser. She never considered herself to be that way. Well, yes, she did work on her flash until it became an obsession, but that was because she had so little else to occupy her.

What she needed to do was to get home, have a long talk with Jack about not going off on wild field trips with enemies of the family, and explain to Declan . . . What the hell did she want to explain to Declan? That in the moments when he forgot about being a blueblood, she found herself drawn to him like a foolish little moth is drawn to a bug-zapping lantern?

Rose drove back to the house. Declan and Jack were still out. She dragged the groceries in and sorted them out between the freezer, fridge, and pantry. A bag of apples and a plastic container of strawberries came up missing. Probably still in the truck. She went outside.

As Rose approached the truck, broken glass crunched under her foot. Glittering shards from a busted windshield lay on the road, stretching to the left in a shiny trail. A quick glance at the truck assured her that her own windshield was intact. Rose crouched and examined the glass. Odd. Not the typical spray or sheet of glass that resulted from a crash. It looked as if someone had smashed a windshield and then carefully poured the pieces out to get her attention. She could've sworn it hadn't been there when she got home.

The sparkling trail ended at an old pine. Rose frowned, looked up, and saw a license plate dangling off a branch on a cord. BOSSMAN. Emerson's license plate. What in the world . . .

She scanned the road. At the far left a chunk of red metal lay on the side, by some bushes. She jogged to it. It was a piece of a red car hood in the precise tomato shade of Emerson's SUV, its edges dark from the blowtorch burn.

Farther down the road, another chunk lay just before the bend. Rose strode to it, passed the curve, and saw a third red spot a hundred yards down. A trail of car crumbs, leading away from the house, toward the Broken. Very well. She jogged back to her truck and started it. She had to see where the car parts led.

FIFTEEN

ÉLÉONORE rose from the table, where a small piece of the beast floated in a jar of formaldehyde. The rest of the body had begun to decompose, and she'd had to bury it when she could no longer stand the smell.

"Talk to me," she whispered. She had tried everything. She had called on Adele Moore, Lee Stearns, and Jeremiah. They looked through their books and diaries, and cast their spells, and burned their herbs. She even made the trip down to speak to Elsie, or what was left of her. Her efforts earned her nothing. The collective wisdom of East Laporte had failed.

Whatever the beast was, wherever it came from, it was evil. On that everyone agreed.

Rumors flew about. To the north, Malachai Radish and his family were gone from their trailer, their place torn apart and left open. Malachai was never the sharpest tool in the shed and his truck was missing, so it was possible he just lost his marbles and took off with his wife and his kids without telling anyone. But Éléonore doubted it. Adele heard rumors of the dogs vanishing into the night. And Dena Vaughn found her livestock slaughtered. Something killed the small herd of pygmy goats and painted the hill where they grazed with their entrails.

They were under attack. Dread sat in her chest like a hard clump of ice. Where would it end? What did the creatures want? She had no answers. The only weapon they had was Rose and her flash.

Éléonore rubbed her face. Rose . . . If it wasn't one thing, it was another. The child just couldn't catch a break.

Lord Camarine bothered her. The boy was a genuine article. Flawless manners. Flawless poise. He'd picked up on the faint trace of accent in her speech when she cursed him and replied in refined, aristocratic French. Not something one could easily falsify. And power. Such great power. When she had gone to visit Elsie, she'd seen the damage to the house. The roof was completely gone and most of the wall, too. Amy said he'd done it in one burst. Expected from the one of the Red Legionnaires, of course. They were the Adrianglian weapon of last resort. She'd heard stories about them when she was a little girl. They fought like demons. Some of them weren't even human. What in the world would an earl be doing in such a legion?

The boy looked like a born rake. He would smash Rose's heart to pieces.

Éléonore sighed. In times like these, she wished for Cletus. Not that the old rogue would be any help. He'd grin and tell her to leave the kids alone so they could have their fun. Cletus always reasoned with his heart while she always reasoned with her brain. But still she missed him so badly.

For a while she sat, lost in thought and memories. When she finally shrugged them off, the tea in her cup had gone cold. She touched the teapot. Cold, too. Oh well.

She would have to learn more about this Declan. And if Rose wasn't there to answer the questions, she would just have to ask Georgie.

That reminded her. She better check on the boy.

Éléonore crossed into the sitting room. The daybed lay empty.

"Georgie?" she called.

He didn't answer.

"Georgie?" Éléonore strode through the house, from the kitchen to the bedroom, through it to the other bedroom, past the bathroom, to the storage room. There he was, staring out the window.

She came up to him and petted the pale blond hair. "What are you doing here, all by yourself?"

She glanced through the window and froze. On the edge of the ward, dark beasts prowled. Two, four, six, more, more . . . They bunched together, crawling on one another, piling into a narrow pyramid. Éléonore caught her breath.

The ward stones were strong and old, but the higher you reached, the weaker the magic barrier became.

The pyramid was now six beasts high. Eight. Nine. The top hound pressed against the ward and toppled into the yard. It fell inside the ward, flipping in the air to land on all fours, shook itself, and padded toward the house.

Georgie looked at her, his eyes huge and terrified. "They're coming."

JUST before the boundary, a narrow overgrown path veered right from the main road. A small red piece of a car door lay at the bend, and another rested a little down the path just in case Rose failed to get the message. She parked the truck and took her .22 out of her bag. She was so close to the boundary, that whoever left the trail of car parts could duck into the Broken when she got near. In the Broken her flash was useless, but her bullets would fly past the boundary just fine.

Rose locked the truck and headed down the trail. A few moments later the dense brush ended abruptly, and she found herself at the beginning of a pasture. A low hill rose in front of her, at the apex of which towered a massive oak. A few decades ago lightning had hit it, shearing one of the branches on the right side. The story went that some knucklehead ignored the rule about standing under the large isolated trees during a thunderstorm, and when the lightning cleaved off a branch, it fell and crushed his horse. Ever since, the giant of a tree became known as the Dead Horse Oak.

Today the tree seemed even more lopsided than usual. A large oblong thing hung from a thick branch on the right side, swaying slightly. Rose frowned. Now what?

The thing moaned.

She squinted and realized what it was: Emerson, wrapped in white plastic and hung upside down by the seat belts of his car.

He moaned again, weaker. Rose took the safety off her gun, took a deep breath, and advanced toward him, slowly, scanning the surroundings as she came. Her eyes strained to catch the quickest glimpse of danger. Her ears searched for the slightest sound. She heard nothing, only wind, crickets, and the distant small noises of the Wood.

Step. Another. Rose shivered. She was almost there.

Emerson's face was the color of a ripe plum. His eyes looked at her, unfocused, but failed to see.

"It's okay," she told him softly. "It's okay. I've got you."

Blood was probably rushing to his head. She had to get him down.

Emerson's lips moved. "Woo . . ."

"Yes?"

"Woo . . . Wolf."

"Wolf?"

"Wolf!" His voice gained a sudden intensity. "Wolf! Wolf! Wolf!"

Wolf? A wolf didn't wrap him in plastic and hang him off the tree. "Okay, okay," she murmured. "Calm down. I'll get you down."

She reached for the seat belts.

A black shaggy wolf emerged from behind the tree. Huge, as big as a calf, it stared at her with two large golden eyes, its glare cold and vicious, and smart. Too smart. This wasn't an ordinary wolf. This was a changeling.

Every hair on the back of her neck stood on its end. Rose became utterly still. There was no other changeling in East Laporte, except for her brother.

Below the eyes, the black muzzle gaped, revealing enormous ivory fangs.

Rose clutched Emerson, pulling him to herself, and flashed. The white arch of Ataman's defense swept around her, severing the seat belt rope. Emerson fell. Two hundred pounds of dead weight hit her, and she dropped him to the ground.

The wolf snarled. It was a horrible sound, fury and bloodthirst rolled into a savage promise.

"You can't have him," she said.

The wolf snapped. Its teeth rent the air a hair away from her flash.

Panic shot through her. The white arch split into three, each whip of white speeding so fast, they blended into a continuous white barrier around her and Emerson.

The wolf halted, puzzled.

They were trapped. She couldn't keep the three arches

moving indefinitely, but to attack him with her flash, she'd have to drop her defense. The gold eyes told her that if she gave him a fraction of a second, he'd tear her to pieces.

Rose slowed down the arches. They became distinct once again.

The wolf panted at her, as if it were laughing, amused by her wimpy efforts to keep it from its prey.

She slowed the arches enough that for a fraction of a second, as each arch passed her, she was unprotected. As the next arch slid to the right, Rose snapped her gun up and fired. The gun spat bullets and thunder.

The wolf dashed to the left, bounded off the oak trunk, and sprinted away, into the Wood. Rose swallowed. At her feet, Emerson whimpered like a child.

"It's gone," she told him in a trembling voice. "It's gone and gone."

She couldn't carry Emerson off the hill. She couldn't even drag him. Her fingers shook. She pulled her cell phone out of the pocket of her jeans. It took her three tries to dial the right number.

"Eric Kaplan, Kaplan Insurance. How may I help you?" the voice on the other end said.

"This is Rose. I'm at Dead Horse Oak. I have your uncle, and I need you to come and get him."

"HURRY, child." Mémère's voice urged Georgie up the ladder. He squirmed up the steps into the attic and scooted aside, offering her his hand. She climbed up, carrying one of Grandpa's guns. They pulled the ladder up and the trapdoor shut with a slap. Mémère slid the latch closed.

It wouldn't help. The beasts would find them. They both knew it.

"It will be fine," Mémère murmured. "It will be fine. We're going to cast a spell . . ."

"They eat magic, Mémère," George said softly. "They like it."

She stopped. "That's what Rose said."

Porcelain shattered downstairs. Icy alarm shot through Georgie. He jerked. Mémère's arms closed about him.

Another dish crashed. Something was moving through the kitchen.

"Be very silent, child," Mémère whispered in his ear. "Quiet like a mouse."

Silence reigned. A long minute passed.

Around them the attic lay dim, empty except for a few boxes. A fine layer of dust covered the floor. Barely any light penetrated through the wooden slits of the closed shutter that guarded a single tiny window.

Georgie felt the hounds' magic. It hovered on the edge of his senses, waiting quietly and patiently, waiting for them to use their power so it could pounce.

The eerie sound of claws scratching at the walls nearly made Georgie jump. He clung to Mémère. She bit her lip and hugged him closer.

He couldn't let the hounds get her. Not Mémère.

But if he opened his mind, their magic would get him. Terror squirmed through Georgie.

Claws skittered on the roof. Something bumped downstairs, directly under them. The beasts knew where they hid. Georgie shivered. His teeth chattered, his fingers and toes gone ice-cold.

A hard punch struck the boards to the left. The scratching grew louder. The beasts dug through the roof, trying to break in.

He couldn't let them get Mémère.

Georgie fought against his fear and forced it down. He leaned back in Mémère's arms. It was time to find lost things.

He quested outward, searching the vast darkness before him with his mind's eye. The hounds' magic pounced on him in a smothering wave, like a flood of slime armed with a thousand mouths. Georgie choked. Something inside him whimpered. The mouths bit into him with tiny sharp teeth, winding about his legs, spiraling up his body. His mind burned with pain. He quested harder, desperate to be heard before the foul magic drowned him completely. Somewhere impossibly far away, Mémère called his name. Her voice was full of tears.

He reached out to Rose, but she was too far away. He couldn't get to her. He had to find someone else.

He searched, his mind staggering under the pressure, until he finally saw it, a bright white star shining in the darkness. With the last of his strength, he touched it.

The beastly magic gaped below him, like the mouth of a horrible creature, and gulped him whole.

JACK sat atop the kitchen island and watched Declan search the fridge with a plate in hand. His stomach growled. They'd spent the whole morning in the Wood tracking down the beasts. Declan called them hounds. They couldn't be killed with a gun, he'd said. The bullets went right through them. The only way to kill them was to tear or cut them apart or to fry them with magic.

He'd tracked the scents for hours, but most of them led out of the Wood, not to it. Declan followed him everywhere. Declan was fun in the Wood, Jack decided. He was quiet and he didn't do stupid things. But now they were both tired and hungry. He thought Rose would be home with lunch, but she wasn't here. Instead he and Declan had to raid the fridge.

"It seems we have enough food for a feast. We can even make our own Edger burgers—" Declan dropped the plate. It crashed to the floor with a thud. Jack jumped at the sound.

"Stay here!" Declan barked, his face terrible. "Don't follow me, don't leave the house! Do you understand?"

Jack nodded.

"I'm going to get your brother. *Do not leave!*"

SIXTEEN

ÉLÉONORE cradled Georgie. He lay limp, his skin cold and clammy. His pulse fluttered like a dying butterfly under her fingertips. She tried to reach him again and again, but he had slipped somewhere deep, far beneath her power.

Below her the house shuddered and snapped, loud with breaking wood and heavy crashes, but none of that mattered. She focused on her hoarse whisper, pouring every iota of her power into the words. "Come on, sweetheart. Come back to me. Come back to your *grandmère*. You don't want to leave me, do you?"

She sensed only darkness.

"Come back to me, baby."

Her magic suffused her. A faint glow spread from her face to her fingertips. In the darkness of the attic and in the darkness that had swallowed Georgie, Éléonore became a beacon.

"Come back to me."

She was so intent on finding him, it took her several seconds to realize that all had gone quiet.

The trapdoor quaked. Someone or something had grasped the pull rope from below and jerked it. Éléonore began to chant soundlessly, gathering the magic around her. She couldn't flash, not like Rose, but she had the old magic. She wouldn't roll over and let them rip her to pieces without a fight.

The next tug tore the latch from the wood. The ladder dropped down.

The magic swirled around her like a death cloud. Malevolent streaks shot through her glow, twisting about her in furious ribbons. The spell would take her life in payment for its services, but she had no choice. Anything to buy Georgie a few more minutes.

The magic hovered at her fingertips, itching to be unleashed.

"It's Declan!" a male voice called. "I'm coming up!"

She saw the blond head rise through the opening. His face was covered in silver spatter.

The death magic vanished, replaced by a single urgent need—to save Georgie.

"Hurry," Declan called.

"He's fading!" She thrust Georgie at him. Declan grabbed the body and disappeared down below. She scrambled after him.

Declan rushed through the house. She followed him, stepping over beast carcasses and shattered furniture. Declan swept the kitchen table clean with a brush of his arm, sending dishes and jars to the floor, and deposited Georgie on the table. He briskly lifted Georgie's eyelid, exposing a tiny line of blue surrounding a black dilated pupil.

"I need a candle," he said.

Éléonore turned, sliding on gore splashed across the kitchen floor, grasped a candle and a box of matches. She lit the candle with shaking hands.

Declan dug into his clothes and pulled out a small pouch. He pulled a small piece of paper from the pouch, sprinkled herbs on it, rolled it like a cigarette, and set the end on fire. A tangy sweet scent spread through the room. She realized what he was trying to do and swept Georgie up, raising his head off the table. Declan held the burning incense under Georgie's nose.

The boy didn't move. Declan gulped a mouthful of smoke, pulled Georgie's mouth open, and blew into it.

No response.

He's gone, she realized. *It's a nightmare. It has to be a nightmare.*

Declan's face turned grim. He grabbed a handful of the boy's T-shirt and ripped it apart, revealing his bare chest. "Lay him flat."

She grasped his hand and saw his magic gather, blazing with white. "No! You'll kill him!"

"This is the only way."

He pushed her aside, thrust his hand against Georgie's

chest, and flashed. The spark of magic slashed through the small body.

Georgie's eyes snapped open, but they were pure white, his eyes rolled back in their sockets. He made a terrible creaky sound like an unoiled door, and Declan thrust the burning herbs under his nose. Georgie inhaled, coughed, inhaled again, blinked, and she saw his blue eyes looking at her.

"Mémère," he whispered and coughed out a tiny puff of smoke.

Éléonore clutched him to her. She smelled his hair, felt his heart beat, and finally understood that he was alive.

"We must move," Declan said briskly. "I can't protect you here. Can you carry the boy?"

He needed his hands for his sword. She swept Georgie off the table. "Hold on to me, darling."

Declan pulled a sword from his back and strode on. As Éléonore followed him, she realized his back was red with blood. Beasts bled only silver.

They crossed the kitchen to the front door. Declan kicked it open. A hound lunged at him from the right and was cut down in a flash of steel.

Declan crossed the porch and nodded to her. She followed.

To the left, near the bushes bordering the lawn, foul magic bloomed like a polluted flower, growing from several beast corpses. The silver blood from their carcasses pooled into a large puddle.

The silver surface shimmered and twisted up in a corkscrew fountain, turning dark and ghostly, flowing into the outline of a man. Éléonore couldn't see his face or any features, just a black shape, like a hole in the normal fabric of the world.

The shade spoke. "I just want the boy. Just a taste . . ."

Declan spun about. A grimace clamped his face. A torrent of white ripped from him, disintegrating the beasts, the puddle, and the shadow with it.

"Come," Declan urged her. "The wards at Rose's house are better. Hurry."

In the distance, Éléonore heard the rumble of a car engine. A moment later a truck shot out around the bend, Rose's face behind the windshield.

ROSE gently pulled Georgie's blanket up and glanced to Grandma. "Are you all right?"

Grandma nodded wordlessly. Rose stepped to her and hugged her. Éléonore was a plump, happy woman, but right then her shoulders seemed fragile beneath all those layers of tattered cloth. She raised her hand and patted Rose's arm gently. "I thought I lost Georgie."

"You didn't."

As long as Rose could remember herself, Grandma had served as the source of her strength. She was the one and only thing that remained constant. Mother, even before her death, had stopped really being there. Grandfather died. Relying on Dad was just asking for heartache. But Grandma was always present, always sure what to do, and if she couldn't help, she would at least make them laugh about it. No humor remained now. She sat on her chair, weak and gray. Even her teased-up hair drooped in defeat. Rose's chest tightened with ache.

"Would you like a cup of tea?" Rose asked.

"No." Grandmother looked at the two boys. Georgie slept. Jack curled next to him, not really sleeping but being quiet, watching Georgie through the narrow slits of his half-closed eyes.

"I just want to sit," Grandma murmured. "I just need a bit of time to understand that they're okay. You go on. See to Declan. His back is all ripped up."

Rose studied her for a long moment and quietly slipped out of the room. In the kitchen Declan sat on a chair by the table. He had shrugged his leather and undershirt off, and his back was to her. Two long, ugly gashes scored his skin. Blood caked in the deep, raw wounds. A cold needle of worry stabbed her. For all his strength, the beasts could've torn him apart in that house.

"I don't suppose you know how to sew the wounds shut?" he asked.

"You're in luck." She stepped into the bathroom and

brought out her first aid kit. "I can take you to the hospital, if you want. I have the money now, thanks to you."

He shook his head. "I trust you."

"Famous last words." She handed him a glass of water and two Aleve gelcaps. "They're anti-inflammatories. They will dull the pain a little bit and keep down swelling and redness. Swallow the pills, don't chew."

"Well, I thought I'd stick them into my nose and impersonate a walrus, but if you insist, I'll swallow them."

Rose blinked. Too much time with Jack and Georgie, not enough adult interaction. Next thing she knew, she'd be threatening to take away his comics if he didn't finish his dinner. "Jack always tries to chew his," she murmured. "Sorry."

"He told me he tried to eat cardboard."

"And candles. And soap." Rose popped open the kit, talking as she worked. "Once, when he was a baby, I was in the yard, hanging the sheets out to dry. He was in the grass next to me. I turned away for ten seconds, and he was gone. By the time I chased him down, his face was covered in purple berry juice. I made him vomit on the spot, and he fell asleep right in my arms. I thought he'd passed out from the poison, and my father had the truck, so I ran with him to Grandma's."

Rose took out a ziplock bag containing a white cloth, spread the cloth on the table, and retrieved three curved needles and twenty pieces of precut thread, each about a foot long. She threaded the three needles, poured water into a pot, put the needles, thread, and a pair of small tweezers into it, and set the whole thing to boil on the stove.

"How did it end?" Declan asked.

"Turned out to be pokeweed. The berries are poisonous, but he hadn't gotten enough of it in him to do any damage. I still remember every step of that run. Worst five minutes of my life."

"How old were you?"

"Sixteen. Come on. I need to wash off your wounds," she said.

He followed her into the bathroom, where she took the shower head out of the holder and rinsed the wounds on his back with lukewarm water. Afterward, they returned to the kitchen, where the light was better, to examine his gashes. "Only the top one needs to be stitched. The bottom one we can hold together with medical tape and butterfly bandages."

She turned off the pot, let the needles cool, washed her hands and arms to the elbows with soap, and opened the bottle of Betadine. "Are you allergic to seafood?"

"No. You can use iodine on me. I won't suffer any side effects."

"Oh, good." She doused the gauze with Betadine and proceeded to clean the gashes. His back remained rock steady. It was a huge back, too, covered with bulges of hard muscle and scars.

"You don't have to be that much of a hard-ass," she said.

"Would you find me more sympathetic if I cried?"

"No." She finished cleaning and bandaging the lower wound. "Last chance for a Broken surgeon."

"No need."

Rose carried the pot over and retrieved the first needle with tweezers. She held it for a minute or two, just to make sure it cooled off, then she brought the edges of the top wound together, clamped the needle, and pierced the edge of the gash. She pushed the needle through, pulled it free with tweezers, and made her first stitch. By now either of the boys would be crying. She would be crying. She'd had to sew up cuts on herself before. Eventually you did get numb to the pain, but the first few stitches hurt like hell. He just sat there. He really was a very scary bastard.

"You're quick," he said. His voice gained a deeper undertone. If she didn't know better, she'd say he was flirting. A man would have to be insane to flirt while she was jabbing sharp metal into his wounds.

"It's not my first time at the rodeo. Do they have rodeos in the Weird?" she asked, trying to distract herself from the fact that she was sticking a huge needle into his living flesh.

"Yes. They're a national sport in the Republic of Texas."

"Texas is a separate republic?" She finished the knot and started the next.

"The Weird and the Broken are mirror images of each other. Same continents, same oceans. In the Broken, the continent of North America is divided sideways."

"What do you mean, sideways?"

There was a tiny pause as the needle slid into his back, but his voice was calm and strain-free. "The countries are horizontal: Canada, United States, Mexico. In the Weird, the division is vertical. That's how the continent was settled. In the east is Adrianglia. In the center is the Dukedom of Louisiana, which is part of the United Kingdom of Gaul."

"Gaul?"

"It's a kingdom of the Old World. Gaulish tribes used to be fragmented into several kingdoms: Celtica, Belgica, Gallica."

France and Belgium, Rose guessed. "Almost done," she murmured. "So what is to the west of Louisiana?"

"Republic of Texas. Then the Democracy of California."

"What about Mexico?"

"It still belongs to Castillia. Spain."

They'd run out of continent, and she still had a few stitches to go.

"How did Adrianglia come to be called that?" She knew already, but she wanted to keep him talking.

"Because it was discovered by Adrian Robert Drake, who claimed it in the name of the Anglian Kingdom. Unlike Columbus of the Broken, he realized he had found a new continent rather than a roundabout way to India."

"For a blueblood, you know a lot about the Broken," she told him, finishing the last stitch.

"I serve the Duke of the Southern Provinces. The Edge touches his lands. I was taught about the Broken, because it's my duty to keep people from escaping into it. I can use a phone, fire a gun, and I know the theory of driving a vehicle, although I would rather not attempt it."

"All done," she said. "You can go into your room and cry now."

"Only if you come with me." He caught her hand into his. The feel of his skin almost made her shiver. "You have a very light touch. I barely felt it."

"Don't try to lie to a professional liar. I need my hand to bandage you."

He held on to her for another long second and opened his fingers. She pulled her hand from his, bandaged the wound, and came around to put away her needles. Declan didn't seem any worse for wear. Still as arresting as ever.

"Thank you," he said.

"No, thank you. For saving Georgie and my grandmother."

All of the pressure and stress came crashing down on her at once. Her resolve broke like a thin glass tube snapping. She fought to keep from crying. "How did you know they were in trouble?"

"The boy called me," he said. "He probably realized that would open him to the hounds' magic. I think he was afraid for your grandmother, so he sacrificed himself."

"Georgie's heart is too big for his own good," she said. She'd nearly lost him. No more. No more strange expeditions. She needed to stay home with the boys and weather this mess. "How many of the hounds were there?"

Declan shrugged his massive shoulders. "A few."

"How many?" she insisted.

"Fourteen. Unfortunately, the house is narrow, and I was unable to rely on my flash. I surmised Georgie and Madame Éléonore might be in the attic. Bringing the house down with magic would have been bad form. It's generally advisable to keep the people you attempt to rescue alive."

He said it matter-of-factly, as if that were the most ordinary thing in the world. He ran into a house full of monsters to save people to whom he didn't owe anything. "I wish there were some way I could repay you," she said, wiping her hands.

"There is."

She looked up. "What can I do for you?"

"You could kiss me, Rose."

She froze, the kitchen towel in her hands, sure she had misheard.

"Surely, I deserve one kiss for saving your brother."

"Why would you want me to kiss you?"

"I want to know what you taste like." A slow smile stretched his lips. "Don't tell me you haven't thought of it."

She had thought of it, but she would die before admitting it. "Can't say I have."

"One kiss," he said. "Or are you scared?"

That same delicious terror that she felt whenever she

thought about touching Declan made it completely impossible for her to move. "Not at all," she lied.

"Then kiss me."

Here was her chance. She could kiss him free of guilt without admitting anything. She wouldn't get another opportunity like that. If she lived to be a hundred and stayed the entire time in the Edge, at least she would be able to say that in her young and wild days, she'd kissed a crazy blueblood from the Weird. She was daring, right? Wasn't that what daring women did?

Rose closed the distance between them and rested her own palms on the table between his hands and his sides. If he brought his arms in, he could trap her. It should've made her more cautious, but it didn't. She was running along the edge of one of Declan's blades. One misstep, and she would fatally cut herself. And she liked it.

It's just a kiss. Stop making a huge deal out of it.

She leaned close to Declan. Their lips were a mere inch apart.

Declan's eyes were terribly green. Like a grass blade with the sun shining through it.

"I'm going to kiss you because you saved my brother," she murmured. "For no other reason."

"Duly noted," he said.

She leaned another quarter inch forward. Their lips almost touched.

"This is so very wrong," she murmured. Her whole body strummed with anticipation.

He leaned his head to her, his voice low. "It's only a kiss. It's not as if I'm asking you to do something . . . indecent."

He certainly looked as if he would like to do something indecent. She licked her lips and kissed him.

He opened his mouth and let her in. Her tongue found his. She stroked it gently and realized Declan held back, keeping himself under tight control. Suddenly she wanted to make him lose his mind, for no other reason than to prove to him that she could. She attacked his mouth. Her tongue darted in and out, her touch light and quick, teasing, never giving him a taste. Declan growled low in his throat, a purely animal sound that made her want to press against him.

She felt the precise moment when his patience finally snapped.

His arms caught her and pulled her to him. He kissed her back, thrusting his tongue into her mouth, drinking her in. Her head spun. He tasted like a drug. Heat blossomed in her chest and rolled down. Her body ached to be touched.

Another moment, and she would strip naked for him.

Rose pulled back. His arms held on to her, but she took a step back, and he released her. "Was that decent enough, Lord Camarine?"

He looked at her like he was about to pounce. "Quite."

"I thought I had to make the kiss memorable," she told him. "It's your reward, after all."

She was burning up. The air around her had turned viscous like glue. She had to gulp it to get any into her lungs.

Declan was having some issues coping with the sudden distance between them. His pants failed to mask a large bulge.

"I better go get some air," she said, turning away from him.

"Wait." She sensed him looming behind her. He leaned in, brushed her hair out of the way, and gently kissed the back of her neck.

A shiver ran down her spine.

He slid one arm across her shoulders and chest, above her breasts, pulling her to him. "Rose," he whispered into her ear, probably fully aware of what effect that small word had on her when he said it. His other hand caught her waist, trapping her. "Stay."

He kissed her neck again, and it took all of her will not to rub her back against him like a kitten eager for a stroke. *Oh, get ahold of yourself. Don't be melting for him—that's exactly what he wants.*

"Nice kiss," she heard herself say. "But no thanks."

She took his hands off her body. "You still have two challenges," she reminded him and escaped through the house onto the porch.

SEVENTEEN

OUTSIDE the sun shone bright, the early afternoon in full bloom. Rose breathed in deep, trying to calm herself. Part of her wanted to run back into the house; the other part laughed in cynical disbelief. Run and do what? Yell, "Here I am, take me, take me?"

She shrugged it off. She had to give it to Declan. The man could seduce. Not that he had to try terribly hard, considering the way he looked and what easy pickings she was. "You'll be completely safe, Rose, blah-blah-blah." Yeah, right. Safe. Eventually she would have to go back there and look him in the eye. She had no clue how she would manage that.

He was staying in her house, which meant some hard-and-fast rules were in order. No watching him while he waved his sword around in the morning. No thinking about him, unless it was about how she would win a challenge and kick his ass to the curb. No—

A man stood in the middle of the lawn, just beyond the ward line. He shimmered lightly, dark and translucent, as if made of many layers of dark panty hose. A hood hid his face, but she saw his hands. They were the mottled bruised color of the hounds' hide.

"It's taken you a while to notice me, my dear," he said. His voice was cultured and soft and he rolled his *r*'s slightly. Just like Declan. "I was right. You're delicious."

What in the hell is that?

She stepped down off the porch and approached the man slowly. He seemed to float out of a puddle of the gray goo that served as hounds' blood, and as she came near, she saw the bodies of two hounds rapidly dissolving into it.

The closer she got, the stronger the stench of the magic

became. A little more. Close enough so her flash wouldn't miss if she had to use it. "Who are you?" she asked.

"I'm Lord Casshorn Eratres Sandine." The figure dipped his head in a smooth bow. "A pleasure to make your acquaintance. Although really, politeness is unnecessary under the circumstances, but old habits die hard, you understand. You must forgive me this small indulgence."

Casshorn, the man who'd adopted Declan's changeling friend. A streak of alarm bit into her spine with icy fangs. That couldn't be a coincidence. She tried to show nothing and keep her voice calm. "The hounds that attack us, do they belong to you?"

"In the strictest sense of the word, they belong to no one. But I lead them and intend to continue directing their actions." He sounded so completely reasonable, as if he were her guest, discussing the latest gossip while drinking tea on her porch. "I am . . . a part of them. And they are now a part of me. It's a most curious symbiosis."

He raised his hand and showed it to her. The beginnings of black claws tipped his deformed, too-long fingers. His skin matched the color of the hounds, just a shade paler. "We are one," he said. A dark curtain of magic unwrapped and surged from him, streaming along the boundary of her ward and flaring up. Bright veins of purple and yellow twisted within it, like capillaries.

The magic flailed and pounded at the ward, trying to break through. She jerked back, but the stones held.

"Why are you killing us?"

"For your magic. Your deaths are incidental to the process. It is very simple, really. Your bodies contain magic. My hounds collect it and bring it back to me, permitting me to produce more hounds, et cetera, et cetera. I must confess, the process of draining the magic awakens baser instincts in me. A need to rend and tear into the flesh. To taste. It's an exquisite, almost painful ecstasy. And no matter how much I indulge, my hunger is never fully satisfied. I can continue on for quite some time without becoming satiated." He laughed softly, and she nearly retched.

"You realize that you're killing people? Whole families. Children."

"Of course," he chided gently and leaned forward to the ward, as if trying to tell her a secret. "To be thoroughly honest, I never cared for people. They are a bothersome lot, preoccupied with duty, expectations, and the minutiae of their lives." He rubbed his fingers as if trying to shake something from them. "I have done that, my dear. I've climbed the mountain of human ambition, and at the top I've found yet another mountain, alas with no lotuses of fulfillment in bloom."

"I think you might be insane," she said.

"Sanity is overrated compared to happiness, my dear. Taking possession of you, ripping sweet strips of flesh from your body and swallowing them whole, sucking on their juice, would make me infinitely happier than all the wisdom and ability to reason that the human race has to offer. And that brings me to the purpose of my visit. You've permitted Declan under your roof."

"And?"

"Declan has a problem. You see, he can't kill me if he doesn't find me. So he dangles you and your brothers in front of me like pieces of delectable candy. You're so . . ." He sighed. "Magical. Tempting. Make no mistake, my dear, I'll kill you. Declan knows it as well as I do. He's simply hoping to force me to kill you on his terms. If he were to go looking for me, he would have to face the wolf, and he doesn't wish it. They were friends once, he and the wolf."

Anger built inside her. "And why would you be telling me this?"

"Your lives are of no use to you." He pointed at the house behind her. "You squat in filth and poverty upon this pitiful chunk of land, like rats on some enormous garbage heap between two thriving civilizations. Why fight, when the conclusion is foregone? No help will come for you. Sooner or later, all of you will be mine."

"I don't think so."

Casshorn looked past her. "Tell her, Declan. Tell her I'm right."

"I see you've added insanity to the list of your shortcomings," Declan's icy voice said.

"Why must you be so unreasonable? I'll have you." Casshorn sighed. "I ate a man last night. Unfortunately, my hounds usually devour their targets, but this man was sent to me as a special gift. I ate him quickly, with much greed, and the rapture of feeling his magic flow into me is the only thing I now have. It is my sustenance, my goal, and my addiction, and I'll do anything to taste it again. There will be no escape. Why prolong the agony? I offer you a chance to become something useful. Nourish me. Become part of me and mine."

"I see." Rose put her hands on her hips. "Here is how it's going to go: I'll kill your hounds, then I'll find you and kill you, and then my brothers will use your head for a soccer ball. That way you'll be converted into something useful. Good-bye now."

She stepped over the ward line to get a clear shot. His greedy magic streamed to her. Her anger exploded in a wave of brilliant white, burning the puddle and the hound's body to nothing. Casshorn vanished.

Rose turned slowly and saw Declan standing on the porch.

"YOU lied to me!" Rose struggled to keep her fury under control. "You pretended to want to marry me, bullied me into these idiotic challenges, and all the while you were trying to kill Casshorn."

"I didn't lie. I just let you draw the wrong conclusions," he said grimly.

Her anger made everything crystal clear. "What's the name of your friend, Declan? The one who turns into a wolf, the one Casshorn adopted?"

"William," Declan said.

Oh, my dear God.

"The man you've met may not be the same William," Declan said.

"Of course it's the same William! I just came back from cutting my ex-boss from a tree, where a changeling wolf had put him! He wrapped him in plastic, hung him upside down, and left me a trail of car chunks so I could find him. William knows who Emerson is. He specifically asked me about him the last time we spoke. What is the matter with the two of you? Do you think this is some sort of a game? That thing was right, wasn't he? We're nothing more than bait to you."

Declan's eyes frosted over with white. "Rose, his mind was oozing out of his ears before he even started this mess. He's unraveling; surely you can see that! He was never a real soldier, or a real scientist, or a real noble, and now he isn't even a real human being. He's blundered into power, and it consumed him, and now he must be put down like a rabid dog. At his end, nobody will mourn, and he recognizes that. You can't believe anything he says."

She brushed his arguments aside. He had lied to her. She actually thought there might be something between them. Yes, she knew better, and yes, the whole challenges deal was a huge strike against him, but everything else about him felt so right. She was so mad, she couldn't even see straight. Mad at him for lying, mad at herself for buying the lie, and mad at the world because once again she was just the means to someone else's end. The anger sat in her chest and hurt.

"Where did you take Jack this morning?"

"I took him to the Wood."

"To what purpose? Don't lie to me, Declan, because I'll go and get my brother and he *will* tell me the truth."

"I instructed him to follow the hounds' trail."

"Are you out of your mind? He's a child!"

Declan's jaw took on a stubborn set. "He's also a changeling. He's smart, cunning, and fast. He was never in any significant danger. I was always within half a mile from him."

"So because he's a changeling, that makes him expendable?" she snapped. "Or is it because he's a mongrel?"

"You're not listening. Jack was in no danger."

"I'm sorry. I seem to have been mistaken. The hounds are just some fluffy, harmless bunnies. That's why an hour ago you bled all over my kitchen."

"That's a completely different situation. I was alone in cramped quarters without my ability to flash. Jack was in the tree canopy under strict orders to run to me the moment he sensed the hounds."

"And much good it would do him. They would be on him in the trees before you could get your sword out."

Declan growled. "You baby the children, Rose. Especially Jack."

She glared at him.

"He's a predator. He's eight years old, and George is ten. Neither is educated in basic self-defense or blade work. George doesn't know how to properly hold a knife. Jack told me he has never ridden a horse. How do you expect them to survive? They can't cling to your skirt forever."

Her voice caught in her throat, and for a second she couldn't speak. "You barge into our life, you practically force yourself on me, and now you question how I raise my brothers. Who the hell do you think you are? You try it, Declan. You try raising two boys when you're goddamn eighteen years old, your mother's dead, your father has taken off, you're working a below-minimum-wage job that makes you fall over from exhaustion every night, while half of your town is out hunting you so they can sell you to the highest bidder!"

"I didn't say you were doing a poor job, but you can't teach them everything."

"Before I throw you out, answer one question," she squeezed out through clenched teeth. "Why us? Why me? Why the whole marrying ruse?"

"The hounds are attracted to magic. I followed their trail to a house," he said. "And then a beautiful girl came out, leveled a crossbow at me, and declared she wouldn't sleep with me. I played along."

"You played along." Bitterness dripped from her words. "Do you have any idea how scared I was? How much I worried that you might drag me off, leaving the kids behind, or that you might kill them? Do you know how much anxiety your playing along has cost me? Get out."

He sat on the porch and smiled, showing her his teeth like a flash of a sword blade in the scabbard. "I don't think so."

"What?"

"We had an agreement. I haven't breached it, so the fault lies with you. Therefore, you must issue a refund, and you can't. You spent the money."

She opened her mouth and clamped it shut. "You'll get your money," she managed finally.

"Until then, I'll remain here. Like it or not, I'll protect you, and I'll use any excuse to do it. More, you're bound by our oath. We both swore to go through the three challenges, and I expect you to issue a second one."

"I'm through playing," she said.

"I'm not. The world doesn't revolve around your whims."

"Leave!" she demanded.

"Hell no. I would be a fool to walk away. You're one of a kind, Rose. I want you, and I'll fight to have you."

"Well, I don't want you."

"Be that as it may, you have to continue with the challenges. If you don't, there will be a magic flashback, and neither of us knows what form it will take. You and I could both die, and where would that leave your brothers?"

Once again she was backed into a corner. "I hate you," she said.

He offered her a pleasant smile. "I'll take that over indifference. Although I do find you much more attractive when you don't scream and throw a tantrum like a child."

"If I don't scream, I'll fry you."

He jumped off the porch and loomed before her. "Do it. You want to take it to the next step, then let's go. But you won't like it. I'm not one of your local boys. I know how to defend myself."

Magic shimmered around her. His power flared around him. She clenched her teeth.

The screen door banged, and Jack's voice recited, "Grandma said to tell you to please fight quieter. You'll wake Georgie."

Rose closed her eyes and forced herself to exhale slowly. She heard Declan releasing his breath and felt the pressure of his magic ease.

"You'll have your challenge as soon as Georgie wakes up," she said calmly when she could speak.

"I look forward to it, my Lady Camarine," he said.

She marched past him into the house and very carefully closed the door.

EIGHTEEN

GEORGIE woke up the next morning around ten. Rose had checked on him three times by then, and when she finally saw his blue eyes looking back at her, her knees went weak and she had to lean against the door frame.

"Well, there you are," she said. "How are you feeling?"

"Okay," he said.

She came closer, sat on his bed, and touched her lips to his forehead. He felt dry and warm. No trace of a fever. "Declan told me you called him."

"He was closer," Georgie murmured. "I couldn't find you. You were too far."

Guilt clutched at her. "I'm sorry."

"What happened?" he asked.

She told him.

"I tried to tell you about the wolf and Casshorn," he said. "But you had to hurry to work, and then I forgot."

"I'm sorry," she said again. "The next time you have something important to tell me, I'll listen, no matter what. I tell you what—I'll go and get us some tea and funnel cake, and you can tell me all about it."

"There is funnel cake?" Georgie's eyes lit up.

"I made some especially for you. You're the hero. Heroes always get funnel cake."

She came back, and he told her the whole story between bites of funnel cake and sips of raspberry tea. The more he talked, the clearer the picture became in her head.

"I see," she said finally. She saw quite well now. Declan following her into the Broken. His stubborn insistence on staying in her house. She was still angry at him. Very, very angry. But certain aspects of his behavior finally made sense.

She regretted her loss of temper. A lot had happened in the last few days: Declan's presence, the hounds, losing her job, the attack on Georgie. Any event by itself was enough to upset her, but together they turned her into an emotional pressure cooker. All of it had to come out somehow. She just wished it hadn't come out quite the way it did, in front of Declan, who no doubt thought she was throwing a tantrum. It's hard to convince someone to listen to you and leave your house when you're raving too loud to be taken seriously.

"So what happens now?" Georgie asked.

"Now I need your help for my second challenge to Declan." She hesitated. "Do you think you're strong enough to walk?"

Georgie nodded.

"I'm sorry to ask this of you, but I need you to come to the porch."

"I need the bathroom first," he said.

"Do you need help getting there?"

Georgie gave her a long look. She sighed and left him to it. When she finally got married, if she ever got married, she hoped her first child would be a cute little girl. A cute, sweet, harmless little girl.

ÉLÉONORE stepped into the kitchen, mentally steeling herself. She had only a few minutes before Rose would return from Georgie's room.

Declan rose at her approach with a polite shallow bow and a narrow smile. *"Bonjour, Madame."*

"Bonjour, Monsieur." She sat into a chair and continued in French. "I would like to speak about my granddaughter."

His face turned cold. The smile remained, but it gained that polite, icy tint the bluebloods adopted when they wanted to strangle the conversation with courtesy.

"I want there to be no misunderstandings," she continued. "This isn't an attempt on my part to broker some sort of tryst between the two of you. On the contrary."

His eyebrows crept up a fraction of an inch. He really was a blindingly handsome boy. "Do you find me unworthy of your granddaughter, *Madame*?"

Inwardly Éléonore groaned. She was out of practice. "I have no doubt as to your pedigree. I merely wish you to understand the situation clearly. If you're willing to listen, of course."

"I'm all ears, *Madame*," he assured her.

Éléonore took a deep breath. "My husband abandoned me a number of times during our marriage. I say this not to gain some sympathy for myself. It's simply a fact. He loved me passionately, but he loved the sea more. Because I suffered without him, I did my best to raise my son with a sense of responsibility for his family. Unfortunately, I failed miserably. Just like his father, John abandoned his wife and children frequently. Growing up, Rose had learned that 'father' is a temporary presence in one's life."

She fell silent. Finding the words proved harder than she realized. "*Pardon.* This is difficult for me. Rose's mother was traumatized by the untimely death of her parents, and in her final years she sought to stave off her mortality by any means necessary, usually by finding solace in the arms of any man who would have her. Eventually even that remedy failed and she died. Rose was an adolescent and the boys were mere babies. Thus, my grandchildren were abandoned both by their mother and by their father."

She glanced at Declan, but his face was earnestly polite and about as transparent as a cement block.

"Then Rose flashed white. You must understand, my lord, it's been over a century since an Edger flashed white. She was just a child, barely eighteen, and not at all equipped to either anticipate or deal with the consequences. Due to her mother's loose behavior, it was assumed that Rose was the child of an out-of-wedlock liaison. Overnight she became a valuable commodity. First, her flash made her desirable as a powerful addition to any family; second, her magic hinted at the possibility of blueblood ancestry; and third . . . my granddaughter is lovely, as I'm sure you haven't failed to notice."

"Indeed, *Madame*."

His tone was perfectly neutral and pleasant. If he *Madame*'d her one more time, she would have to throw something at him.

"Rose had a terrible life," Éléonore said bluntly. "For almost a year, she was literally hunted. The Edger families wanted her for her power, the borderland blueblood families wanted her for breeding, and those who didn't want her, hated her. Envy can be a terrible thing. Her mother's exploits already made her a pariah, and her flash only exacerbated the problem. What few friends she had abandoned her. Her boyfriend—who is a terrible creature—betrayed her. We had weathered a siege and arson and being shunned. The slaver was by far the worst. He had arrived under the pretense of courting Rose, promised her the security and acceptance she so desperately wanted, and nearly won, if not her heart, then at least her mind. Fortunately his identity was discovered, but the damage was done. She has learned the lesson again and again: people, men in particular, cannot be trusted. I watched this damage happen, and I was powerless to stop it. Finally after a year of this chaos, things have calmed. My son was there for her during that year. Even he understood that his family couldn't survive this storm without him. That is the longest he had ever spent with his family. However, as soon as pressure lessened, he escaped. He ran away from his own children in the middle of the night, once again abandoning the boys to Rose's care."

She took a deep breath. "It was the final betrayal, my lord. It wounded Rose very badly, and she's determined to spare her brothers this hurt at all costs. She put her life on hold, so her brothers would never know what it's like to be abandoned. A young girl is a creature of dreams, my lord. A woman with one foot in the world of fantasy, searching for the face of true love in every handsome boy she sees. Rose has no fantasies. One would expect a woman who has gone through her trials to be bitter and angry, but she isn't. She's kind, sweet, selfless, and generous, and I thank my lucky stars for this every day."

Éléonore rose, buoyed by her anger. He got up as well.

"I'm sure that you're successful in your pursuits of female attention," she said. "I'm sure that there is a trail of broken hearts in your wake, and you probably look at it fondly, remembering your past conquests. For some young women, being swept off her feet by a man such as you might be thrilling. It might even be a good lesson in the nature of the male species. However, Rose has no illusions to soothe her and no parents to reassure her. If you break her heart, it will shatter my granddaughter. It will destroy her utterly, turning her into a bitter wreck. So I implore you, my lord, to leave her in peace. You don't need her as your trophy. And if you won't, I swear to you that I'll curse you with my dying breath. We both know the power such a curse carries."

Declan bowed. "I'll take it under advisement."

She growled under her breath and stomped into the depths of the house, not sure if she had accomplished more harm than good.

ROSE stuck her head into the kitchen. Declan sat at the table, his eyes lost in thought. A smile curved his lips.

"Come outside," she said. "We need to be in the yard for the next challenge."

He followed her to the porch, where she sat in a chair and he leaned against the rail. She stared at the trees shrouded in morning fog.

Declan cleared his throat. They had managed to keep from saying a single word to each other during breakfast, but now he looked as if he had something to say.

"I lost my temper yesterday," he said. "My sincerest apologies. It won't happen in the future."

"I'm also sorry. I shouldn't have been quite so . . . dramatic."

They looked at each other.

"My behavior aside," he continued, "I meant everything I said."

She stuck her chin in the air. "So did I."

"Very well."

"Indeed."

He sat back down, and she picked a spot as far from him as the porch steps would allow.

"Also," he said after a small pause, "your funeral cake was delicious."

"Funnel. Funnel cake. I'll get you the recipe. It's similar to pancakes."

"Thank you."

They sat in silence. She broke it first. "Don't you think it's dangerous to do this challenge, with Casshorn waiting for the right opportunity?"

"We've destroyed a large number of his hounds," Declan said. "Since I'm his primary target, he'll need to build up his forces before he attacks again. We're safe for two days, maybe three."

Probably longer than that, Rose thought with a small sense of satisfaction. Yesterday, after the fight with Declan, she'd spent nearly all of the minutes remaining on her cell phone. Her words didn't carry much weight in the Edge, but Grandma's did, and now they knew the name of their menace and what he wanted. It would be difficult for Casshorn to find prey in East Laporte come nightfall.

"So he's vulnerable now," she said. "Why don't we go after him?"

Icy green eyes fixed her. "*I* would go after him. But I have no idea where he is, and your brother was unable to find the scent trail during our last excursion."

"Of course. Blame the child for your failure."

"I blame no one. How would you feel about a side bet on this challenge?"

"No more deals, Lord Camarine. You can't be trusted."

He seemed unfazed by her snippy remark. "If I win this challenge, I'll remain in your house and your family will assist me in my efforts to dispatch Casshorn. If I lose, I'll sign writs of citizenship for the three of you. The writs would make you legal citizens of the Weird. You could seek em ployment there. The children could attend school."

She clamped her mouth shut, biting a caustic reply. Her mind spun through the possibilities. "That will just put us in a place where you have the most power."

"On the contrary. First, I have sworn to leave you alone if I fail. Second, the laws of the Weird will protect you, given that you'll be a citizen, and you can have me arrested on stalking charges if I show up on your doorstep. Think about it, Rose. You've lost your job, and you aren't likely to find another. And no matter how much you force the boys to pretend that they have no magic, they do. They can't live in the Broken; they would slowly suffocate without magic. Look behind you." He raised his arms, encompassing the house. "This is what you've settled for. Do you actually want to make something of yourself?"

He pushed all the right buttons. "What guarantee do I have that this writ isn't a worthless piece of paper?"

"I'll affix the Camarine seal to it. As an earl, I have the authority to do so."

"You're not a real earl. The Earl of Camarine is a courtesy title."

He stared at her. "And where did you come by that little tidbit?"

"I read it in a book," she said, trying to freeze him with her voice. "Even us ignorant types do read occasionally."

"Apparently not very well," he said. "A courtesy title is awarded for meritorious service and a couple of other things. A peer titled by courtesy has the same executive peer powers as a full peer. Check your book."

"Don't move."

She stomped into the house and almost ran over her grandmother.

"Is everything all right?" Grandma asked.

"Everything is perfect." Rose climbed to the attic, grabbed the enormous *Encyclopedia*, and wrestled it down. If he was lying, she would rub his nose in it.

She dragged the dusty tome onto the porch and dropped it on the boards.

For the first time this morning, Declan displayed some emotion besides stony determination. "Good God, where did you find that antique?"

"None of your business." She had traded a Rand McNally Atlas, two jars of saffron, and a three-liter bottle of Pepsi for it. Rose flipped the pages to the index and found "Writ of Citizenship, Adrianglia, 1745."

"It looks over two centuries old," Declan said.

Rose turned to page 1745 and read out loud. "'Writ of Citizenship—a document legally conferring all rights and obligations of Adrianglian citizenship. A Writ of Citizenship may be issued by the following authorities: the Office of Census, secured by the Seal of the Minister of Population; the Office of Domestic Affairs, secured by the Seal of the

Minister of the Realm; or a Peer of the Realm, secured by that Peer's House Crest. Only peers of rank Earl or above have the right to issue a Writ of Citizenship. The following is the list of peers possessing such authority as known to the publisher on the date of publication of this volume.'" She scanned the list and ran into "Earl Camarine."

"Satisfied?" Declan asked dryly.

If she passed on this chance, she would be forever kicking herself. Was there a downside to this?

"Do we have a deal?" he asked.

"We have a deal." It nearly killed her to say it. Rose forced herself to smile. "You'll never win this one."

Georgie chose that moment to step out onto the porch. He saw Declan, walked over, and simply hugged him without saying a word. Declan's eyes went wide. Slowly he put his arms around the boy.

It was an odd moment, a thin, fragile, blond child in the arms of a much larger, stronger blond man. A vision of the future that could have been Georgie's if his magic didn't betray him.

Rose sighed and headed to the shed. "Georgie, tell the blueblood about Grandpa Cletus."

Declan let go, and Georgie sat on the porch next to him.

"He's very tall," Georgie said. "He was good with swords. He had several."

"Like mine?" Declan asked.

"No. His were long and thin. Mémère still has them."

"Rapiers," Declan guessed.

Georgie nodded. "He used to laugh a lot and tell us stories. He was a pirate."

"A privateer," Rose corrected, nudging the last ward stone out of the way. "Georgie, are you up to holding Grandpa?"

Georgie nodded.

Rose grasped the heavy dead bolt with both hands and jerked it aside. The door flew open, and Grandpa Cletus charged out, dragging the chain behind him.

Declan leapt to his feet and over to Georgie, a knife in his hand.

Grandpa reached the end of the chain. The collar jerked him back, and Grandpa flew off his feet. Instantly he rolled over and snarled like an animal, clawing at the empty air with his long fingers. His tangled beard trembled as he strained on the chain and bit the air with yellowed fangs.

Rose sighed.

Grandpa's pointed ears twitched. He spun and lunged at her. She stood her ground. A foot away from her, he ran headfirst into an invisible wall and crumpled to the ground.

"No," Georgie said.

"But I want my pint money," Grandpa moaned.

"No," Georgie repeated sadly. "You better sit down."

Grandpa sat cross-legged, rocking back and forth.

Declan jumped off the porch and approached them, peering at Grandpa. "Were his ears always pointed?"

"It happened after," Rose said. "The beard and hair also. He was clean shaven when he died. And the claws. Those also grew after death."

"What's your name?" Declan asked.

"Please answer Declan," Georgie said.

"Caedmon Cletus Drayton," Grandpa said sadly. "Caedmon from the British *caed*, meaning 'battle.' Cletus from the Greek *kleitos*, meaning 'illustrious.'"

"He retains his memories?" Declan asked, his voice neutral.

"Bits and pieces." Rose reached out and patted the matted mane of Grandfather's hair. "Mostly he wants to go down to the pub. Sometimes it's the tavern and he has to meet his friend Connor before their corvette, *Esmeralda*, sails from the harbor. He remembers who we are and he remembers . . . the woman you saved with Georgie. He'll cry if he sees her or if I mention her name."

She felt close to tears herself and swallowed a clump that blocked her throat. "Georgie doesn't like to let things die."

Declan's green eyes studied her. "There are others?"

"No humans. Birds. Kittens. Little creatures he felt sorry for."

Declan's face darkened. "How many?"

"We don't know. He hides them."

Georgie looked away to the grass.

"My brother has a very good heart," Rose said. "But he can't let go of the things he brings to life. We tried explanations, rewards, and punishment. He knows that he's dying, because keeping all those creatures alive is sucking the life out of him. But he doesn't know how to let go. You wanted a challenge. Here it is. Save my brother from himself."

DECLAN sat next to Georgie while Rose herded Grandpa back into his shed. She heard Declan's quiet voice. "You didn't want your grandfather to die?"

"No."

"All things die, George. That's the natural order of the world."

Good luck with that, Rose thought. They'd had this talk a dozen times. It led nowhere.

"Who decided?" Georgie said softly.

"Nature. It's a way for humankind to survive."

Georgie shook his head. "It doesn't have to be like that. I don't want it to be like that."

He got up and went inside.

Declan sat, frowning, his arms resting on his knees. When she passed him on her way inside the house, he said, "I'll need some supplies. Would it tax you too much to obtain them for me?"

She stopped. He actually had some sort of a plan. "What do you need?"

"Blue candles. A metal bowl or a large pot. Certain herbs. A basin, the larger the better. Some other things."

That seemed pretty specific. "How sure are you that the hounds won't attack?"

"Very sure."

"In that case, put on the clothes Amy gave you. I'll take you to Wal-Mart."

Ten minutes later, they were both in the truck. Her cab wasn't that small, but Declan made it seem cramped and tiny. She started the engine. "Have you ever been in a car before?"

"No."

Rose nodded at the guns. "Can you use a gun?"

He picked up a rifle, locked, and loaded.

"Good. Keep the rifle out of sight and please buckle your seat belt."

They drove in silence for a couple of minutes. "Why the sudden benevolence?" Declan asked.

She avoided looking at him. "How long do you think George has?"

"It's hard to say. I don't know what his capabilities are and how much drain he's under or for how long. But judging by his physical weakness, I would say he has less than six months. He's featherlight. He can't do more than two push-ups and he tires very quickly. I thought he was anemic."

"There's your answer," Rose said. "I hate to say it, but if you truly think you can convince my brother to stop his slow suicide, I'll help you, even if it costs me a challenge."

She drove on. "When did you have a chance to see him do push-ups?"

"Two days ago while you were cooking dinner. I gave each of them a knife and put them through some basics. Jack is a born killer. George had to sit down after a couple of minutes."

"It won't help you," Rose said.

He raised his eyebrows.

"Making friends with the children won't help you," she clarified. "We won't leave with you."

"I made friends with the children because I wanted to do so. Not everything I do is calculated. Although I understand why you would think that."

"Oh?"

"I spoke to Madam Éléonore at some length this morning, while you were with George."

Oh, really? He really did get around, but if he thought her grandma would join the Declan-worshipping parade, he had another think coming. "What did she tell you?"

"Many things. Your grandmother is very conflicted. She's unsure if she should encourage or discourage me, so she has done a bit of both."

She glanced at him. Their stares connected, and she didn't like what she saw in his eyes: they were resolute and determined. Disturbed, she turned away to watch the road.

"It's difficult for you to trust anyone," he said. "I contributed to this by my deception. For this, I'm sorry. But it was necessary."

"You keep saying that, but you don't tell me why."

He said nothing.

"That's very illuminating," she said. "You knew the creatures were a threat to the whole Edge. I know we're nothing to you, but couldn't you have at least tried to warn us out of common decency?"

"I did," he said. "You have no law enforcement and no central authority, so as soon as I crossed into the Edge, I went to your church. Your priest seemed like a reasonable man. I told him that the Edge needed to be evacuated. He nodded, pulled out a gun, and unloaded twenty-two shots into me. When he realized the bullets weren't hurting me, he threw his sidearm at me and called me an agent of Lucifer."

Rose winced. "That's because George Farrel, the local preacher, is borderline insane. He preaches hellfire and damnation every Sunday and checks the church for the rogue angels that fought against God with Satan. He's convinced they're out to get him. He probably thought you were an evil angel."

"I see," Declan said dryly.

"Nobody goes to his church except for some old ladies," she said. Not that it helped the situation any.

"Next I went to the largest house I could find. My logic was that anyone who owned a house of that size would have some roots within the community."

Rose's heart sank. There was only one large house next to the church. "Which house? The Ronn house, with the blue roof?"

"Yes."

She almost cringed. "The dogs."

He nodded. "Yes. The owners set a pack of dogs on me. I suppose they were also expecting agents of Satan?"

"No, they have a meth lab in the house. They're producing illegal narcotics. They're high all the time, and they're paranoid the cops from the Broken will somehow get into the Edge and raid the place. Did you try anyone else?"

"As I crossed the road to the next house, a woman tried to run me over with her truck."

"You were in the middle of the road!"

Declan's face was still impassive. "At the next two houses, I was ignored. They saw me and hid inside. I decided not to waste any more time and began tracking the hounds. It took me a day and a half to untangle the different tracks. One of them led me to an isolated house. A woman emerged—the same one who had tried to run me over—and declared that she would not marry me and I better leave or the two kids at the windows would shoot me."

Rose struggled for words. He had really tried. He'd tried more than many other people would have in his place. "You must've thought the lot of us was insane."

"The thought did cross my mind. I went along with you because I needed a foothold in the Edge at any cost. I knew that the hounds were drawn to your family because their magic lingered in the area, and contrary to your assertions of yesterday, I don't want anyone to be hurt. You gave me a very good idea of what you expected a blueblood to be. If I went along with your expectations, I thought I could reasonably predict your reactions. And I wanted to know why you wouldn't marry me. I found you intriguing."

Aha. Intriguing. She would buy that for a dollar. Next thing she knew, he'd try to sell her some intriguing oceanside property in Nebraska.

"Declan, I spoke to Georgie, and he told me what Casshorn said. I thought about it, and I realized that Casshorn was right: I *am* bait. Except it's not you who is doing the baiting, it's him. He's using the threat to me as a means of keeping you put. You can't go out looking for him, because you're worried he'll attack me or the boys. That's why you followed me into the Broken, that's why you insisted on staying at my house, that's why you timed your expedition with Jack for the morning when I was going to spend most of the time in the Broken food shopping. You're trying to do it even now. You've dangled those writs in front of me to make sure that we can escape into the Weird if you fail the challenge and can't defend us."

One glance at his face told her she was right. She parked.

"Why are we stopping?" he asked.

"We're at the boundary. You might not survive it if we cross it in a vehicle—it's too fast." She unbuckled her seat belt. "Look, I understand why Casshorn would view me as bait. He thinks I'm trash and a whore and that I'll just sit on my hands, content to let you guard me until he decides he's done playing. What I don't get is, what exactly makes you think that I will stand for it?"

Declan unbuckled his seat belt and leaned over, too close, blocking out the world.

"What are you—"

His lips touched hers, warm and inviting. She was still furious at him, but somehow her anger didn't stop her from opening her mouth and letting him in. No, it drove her to him, and she kissed him back, caught between the urge to slap him and the thrill of tasting him. His arms closed about her and he pulled her to him. She wasn't sure if she was trapped or shielded or both, but it made her feel happy and she kissed him.

The sound of a car horn blared at them. They broke apart. A red truck roared past them, its windows down. Rob Simoen screamed some obscenity at them and sped past the boundary into the Broken.

Declan growled. "I'll have to kill him one day."

Rose pushed on his chest with her hand. "If you let go of me now, I'm going to chalk your mauling of me up to temporary insanity."

He kissed her again, lightly brushing her lips.

"Declan!"

His grass green eyes laughed at her. "I wanted you to be sure that I wasn't temporarily insane."

"You can stop pretending now, remember?" she said. "I know you didn't come here for me. You came here because of Casshorn, so no need to keep up the seducing charade. I find it bothersome."

"This is probably the point where I should be suave," he said. "I used to be able to do it, but somehow my skills leave me when I'm with you."

"Oh, please." She rolled her eyes.

"I should be more polite about this, but I don't think you'll understand me unless I speak directly," he said.

She'd heard those words before. It took her a second, but she remembered where—she had said them to him outside of the Burger King.

"You're a prickly, stubborn, spirited woman."

"Don't forget crude, rude, and vulgar."

"Only when it suits you. You're sly when occasion calls for it, direct to the point of forgetting tact even exists, sarcastic, fierce, I did mention stubborn, didn't I?"

"Yes," she said dryly.

"You're also smart, kind, gentle, beautiful, and always cling to your personal integrity, even when it's in your best interests to abandon it."

A little warm feeling spread through her chest, and even her natural suspicion that he was lying couldn't quite extinguish it. Where was he going with this?

"You're also quite funny," he said.

"Oh, I amuse you?"

He gave her one of his devastating, slightly wicked smiles. "You have no idea."

Arrogant ass. "And all of that means what?"

"Just that I mean to have you."

She frowned at him.

"I mean to have you, Rose, you and all of your thorns. I'm a disagreeable and stubborn bastard, but I'm not a fool. You didn't really expect me to pass you up, did you?"

Heat flooded her face, and she knew she flushed. Declan laughed.

"Well, you can't have me," she parried. "You lied to me. I don't trust you, I'm not leaving with you, and I'm not sleeping with you either. Now let go of me and get out of the truck, so we can get through the boundary and get this trip over with."

They faced the boundary together. It would be difficult for him. Most people from the Weird had difficulty adjusting to the Edge, let alone the Broken. But he had done it once before and showed up in the Burger King to open a glorious can of whoop-ass for Brad. Still, she had to be very careful.

"What happened when you tried to cross the last time?" she asked. "It's important."

"Pain," he said. "I went into convulsions. I think I might have stopped breathing, but my recollection is murky."

This would take some work. Rose gripped his fingers tighter. "We'll do this easy and slow. Just follow me, and if you feel like you might be blacking out, tell me."

She anchored her magic through her palm to his and took a tiny step forward. He followed her. A small portion of magic drained from him, and she replaced some of it with her own. It felt like hooking a vein in your arm with tweezers and pulling it out slowly.

Another step. Again she cushioned the magic drain.

Declan was perspiring.

One more step. Rose felt her body quake. The shock traveled down her arm, and he glanced at her. She gave him a bright, reassuring smile.

Slowly, little by little, they passed across the boundary, and when the last spark of magic died within Declan, she gave him all she had. Another breath and they were through.

Declan stumbled and shook his head. "That was considerably easier. Rose?"

She sank onto the grass, struggling against sharp pain in her stomach. "Give me a minute."

He knelt by her. "Are you all right?"

She cradled a spiky knot in her stomach. "Fine. Just aftershock. Taking someone across the boundary takes a bit of effort, that's all."

He picked her up.

"There's no need to hold me," she told him. "It's just harmless pain. It's passing already."

He ignored her. "What would've happened if you'd let go?"

"You would've died," she said. "My magic would've torn out of your body, and the shock would've killed you."

"You missed your chance to do away with me."

"Drat," she said. "I guess there's always next time."

A moment later she made him put her down, crossed the boundary, and got her truck.

Despite it being Sunday morning, when a good number of the Broken's citizens flocked to churches, the Wal-Mart parking lot was crowded.

She swiped a cart. They walked in side by side, and Declan stopped. His eyes surveyed the crowd, taking in the electric lights, the bright colors of the packages, rows of gleaming primary color picnic glassware on his right . . . He reached for her and firmly took her arm.

"What?"

"Too many people," he said quietly. "Too loud."

His face closed in, and she was sure that if they had been in the Edge, his eyes would now glow pure white. He resembled a soldier in enemy territory, expecting a sniper's shot from behind every aisle and a land mine under every floor tile. His magic remained in the Edge; his swords and rifles and even her gun stayed in the car. It was a lot to take in.

She slowly pushed the cart to the side, to a display of fresh flowers. "Let's stop here for a little while."

They stood together, watching the crowd. After a few minutes the tension in Declan's shoulders eased.

"Better?" she asked him.

"Yes."

"Let's try walking," she said. "We'll take it easy."

They moved down one of the wider aisles. A couple of young girls coming the opposite way gawked at Declan, giggled, and scooted out of the way. Rose glanced at him. He had forgotten his ball cap in the truck, and his hair fell down over his shoulders, clasped together by a piece of leather cord. His broad shoulders strained his green sweatshirt. He'd pulled the sleeves up to his elbows to reveal forearms corded with muscle. The jeans molded to his long legs. The Broken stripped him of the dangerous power-sharpened edge and haughty perfection. Here he was just a man, a bit rougher about the edges and a lot sexier than most, but knitted from the same fabric as all the other people instead of being carved from a glacier. And the air of menace that lingered about him made him devastating to all things female.

An older woman at the jewelry counter nearly dislocated her neck, trying to get his attention. A housewife fussing over a little girl in a cart looked up as they maneuvered around her and simply stared, openmouthed. A woman at the clothes rack raised an eyebrow, tugged her low-cut white blouse lower, and followed them with a determined look on her face.

Just what they needed, more attention. Rose took a sharp turn into the aisle running between the shoe section and sporting goods and glanced behind her. Six women, some discreetly, some openly, followed them. It irritated her to no end.

"I should've made you wear a hockey mask," she murmured.

Declan glanced back and unleashed a dazzling smile. One

of the younger girls squeaked like an unoiled door. Some-body mumbled, "Oh, Lord."

"Stop that!" Rose snapped.

"Stop what?" He turned to her, and she found herself on the receiving end of that same smile. She could've stared at him for a year and never gotten tired. "That," she said firmly. "Quit it."

"Is it upsetting you?"

The adoring crowd seemed to have grown. "You're going to cause a riot."

"You think so? I've never created a riot before. I did cause a brawl at the last formal. A large number of young women there actually arrived with the expectation of seducing me into matrimony, and a couple of their mothers came to blows. It was hilari— I mean, dreadful. Simply dreadful."

"Yes." Rose sighed in mock pity. "It's awful to be rich and mind-bogglingly handsome and have women fawn over you. My heart bleeds for you. Poor dear, how do you manage?"

"So you do think I'm handsome."

She actually stopped for a second. "Declan, I'm not blind."

He looked disgustingly smug.

"Oh, get over yourself."

"Not just handsome but mind-bogglingly handsome," he said.

He'd never let her live it down. She spun about and fixed their audience with a look of withering scorn. "Ladies, have some decency."

The crowd scattered.

"And now you're feeling possessive."

"I think I liked you better as an icy blueblood." She shook her head and dropped another set of blue candles into the shopping cart.

NINETEEN

ROSE surveyed Declan's preparations from the porch.

A Sand-n-Sun inflatable pool, twelve feet across and about three feet high, sat in the middle of the lawn. The water shone under the afternoon sun. To the left, Jack sat in a pine tree, staring at the water with a wistful look on his face. Georgie stayed inside. He would never refuse to come out—he was too polite for that—so he quietly hid in the attic, probably hoping they would forget about him.

The screen door swung open, and Grandmother came to join her. Éléonore looked better. Her hair was teased back up, and she had gained a bit of spring in her step. She stared at the lawn.

"What is that boy doing?"

"According to him, he's implementing his plan to have me. With all my thorns."

Grandma blinked. "He said that?"

"He did." And she was a stupid fool, because every time she thought about it, her heart beat faster.

"He's trying hard, no?"

Rose nodded.

Declan had bought a measuring tape and very carefully measured the distance from the pool, marking the points with white paint. Next he cut several sticks about two feet tall, sharpened both ends, and hammered the sticks into the marked points. He impaled the candles onto the sticks and then strung white clothesline between them. From the height of the porch, the clothesline formed a complex geometrical figure, a seven-pointed star enclosed in a circle, with the pool in the exact center.

"Well, it's a sigil," Grandmother said.

Rose had tried to study sigils before. Mystical signs, sigils were most often used in summoning and alchemy. Some of them signified true names of magical beings, and some channeled magic into patterns. It was boring as all get-out, but she'd forced herself to learn the basics.

"Looks like he used a single piece of string," Grandmother murmured.

Rose found the knot and tried to follow the clothesline with her gaze. The stretches of string crossed, under, over, under again, and came back to the same first post. "Yes," she said.

"Definitely a sigil," Grandmother said.

"Grandma?"

"Mmm?"

"Did the boys tell you about Casshorn?"

Éléonore's eyes darkened, taking on a strange, predatory aspect. "Yes. Yes, they did."

"He's in the Wood," Rose said.

Magic swirled around Éléonore, dark and frightening, like black wings. "Of course," she said evenly, her face terrible. "Where else would he be? Thinks he can hide in our backyard, does he? We'll find him. And once we do, I'll bring the power of all of East Laporte onto his head for daring to touch my grandchildren. I'll see him weep bloody tears before this is over."

Rose shivered.

Declan emerged from the driveway, carrying the grill from the truck. He set it at the starting point of the star, dumped some charcoal into it, and brought over the large metal bowl filled with powdered herbs.

There were so many things they didn't know yet. And Declan was their key to finding them out.

"He has half of my supply room in that bowl," Grandmother said. Rose snuck a peek at her—the dark magic was gone, as if it had never been.

In the yard, Declan drenched the charcoal in lighter fluid and lit it. The flames surged up, licking the briquettes.

"Do you think he can help Georgie?" Rose asked.

"We've tried everything else. He can't hurt, I suppose." Grandma sighed. "But if you don't want to leave with him, you should stop helping him."

"I'm doing it for Georgie."

"I know, child. I know." Éléonore petted her shoulder and went inside.

Rose hopped off the porch and approached Declan. He spread the coals with an oversized fork and glanced at her through the cloud of sparks.

"Are you planning to summon a demon?" she asked.

He grimaced. "No."

"Just checking."

He threw a handful of herbs into the fire.

"But you are summoning something?"

"An image. I'm also binding it to the water." He tossed another handful into the fire. The greedy flames pounced on the herbs, sending aromatic smoke into the air. "Problem is, I have to reach across the boundary into the Weird. That will take a fair amount of magic. I'll need a sacrifice. Just not sure if what I have is enough."

The first hesitant traces of magic swirled along the clothesline. The water in the pool darkened.

Declan began to intone something in a steady monotone. She didn't recognize the language, but she felt his effort and the roiling current of magic vibrating within the sigil.

He chanted for almost a half hour, his face quaking with the strain. She sank next to him on the grass. The sound of his voice lulled her into a kind of trance. Shrouded in clouds of fragrant smoke, he seemed otherworldly, like some arcane sorcerer from a fairy tale.

Then Declan clasped his hair in a tight grip, drew the knife, and sliced it off.

"Aaaa!" It happened so fast, all Rose could do was gasp.

"What?" He threw the hair into the flames.

"Your hair!"

"That's why I grew it," he said, glancing at the water in the pool. "Power reserve. Three years' worth. But it's not enough."

Rose stood up, gathered her hair, and held out her hand.

He handed her the knife. She severed her hair with one sharp stroke and threw it in the fire.

"Most women would rather die than cut their hair," he said.

"It's just hair," she said. "I would sacrifice a lot more to keep Georgie alive."

The water within the pool bubbled up, rising, twisting into a huge translucent dome.

Something bumped Rose's elbow, and she jumped. "Jack!"

He regarded her with solemn eyes and held out his hand.

Declan passed her the knife, and she handed it to Jack. He sliced a lock from his head and tossed it into the fire. It went up in flames.

"Smells awful," Rose said, ruffling Jack's hair.

The water swirled, geysered up one last time, and snapped into shape.

SOMEONE was coming up the attic stairs. Georgie looked away from the picture. The attic belonged to him and Jack. It was a wondrous place. Huge piles of junk gathered against the walls: books, weapons, rusty contraptions, drawings, parchments . . . Down in the house, Rose cleaned up any hint of dirt and clutter, but here everything was messy and dusty. He liked it up here. It was quiet, and he could dream. Sometimes he imagined himself to be a pirate like Grandpa in the hull of his ship filled with treasure. Sometimes he was an explorer like Dad. Sometimes he was a demon . . .

A blond head emerged, followed by the rest of Declan. His long blond ponytail was gone, and his head looked lopsided, the hair on one side longer than on the other.

The blueblood paused for a moment, taking in the gloom and treasures, and looked at Georgie on his seat on a punching bag by a narrow window. Georgie sighed. There would be another talk about letting things die and "take their natural course." He'd nod and do what he always did. A waste of time.

Declan crossed the floor, crouched by him, and looked at the metal frame in his hands. George offered it to Declan.

Grandpa Cletus stood in the picture. Very tall and redheaded, he wore loose dark pants and a light shirt, with a triangular hat set at a jaunty angle. A carbine, an ancient musket, rested across his shoulders, the stock held in his right hand, the barrel passing behind his neck. In his other hand, he held a long rapier, leaning on it slightly as if it were a walking stick. His eyes were alight with crazy mirth. Grandma said he looked like a grown-up version of Jack, wrapped in pirate garb. When he first dragged this picture down to show her, she clicked her tongue and said, "Fiercely loyal and utterly unreliable." She didn't smile for a whole day after that, and he hid the picture in the attic with the rest of his stuff.

"Grandpa," George said, in case Declan failed to figure it out.

"I see."

"What happened to your hair?"

"I got tired of it."

George nodded and looked at him, waiting for a lecture.

"I've made something for you," Declan said. "I'd like it if you came to see it with me."

George followed him outside. A kiddie pool was in the middle of the lawn. Around it was a big complicated design made with rope and sticks. They climbed through the ropes. Declan stepped over the lines, while George ducked underneath, and they stood together at the rim.

A transparent dome rose in the middle of the pool, all the water bound together tightly by the magic. Within the dome sat a small settlement of crooked huts. Fields and forest surrounded it, giving way to a green plain. The top of the dome glowed with soft silvery light, and he could see every detail of the village, from the stones on the well to tiny creatures scurrying about. Shaped like little human-looking foxes with red, brown, and black pelts, the creatures went about performing small tasks, carrying water, tending the fields, fixing the thatched roofs. Georgie stared, mesmerized.

"What is that?" he asked finally.

"It's a willworld. Do you know what a computer is?" Declan asked.

"Yes."

"This is similar. It's the Weird version of it, only unlike a computer, the willworld has a very specific purpose. It only does one thing, but it does it really well. I made it for my graduation project when I finished gymnasium."

"Did it take you a long time?"

"A couple of years. The willworld itself is back at my house. This is just a facsimile . . . a copy. It's an exact image of the device, made of water and magic and linked by magic to the original. You might say it's a three-dimensional reflection. For all practical purposes, it's pretty much like having the real thing at your disposal."

George watched the foxes as they carried long stalks back to their huts. "Are they alive?"

"No. They're magic constructs. Strictly speaking, they don't actually exist. If you were to break the dome, you couldn't pick one up. The whole thing would simply go dark. Look here."

Declan walked over to the side, where a watery control panel protruded from the dome. "The willworld is a simulator. It lets you study the progress of civilization and see how it might develop. You control the world. You can make it rain or you can cause a drought. Here." He turned a dial.

Water rose within the dome, streaming over the fields. The foxes climbed atop the huts. He turned the dial the other way, and the waters fled.

Declan tapped the keys. The inside of the dome swirled and formed a small white-walled city with gardens and carved white towers. "This is a standard city, a kind of default. Everything is going well. There is plenty of food, the weather is mild, and the civilization prospers."

Georgie watched the city for a few minutes. Tiny foxes in bright robes lectured before their students in the gardens, strolled through the marketplace, and danced in a square while two other foxes played oddly shaped instruments.

Declan pressed another key.

"See this sign?" He pointed to a horizontal double loop in a small window. "I just set their generation length to infinity. They are now immortal. They can kill each other, but they won't die of natural causes. I also sped things up a little, so we don't spend all night watching a single scenario. Now this city is stored within the willworld. Anytime you wish to return to it, push this button right here and the world will be reset."

For the first few minutes nothing happened. Then the city began to grow. It filled the fields, spreading, sprawling, growing higher and higher. In twenty minutes the city completely swallowed the dome. Streets became tunnels. Towers turned into tall contraptions. Creatures stumbled about in crowded streets. The city had grown filthy and dark, its buildings decrepit.

"What's happening?" George whispered.

"Overpopulation. There are too many of them. There is not enough food or space. The old ones won't die, and they keep making more children."

In thirty minutes, the creatures began falling on the streets, crawling through the filth, searching for scraps of food. Declan reached to reset the dome.

"No. I want to see," George said.

"It won't be pretty," Declan warned.

"I understand."

Declan let it go.

Fires broke out. The creatures formed gangs and began ripping each other apart, feeding on the severed limbs.

George stumbled away from the dome and closed his eyes.

"Are you unwell?" Declan asked.

Georgie shook his head. They ate each other. The little foxes ate each other.

"Let us continue then. Take two."

George looked at the dome in time to see the darkness swirl. The perfect little city reappeared.

Five minutes into it, one of the foxes began to cough. The cough spread, first to the neighbors, then farther, engulfing the entire city.

"The plague," Declan explained. "They're sick, but they can't die. Sometimes death is the only way to stop the spread of infection. This sickness can't quite kill them, but there is no cure."

They watched the foxes shamble about in the dark, coughing in misery. When they started falling from exhaustion, George asked him to reset the dome.

The third try went well for the first ten minutes, and George began to have hope, until a group of older foxes started smashing the new building with sticks.

"Why are they doing that?" Georgie asked.

"They don't want the city to change," Declan said. "They've realized that if they keep growing, they'll run out of space."

Five minutes later, some foxes were chained, marched to the lake, and forced into the water.

"Why?" Georgie whispered, watching them drown.

"They are probably the ones who wanted the city to grow. The others must have decided that the population should remain the same. The city can only support so many foxes. This is their way of controlling it."

"But . . ." George bit his lip, as the foxes brought out little fox babies and one by one threw them into the lake. That was just about enough of that. He marched to the control panel and hit a reset button.

Declan straightened. "I'm going to go inside now. You know how to reset the dome back to default. The spell will probably hold through the night, but I doubt we'll get more than twelve, fifteen hours from it, so if you want to run it a bit more, best to do it now."

GEORGIE felt Rose's arms close about him. She hugged him. "It's almost midnight. You should come inside."

He shook his head. "It's okay," he said, staring at the dome. "A little longer."

"Declan and I decided to sleep on the porch tonight to keep an eye on you. If you run into any trouble, you come and get one of us, okay?"

George glanced back. On the porch, Declan and Grandma were arranging some blankets.

"Okay," he said, reaching to the control panel. If he reset it just one more time, maybe it would be fine. It had to be fine. There had to be a way for it to end well.

ROSE awoke when the first hint of sunrise colored the sky. Georgie sat on the steps, hugging his knees. She stirred. At the other end of the porch, Declan's eyes snapped open. He looked at her from above the back of a small lynx who curled by his side. Jack must've taken off his bracelet in the night. Probably to keep an eye on his brother.

Rose untangled herself from the blankets and went to sit by Georgie.

"How long did you stay up?"

"The whole time."

She glanced at the pool. A beautiful city shimmered within the dome. Declan had explained the concept to her last night, while she trimmed his hair so it didn't look lopsided. She had watched Georgie from the window for about an hour, while Grandma hemmed and hawed and threw up her hands in disgust trying to trim Rose's own butchered hair into some semblance of a decent haircut. In that hour, Georgie had cried twice. Rose had desperately wanted to go and comfort him. But her sympathy would do more harm than good. Something profound was happening to Georgie, and he had to go through it alone.

Now, as he sat next to her, he seemed older. Somber and almost grim.

"It went wrong every time." He wouldn't look at her.

"The city looks fine now," she said.

"That's because I let them die. I set the dial back to fifty years. I had to. There was no other way."

She hugged him and kissed his hair.

"Life is so precious because it's short," she said. "Even the most resilient people are fragile. Life isn't about dying or not dying. It's about living well, George. Living so you can be proud and happy."

Georgie hunched his shoulders.

"I'm ready," he said. "I just want to see them all. For the last time."

Behind them, Declan rose quietly and picked up his sword.

They released Grandpa from the shed and headed into the Wood, Jack padding ahead, a lithe, feline shadow, then she and Georgie with a look of intense concentration on his face, then Declan, and finally Grandfather, snarling and mumbling to himself.

They came to a large clearing, where last year Donovan's trailer had burned to the ground, nearly setting the entire Wood on fire.

Georgie sighed and spread his arms.

A minute passed. Then another. Sweat beaded on Georgie's forehead.

A rustle troubled the bushes. The branches bent, releasing a small raccoon into the open. A bird swooped down and landed on the right. A litter of young kittens scampered into the open, followed by an old three-legged black Lab. Several squirrels emerged, scuttling ... A puppy with an oddly shaped head ... They came and came, dozens of mangled, broken creatures, repaired by Georgie's will. They came to their master and sat in a semicircle around them.

Rose drew a sharp breath. So many. Oh, dear God, so very many. *It's a wonder he's alive at all*

Georgie approached Grandfather sitting in the grass and hugged him.

"It's time to leave," he said.

The creature who used to be Cletus looked at him with rheumy eyes. "Will I see you again?"

Georgie shook his head. "No."

Grandfather hung his head. "I'm tired," he said.

Georgie rested his hand on Grandfather's shoulder and looked at the wall of creatures.

"Wait!" Grandma's voice rang.

Rose turned. Éléonore stood behind them on the path. She swallowed and slowly walked past them. Grandfather saw her. Tears swelled in his eyes. Éléonore stood by him, and he hugged her legs. She patted his matted hair.

"Okay," she said, her voice trembling. "You can do it now."

Georgie's lips shaped one quiet word. "Bye."

A faint sound emanated from the semicircle as if the undead who couldn't breathe exhaled in unison.

The creatures dropped to the ground. Grandpa toppled forward softly. A sweet sickening reek of decaying flesh filled the clearing. Rose gagged. The beasts melted, their ruptured carcasses leaking fluids into the ground. Another moment, and they decomposed down to their bones.

By Éléonore's feet, Grandfather had become dust. She emptied one of the herb pouches she carried in her pockets and gently scooped some of the powder into it.

Georgie swayed. Before Rose could reach him, Declan picked him up. "Is that all?" he asked.

Georgie nodded.

The four of them turned and headed back to the house.

"Rose?" Georgie raised his head from Declan's shoulder.

"Yes?"

"I'd like to be George from now on," he said.

"Okay," she said. "That will be fine, George."

He nodded and said, "I'm hungry."

TWENTY

ROSE sat on the porch, a cup of tea in her hand. Inside, George ate like he hadn't eaten in years, and Grandma was overjoyed to pile more food into his and Jack's dishes.

The screen door opened, and quiet steps approached her. Declan sat next to her on the steps.

For a long minute they said nothing, then she leaned to him and brushed his cheek with her lips. "Thank you for saving my brother."

She pulled away before he could touch her.

"You don't seem happy," he said.

"I am. It's just . . ." She ducked her head. "I've lived with this fear for so long. He started raising things when he was six. He's ten now. For four years, I watched him fade. I know that it hampered his growth. He probably never will be as tall or strong as he should've been."

"Children are resilient," Declan said. "Given the right diet and exercise, he'll hold his own."

"I've tried to help him," she told him. "I've done everything I could think of. Once Grandma and I put him to sleep for ten days, hoping that all of his creatures would die. But they just kept on sucking the life out of him. This will sound so terrible, but I'd convinced myself he couldn't be helped. I think that's the only way I could deal with it. I never stopped hoping and trying, but deep down I sort of came to terms with knowing that one day he would just burn down, like a candle." She covered her face. "You saved him. You saved Georgie. I'm so grateful. I don't want you to think that I take it lightly. It's just that I don't even know what to say. I'm scared to believe it. I should've tried harder . . . I should be thrilled, but I'm just so . . . lost. Stunned."

"Like a runner whose race had been cut short," Declan said.

"Yes. It's selfish and terrible of me, and I'm ashamed of it. I don't know why I'm even telling you this."

He pulled her to him, wrapping his massive arm around her back. She pushed away.

"Let me hold you," he said. "I won't 'maul' you. You need it. Just sit with me."

There was a quiet strength in the way he held her, and she drew on it, wrapped up in his warmth and the scent of his skin. She'd never had anyone to lean on, not like this. He made her feel so safe that she was afraid to let go, terrified that she would break into tears if she did.

"I felt that way when Casshorn rescued William," he said. "And felt like scum for it. I was sure nothing good would come of it. I knew it then, but what could I say? No, Will, take the death instead?"

"Why did Casshorn do it?" she asked.

"Me. I think he was planning the beginnings of this insanity back then. Casshorn is older than me by three decades. He's well trained and he's dangerous and skilled, but he always lacked the perseverance and discipline necessary to truly master a weapon. In his best moments, he's brilliant, but it will do him no good in a direct fight. If we cross blades, I'll cut him down. He's well aware of it. He wanted William to use against me. William's deadly with any blade, especially knives."

"But William is your friend."

There was a tiny pause. "After William was released, I met him at one of the formal dinners His Grace gave. He came as Casshorn's adopted son. He wouldn't speak to me."

Rose glanced at his face. "I'm so sorry. Did you ever find out why?"

"No. I don't know if he was angry because I failed to secure his release or if it was something Casshorn told him about me. The next thing I knew, both of them were gone. You spoke to him. What did he say?"

"He mostly tried to get me to go out with him. The last time he spoke, he told me he wanted me because the boys and I were together. He said he never had a family and always wanted one, and we fit the bill."

"Well, he'll have to do without," Declan said with the warmth of a glacier. "You're mine, and he can't have you."

Well then. "That sounds pretty final. Do I even have a say in this?"

"Of course you do," he said softly. "If you say no, I'll have to accept it."

Sure, he said that now. But the oath he swore was very clear. If he won the challenges, Declan gained the right to her. She would be his possession. Not a wife, not a friend, a lover, or an equal. A possession.

Declan always planned things out. He didn't know her at the time he swore the oath and probably thought she was unhinged. He had phrased his oath to gain as much as he could with minimal risk, relying on his presence and her fear to carry it through. If only she had called his bluff. He wouldn't have hurt the boys, not in a million years. He would've walked away. But then she wouldn't have gotten to know him. Rose tried to imagine him leaving on that day without another word. Her throat constricted. Her heart beat faster. She leaned a little closer to him, seeking reassurance that he was still here in spite of herself and realized a simple fact.

She was in love with Declan Camarine.

But loving him and being with him weren't the same thing. He was still a blueblood, and she . . . She had no dowry and no pedigree. She didn't fit into his world any more than he fit into hers. He wanted her. She was a challenge, and just like Grandma said, Declan couldn't resist. And once he got her, what then? One day they would wake up next to each other, and he would be Earl Camarine, lord of a dozen places with names she couldn't remember, and she would still be only Rose.

She swallowed. In her head she pictured him walking out the door, never to come back. The anxiety squeezed her heart in a lead fist.

"There is no hope for us," she said softly.

"There is always hope," Declan said. "As dangerous as Casshorn is, he's also irrational, and that weakens him."

She shook her head and forced herself to pull free of him. He didn't understand. He concentrated on the biggest threat, and it would do her good to do the same. For now, she had to keep her worries to herself. Casshorn had to come first.

"As far as William goes, I don't know what the devil he's doing, but I doubt he's helping Casshorn," Declan said.

"What makes you think that?"

"William is a decorated veteran with over a decade in the Legion. Casshorn couldn't hack it in the Legion longer than six months. Hell, he couldn't hack it in the research branch of the Airforce." Declan shook his head. "All he had to do was study wyverns, and he failed at that. I have no respect for him, and I wouldn't suffer his orders. I don't see why Will would."

"So why is he here, then?" She frowned.

"I don't know." Declan grimaced. "I know what I'm going to do once I find him."

"And that would be?"

"I'll beat him bloody."

She blinked.

"I walked away from eleven years in the Legion to pull his ar—him out of the fire. One would expect a thank-you or at least a cordial demeanor. Failing that, one would expect some small courtesy for old times' sake, such as a note perhaps, something along the lines of 'My adoptive father is about to make off with a world-destroying device, so he can kill us all. Just thought you'd like to know.'"

"Maybe he didn't know."

Declan gave her a hard look. "He knew."

"A little of you is pissed off because he didn't go all to pieces thanking you for saving him," she said.

Declan swore. "I couldn't care less."

"It bothers you. It would bother me, too."

A man appeared at the end of the road. Slight, a bit disheveled, he wore black pants, a red polo shirt, and a dark leather vest over it. The shirt and pants sagged on his thin frame. He was balding, and the remains of his short hair and a neatly trimmed, short beard were liberally salted with gray. His face radiated calm kindness, and he smiled at them as he came down the road, leading a horse to the house, but his hooded eyes were solid black.

Declan focused on the man with predatory alertness. "Who is that?"

Rose sighed. There went her chance to talk. "That's Jeremiah Lovedahl."

"Why is he coming here?"

"Supposedly he's coming to take Grandmother and the boys to Wood House. It's a heavily warded shelter deep inside the Wood."

"You seem skeptical," he said.

"He has an agenda," Rose said. "The Edge is very much an 'every man for himself' kind of place. But once in a while we run across a threat that's too much for any one family to handle on its own. At times like this, people like my grandma and Jeremiah step forward. They're our elders. There are six of them, and when they agree on something, East Laporte usually pays attention."

"They won't compel you to obey, but they issue advisory opinions?" Declan asked.

She nodded. "Something like that. After we had that fight, I called them for Grandma and they had themselves a huddle. They've realized that we're too weak to fight Casshorn directly, so they're trying to outsmart him. First step is to deprive him of food, so to starve him and the hounds, they 'advised' getting the hell out of town. Last night everyone with a drop of sense packed up, and this morning, they all drove out as if to work in the Broken, but none of them are coming back. Some holdouts remain, as usual, but what are you going to do?" She shrugged. "The Edgers are outcasts. For some of us, our house and land are all we have. I swear, you could have a wall of fire sweeping through East Laporte, and some of the harder heads would hole up on their property. They'd rather die than leave."

Jeremiah tied his horse to a tree.

"So what does he really want here?" Declan asked.

"Jeremiah hopes to convince you and me to come with him to Wood House, where the rest of the elders are. They want to know more about Casshorn, so they want you to help them with that. I'm to come as their protection against you and Casshorn both. You make them nervous."

His green eyes studied her. "Do you want me to come?"

Rose pursed her mouth. "It's up to you. I don't want to ask you to do something you don't want to do, but yes, I would like you to visit Wood House. The elders are old and full of magic. They can't attack Casshorn or the hounds directly, because the hounds absorb any magic less intense than a flash, but I wouldn't discount them. And we don't have a lot of allies."

"We? Do you include yourself in my fight?"

"He's destroying my home, eating my neighbors, and wants to kill my family. I told you before; I don't intend to sit on my hands. And you need me, Declan. You need my flash."

He gave her a pointed stare.

Rose rolled her eyes. "Oh, the blueblood look of scorn. Whatever shall I do? I do declare, I feel faint."

Declan growled under his breath.

She patted his hand. "It's not too late to reconsider this whole 'I'll have you, Rose' business."

"Nice try," he told her.

Jeremiah came up to the porch. "Hello, Ms. Drayton." His accent was the old Southern, slow, refined, swallowing his *r*'s as if he'd just stepped off some plantation in Virginia.

"Hello, Mr. Lovedahl," she said. "Would you care for some iced tea?"

"I would, thank you."

When she returned from the kitchen with two glasses, Jeremiah smiled at her. "Lord Camarine and I were just discussing the defenses of Wood House. He mentioned he'd like to see them for himself."

"Did he now?" Rose smiled pleasantly and handed out the tea.

"Will you be joining us?" Jeremiah asked.

"I'd be delighted," she said.

ROSE walked next to Declan, picking her way through the forest floor thick with centuries of autumns. They formed a narrow procession: first, Jeremiah, leading the horse loaded with their bags, then Grandma, then Georgie, and then she and Declan, bringing up the rear. Jack had gone cat as soon as they set out, and he slunk along on their flanks. Once in a while she'd catch a glimpse of him, creeping over a log or scrambling up a tree, but he blended in so well, she wasn't even sure if she truly had seen him or if she just imagined it.

They were only twenty minutes into the Wood, but the change was startling. The forest here was older. Colossal trees towered above them: enormous pines, straight as masts, venerable Edge oaks, pale poplars ... The forest was grass green, and emerald, and yellow. Patches of velvet moss climbed up the bark and sheathed the forest floor, so bright that when the sunlight spilling through the breaks in the canopy struck it, the moss nearly glowed. In the shadows, Granny Rose lichens bloomed on trunks and boulders like vivid scarlet peonies, and in the deeper gloom between the twisted, massive roots, delicate lady's slipper flowers stretched on thin stalks, and yellow-, brown-, and red-capped mushrooms the size of footstools squatted in clumps and rings. The air smelled of life, greenery, and magic. It filled Rose's lungs and carried away worry. She smiled quietly to herself and kept walking, following Jeremiah and Grandma along the trail she could barely see.

"I'm too old for this," Grandma murmured.

"I do recollect that you made this same trip all by your lonesome earlier in the week," Jeremiah said.

"Well, that's true," Grandma murmured.

"I was always of the opinion that some women improve with age," Jeremiah continued. "Like fine wine."

Rose rolled her eyes. Jeremiah Lovedahl was putting the moves on her grandmother. What was the world coming to?

They reached a grove of pines. The trees stood very dense here, the stubby broken branches near the roots supporting pale clusters of bone wind chimes. Each chime consisted of a skull, suspended from a metal ring among an assortment of small bones. Past the chimes, the forest stood unnaturally still. Not a single pine needle moved.

"Is there a spell on the trees?" Declan asked softly.

"Bone ward," Rose murmured back. "Very old, very strong."

They came to a halt at the trees marked by chimes. Most skulls were possum, wolf, lynx, but three were human, and one, heavy-jawed and oddly flat, had two thick fangs curving down like sabers. Declan nodded at the bizarre skull. "Troll."

"That's correct," Jeremiah said. "One came our way from the Weird about fifty years ago. Killed two little girls and ate them."

"How did you manage to bring him down? Their hide's too thick for a bullet, and they're immune to most poisons."

Jeremiah plucked a wide triangular leaf from a low branch and held it up. It was slightly larger than his hand. "Forest Tear. If you boil the sap of the tree, it makes glue, clear, odorless, and very strong. We served the troll a freshly slaughtered cow on a blanket of these leaves dipped in glue. Trolls are dumb creatures. He got down on all fours to eat his feast, and the leaves stuck to his feet and hands. He tried to shake them off, and when that failed, tried to pull them off with his teeth and got a leaf stuck to his face for his trouble. Then he panicked and rolled, until he was completely covered. The original plan was for him to suffocate to death, but he somehow got to his feet and ran blindly, until he knocked down a power line pole and got himself electrocuted."

"I'm beginning to see that one doesn't disturb your town without consequences," Declan said.

"Oh, we're just simple country folk." Jeremiah gave him a mild smile. "We don't take kindly to having our children murdered, but really we keep to ourselves. We're mostly harmless."

Magic streamed to him, gathering about his body in a deep red cloud. He raised his hand up to the sky. His black eyes narrowed to mere slits, and he barked a single word. "Break!"

The magic shot up and vanished. A moment later a long serpentine body crashed through the canopy and thudded to the ground. A leech bird. About five feet long and pale blue, it resembled a stork, but instead of the normal feathers, its tail split into two long, snake-like whips, tipped with blue tufts. The leech bird flailed in convulsions, slapping its broken bat-like wings on the ground. It had no beak. Instead, its jaws were very long and narrow, full of sharp needle-teeth. Magic spiked from it in dangerous bursts, but they fell short of Jeremiah.

"Dreadful creatures. Foul magic, too. Common wisdom says you'll turn into one if bitten. I haven't witnessed that

happening in my lifetime, but I wouldn't discount it."
Jeremiah raised his rifle and shot the leech bird twice. It
jerked and became still. He waited a minute or two, approached the carcass, then pulled out a machete from his belt
and hacked the head from the bird in a single chop. He
picked it up and tossed it at the ward. The head crashed into
the woods and vanished. Wind stirred the chimes. Bones
rattled against each other with a dry clatter.

"It takes blood to open it," Jeremiah said. He hacked at
the leech bird, carving it like a chicken, and nodded at the
bloody chunks. "Each of you, take one and pay your dues.
Quickly now before the blood cools."

One by one they fed the carcass to the ward. When Jack
descended from the trees and dragged the last piece to the
spell and pushed it in with his furry head, the chimes froze,
but beyond them the Wood came to life, as if someone had
pressed Play on an invisible remote. Branches shivered.
Small red leaves fluttered to the ground here and there,
breaking free from the vine garlands dripping from high
branches. Magic bloomed like a flower.

"Come," Jeremiah ordered.

In they went. The Wood grew darker here, older, harder.
You'd never guess the town roads were only a half hour
away. The trees were truly enormous now. It would take several people with their arms outstretched to enclose one of the
trunks. Odd creatures skittered in the branches: some small
and furry, some scaly, some with eyes that glowed orange
and red. Jack spat, and hissed, and promised trouble in his
cat language, until Declan picked him up to keep him put.

Twenty minutes later, they finally reached Wood House. It
sat on top of a low man-made hill, shaped like a pyramid
with its top chopped off. A wooden palisade, centuries old
and slathered with clay to protect it from moisture and fires,
surrounded the apex of the hill. Moss and underbrush hugged
its roots, trying to climb up the palisade, and pale flowers
thrust through it to the sun, as if a wave of greenery had
crashed against the wooden walls. Rose remembered coming
here only once, when she was very small.

They climbed up the side of the hill, using ancient stone
blocks placed there like giant steps. The wooden gate swung

open with a creak. A weather-scarred totem pole stood to the right, next to a bonfire pit filled with stones. A tall oak rose straight up, a small wooden lookout platform sitting in its branches like a tree house. To the left, a big log cabin waited for them, its walls so layered with moss and lichen that the building seemed to have grown from the Wood's floor, and behind it a scattering of smaller buildings only intensified the illusion: the structures sat together like toadstools in a ring.

The wooden gate behind them shut, and Rose turned to see Leanne sliding a heavy wooden beam across it. A few other familiar people walked in the yard: all about her age, most single and magically adept. The Edgers with the least to lose, she realized.

"Welcome to Wood House," Jeremiah said.

TWENTY-ONE

LEE Stearns claimed he was half–Cherokee Indian, but his hair, skin, and face said he was whiter than the Pillsbury Doughboy, and rumor had it that both of his parents were about as Cherokee as pizza. It wasn't something people dared to say to his face or behind his back. His skin was smooth and pale, almost satiny, despite his advanced age. He looked at the world with watery blue eyes, and his hair was corn silk blond. It was as if the sun had bleached him. Lee drew the eye. He was also known to lose his temper if he thought people stared at him too much, and as Rose found a seat across from him at an old wooden table in the Wood House hall, she took care not to look at him too long.

Gaping at the other five elders wasn't a good idea either. There was a lot of power in the room, and they looked far too somber to tolerate foolishness right about now.

Rose glanced to her grandma. Éléonore gave her a careful smile. Rose looked at her hands.

She was terribly aware of Declan, sitting very still next to her, about as perturbed as a granite crag. At least the children were amused from the meeting. Leanne had brought Kenny Jo to Wood House, probably so the elders could question him. George and Kenny Jo decided to call a truce for the time being in the name of exploring Wood House. They got off easy.

"Why don't you introduce us to the young man, Rose?" Jeremiah said.

Rose cleared her throat. "Directly across from us is Adele Moore."

If Grandma pretended to be a hedge witch, Adele was one. She was tall for an older woman, with skin the color of coffee grounds. Her hair streamed down to her waist in long gray dreads, each lock woven with bead strings and leather cords tingling with small bone and wood charms. Her clothes were layers of threadbare fabric, green, olive, and brown. She wore a dozen necklaces, some of dried mushroom caps stuck onto a thin thread, some of dried blossoms, some of discarded snakeskin, and one or two of tiny, cheap beads probably bought at Wal-Mart, of all places. Her face was wrinkled, and her hair had lost its color, but Adele's eyes were quick and young.

"To the left of Adele is Emily Paw, Elsie Moore's niece."

Emily looked a lot like her aunt. Haggish and slight, she resembled a dried-out crow. Her mouth drooped downward, and in all of her twenty-two years, Rose had never seen Emily smile once. Of all present, with the exception of herself and Declan, Emily was the youngest and looked the oldest.

"You already know Jeremiah and Grandma," Rose continued. "The man on the right is Lee Stearns. Next to him is Tom Buckwell."

"Hello." Tom Buckwell sounded like an ornery bear and looked like one, too. Big, almost seven feet tall and three hundred pounds heavy, he sat hunching his thick shoulders. He was also the hairiest man she had ever seen. His reddish beard was always tangled, his hair long, and the hair on his muscular forearms resembled fur. Rumors said that if he got drunk enough, he sometimes got his jollies by stripping naked and scaring hikers out in the Broken into thinking he was Bigfoot. Tom was also Fred Simoen's uncle, once removed.

"And this is Earl Declan Camarine," Rose finished finally.

Silence fell.

"How do we know you are who you say you are?" Lee asked.

Declan shrugged. "You don't."

"Then how do you expect to prove yourself?"

Rose tensed. She'd expected the question. It was natural that they would want to test him, but testing Declan was like trying to pet a strange pit bull.

Declan's eyebrows crept up an eighth of an inch. "I don't have to prove anything. I came to you because Miss Drayton convinced me it would be beneficial to my cause. I'm here to kill Casshorn. I have no other purpose or agenda, and once I'm done, I'll return back to where I came from. It's up to you to accept me or not."

It really was amazing how Declan could shift into blue-blood mode. His tone wasn't exactly imperious, but it made it seem as if his words were cast in stone.

"What Lee means is we would like to see some proof of your power," Grandma said. "Please, indulge us."

He bowed his head. "As you wish, *Madame*."

Magic stirred within Declan, like a lazy monster, awakening slowly, stretching, testing its claws. It built stronger and stronger. A white glow rolled over his irises. It was as if the side of the room where he sat had darkened, but the magic within him glowed, swelling, rising, terrifying and impossibly strong like a hurricane.

The tiny hairs on the back of Rose's neck stood on their ends.

Declan's eyes blazed white. A ghostly wind brushed Rose. She could actually see it—a thin veil of pale glow, streaming about Declan, winding against him.

She reached out and put her fingers on his hand. He glanced at her with his star-eyes and pulled the magic inside himself, sheathing it like a weapon. She wasn't sure what was more impressive: the sheer magnitude of his power or the ease with which he controlled it.

Lee opened his mouth and clamped it shut. Grandma looked pained. Up until now, some of them probably thought they could take care of Declan if it came to that. Now they knew that all of them put together could slow him down, but killing him would be another matter entirely.

Adele leaned forward. "We would hear about Casshorn," she said. "If it's at all possible, Lord Camarine."

Declan leaned forward. "What I say here mustn't leave this room. If it does, I'll have to return, and I won't be alone," he said.

Heads nodded around the table.

"It goes back to the Empire of the Sun Serpent," Declan said. "In the Broken, settlers from the Eastern half of the world came to the West and killed the native tribes, who lacked technology and the means to effectively resist."

Lee looked like he was about to say something but thought better of it.

"In my world, the opposite was true. This continent was home to a powerful empire. Its people called itself *tlatoke*, and they called their realm the Kingdom of the Sun Serpent. Their magic was born in the jungle, and it was extremely powerful and difficult to counter. About sixteen centuries ago they crossed the ocean and began raiding the Eastern continent, terrorizing the coast of Anglia and what is now the Gaulic Empire, all the way south to Etruria. They killed, raped, stole slaves, and demanded bowls of gold dust in tribute. This continued for approximately two hundred years, until they abruptly stopped. Usually raids die down gradually, but the *tlatoke* simply vanished."

Declan paused.

"Something screwed up the kingdom of the shiny snake," Tom Buckwell said.

Declan nodded. "The raids had spurred research. A century later, the peoples of the Eastern continent had developed the means to cross the ocean, but the fear of the *tlatoke* was so great that almost three hundred years passed before the first voyage took place. When the first war fleets arrived at the Western continent, they found no *tlatoke*. Plenty of ruined cities and temples, but no people. More, a lot of the magic-saturated flora and fauna one would expect was gone. The woods were young. Even now it's difficult to find a thousand-year-old tree. The species of plants and animals that did survive had developed great defenses. Western animals are bigger and stronger than their Eastern counterparts, and something as sluggish as a vampire vine has evolved into an active predator."

"What killed the *tlatoke*?" Jeremiah asked.

"It is unclear. The searches of the ruins didn't provide any definitive answers. If something did kill the inhabitants, they were consumed, because no intact skeletons remained. But the researchers did find signs of struggle. Broken furniture. Holes in the walls. Claw marks."

"The hounds," Grandma said.

Declan continued. "Eventually survivors were found, isolated bands hiding out in the wilderness. They were almost unrecognizable. Legends said the raiders had worn steel armor and brightly colored robes, but their descendants had regressed into primitivism. The use of magic and cultivation of crops were forbidden. The former *tlatoke* lived in small nomadic groups, wore furs, and hunted with bows and spears. In three hundred years, they managed to fall from a glorious, advanced civilization to people who no longer remembered how to read the writings of their ancestors. Their oral traditions persisted, however, and their legends spoke about a gift from the Sun Serpent, which then turned on them and destroyed their kingdom. Even in the Weird, gods don't actually interfere in the lives of the mortal men. We pray to them, but we have yet to see definitive proof they exist. So nobody was quite sure where this gift came from. Perhaps it was manufactured by *tlatoke* priests. Perhaps it fell from the depths between the stars as meteorites do. Perhaps it was an artifact of a forgotten nation. Whatever its origin was, the gift destroyed the *tlatoke* civilization and vanished."

"What happened?" Rose asked.

"The continent was settled. New countries sprang up. Some, like Adrianglia, won their independence from their mother states. The *tlatoke* became a bizarre historical mystery. Then, about three hundred years ago, the great-grandfather of the current Duke of the Southern Provinces decided to drain a mire pond. As the pond was drained, a strange egg-like object emerged, sheathed in clay. It was too heavy to move, and so His Grace ordered the shell broken. Under the clay lay ceramic, followed by a layer of pure iron, then more ceramic, then lead. Finally when all the layers were cut through, His Grace found a strange device. As soon as the device was touched, it came alive and produced the first hound. The hound killed one of the workers. The magic it absorbed then streamed back into the device, and a second hound was born."

"You should've destroyed it," Emily Paw said.

"We tried," Declan said. "The device absorbs magic. It's impervious to fire. Attempts were made to crush it and encase it in molten metal, but they were unsuccessful. It's made of a material not found in the Weird. As far as we know, its function is simple: it pulls magic from its environment and produces hounds, which then collect magic and return it to the device. We don't know why it does what it does. We know human beings are the hounds' preferred prey. We know it can't be stopped."

"Is that what killed the Weird's Indians?" Tom Buckwell asked.

"That's what some believe. The device was classified as an 'imminent threat to the realm.' A bunker was built, mimicking the original object: several layers of iron, lead, ceramic, and glass were arranged in such a way as to provide maximum isolation from the environment. The device was placed into the bunker. Its existence was kept secret from the general public to prevent panic or terrorist acts."

Lee Stearns snorted. "Of course."

"The bunker is located in Beliy Forest," Declan said. "It's an ugly, inhospitable place, and nobody in their right mind trespasses there. The structure itself sits on a slab of ceramic, and the forest is burned, salted, and fenced off for a mile around the bunker. Once every two weeks a crew made up of members of a secret branch of the Duke's personal guard travels to the bunker and destroys any encroaching plants or animals to prevent the device from accessing environmental magic. Approximately two weeks ago, Casshorn Sandine, brother of the current Duke, broke into the bunker and stole the device. It was brilliantly done: he had been secretly cutting a narrow trail into the forest for the last year and a half, ending it about twelve miles from the bunker. He then compromised the bunker and airlifted the device twelve miles to the trail by means of an Airforce wyvern he had stolen from a local armory. The device killed the wyvern but not before it got Casshorn to his escape route. He loaded the device onto a cart and drove it out of Adrianglia into the Edge."

"I think we all could use something to drink," Adele said.

ONCE iced tea had been distributed, the mood in the room lightened and Rose breathed easier.

"Why would Casshorn do it?" Adele asked, sipping her tea.

"Why is good, but I want to know how come the beasts aren't killing him," Grandma said.

Declan drained half his glass. "It's difficult to understand Casshorn. He's mad, but he has flashes of genius. He's amoral, but he takes pains to be polite. He's failed at everything he ever tried. Casshorn expressed the desire to be a duke like his father. Centuries ago titles used to be hereditary. Now titles are administrative posts that carry a great deal of civil and military responsibility. One can't inherit a title. One must earn it and pass the requisite examinations proving his or her competency in order to claim it. The higher the rank, the more stringent are the requirements. Sons and daughters of nobles often receive very specialized education from birth in anticipation of trying to assume the title. They have an advantage, because they watch and learn as their parents govern, in the same sense as the baker's son knows about baking bread from watching his father make it. But no matter how good their test scores are, nobody, not even an heir to the throne of Adrianglia, can assume a title without first providing service to the realm. Some choose civil, some military, but all have to serve. The mandatory period of service is seven years in the military and ten for the civil service."

"Military for you, I take it?" Tom Buckwell asked.

Declan nodded. "Casshorn passed the examinations at fifteen. Did spectacularly well, in fact. All that remained was the period of service. Casshorn attempted the Airforce, because it is considered the most cerebral of all military occupations."

"Airforce like planes?" Lee Stearns asked.

"Airforce like flying beasts," Declan said. "Wyverns, manticores, and so on. Within a year Casshorn was booted from the Airforce Academy for plotting to kill one of his instructors. That effectively barred him from any military branch except for the Red Legion, who will take anyone. Whether you're a wanted criminal or a certified lunatic—they don't care. They can take an average person and in two years turn him or her into a mass murderer. Just deploying them often causes panic in the enemy. The Red Legion discharged Casshorn in six months, deeming him completely unsuited to military service."

"To screw up like that takes talent." Tom Buckwell shook his head. "He must be special."

Declan grimaced. "He certainly thinks so. With the military crossed off his list, Casshorn attempted the civil service. He was fired from Elizabethian University for plagiarism, having served a little over twenty months. Two days later, someone set the campus on fire. Then Casshorn took a sabbatical for three years. Then he attempted manufacturing research. To make a long story short, in the meantime Casshorn's younger brother, Ortes, finished his seven years, serving in the Andrianglian Navy with distinction, and Casshorn hadn't even managed to pass a half mark. Their test scores were tied. Because they were siblings, Ortes had the option of signing a waiver to give his brother five years to complete the service requirement. A peer title can't remain vacant for long. All peers have duties, and someone has to fulfill them."

"So what happened?" Rose asked.

"Ortes was willing to sign the waiver, if his father wished to give Casshorn another chance. The Duke decided he needed to think some more on the matter and invited his sons to Yule Dinner at the ducal manor. Most of the nobles and their families were present at the celebration. I was eight, and I remember it vividly. Casshorn's demeanor was bizarre. He seemed not to know where he was. Midway through the evening he stood up and started talking. He ranted like a lunatic and attacked Ortes's wife, calling her a whore and blaming her for a number of odd and illogical things. Apparently, years earlier, when Ortes and Jane were affianced, Casshorn had made some advances toward her and she turned him down, but to hear him tell it, the incident had happened earlier in the evening, not nearly a decade ago. Obviously, no waiver was signed, and Ortes became Duke shortly after his father retired. Casshorn later claimed that someone had added a narcotic to his drink, but by then it was too late, and he seemed to accept it. Apparently, he found a new way of obtaining the power he always wanted."

Jeremiah frowned. "Why the Edge? Why our small neck of the woods?"

Declan rested his arms on the table and leaned forward. "The Edge has no strong police or military force. Any resistance he encounters will be fragmented, since nobody but Edgers care what happens between the worlds. As to what his purpose is, I don't know. I think he may have started with some idea of conquering the Edge, building up an army of hounds, and avenging himself on all the people who wronged him in Adrianglia. However, whatever he has done to earn immunity from the hounds is changing him. I'm not sure how much of his humanity remains."

"I think his conquering plans bit the dust," Rose said. "He simply wants to absorb magic and eat us now. He kept his face hidden, but his hands looked like paws. He has claws instead of nails. If he conquers the Edge, it will be so he can feed."

"He can't be reasoned with," Tom Buckwell said.

Lee turned to him. "How do you know?"

Tom's bushy beard moved around a bit. His face looked sour. "Fred Simoen sent Brad Dillon up to him with gifts."

"He what?" Grandma drew from the table in shock.

"I told him not to do it," Tom growled. "I said from the get-go that it was a lousy idea and it wouldn't end well, but there was no reasoning with him. Fred thinks he can buy the world."

Rose thought of Casshorn raving on about the delicious man he had received as a gift. Nausea squirmed through her. "Casshorn ate Brad, didn't he?"

"He sure did," Tom said. "At least that's what Fred said, before he and the whole clan peeled out of the Edge like their arses were on fire."

Rose rubbed her face. Brad was slime, but to die like this . . . Nobody deserved that. She thought of the boys being eaten and had to clench her hands under the table.

Declan's large hand settled on her fist. He rubbed her hand with his dry warm fingers. "So you do know where Casshorn is?"

Silence fell around the table.

"He's in Moss Ravine," Adele said. "The Wood started dying there about six days ago."

Lee threw his hands in the air. "And he needs to know that why?"

"It's his mess," Emily creaked. "Let him clean it up."

"That's a real good point." Lee swung to Declan. "Why aren't more of you fellows here taking care of this problem? Why is it you're here by your lonesome? It's your mess."

"Technically, the Duke has no jurisdiction in the Edge," Declan said. "So it's your mess at the moment."

"But they did send you," Jeremiah said.

"Oh, come on." Tom Buckwell slapped the table with his big hands. "He's covert ops, if I ever saw one. They ain't gonna send a battalion to help us out, because that would mean they'd have to admit that Duke's psycho brother made off with their supersecret apocalypse machine, which they weren't supposed to have in the first place. They sent one guy, a killer, and if he fails, they're gonna deny they ever knew anything about the whole deal."

"Not quite," Declan said. His hand still stroked Rose's under the table. "I have a time limit. If in a fortnight I don't inform His Grace that Casshorn is dead and the device is destroyed, the Duke will take further measures."

"The Red Legion," Grandma said softly.

Declan nodded.

"What does that mean?" Lee Stearns asked.

Grandma's mouth flattened into a severe line. "When the Red Legion comes through, nothing remains."

"You may hide in the Broken," Declan said, "but they'll purge East Laporte. It will be like you were never here."

Lee glared. "They have no right!"

"Think," Tom Buckwell said. "Fifty fellows just like him. They'll come and wipe the place out, so we have nothing to come back to. That's what the U.S. did in Korea. They don't want us sitting in East Laporte spreading rumors of their doom machine. And he"—Tom stabbed his finger in Declan's direction—"he's the one who's gonna carry the responsibility for us getting wiped off the map on his soul. It will be his call. Nobody wants to make a call like that."

"Why are you here?" Adele asked softly. "Why did you choose to be the one?"

"I have my reasons," Declan said.

This wasn't going to get them anywhere. "There is a changeling," Rose said, ignoring Declan's sharp glance. His hand abruptly left hers. "Casshorn has some sort of hold over him. His name's William."

"Is he the one who hung Emerson on Dead Horse Oak?" Emily Paw asked.

Rose nodded. "Declan and William were friends, and he wants to save him."

"An army buddy, I bet." Tom Buckwell nodded. "Figures. It's good for us. Makes it nice and personal, so you'll fight harder. You got a plan?"

"I can take Casshorn in a one-on-one physical fight," Declan said. "But he knows this. I need to separate him from the hounds. Since the device produces the hounds continuously, one at a time, the only way to get Casshorn alone is to rapidly destroy a large number of his beasts. Unfortunately, he seems to be directing their actions. He may not be fully human, but he would recognize a trap. I would know more if I could survey his position and see what sort of odds we were facing."

Jeremiah rose. "I think we've heard enough. We need to confer. Let's let the young ones get some air."

AS the wooden door shut behind her and Declan, Rose blinked against the sunlight and sank on the porch. "Well, that went as well as it could."

"You told them about William," he said.

"Yes, I did. Words like 'duty' don't mean much to them. They understand friendship and family. They wouldn't touch you because you're powerful and they're afraid of retribution from the Weird. They can't hurt the hounds, because they absorb magic. But they could hurt William. With things the way they are, if they saw a strange changeling, they might act first and ask questions later. They're all cursers, Declan. You saw what Jeremiah did to that bird, and you know what my grandmother tried to do to you."

She faced the weighty look in his eyes. "I know it's a private thing between you and him. But it was best they knew. They might not hurt him now."

"Why the sudden love for William?"

"Are you jealous?" She narrowed her eyes.

"You didn't answer my question."

"I worry about William, because he's important to you," she said. "Because I feel that until the two of you settle things between yourselves, it will eat at you. And if William's truly helping Casshorn . . . You'll have to kill him, won't you?"

"Yes," Declan said.

He would have to kill his best friend. Rose looked away, at the trees, at the grass, at her hands. Her stomach churned. It had all gone so wrong somehow, and so fast, and fixing it seemed impossible. Two weeks ago, life was a normal drudgery, and seemingly overnight, her stable world became the place where demonic creatures hunted small boys so they could eat them and the man she loved had to pick between his survival and the life of his best friend.

She was caught in an ugly dream and couldn't wake up, and the fear that clung to her every second was worst of all. She was scared for the boys and Grandma and terribly frightened for Declan, so badly it hurt inside, as if her bones ached. If she let herself dream just a little, she glimpsed a hint of fragile happiness that might even be hers, if not forever, then for a little while, and it was about to be ripped away from her. She was so sick of being scared. "You said you were a Marshal. Is this what you do?" she asked. "This is what your job is like?"

Declan nodded.

"And it's always like this?"

"This is probably the worst," he said. "But yes, there are always choices I don't want to make. It's my duty as Marshal. A lot is riding on my back right now. If I fail to kill Casshorn, people will die, the Duke of the Southern Provinces will be dishonored and possibly have to step down, your town will be wiped out, and I'll lose you. And I don't even know if I have you."

Rose chewed on that. Did "I don't even know if I have you" mean "I don't even know if you like me" or did it mean "I don't even know if I'll win the challenges and get to own you"?

"You won't lose me just because you've failed," she said.

"If I fail, I'll be dead," Declan said.

Suddenly she was angry. All that worry and fear mixed in her, and him talking so calmly about dying squeezed it together into pure fury. She was furious at Casshorn for putting them all through it. "Oh no, you won't."

His eyebrows crept up.

"You'll survive this," she told him. "I'll be right there to make sure you'll make it out alive, even if I have to drag your bloody body out of the Wood on my back. I still have a challenge left, and I *will* stump you with it. You won't rob me of my victory, Lord Camarine."

A light sparked in his eyes. "I'll have to postpone my dying then."

"You do that," she told him. "I don't know what will become of this thing between you and me, but no brainsick blueblood crackpot is going to take away my chance to find out."

"Have you made up your mind, then?" he asked.

"About what? About surrendering to your manly charms?"

"Yes."

"Not yet," she said. "I'm still thinking about it."

"Is there anything I can do to persuade you?" He leaned forward, a dangerously focused expression on his face. His green eyes turned warm and wicked, and she froze, snared in his stare.

"I can't think of anything," she murmured.

He was close, entirely too close, only a couple of inches away. She saw his lips, curving in a sly smile, a network of thin scars by his left eye, his long eyelashes . . .

"Are you sure, Miss Drayton?" he asked, his voice low and husky.

"I'm sure," she whispered, and then he closed the distance between them.

His hand cupped the back of her head, and he kissed her. She opened her mouth, tasted iced tea and Declan. He smelled of sweat, mixed with light sandalwood musk and sun-kissed skin. She would recognize his scent anywhere, just as she would recognize the strength in the arms around her. He held her as if daring the world to come over and make an issue of it. She let herself sink into that embrace, sliding her hands up the hard muscles of his chest to his neck and to his short hair. He pulled her closer, kissing harder, hungrier, and she licked the inside of his mouth and molded herself to him. Declan growled, a very male possessive sound that sent a thrill from her neck down her spine.

The floor behind them creaked. They broke apart a frac-

tion of a second before the door swung open. Rose stared
straight ahead, trying to catch her breath.

"Well, it took some doing, but they decided to help you,"
Grandma's voice said behind her. "We have a plan, or some
semblance of one. Tom's coming out to explain it to you.
He's all excited at playing soldier again. What exactly happened to the two of you? You look like you got into my pantry and ate all of my jam."

"We're fine," Rose managed, stealing a glance at Declan.
He looked halfway between shell-shocked and frustrated.

"All right then." Éléonore's tone plainly said she wasn't
sure what they were selling, but she sure as hell wasn't buying it. She lingered for another long breath, shook her head,
and went inside.

"We need a barn," Declan said.

"What?"

"A barn," he said, with the gravity of a commander planning an attack. "We need a barn or one of those storage areas
for the Broken vehicles."

"A garage?"

He gave her a short nod. "A private, relatively remote lo-
cation, with thick walls to dampen the sound and preferably a
sturdy door I could bolt from the inside, keeping your grandmother, your brothers, and all other painfully annoying spec-
tators out . . ."

Rose began to laugh. A make-out bunker . . .

"I'm glad you find our dilemma hilarious," he said dryly.

Tom Buckwell emerged onto the porch then and squeezed
his giant body between the two of them. "Here's the deal.
Attacking Casshorn head-on is straight out, because he's got
too many hounds with him, right?"

"Right," Rose said.

"To get to Casshorn, you need to nuke the hounds. To
nuke the hounds, you have to separate them from Casshorn
or attack him at his lair. This is what guys in the Broken call
a catch-22. Here's how I'm going to make your day . . . you
do have ranks in the Weird, don't you?"

"We do," Declan said.

"What was yours?"

"Legionnaire First Class."

"What is that? Is that like an officer?"

"No," Declan said.

"An NCO, then." Tom grinned. "I was a Staff Sergeant myself. Suppose I call you 'Sergeant,' would you go with that?"

"That will be fine," Declan said.

"Good then, Sahgent."

Rose rolled her eyes. Funny how "sergeant" became "sahgent" all of a sudden, and Tom had morphed from a surly bear into Declan's best buddy, all smiles and camaraderie. It was a classic Edge tactic. She'd seen it employed with outsiders before. The six elders didn't know Declan, they had no way of verifying the information he'd given them, and they were afraid of him. So Tom Buckwell had chosen to play a "friend," hoping to establish common ground, get into Declan's confidence, and stab him in the back if necessary. With some men, it might have worked, but Declan had good instincts and Buckwell was laying the none-too-bright we're-all-just-army-buddies on too thick.

"Casshorn might be a goner, but he was human to begin with, so he's still vulnerable there. We build a trap, and the elders will curse his arse into sleep. No matter how inhuman he is, the six of us aren't without skill. We'll hold him at least for a few hours. Meanwhile you and Rose here lead the hounds into the trap, kill them off, and then go after Casshorn. Good plan, yeah?"

"Great plan," Declan said. "What kind of a trap?"

"Haven't thought that far yet," Tom said.

"How are you going to curse him?" Rose asked. Sleep would be the obvious choice: unlike pain curses, it was subtle. Casshorn wouldn't even know anything was wrong. He'd simply get tired and fall asleep. "To cast sleep, we need a thing of his. Hair. Piece of clothing."

"Haven't thought that far yet," Tom said.

Some plan. Rose sighed. Over half a millennium of experience between the six of them, and this was what they came up with.

"Trap first," Declan said. "Without the trap, we have no plan. Bullets don't work against the hounds. They go straight through their bodies. Dismemberment works. Flash does, too, but we have only two flashers. Fire, but they know to steer clear of it."

"So it has to be something subtle. Can we poison them?" Tom asked.

Declan shook his head. "I doubt it. I know that the first time it was found, they had tried hemlock and arsenic on hounds with no result. Ideally, we need a slow-acting trap, something that would kill them slowly or in a gradual fashion so as not to alarm Casshorn out of his sleep."

"Like drowning?" Tom asked. "Lure the hounds out into a lake and drown them one by one?"

"Possibly. Unfortunately, they can hold their breath for a long time, and they're good swimmers."

Silence fell. Leanne wandered over and came to sit in a rocking chair.

"Too bad we couldn't electrocute the hound like that troll," Declan said.

"Oh, now that is a capital idea, Sahgent." Tom nodded. "Except we don't know if electricity works against then."

"It does," Leanne said. "Before Karen Roe left for the Broken, she told me she killed a hound with electricity. Tasered it to death."

"How do you Taser something to death?" Tom's eyebrows rose.

"Her mom got it into her head that Karen's house would get broken into and bought her one of those expensive gun-looking Tasers," Leanne said. "You pop a cartridge in and fire, then you disconnect the cartridge and reload. She's kind of hard to buy for, so every Christmas or so the family would get her some of those cartridge packs. They're like sixty bucks for two. She shot the beast once, but it didn't croak, so she just kept reloading the cartridges and shooting it until it stopped wiggling. She said the damn hound cost her over two hundred bucks."

"Well, we can't take time to Taser them, and I just don't see how we'd be able to stick each one of them with a live wire. They'd overrun us," Tom said.

"Why don't you just put the two together? Drop a live wire into a lake and electrocute the lot of them until they drown?" Rose asked.

The men looked up, and she found herself on the receiving end of two stares, one green, one brown.

"What?"

"That's a good plan," Declan said.

"It might work," Tom said.

Declan glanced at him. "Is there a large enough lake nearby?"

"Laporte Pond," Tom said.

Declan got up. "I need to see it."

Tom nodded. "It's perfect. It will take us a good hour to get there on foot, though, so if we want to go today, best to do it now. I need to check on my daughters anyhow, make sure they cleared out. Holly, I'm not worried about, but Nicki meanders like molasses in January. She was supposed to be out this morning, but I bet she's still there, squatting on her bags like a mother hen."

"I'll come, too," Rose said, "If you're going to curse Casshorn, I'll have to pick up a couple of things from Grandma's. The boys are reasonably safe here for the time being."

Leanne sighed. "That's all good, but how are you going to make the hounds go into the water?"

Declan's face was unreadable. "We'll use bait."

"Like what?" Leanne frowned.

"One of us," Rose said. "The hounds are attracted to magic. He means me or him, Leanne. One of us will be bait."

TWENTY-TWO

ROSE hugged herself and peered at the placid, tea-colored water of Laporte Pond. Twelve hundred feet long and close to five hundred feet across at the widest spot, the pond sat in a depression just west of town. Tall grayish cypresses flanked it like guards, their bloated trunks blocking the shore completely except for the far west end. A broken, dilapidated dock jutted sadly from the center of the pond.

Next to her, Declan crouched and dipped his fingers into the water. Tom Buckwell gave him a wide berth. Declan wasn't buying all his "Aw, shucks, Sahgent" nonsense, and she suspected Buckwell realized that as well, because he watched Declan the way one would watch a large predatory animal.

"There used to be a rowboat," she explained. "You could take it to the dock and fish. The boat sank about two years ago, and nobody bothered to get another one. And you can't really swim in it—too much algae."

Declan pivoted on his feet and glanced up to where twin power lines were etched against the sky.

"We're stealing power from the Broken," Tom explained. "Used to be there was no way to run a power line into the Edge. But about fifty years ago, the boundary crawled out farther into the Broken, about forty feet or so. Nobody knows what caused it, but when it was done crawling, we found a power pole in the Edge and the line was live. We got together and made a deal with the local co-op that owned the pole. We pay them a shitload of money, and they don't ask what's draining their power."

Declan looked at the dock. Rose followed his gaze. The dock wasn't very big. Twelve by twelve feet. Old tires hitched to its sides bobbed in the water. Either she or Declan would be on that dock, flashing to get the hounds' attention. She'd been thinking about it for the last two hours, and the more she thought about it, the more certain she became that she should be the one. She could do it. Get on the dock. Electrify the pond. Flash a few times to attract the hounds and watch them pile into the deadly water. Simple enough. How hard could it be, right?

She pictured herself on the dock, surrounded by hounds. And what if electricity didn't work on them? Alarm squirmed through her. No, it was a mistake to think like that. She raised her chin up a bit. It would be fine. Even if the electricity didn't kill them, it would be fine. She had more than enough flash to deal with them.

If she stood on the dock instead of Declan, he would be safe. He could go after Casshorn while she dealt with the hounds. Casshorn would be asleep, and Declan would have an easier time dealing with him. If she could just occupy the hounds, he might come out of the fight alive.

Rose hugged herself tighter and glanced at Declan. He was looking at her.

"A man who knows what he's doing could hold that dock for a long time," Tom was saying. "I figure we cut the line there." He pointed at a break between two cypresses. I know some fellows in town who work at a tire-retreading plant. We can get some bias tire tread—the stuff comes in rolls—and roll it out on that dock to insulate it and keep you from slipping into the water, 'cause if the beasts get to the dock, you'll be standing in some slimy gore. We'll get you some rubber-soled boots, and you'll be good to go."

"There is no need for him to be on the dock," Rose said. "I can do it. I'll be fine. My flash is almost as powerful as his."

Tom made a low grumbling noise into his beard.

"Casshorn will be asleep," she said. "His hounds will be occupied. It's the perfect time for Declan to go after them."

"No," Declan said.

"Declan, this makes total sense," she said.

"No."

Tom shrugged. "If he says no, it's a no. It's his show."

"Why the hell not?" She crossed her arms. "It's a good idea. You won't get another clean shot at him like that, Declan!"

He simply rose. "I'll escort you to your house."

Tom furrowed his eyebrows at them. "Well, you sort it out between yourselves. I'll swing by my daughters' places and pick you up at your house in about an hour. Two, if I have to drag Nicki out of the Edge kicking and screaming."

THEY didn't speak on the way to Éléonore's house. Adele had plenty of supplies at Wood House, but any self-respecting curser preferred to use her own. If nothing else, Grandma would feel better with familiar things. Rose collected the twigs and herbs while Declan stood guard over her, and she had to restrain herself to keep from smacking him to get the grim expression off his face.

They returned to Rose's house in silence. "Would you like some tea?" Rose asked as they went up the steps.

He nodded.

She went into the kitchen. He had no reason to be stubborn about it. Her plan made perfect sense. It also had one added benefit, which she decided wasn't important enough to mention. If things went wrong—and they were bound to go wrong when you're standing on a rotting hunk of wood in the middle of an electrified lake surrounded by monsters—if things went wrong, she would go down alone. Declan would still survive to fight another day. He had more of a chance against Casshorn than she did.

It was a good plan. She just needed Declan to see it.

She poured the boiling water into the teapot, set the tea to steep, and went in search of him.

She found him behind the house, at the woodshed. He sat on the bench, his larger sword on his lap, and he slowly, methodically drew a soft cloth along the blade.

Rose sat on a tree stump scarred with the strikes of countless wood axes and waited. He ignored her.

"My way is a good way, Declan. You know it is. My control is better than yours. I'm more precise."

He glanced up. His eyes were pure white. Great, his

brights were on, but nobody was driving. She had to make him see reason.

"Is this some sort of blueblood chivalry thing? Because I have news for you, you can't exactly afford to be chivalrous, Declan. Right now, you're an army of one with me as your National Guard volunteer unit. You have to let me help, and this is the best way to do it."

He said nothing.

"At least talk to me, damn you!"

He set the sword aside and walked to her. The determination on his face shot a bolt of alarm down her spine. She backed away. He caught her and pushed her back lightly. Her back pressed against the wall of the house. She realized that for the first time they were truly alone, with no risk of interruptions. Well, if he thought he could bully her into backing down, he had another think coming.

"Rose."

Rose jerked aside, but he barred her escape with his arm. "You're stronger, I get it," she ground out. She tried to push him aside, but she might as well have tried to push a train. He didn't move an inch.

"Rose," he said softly. "Look at me."

She glared at him. Their stares connected, and there was something so arresting and possessive in his grass green eyes that words died on her lips. He looked at her like she was some great treasure. Like nothing else mattered.

He looked at her like he loved her.

Warmth touched her cheeks, and she knew she blushed. He looked her over, studying her neck, her eyes, her throat, slowly, taking his time. She was locked in his arms. The heat of his body seeped through the thin fabric of her shirt. She smelled him, that very familiar scent of sandalwood, and clove oil he had used to clean his sword, and sweat. His chest pressed on her, the muscles hard but supple, and her nipples tightened. She was caught.

"I'm going on that dock instead of you," she said.

"No."

"You don't understand."

"I understand perfectly."

His big body braced hers. His hips kept her pinned. He

raised his hand and slid his fingers up the side of her neck in a long caress, up her chin, and to her lips. She shivered. He brushed her lower lip with a calloused thumb.

"Kissing me won't make me more agreeable," she whispered.

"I'm not trying to make you more agreeable." His voice was rough and low. "I just can't help myself."

The muscles on his arms flexed, and she realized Declan was fighting for control.

He swallowed, his eyes dark.

A million reasons to get away streaked through her head. He was a blueblood, and she was an Edge mongrel. He lied to her. He wanted to own her. They had no future together. He ... If someone told her that right now in this very moment, trapped between the wall of her own house and Declan's rigid body, that she could have one thing and one thing only before she died, she would choose to be with him.

Nothing good ever happened to people who didn't take chances.

She kissed him, molding herself against his large frame, supple softness to his hardness.

His control snapped. He lunged for her, pushing her against the wall, and kissed her back, furious and passionate, drinking her in. The echo of the kiss rolled through her body, dragging a low moan from her. She slid against him, working her hands up the hard muscles of his back.

He pulled her to him and buried his face in her neck. His teeth and tongue played with her skin, rasping over the sensitive spot on her pulse, painting heat over her flesh. Warmth spread through her. Declan kissed her again and again. Her body tightened. He ground into her, and she slid up and down with him, giving soft resistance to the hard thrust of his erection.

His voice was a hot breath in her ear. "God, I want you."

"I want you, too," she whispered. She wanted him so badly that every time he touched her, she wanted to hold on to him to keep him from letting go. The thought of him standing on that dock, collapsing under the weight of hundreds of hounds, almost made her scream in frustration. He wasn't going to die there. "I'm still going on that dock."

His voice was low and so suffused with need, it was almost a snarl. "I know. I'm coming with you."

"What?"

"We'll do it together."

He thrust his hand under hers, pushed her bra down, releasing her aching breast, and brushed the nipple. A jolt of pleasure, intense and unexpected, rippled through her.

"I can handle the hounds. You don't have to . . ." she whispered.

"Yes, I do."

He kissed her again, stealing her breath, and nipped her lip with his teeth. She pulled at his T-shirt. She wanted him naked, she wanted to feel his skin against hers.

He pulled away from her and swept her off her feet. "Bed."

She wound herself about him, kissing his neck and the corner of his jaw. "Good idea."

They tore through the house and into the bedroom. He dropped her on the bed, grasped the fabric of her T-shirt, pulled up, and the old worn-out cotton tore in his hands. "Sorry."

"I have another one." She pulled off his shirt and ran her hands down his body, from his chest over the hard ridges of his stomach, and then she was sliding him out of his jeans and rubbing her hand down the hard shaft of his erection. He made a raw animal sound in his throat and stripped the last shreds of clothing from her. For a moment she saw him towering above the bed, tall, golden, knitted with carved muscle.

She was too hot and too wet and too impatient.

He lunged for her, and she met him halfway, kissing, rubbing, stoking the fire inside both of them. His tongue played on her skin. He cupped her left breast, stroking the nipple with his fingers until it ached. She moaned. His hips slid between her legs. He dipped his head down and caught her nipple in his hot mouth, sending a wave of pure pleasure through her. She dug her fingers into the hard muscle of his back and arched herself, welcoming him. "Now," she whispered. "Now, Declan, don't wait."

He heard her. His lips found hers. He thrust into her, and she gasped. Her body resonated with pleasure, wanting, demanding more. She ground against him.

He thrust again and again, deep, hard, building to a rapid fiery rhythm, his weight a steady sweet pressure on her. She was full, so wonderfully full of him, and she wanted more.

She kissed his jaw and his throat, and he thrust harder. She clawed at his back, taut with strain, and the aching need within her blossomed into a cascade of bliss. She felt herself rising higher and higher, propelled by his thrusts and lost in the hot glide of their bodies, until something within her snapped. Pleasure drowned her, smothering all thought. She screamed his name. Her body screamed with her, gripping him, pumping. He clenched and emptied himself into her with a hoarse growl. They lay together in a hot, sweaty tangle, and for a while, lost in the aftershocks, she couldn't tell which limbs were hers and which were his.

"That was not the way it was supposed to go," he said, his voice still raspy with echoes of lust.

"How was it supposed to go?"

He pulled her to him, closing his arms around her, and Rose sank into him, implausibly happy. He ran his fingers along her arm. "Slow and sensuous. Sophisticated."

She turned on her side and kissed him. "How terribly inappropriate of you, Earl Declan Riel Martel Camarine."

"You've remembered my name. I feel the need to celebrate this momentous occasion."

"I thought we just did that," she murmured, out of breath. "But if you insist on a do-over, I'm sure we can do this again in the near future."

"Do you know what happens when you overflash?" he asked softly.

"No."

"I've done it once." He pulled her close, his muscled arm under her breasts. "We were trapped in a field while the Gaul's summoners ran a horde of marloks at us. They're simian animals, large predatory apes. There was no cover and no support. There were just the five of us, and we stood back to back and flashed. I remember my mouth was full of blood. My vision wavered. I felt like my arms were stretching out into the distance."

"What happened?"

"William went into *rending*. Changelings do this once in a

while, especially after puberty. They lose touch with reality and go berserk. He went crazy, and we just hit the ground, because when he *rends*, he kills everything. I'd asked him about it once, and he told me *rending* is going to the place where there is no God. Make of that what you will. When he finally wore himself out, the five of us were the only things alive on the field."

"What would've happened if you had kept going, had kept flashing?" she asked.

"I would've died. I wouldn't have even known it. You'd think that you could push just a touch further, and then the world would fade and so would your life." He kissed her cheek. "I won't let it happen to you."

She frowned.

"You don't know when to stop," he said. "You overdo it. I've watched you flash for two hours straight, when you were trying to get Ataman's defense down. You have no clue where your limits are."

She rose on her elbow. "Declan . . ."

"There were times when I've deferred to you. The time when you stopped me from going after Simoen or the time when you told your elders about William. I did so because you understood the situation better. It's your turn to defer to me. I know what I'm talking about, Rose. I was a professional soldier for over a decade. You're brilliant, but you need training. If you go on that dock alone, you'll die, and I won't let it happen."

"No." She pushed away from him. "Don't you see—"

"I see." He pulled her back and kissed her. "You'll magnificently kill the first wave of the hounds, and then the second wave will tear your throat out, and everyone will cry at your funeral and describe how you laid down your life for the good of your neighbors."

She recoiled.

He reached over, picked up her hand, and kissed her fingers. "We do this my way. We both survive, and then we deal with Casshorn." His stare fixed her. "Promise me, Rose."

What he said made sense. She wasn't too proud to understand that, and she still got what she wanted—he wouldn't be on the dock alone. "Okay," she said simply. "We'll do it your way. But we still need something from Casshorn for this curse to work."

Declan's eyebrows furrowed. "Do you think George is strong enough to reanimate a creature? Only for a short while."

"He might be," she said. "We'll have to ask him."

"If he can do it, then I might have a plan."

His hand wandered down her body, stroking. He kissed her, and she slid tighter against him.

"Rose?" Tom's gruff voice called from the porch.

Declan swore.

GEORGE sat on a fallen log and looked at the three dead crows lying on the ground before him. Sad, black bodies. Lifeless. They had been carefully killed, with a bow and arrow. Not a lot of damage to repair.

Behind him, Jack sniffed at the air. He probably thought the birds would make a nice snack. To the right, Mémère and Rose sat on an old wooden log.

"I can't believe you're going to make him do this." Mémère was angry. Her cheeks were flushed.

"He'll raise something again, sooner or later," Rose said.

"But not so soon!"

Rose was using her "reasonable" voice. He never won an argument with that voice.

"When would it be not too soon?" Rose asked.

"I don't know!" Mémère waved her arms. "Not now."

"If it was up to you, not too soon would mean never."

"And what's wrong with that?"

"You can't expect him never to use his talent again," Rose said.

"George," Declan said.

George looked at him, crouched by the crows.

"What I'm about to ask you to do is called combat necromancy. We're going to play some games first, and then we'll do the hard part. Understand?"

George nodded.

"Before, when you raised things, you felt a connection between you and them, right?"

George nodded again. It felt like having a fish on a very thin line, always shivering and tugging the line, but not too hard.

"And sometimes you stopped them from doing things. Like the time you stopped your grandfather from attacking Rose."

George nodded again. He could do that. He didn't do it very often, because he wanted things to be alive and do things on their own, but yes, he could do that.

"I want you to take it a step further," Declan said. "I'd like you to raise one of those birds and keep a very good control of it. You have to understand that this bird is raised for this one mission only. Once the mission is over, you must let it go, because it did its job and it deserves to rest. Do you understand?"

George nodded.

Declan kept looking at him.

"I understand," George said.

"Go ahead," Declan said.

George touched the bird on the right. She was the smallest, and he felt sorry for her the most. The bird pulled at his magic, it stretched, snapped, and Georgie recoiled, biting his lip. It always hurt when he raised something. He couldn't see the arrow hole under the feathers, but he felt it, and he fed a little of his magic down the line, closing it up, nice and neat, just in case.

The bird shivered. Slowly, she stretched one leg, then the other, rolled, and got to her feet.

Mémère sucked in her breath. "Now you've done it. You've started the whole thing over again."

"Very good." Declan rose to his feet and moved to stand by the bird. "I want you to close your eyes and turn around, keeping the bird very still. I'm going to touch the bird, and I need you to tell me when I do."

George closed his eyes. A faint touch disturbed the magic. "Now," he said.

"Very good," Declan said. "What am I doing now?"

"You're pinning the wings to the body."

"I need you to tell me when you feel me let go."

A long moment passed. The pressure on the crow vanished. "Now!"

"Excellent. You can turn around now."

Declan walked away until several yards separated them. "Try to make it walk toward me."

"Her," Georgie corrected. "It's a girl bird."

"Sorry. Please make her walk toward me."

George tugged on the line. He'd never before tried to make a bird walk. Stopping the creatures from moving was easy. This was harder. The crow stumbled and spun in place.

"Take your time," Declan said.

George concentrated. The longer he focused on the magic between them, the more complex it became: at first it was a line, then it was a whole bunch of thinner lines, woven together, and then the lines fractured into a glowing web that clutched at the bird. He tried to tug on the web. The crow jerked and fell into the dirt. Georgie shook his head, trying to clear his vision.

"It's all right, Georgie, you don't have to do it," Mémère said.

"Grandmother, let him be," Rose said. "Please."

George sighed. This just wasn't the way to do it. "Get over to Declan," he whispered.

The crow picked herself up and spread her wings. She took to the air, flew a few feet, and landed on Declan's shoulder.

"Sorry," George said.

"It's good," Declan said. "Try it again."

George nodded. It took him a good ten minutes to figure out what he needed to do. He had to concentrate very closely on the path before the crow to get her to walk. If he let up, she would fly over to Declan. When the crow had finally done her little walk, George let out a happy sigh.

"Tired?" Declan asked.

"No."

"New game, then." Declan opened his hand and showed him a small reddish rock. He tossed the rock into the dirt. "Can she bring it back?"

The crow swooped, grasped the rock, flew back, and dropped it into Declan's palm. George smiled.

Declan raised his eyebrows. "This is supposed to be harder than walking the bird."

"It's easier for me." All he had to do was to concentrate on the rock and then on Declan.

"He used to make the birds steal cherries for us," Jack said.

Declan bent back and hurled the rock into the bushes. The crow took off from his shoulder and followed the path of the rock, perching on a branch. George frowned. He couldn't see the rock from where he sat.

"You can't find it?" Declan asked.

"I have to look through her eyes to find it," George said quietly.

"And you don't like doing that," Declan said.

George shook his head.

"Because you forget you're not a bird when you do it? And it's hard to remember how to get back?"

George startled. "How did you know that?"

"My aunt is a necromancer. What I'm asking you to do is called necromantic possession. There is a trick to it. If I promise you that I can help you get back to your body, will you try it?"

"Rose!" Mémère jumped off the log.

"George, you don't have to do it, if you don't want to," Rose said. "It's your choice. Nobody will be angry if you don't."

George thought about it. He'd done it only once with a cat, because Jack was a cat whenever he wanted, and he had never been one and wanted to know what it was like. The only reason he had returned to his body at all was because Jack found him, sitting still in the yard, and tackled him from behind, knocking the wind out of him. The worst thing was that he couldn't even remember what it was like to be a cat. He just remembered the vague, scary feeling of looking and looking for something and not being able to find it, and knowing that he was looking for his own body.

He wanted to know what it was like to be a bird.

George looked at Declan. "Okay," he said.

"Whenever you're ready." Declan nodded.

George looked at the crow, grasped the line of magic stretching between them, and pulled, propelling himself into the black body.

The world exploded into colors for which there was no name. For a long moment, he sat still, lost in the vibrancy and shimmering glow of the leaves, until something nudged him gently from the back of his mind.

The rock.

He was supposed to find the rock.

He hopped off the branch into the leaves and searched the ground. There it was, glittering with a dozen hues. So pretty. Pretty, pretty rock.

He took it into his beak and crashed through the bush. The sunlit grass was so beautiful. In the distance, he saw figures: two standing together, crystal clear and glowing, one stronger, the other weaker. Words surfaced in his mind. Rose. Mémère. He wasn't sure what they meant, but he knew they made him feel good. He saw another figure, smaller, with an odd tint to it. He knew it as well. Jack. A fourth figure waited to his right, the largest of them all. Declan. He had to do something for Declan. He felt drawn to him, and he didn't know why. He spread his wings and flew to him, landing on his arm, Declan warm and rough under his claws. The rock fell from his beak.

There was a fifth figure, one he hadn't seen before. It slumped on the ground, curled into a ball. There was something oddly familiar about it, but it didn't glow like the others.

Declan opened his mouth and made a noise.

Ice slammed into him. He cried out, the world swirled, and George jerked up, gasping. His face was wet. Next to him, Jack stood with an empty bucket.

Rose's arms closed about him. They felt so comfortable and warm.

"Shock breaks it," Declan said. "Doesn't take much, especially if he didn't spend a lot of time in the other form. The longer he possesses something, the more intense the shock has to be. We had necroscouts who'd burn each other to get out, but that was after hours of immersion. We'll only need a minute, if that."

"You okay?" Rose asked.

George smiled, the swirl of colors slowly fading in his head. "I remember this time," he said. "I remember what it's like to be a bird."

TWENTY-THREE

THE deeper one dived into the Wood, the darker it became. The trees grew taller and thicker, their trunks rising high above like colossal textured columns. Their branches spread and twisted, bound together by moss and lichen and bright blue bunches of horsetail vines, dripping down like the hair of phantom tree spirits. The canopy formed its own separate level, removed from the forest floor, and as Rose found her way through the Wood, she glanced around once in a while above to make sure Jack hadn't gotten away from Grandma. He was none too pleased at staying behind.

She looked at Declan, who strode on, seemingly at home in the wilderness. He carried a small pack. In the pack, two crows rode, carefully secured. Back at Wood House, George had reanimated both. He didn't possess them at the moment, but he would sense when they were free and take them over.

It was a simple plan. They would get close enough to Casshorn, wait for the right moment, release the crows, and let George use them to steal an item. Then the crows would fly away and they would chase them, retrieve the item, and get away, hopefully alive.

George would be allowed only five minutes of possession. Five minutes later, ready or not, Grandma and Jeremiah would awaken him. Five minutes was a safe enough time limit, according to Declan. She didn't want to put George through it, but they had no choice. It was a flimsy plan all around, but it was the only one they had.

She'd spoken to Jeremiah and Leanne. Once George awakened and they no longer needed his gift, Jeremiah would take him and Jack and Leanne and her son out into the Broken, supposedly to get supplies. She had given Leanne enough money for a decent hotel room. With her strength, Leanne would be able to handle the boys. No matter what would happen in the Edge, her brothers would be safe.

The Wood thrived around them. Life reigned here. A hundred small noises filled the silence: birds bickering, squirrels screeching angrily at Edger ermines that came to steal babies out of their nests, badgers grunting heavily, and the careful coughing bark of the fox sounded so near yet far. Edger moss sheathed the trunks, its lady's-slipper-shaped flowers all but glowing with pastel reds, yellows, lavender, and purple. Fallen trees served to anchor new life, sending shoots up and giving purchase to vines. The perfume of countless flowers and herbs floated in the air, mixing with animal scents. Even the light, filtered through the canopy, was verdant and emerald green.

In the chaos of the Wood, she and Declan were just two small motes of life. At other times, she would've loved to sit and listen to the Wood breathe, but today she didn't have that luxury.

"Careful," Rose called out, when Declan paused by a patch of bright pink grass that had broken through the carpet of pine straw and dirt-hugging creepers. "Very poisonous."

She reached to the nearest vine, snagged a handful of pale yellow berries, and handed some to him. "False cherries," she said.

He popped one into his mouth. "Tastes like the real thing."

She could find no fault with the way Declan moved through the woods—like a wolf, soundless and light on his feet. His face had closed in again. The hardness around his mouth was back and so was the cold, distant stare.

She had insisted on coming with him against Éléonore's wishes.

Her grandmother had been beside herself. "Why do you have to take him there?"

"Somebody has to. He doesn't know the Wood."

"Let Tom or Jeremiah do it."

"We might have to run out of there like a bat out of hell,

and I can run much faster than either Tom or Jeremiah, and I flash hotter. Besides, he trusts me. He'll be comfortable with me."

Éléonore had pursed her lips. "I wish you wouldn't. I only have one granddaughter."

Looking at Declan, Rose got a feeling that he also wished she hadn't come. "My helping you bothers you that much, huh?" she asked finally.

"I wish I didn't have to rely on you."

"You didn't twist my arm. It's my home that's invaded and my family who is the target."

"I understand that." He shook his head. "The point of being a professional soldier is so civilians don't have to fight. We do the things we do so people like you can go to sleep safe. And here I am, relying on a civilian woman and a child's talent. Yes, it bothers me. As well it should."

"If I go away with you—" she started.

His head came up sharply. He looked at her.

"If I go away with you and if we decide to be together, eventually you'll go away on some mission and I'll be left at home, pacing and biting my nails, hoping you'll come back alive."

"It's not always quite that dramatic," he said quietly.

"But it's often dangerous."

"Yes," he admitted.

"What would I have to do to come with you?" she asked.

He gave her a frosty stare. "You would have to pass some security examinations and competency tests to be registered as one of my operatives. It's a bad idea. I would be more worried about you than about the mission."

She smiled. He didn't say no. "I suppose I'll just have to learn to be good enough so you don't worry so much. I hope you're a good teacher."

"You're an impossible woman," he growled.

"Hey, I didn't show up at your house demanding you challenge me. You were the knucklehead who picked me, so you only have yourself to blame."

They halted in unison. They stood at the edge of a narrow meadow. The Wood beyond it had lost its vibrant color. The trunks stood bare and grim, and the underbrush had shriveled to a limp tangle of wilted leaves. The magic was gone. The forest lay dead and oddly preserved, as if mummified. A taint of foul magic, alien and sharp, stained the dead trunks and withered grass. If it had color, it would drip from the Wood like purple putrid slime. The evidence of the hounds' presence.

"It's frightening what they do," Rose said.

Declan's arms closed about her for a brief moment and crushed her to him. He let her go almost immediately, but he'd packed so much into that one fierce hug: want, need, worry, reassurance . . . He'd protect her with his life. Strangely, it made her indignant. Nobody should have to be in the position of having another person give up their life for them. She didn't want the weight of Declan's death. The fear took a backseat, and cold anger started driving. Casshorn. If she had any hope for the future with Declan, or even without him, she had to destroy Casshorn and the hounds. That was the only way.

Declan would be there, fighting to the last. She had to do the same.

Together they walked into the blighted Wood.

TWENTY minutes later, Rose lay next to Declan on the edge of a ravine. Below them, the ground dropped off sharply. A strange contraption sat in the center of the ravine's floor, a tangled mess of gears and moving parts, as if an enormous clock had gotten violently sick and vomited all of its insides before turning inside out. In the center of the device hung an oblong cluster of pale silvery glow, like a large batch of cotton candy woven of luminescent fog.

Around the device, hounds lay side by side, packed tight like matches into a box. Rose tried to count them. Hundred and twelve. Hundred and thirteen. Hundred and . . . too many. *If they see us, we will be torn to pieces.*

The magic rising from the ravine nearly made her gag. It filled the gap, crawling along the ground and up the slope, as if it were too heavy to dissipate. She felt the mere traces of it, but when they slithered past, her whole body recoiled from the contact. She wanted to jump to her feet and run back into the Wood, to jump into a lake or to grab a handful of mud and scrub herself just to scrape the slimy patina off.

She clenched her teeth and lay absolutely still, afraid to breathe. Her mind painted a horde of hounds streaming up the wall of the ravine. She imagined wicked dagger teeth ripping into Declan, tearing flesh off his bones. All of what they were, all their fears, worries, happiness, all that made them human, didn't matter. To hounds, they were just magic-infused meat. Cold descended on her, locking her muscles. Her heart hammered.

Declan's hand came to rest on her shoulder. She looked at him, wide-eyed, and saw calm, steadying strength in his eyes. He didn't lose his head. He didn't seem afraid. She held on to his courage like a crutch and exhaled her panic in tiny, silent breaths.

Something stirred on the floor of the ravine.

Declan focused on the movement. His eyes turned glacially cold.

A clump of the hounds parted, and a tall figure rose, swaddled in a long cloak.

Casshorn.

There he was. They finally found the sonovabitch. Triumph filled her. Thought he could hide, did he?

Casshorn swayed, as if woozy, but righted himself. He flicked his fingers, and the hounds parted before him, clearing a path. Slowly he dragged himself to the device.

She stared at his back and wished him dead. If they were within flashing distance, she might have tried frying him.

The device emitted a screech of metal rubbing against metal. Gears whirled.

Casshorn crouched down and picked something off the ground.

The glowing cone in the center of the device split open. A dark object slid out, wrapped in a membrane laced with thick purple and yellow veins. The object fell to the ground with a wet thump and squirmed, stretching the membrane.

Casshorn approached it and pulled a large, wicked-looking hook into the light. A thick chain stretched from the hook, disappearing into a dead tree to the left.

The thing in the membrane wriggled. With a brutal strike, Casshorn stabbed the hook into the membrane and kicked a lever protruding from the wooden block next to him. The chain snapped taut, dragging the membrane sack across the ground and jerking it in the air, to the tree, where it hung suspended three feet from the ground.

Casshorn scratched at the membrane, brushing it away, revealing a fully formed hound writhing upside down on the hook. He grasped the beast by the head, and she saw Casshorn's hand. His fingers had grown very long, and on top of each one sat a two-inch black claw. Those claws dug into the beast's neck, but the hound did nothing to resist.

Casshorn struck. His claws sliced the hound's throat. A stream of gray spilled from the wound. Casshorn picked up a cup from the ground and held it under the stream. The liquid splashed into the cup and onto his hands. A few seconds later, the hound stopped jerking. The stream of fluid died. Casshorn wiped his hand on the beast's back and brought the cup to his lips.

Her stomach clenched. Rose clamped her hand over her mouth to keep from vomiting.

As Casshorn lifted the cup, the cloak slid off his shoulders. He was nude underneath it. He was very tall with broad shoulders and a large chest, but inhumanly thin and corded with tight muscle like a greyhound. Splotches of yellow and purple stained his skin. His arms and legs were disproportionately long.

Casshorn tipped the glass, turning, and she saw his face. He must have been a handsome man at some point. She still glimpsed echoes of it: the large hooded eyes, the square line of the jaw, the shadow of what had once been a broad, strong, masculine face. He must've looked similar to Declan in the past, but no longer. A network of veins stood out on his temples, like rope threaded under his skin. His long hair, still golden blond, had thinned and now dripped from his scalp in isolated clumps to his chest. His face sagged and wrinkled, and when he opened his mouth to swallow the contents of the glass, she caught sight of his teeth. His mouth was filled with bloodred fangs.

Casshorn emptied the glass. So that's how he did it. He paid for the immunity to the hounds' magic with his mind and his body.

Declan's strong fingers pressed on her arm. She glanced at him. His gaze was fixed on a point well above Casshorn, on the other side of the ravine. She looked and bit back a gasp before it had a chance to escape.

A wolf lay in the brush, solid black and huge, like a nightmare come to life. In her memory, he'd been enormous. She'd thought fear had played tricks on her, making him larger than he really was, but no, he really was that huge.

Declan's lips moved, and he mouthed a silent word. *William.*

The wolf shifted his gaze and saw her. His eyes flared with amber. His black lips rose in a silent snarl, and William showed them a mouth full of fangs. Rose shivered.

Something wasn't right. If William was in league with Casshorn, then what in the world was he doing hiding in the bushes?

A crash made them glance down. Casshorn had hurled his cup at the device, and it bounced off. He leaned back, dragged his clawed hands through his thinning mane, and began braiding it in a mechanical fashion, the way he must've done a thousand times. He'd managed to plait a couple of inches when the entire thing slid off his head, leaving him bald. Casshorn stared at the hair in his hand in disbelief and flung it from him. It caught on one of the gears and hung there.

They couldn't have asked for a better opportunity. Rose grabbed Declan's arm, clenching her fingers until he looked at her and whispered so quietly she could barely hear herself. "Hair. His hair."

Casshorn sank into the dirt. The sea of hounds brushed against him. He hugged one and put his cheek against the pale hide. The beast lay down on its side, and Casshorn lay atop it.

Declan nodded and reached to the pack next to him. Carefully they unwrapped the crows. Rose prayed George would see the hair. She'd stressed what he had to look for: clothes, a brush with hair on it, personal items, silverware . . . Hair, that much hair, just fresh off the body, was any curser's dream. Only blood was better and only short-term—it rotted too quickly.

The wolf's gaze burned her as they worked. The ravine ran almost two miles in every direction of tough wooded terrain. She knew William wouldn't be able to get to them, but the way he stared at them made her want to scream.

Rose clenched her bird. By now George would feel them handling the crows and would be paying attention. She pointed the bird so the hair was directly in front of it and whispered over and over, "Hair, hair, hair, hair, hair . . ."

Declan released his bird. A moment later she let hers go. The crows swooped down like two black rocks. Declan's crow plunged and came up, its claws caught in the fabric of Casshorn's cloak. "No," she whispered. "No, no, Georgie . . ."

A hound snapped up its head, then another. A dark body lunged up, and the crow went down.

The second bird made a slow circle above the hounds, turned, veered left—he was going after the cup. Rose's heart hammered. She squeezed her hands into fists, willing the bird to turn right.

At the last moment, the crow dropped right and snagged the braid off the gears.

A tendril of dark magic snapped from the device, stinging the bird's wings. Rose held her breath. *Come on, George, come on, you can do it.*

The crow faltered, jerked, beating its wings furiously, and flew up, higher and higher, disappearing beyond the trees heading back to East Laporte.

Rose dropped her head facedown into the dirt. He did it. Her brother did it.

Declan's hand gripped her shoulder and jerked her up, hard. In the ravine below them, the hounds were rising. Declan's face was dark. At the other end of the ravine, William retreated, crawling away.

They slithered from the cliff. Ten feet. Twelve. Fifteen. Twenty. Declan hauled her upright and breathed one word.

"Run!"

They dashed through the woods, running as fast as the terrain would allow. The tree trunks flew by. She leapt over the branches and crashed through the brush.

"Faster," Declan called directly behind her.

Rose squeezed out a burst of speed. The air seared her lungs. Her side began to hurt. She kept running. The woods blended into a blur, punctuated by her hoarse breaths.

They burst into a small glade. Declan caught her arm and spun her around. "We make a stand."

She doubled over, trying not to vomit. He didn't even look winded.

Declan pulled a sword from the sheath on his back and turned it over once. "Use short-range flash," he said. "The less noise we make, the better."

The first hound padded out of the bushes into the open. It tensed, the muscles along its long limbs contracted, and it leapt into the air.

Declan swung. The blade cleaved the hound in two, and he sank flash into the ruin of the body. Acrid fumes surged from the hound's carcass. Rose coughed and moved away from him. Short-range flash. She could do that.

A hound burst through the shriveled brush. It made for her, jumping in great leaps, maw gaping, bloodred fangs ready to rip. The four eyes glared at her with luminescent gray. The hound lunged, and Rose flashed. Her short, controlled burst of magic cleaved across the creature's shoulder all the way deep through the chest. The top half of the beast slid aside, betraying a glimpse of soft purplish innards filled with gray slime, and crashed to the side.

Another hound dashed at her from the right. Rose flashed again and watched its head roll through the dead grass.

A dark flood of the beasts came loping through the Wood, stark against the dull, magic-drained trees. It headed straight for them. In a moment they would be overwhelmed.

Rose leaned back and took a deep breath. A line of magic thrust from her, curving to the ground. It split into three and began to circle her.

The foremost beast sprinted, muscle flexing under the

bruise-colored pelt, legs pumping, horrible teeth bared. It
leaped at her and fell aside, cut in three pieces.

They made right for her. With her flash blazing bright, she
made an irresistible target. She concentrated on rotating the
arches as fast as she could, slicing through the hideous bodies until the ground grew wet with their gray sluice. To the
left, Declan struck at the stream of hounds, his blade a lethal
whirl. He cut with deadly precision, fast and unstoppable.
Every time his sword sliced, something died. He was absolutely beautiful.

The last hound paused on the edge of the clearing. Rose
dropped her flash and sent a single sharp bolt of blinding
white at it. Declan flashed at the same time, the two flashes
connected, and the hound went down.

The clearing was wet with gray blood and littered with
smoking bodies.

Declan looked her over. "Unhurt?"

She nodded.

"How many did we kill?" he asked.

She surveyed the carnage. "Fifty?"

"Twenty-two." He wiped his sword and slid it back into
his sheath.

"Only twenty-two?" She couldn't believe it. It seemed
like many more . . .

"Twenty-two." He took her by the arm. "Run. Before the
rest get here."

They ran through the woods.

"I don't think William's helping Casshorn," she said.

"I don't think so either."

"Then what is he doing here?"

"Hell if I know."

If William had been in league with Casshorn, he had only
to make a noise, and the entire swarm would've been on
them.

"What was that?" Declan asked.

"What?"

"The sphere of flash you did back there?"

"It's a modified Ataman's defense," she told him. "When I
saw William for the first time, I got scared he'd get through
and split the arch into three. For some reason, I can rotate

them a lot faster this way. Why, you never saw something like this before?"

"I don't think anyone has ever seen anything like this before," he told her. "Keep running."

THEY reached the palisade in record time. Grandma waited inside by the gates.

Declan did a little bow. *"Madame."*

"Yes, yes," she told him with a sour face. "Tom wants to see you inside."

Declan nodded.

"Did you get the hair?" Rose asked.

"We have it."

Declan disappeared into the building. Rose collapsed on the ground. She lay on her back, her arms and legs flung wide. Her body felt like wet cotton put through a washing machine.

"Are you all right?" Éléonore's face blocked the sky.

"Fine," she said, breathless. "I'll just lie here for a bit. He's made of iron: he runs very fast and never gets tired."

"The hooligans escaped," Éléonore said.

"What?"

"Jeremiah called me on your phone. He took them and Leanne with her boy out into the Broken, just as agreed. They sat all quiet and nice, until he stopped to make a right onto the freeway at the gas station, and then they threw the truck's door open and bolted."

Rose closed her eyes and groaned. *Why me?*

"Jeremiah and Leanne tried to catch them, but they're gone."

"They went back to the house." Rose pushed off the ground and sat. She felt a thousand years old. Where else would they go? "It's Jack's fault. He's convinced we'll all fail to fight Casshorn without his help, and he must've talked Georgie into it. I'll get them and take them out to Leanne. I doubt they'll come out for anyone but family, so it's either you or me, and it will have to be me, since you'll be cursing Casshorn."

"Hurry," Grandma said.

"All right." Rose pushed herself to her feet.

"Go!" Éléonore waved.

Rose headed for the gates. She briefly considered getting Declan but decided against it. He'd need to protect the palisade while they cast their curse, and she knew the Wood like the back of her hand. She'd be back in a couple of hours, after she dropped the boys with Leanne. The boys had to be taken to safety, and the faster she managed it, the better it was for everyone involved.

TWENTY-FOUR

ROSE jogged at a brisk trot down the road. Her body ached. There was clearly wisdom in all that running Declan did in the mornings. If she ever hoped to keep up with him, she'd have to take up running, even though she hated it with a passion. She walked a lot, but there was a world of difference between walking a few miles down the road and running for your life. And cleaning offices for ten hours a day didn't exactly improve her athletic ability. She'd have to ride better, too. She did well enough at slow speed, but a canter would have her hanging on for dear life, and the gallop was right out.

She recalled Declan being all indignant about the boys not being able to ride a horse. Like everyone had a damn horse in the Edge. The only reason she knew how to ride was because Grandpa had insisted on keeping his half-blind old mare, Lovely. She remembered riding her as a child. Lovely died a few years back, and Grandpa had never replaced her.

She wondered if Grandpa Cletus would've approved of Declan.

Rose rounded the turn and glimpsed the house. She braced herself. There would be angry yelling and tears. She'd get her way in the end, but it would take some harsh words.

A tall, dark-haired man stepped into the road from between the shrubs. He wore jeans and a black leather jacket over a faded T-shirt. Wild eyes looked at her, glowing like two pieces of amber.

William.

Rose halted.

He made no move to approach her. His face was grim, his mouth a severe line. "The kids are safe," he said. "I've watched over them."

Fear trickled down her neck. She reminded herself that she could fry him with her flash at any moment. "Why are you here, William?"

He shook his head. "I don't know."

She searched his face and saw a blank uncertainty tinted with wariness. That's exactly what Jack looked like when he blundered into the unfamiliar territory of human emotions and clenched up, not knowing what to say or do next. If Jack was any indication, William was stretched to his limit. He could snap and lash out at any moment.

"Come sit with me," she said, keeping her voice calm. "We'll talk."

He followed her to the house. She removed the ward stones, letting him in, and pointed to the porch chairs. He sat on the steps instead, and she sat on the other side, keeping enough distance between them. She glanced at the kitchen window and saw two faces. They ducked, but not before she hit them with a first-rate scowl.

Rose looked back to William. He was at an emotional cliff, and one wrong word or look could push him over. She'd talked Jack from this same edge more than once. Of course, an eight-year-old boy and a trained killer approaching his thirties were two different things. She'd have to tread very carefully. Honesty was paramount. Jack instinctually sensed her lies, and William would probably do the same. It was best to stay away from subjects that might agitate him.

"I saw you with Declan," he said. "Are the two of you . . . ?"

There went the careful treading. "I love him," she said.

"Huh." He dragged his hand through his hair. "Does he love you?"

"I don't know. We didn't discuss it, so he doesn't know how I feel."

"Why him? Why not me?"

He had delivered the questions in a perfectly neutral tone, but she glimpsed the emotion behind it—a lifetime of rejection. He deserved an honest answer, and she took a moment to think about it.

"It's difficult to explain. We're alike in many ways. You wouldn't think it, but we are. He makes me feel wanted and safe, and he makes me laugh . . . He also irritates the daylights out of me. I almost flashed at him at one point." She paused. "It's very hard to break love down to explainable pieces, William. It's a force, a feeling. You know when you feel it and you know when you don't."

"So you feel nothing for me?" The question was delivered in a flat, neutral voice.

"That's not quite right," she said. "I don't know you well, but there are things I like about you. I like that you're honest. I like that you're patient and kind to the boys and that you've watched over them. I didn't like that you hung Emerson upside down on the tree and then scared me half to death."

"I was frustrated," he said. "You weren't happy."

He had made her a present and didn't understand why she wasn't thrilled. Just like Jack. "I appreciate the thought behind it. I still wish you hadn't done it."

William gave her a suspicious look.

"Once George and an older boy got into a fight. The older boy hit George in the mouth and knocked him off his feet. Jack decided to jump in. He beat the older boy very badly. Broke his nose and knocked out a tooth. He thought he was a hero. I grounded him for a week. If he had punched the boy and left it at that, I would've let it go. But he had done too much. Hanging Emerson off the tree was too much." She sighed. "Believe it or not, Declan and I had this same discussion. I don't want anyone to fight my battles for me. It's my business, and I'd like to handle it myself."

He considered it. "Fair enough."

"I do have feelings for you," she said. "Gratitude for trying to watch out for the boys and for checking on me when I'd lost my job. But they aren't the same feelings as I have for Declan. When Declan's gone, I miss him very badly. It's like something isn't quite right with the world."

"I get it," he said. "But what does that make you and me then?"

"We could be friends," she said. "Friends make the world bearable. It's an honor of sorts. Of all the people that a person knows, they pick you to be their friend, and you try to be worthy of that friendship. Or at least I try. I don't really know you, but I feel we could become friends if we had more time."

William's face darkened.

"You can tell a lot about the person by the company they keep," Rose said. "For example, you have a friend—Declan. You must be a glutton for punishment."

William said nothing.

"He's been trying very hard to find you," she said. "That time when you were on the phone with me and I wouldn't give it to him, he almost bit my head off."

No response.

"What's the deal with you and Declan?" she asked gently.

"We were in the Legion together," he said. "Did he tell you that part?"

She nodded.

"It's easy to be in the Legion." His voice went dull and toneless. "They tell you when to get up, when to sleep, when to eat. What to wear. Who to kill. All you have to do is be where they tell you when they tell you and don't ask questions. We were in for a long time. Most people don't survive that long. He kept to himself, I kept to myself. We'd talk once in a while. Never said much, but he had my back and I had his. He dragged me out of a burning ship once and swam through the night until a cutter picked us up. I was out of it, a dead weight. I asked him why he did it, and he said because I'd do it for him. I thought he was like me, you see? A damaged twisted sonovabitch with no place to go."

He looked up. His eyes were full of fury.

"Do you know he has a *family*? His parents love him. He has a mother, and she loves him. His father thinks the sun rises and sets on Declan's word. They're proud of him. He has a sister, and she loves him, too! I went to see them when I became a noble, and she hugged him. He stood there, and in my head I saw all the blood we spilled dripping from him, and I knew that they wouldn't care. All this time I was thinking he was fucked up and alone like me, just hid it better. But no. The bastard could've left the Legion anytime and they would take him back and love him anyway. You tell me, what kind of a sonovabitch walks away from a family like that?"

She didn't know what to say. "It isn't his fault that he has a family, William," she said finally.

"No. But I can't forgive him for it. I have nothing. The clothes on my back? I stole them. What you see is everything

I own. The Legion was everything I had, until they took it away from me. Even that Declan threw away."

Rage emanated from him. William would kill Declan if he got his hands on him; she was sure of it. She had to steer him away from violence. "Declan didn't want to leave the Legion. He doesn't care for being a noble. He doesn't want the responsibility. He did it to help you."

"I didn't ask him to do it," William snarled.

"But he did it anyway," Rose said. "I didn't ask you to attack Emerson, but you did it anyway."

"It's not the same."

"It is. Sometimes people try to help us even when we don't want the help. What would you have done in his place, William?"

"I would've broken him out," William said.

"And some people would've died in the process, you would be wanted criminals, and then Declan would be pissed off at you."

William leaned back. A long growl reverberated in his throat.

"Why did you follow Casshorn out here?" she asked. "Because you knew Declan would come and you'd get a chance to fight him?"

"No. Once Casshorn 'adopted' me, he started hinting that he wanted Declan out of the way. I told him no. The thing between me and Declan would happen on my terms. It didn't sit well with him. He gave me a house on the edge of some woods, made sure food was delivered to me, but other than that, he let me be. Then three weeks ago he invited me to come with him 'on a little adventure.' I declined. He smelled . . . odd. After he left, I went to his place and broke into his study. He had papers prepared blaming me for this entire mess in case things went sour. So I tracked him down, but he had too many hounds by the time I found him. He tried to hunt me, and I went into the Broken."

"So you're here for revenge?"

William shook his head. "No. What he's doing is treason. I swore to protect the realm." He looked at her. "There are rules I will never break. They're in me too deep. Treason is unthinkable."

"Declan's here to enforce the rules as well. If the two of you murder each other now, Casshorn will win."

William growled again, a purely animal sound of warning and contained aggression. Every hair on the back of her neck stood up.

Rose forced herself to sound calm. "Casshorn's gone insane. He wants to eat the boys. I don't want my brothers to die. I don't want to die either. Is there any way you and Declan can act like adults and postpone your reckoning until we kill him?"

William gave her a wary look. His eyes had cooled to an almost normal light brown.

"You've waited this long. Surely you could wait a little longer. Please?"

He leaned back and sucked in the air through his nose. "All right."

"Thank you." Rose smiled.

William's head snapped up. He bared his teeth, his eyes flashing amber.

A moment later she heard it, too, a thudding of horse's hooves. A rider burst from around the curve: Declan atop Jeremiah's dark horse.

Rose stared, speechless. He just had to show up right this second.

Declan brought the horse to an abrupt halt and dismounted in front of the house. "Hey, Will."

William inhaled deeply. "Declan. How did you know?"

"The boy called me."

She whipped about and saw George's face go white in the window when he saw her expression. Little fool.

Declan unbuckled his sheath and leaned it and the sword against a shrub. William pulled out a large bowie knife and thrust it into the porch. "You're good?"

"Yes."

"Good."

William blurred. He struck so fast, she failed to see it. Declan dodged and rammed his elbow into William's ribs. William spun, snapping a kick. Declan jerked back, and they broke apart.

They clashed in a whirl of kicks and punches, too fast to

follow, dancing across the grass, lethal and quick. William hammered a savage jab into Declan's ribs. Declan grunted and smashed his elbow into William's face.

Whatever it was between them apparently couldn't be resolved with words.

Behind Rose, the screen door opened and closed carefully. Jack and George came over and sat next to her.

On the lawn, William knocked Declan to the ground. Declan rolled up, and William sank punches into his face, one, two, three. Declan dropped to the ground, coughing, and kicked out, swiping William's legs from under him. William crashed like a log, and they both leapt to their feet.

"Why are they fighting?" Jack asked.

William jabbed his fingers at Declan's side.

"They're close friends," she said. "Like brothers. It's easier than talking things out."

Declan caught William's arm

"Oh." Jack nodded. "Like me and George."

"Like that," she said.

William hammered his elbow into Declan's stomach and broke free.

Rose put her arms around her brothers, and the three of them watched, cringing and making sucking noises when something crunched. What else was there to do?

Declan kicked William in the head. William staggered, shook his head, and launched a whirlwind of lightning-quick jabs. Declan blocked, and William sank a sharp punch into Declan's midsection. The blueblood grunted and rammed his head into William's face. Blood poured. They staggered away from each other, out of breath.

Declan bent over, shielding his side with his arm. William rubbed his face and raised his bloody fingers as if to say something. His knees gave out, and he dropped into the grass.

Declan sank down.

"That was awesome," George said.

Jack offered no commentary, apparently too overcome with the coolness of the fight.

"Are you done?" Rose called out.

Declan glanced up. "Will?"

William waved his bloody hand.

"Yes, we're done," Declan said.

"Good," she said, getting up. "Jack, help William inside the house to wash the blood off his face."

She crossed the grass to Declan. "How are you?"

"Perfectly fine," he said.

"Are your ribs broken?"

"Probably not. Cracked at most. We fought very carefully."

"Did this settle anything?"

"It made me feel better," he said, sitting up. "Did you see me kick him in the kidneys?"

"I saw."

Declan gave her a sharp predatory smile. "He'll feel it tomorrow morning."

JACK watched William wash his face in the sink. The water ran red. The scent of blood, sharp and salty, was everywhere in the room. Jack didn't care for human blood. It made him jumpy. The skin under his bracelet itched. He scratched at his wrist and fought the prickling pain of his claws wanting to come out. He couldn't help it. William was bigger and stronger and bloody. He was a threat. A very nasty threat.

That fight was the best thing he had ever witnessed in his whole entire life.

"You got a towel?" William said.

Jack pulled a towel from the kitchen chair and brought it over to him. William pulled it from his fingers, wiped his face, and glanced at him. William's eyes flared with gold. *Wolf,* shot through Jack's head. He'd known William was some kind of changeling because he saw his eyes glow while he and George watched William talk to Rose, but he didn't know what kind. Now he knew.

William lunged at him. Jack jerked back, but William caught him and dragged him up to his face.

Jack jerked, but William's hands held him like big iron pinchers.

William stared into his eyes, his face completely white. "Show me your teeth."

Jack hissed.

"You're like me," William whispered. He looked like someone had hit him in the gut.

"No," Jack told him to make him feel better. "You're a wolf, and I'm a cat. We're different."

William swallowed. "You live here?"

Something was wrong with him, Jack decided. Of course he lived here. But William was a big wolf, and it wasn't wise to make him mad. He simply nodded.

"Do you have a room?"

Jack nodded.

"Where?"

Jack pointed with his head. His arms were still clamped to his sides by William's hands.

William strode through the house, carrying him, stepped into his room, and sagged against the door. All the strength must have gone out of his arms, because they let go, and Jack squirmed out and landed on the floor.

William stared at his room. Jack looked, too, just in case there was something surprising there that William saw and he didn't. It was a regular room. Two beds, one for him, one for George. Rose had made them both blankets with a crochet hook. His was blue and black, and George's was red and black. He liked the blankets because even after you washed them, they still smelled like Rose.

He looked past the beds to the windowsill, where the seven-inch plastic Batman duked it out with Superman. In the corner, a beat-up shelf held some matchbox cars, books, and more figures. Jack went over to the shelf and pointed out the guys. "This is He-Man," he said. "He's my favorite. Rose bought him at a flea market, because I liked him."

William just watched him. His eyes looked huge, and they were glowing.

"This guy, I don't know what he is, but I like his armor. I think he might be like a knight. Only I don't have a sword that fits into his hand, so he has a gun. So he's a gun-knight, I think."

Jack made He-Man and Gun-Knight fight a bit and looked at William. William didn't look any better.

"I think you might be not right," Jack said. "That's okay. I get like that sometimes. When I'm real scared and I just want to hurt something. It's okay. The important thing is don't panic."

He came over and took William's hand. Rose was better at this than he was, because he never had to do it for anybody else, but he remembered what she did. "You're safe," he said. "You're in a good place. Nobody can hurt you here. You don't have to be afraid." He hesitated. "There is some mushy love stuff that goes here, but it probably won't work for you. The important thing is, this is a good place. It's safe and warm, and there is water and food. And you don't have to be scared, because there are ward stones and they keep bad people away. And Rose won't let anybody hurt you."

William looked like he might be sick. This called for emergency measures. "Stay here," Jack told him, ran over to the fridge, and brought him a chocolate bar. "Eat this," he said. "Rose gives me one when I get not right. It makes you feel better."

William's hand shook.

"I'll get Rose," Jack said.

"No." William's voice sounded like he had eaten some rocks. "I'm good. I've got it."

He got up to his feet and handed him the chocolate. "You eat it," he said and walked out onto the porch.

Jack looked at the chocolate bar. It smelled so good. But chocolate was for emergencies. He sighed and went to put it back into the fridge.

When he came outside, William was leaning against the porch next to Declan, who sat in the grass. Rose was chewing George out for something. Jack went over to Declan and sat by him.

"How long have you known?" William said.

"I came across them my second day here. Casshorn's hounds attacked him, but he hadn't turned, so I wasn't sure at first."

"It hurts to change shape here," William said. "You go into a fit."

"That's what I gathered."

The muscles along William's jaw went tight. "Are you sending him to Hawk's?"

Declan shook his head. "If she comes with me—and she hasn't said she would—he's staying with us. No Hawk Academy, no special schools, no empty rooms. His childhood will be as normal as is in my power to make it."

William didn't look like he believed him.

"He's lived with them all his life," Declan said. "You think she'd let me send him off?"

They both looked at Rose.

"You got me for this fight," William said. "For the boy. After that, I'm gone."

Declan nodded.

"You have a plan?"

Rose came up to them. Jack tensed, but no chewing-out seemed to be forthcoming.

"Several locals are cursing Casshorn into sleep as we speak," Declan said. "Once he's out, we're going to send an electric current through a local lake. The current should be strong enough to weaken the hounds. Rose and I will wait for them on the dock in the middle of the lake. We'll flash a few times to pull them to us and kill the survivors. Once the main body of the hounds is gone, we go after Casshorn."

William squeezed his eyes shut and shook his head.

"If you have a better plan, be my guest, don't keep it to yourself," Declan invited.

William leaned back and stayed quiet for a few minutes. "Flashing won't be enough. You need to draw as many hounds as you can to you."

"You want to run it?" Declan asked.

"Who else? You're too slow."

"What do you mean?" Rose asked.

"He means that he'll turn into a wolf and draw the hounds to us," Declan said.

"That's suicide," she said flatly.

William grimaced. "This is coming from a woman who's willing to crawl onto a dock in an electrocuted pond."

"How do you even know what 'electrocuted' means?" Rose asked.

William glanced at Declan. "You didn't tell her?"

Declan shrugged. "It didn't come up."

"We had training in industrial sabotage," William said. "In

case of a conflict between the Broken and the Weird, the Legion will send soldiers into the Broken and they will cripple the industrial centers."

"The Broken runs on electric power," Declan said. "Destroy the power plants, and everything stops. No power equals no water, no communications, no logistics, nothing. Even fuel is pumped by electric pumps. Take away electricity, and you'll have anarchy."

"The Weird has a lot less people than the Broken," William said. "If it comes to war, destroying their infrastructure is our only option."

"You're scaring me," Rose said.

"Don't worry," Declan told her. "The probability of an actual conflict between the two dimensions is rather low."

"It's mostly a precautionary measure," William said.

"You have to be prepared for what your enemy could do rather than what they might do," Declan said.

William nodded.

Rose didn't look convinced.

TWENTY-FIVE

ÉLÉONORE sensed the approaching steps a moment before a careful knock on the door broke the silence. She put down her pestle and went to get the door. Technically Emily should be the one to do it, given that she was the youngest, but Emily was cooking a dead cat over the stove and had to keep stirring it. It smelled ghastly enough as it was. No need to add burned stench to it.

Éléonore opened the door and looked at a familiar-looking young woman. Ruby, she remembered. One of Adele's great-grandchildren.

"There is a man here to see you," the girl said.

A man? In Wood House? How in the world did he get past the wards? "Me or your great-grandma?"

The girl bobbed her dark head. "You, Mrs. Drayton."

Éléonore wiped her hands on her apron and stepped out.

A man waited in the yard. Dark-haired, tall, about Declan's age. He looked up, and his eyes shone with wild amber. Alarm shot through Éléonore. Like looking into the eyes of a feral beast. "You would be William, then," she said.

He nodded.

"Are you here for yourself or for Casshorn?"

"For Jack," he said.

"I see." She didn't, but that seemed like the right thing to say.

William sat into the grass. "Tell me when the curse is ready. I'll draw the hounds to the lake."

Éléonore nodded and went inside. Something had happened. She would have to ask Rose about it, but not now. Now they had old magic to court.

Two hours later, she staggered out onto the porch, pale

and exhausted. He sat in the same spot. "It's done," she gasped. It had taken all of their strength, too. "Go fast. The curse won't hold him for long."

William pulled off his shirt, then his boots. His pants followed, and he stood naked on the grass.

His body twisted, muscle and bone stretching, flowing like molten wax. His spine bent, his legs jerked, and he crashed into the grass. A violent tremor shook his limbs. His fingers clawed the air. Newly formed bone, wet with lymph and blood, thrust through the muscle. Éléonore fought a shudder.

Flesh churned and flowed, encasing the new skeleton. Dense black fur sprouted and sheathed the skin. A huge wolf rolled onto his feet.

"Open the gate!" Éléonore called. Some young one slid the wooden beam aside and wrenched the gate open.

The wolf panted once and dashed into the Wood.

Éléonore watched him go. A terrible dread claimed her, squeezing her chest with a cold fist, and she sank down into a chair. This wouldn't end well.

THE pond lay placid, its silt-muddled waters opaque and green. The afternoon had ripened into early evening, but they still had at least a few hours of sunlight. From her vantage point at the nose of the small inflatable boat, Rose saw the dock very clearly. Layers of ribbed tire rubber sheathed it, covering the wood completely. She might die there. All the times in her life she'd thought of dying, she hadn't pictured her demise on a dock covered with black rubber. At least the boys were safe. She took them out to the Broken to stay with Amy Haire. They didn't like it, but they both realized this wasn't a good time to argue with her.

Behind her, Buckwell and Declan rowed quietly. The dock grew closer and closer.

She clenched her hands to keep them from shaking. Ten minutes ago Jeremiah had called her. Her phone finally died, cutting him off in mid-word, but not before she got the message: the curse had been placed. Casshorn was asleep. William took off into the woods as soon as he heard, and now she was in a small boat, heading to a dock that looked more and more like a death trap.

"It's not too late to back out," Declan said.

She shook her head, stealing a glance at him. A relaxed expression held his face. His body betrayed no tension. She didn't know if he didn't feel fear or if he hid it well, but she had to do the same. If she fell apart, she would be a distraction. The whole point of her forcing her way into this situation was to let him save his strength.

She rolled her eyes at him. "Not a chance."

Declan smiled at her.

"We had a saying in the army," Tom Buckwell said. "Often wrong, but never in doubt. Once you decide what you need to do and how to go about it, you can't afford to second-guess yourself. You just do it."

The dock loomed before them. Rose got up and caught a wooden support, bringing the boat alongside of the dock. Declan caught the edge and pulled himself up. Rose gripped his hand, and he lifted her onto the dock. She stomped her feet in Leanne's rubber-soled boots. They were a size too big, but she didn't own any electrical hazard boots and they would have to do. This whole idea seemed amazingly stupid now.

William was in agreement with her. When they told him of their plan, he'd shut his eyes and shaken his head. The fact that she'd come up with this harebrained scheme only made the whole thing more ironic.

Buckwell passed Declan his swords. "Don't touch the water once the power lines come down. We'll be over there." He pointed to the shore behind the dock, where the roof of the church cut across the sky. "If any of them make it past you up the road, we've got machetes. And I've got my chainsaw. I've got six people down there, and every one of us should be able to see the beasts."

Declan nodded. "Good luck."

"Same to you." Buckwell took off.

She wanted to jump into his boat. Hell, she wanted to jump into the water and swim ashore.

"Scared?" Declan asked.

"Yes." She saw no point in lying.

"Good. It will keep you ready."

They watched Buckwell land and pull the boat out. Behind him Thad Smith waved his arms. Leanne appeared on the bank, gripping a huge severed cable with rubber gloves. She hurled it into the water. A loud sound popped, like a thunderclap.

A small fish surfaced by the dock, white belly up.

"Now we wait," Declan said.

Rose shrugged her shoulders, trying to break free of the pressure that clamped her.

"Remember, stop the moment your vision blurs," he said. "Pushing any further is asking for trouble. Don't be stupid."

She nodded.

No wind troubled the greenery around the pond. Somewhere in the distance an Edger warbler sang out a trilling note. Mockingbirds screeched.

"So, regarding that tidbit about your having a fertile imagination when it came to private activities," she said, fighting off anxiety. "Was it another lie?"

"Depends on how you look at it. It's not exactly a lie, and if you come with me to the Weird, you'll find that rumors of my 'creativity' when it comes to bed games with the opposite sex do exist. I started them myself and managed them very carefully. The trick with rumors is to feed them once in a while, so they don't die."

"Why would you do something like that?"

"Because I don't particularly feel like being appraised like a side of beef by every enterprising young lady shopping for a husband. Despite my unfriendly demeanor, I'm wealthy, handsome, and a peer."

"All that female attention. Poor you."

Declan grimaced, his face turning cold. His voice became saturated with hard cynicism. "There is a great deal of difference between female attention and a never-ending assault of sugary pouts and 'marry me, marry me, marry me.' 'You looked at me, can we get married now? You laughed at something I said, should I order a dress? You kissed me, I shall summon my father; he will be overjoyed to hear of our engagement.' This way the only woman who tolerates being alone with me doesn't mind having her reputation sullied, because she's either in the market for a lover or she's looking for a patron to support her. Quite frankly, I prefer it this way. No painful confusion, no complicated explanations."

She stared at him.

"What?" he asked.

"Nothing, Lord Camarine. Absolutely nothing."

A long eerie howl cut through the evening. Rose jerked. A flock of birds burst from the distant branches. William was close, with the horde of hounds on his heels.

Declan raised his hand and shot a burst of white magic into the sky. She added her own flash and then shot another, just in case.

She sensed the magic first. It swelled like an icy tide along the pond's edge, drenching the brush and rolling across the water. Tiny hairs on the back of her neck stood on their ends.

The magic slimed her in a clammy wave. Tiny needles prickled at her pores. Inside her, an instinctual alarm wailed, *Run away! Run away as fast as you can and don't look back!*

A dark body burst through the brush. Amber eyes glared at her, and the enormous wolf dashed to the left, veering around the lake. She flashed again.

The first hound pushed through the branches. God, that was fast.

Another appeared. Another The first ten or twelve. The advance guard. Rose fought rising panic. She had to do this, she reminded herself. There was nobody else to do it. There was no escape anyway. For some reason that thought calmed her. It was very simple, just like cleaning an office: she had to do a certain amount of work before she could go home. No need to fret about it.

"What did I say?" Declan asked quietly.

"Not now." She raised her hand and let a string of white magic play on her fingers, taunting the beasts.

The hounds entered the water. They swam like dogs, but their heads remained underwater. Did they even need to breathe? she wondered.

Please work. Please work.

Please.

Midway through the lake, the foremost hound shuddered. It struggled for another six yards and sank. She breathed a sigh of relief. Two more drowned. The fourth one persevered and kept on, heading right for them. One in four. Better odds than she'd hoped for.

The surviving hound clenched the wooden support. Sluggish, it crawled up slowly. The moment its head rose above the edge of the dock, Rose blew it off with a sharp slice of white.

"Too much," he told her. "Reduce the intensity. We have a long way to go. Why are you mad?"

The rest of the hounds braved the water.

"Rose?"

She recognized the persistent tone. He wouldn't let it go. "You just said that the only women you favor with your attentions are either sluts or whores and that you prefer it that way. I'm just wondering where I fit in. I would hate to create any painful confusion for you."

His long blade cut through the air and sliced an emerging hound in half. He kicked the pieces into the water.

"You're neither."

She said nothing.

Declan squared his shoulders, eyeing the approaching hounds. "When I was a child, I watched an iren-play called *Aesu's Rage*. It's similar to a motion film from the Broken. It's the story of Aesu, a leader of a small tribe, who takes on an enormous empire and succeeds against all odds. I vividly remember one scene in it: Aesu, huge in his spiked armor, was about to go into a battle he couldn't possibly win. He stood there in his tent, caressed his wife's face, and told her, 'You're the measure of my wrath.' I was twelve years old, and at the time I thought it was a remarkably asinine thing to say."

A third hound reached the dock. An ugly head broke the water, and Rose flashed, cutting the dark skull in two.

"Over the years I'd come to understand what the scene meant, but now I finally feel it, very sharply." Declan decapitated the emerging hound with two quick precise strokes of his blade. "And I would never tell you this, if you hadn't insisted on coming on this dock, because that means you feel it, too. This used to be about honor, and duty, and my dislike of Casshorn. Now it's about you."

"Me?" She tried to concentrate on the next group of hounds swimming through the water.

"I would give all of myself to keep you safe. To do that, I have to kill Casshorn. It's a simple trade. Casshorn has to die, so you can live. Two sides of the same coin. I love you, and you're the measure of my wrath."

"What did you say?" She flashed too hard and missed the hound.

He stepped in and sank a focused shot of white into the three bodies squirming in the water. "I said I love you, Rose. Easy on the flash."

ROSE swayed. She gritted her teeth and stood her ground, fighting to remain upright. The magic inside her no longer thrived and filled her up. She had to reach deep to pull it out. She was draining the last of her reserve.

"Are you all right?" Declan's voice asked.

"Fine," she said.

Dark bodies bobbed in the murky waters around the dock, their silvery blood sliding across the surface of the lake like an oil rainbow. The silver wet the rubber under her feet, and she had already slipped once and barely caught herself.

They kept coming. Two, three at a time, a fraction of the horde unaffected by electrocution, swimming through the dark stream of cadavers and climbing on the dock, teeth bared, eyes glowing. Next to her, Declan swung his sword, mechanical, silent and unstoppable. Like a machine.

Another hound. Flash.

Flash.

Flash.

Her heartbeat thudded like a hammer in her temples. One flash too many. Her vision began to blur. To push any further would be stupid. "I think I'm done," she said and pulled out the machete Buckwell had given her.

A hound crawled onto the dock, and she hacked at it. Gray goo sprayed the rubber.

"Will they never end?" she whispered. She was so tired.

Declan's hand caught her waist. He pulled her to him and kissed her, his lips warm and dry. "It's over. There are none left. They're pulling the cable out."

"We're done?" she asked.

"Yes."

The surface of the lake was gray with the hounds' blood. Bodies bobbed in the water. "You were right," she said softly. "I never could've killed them all by myself."

"What did you say?"

"I said you were right . . ."

He gave her a dazzling grin. "One more time, my lady?"

"You were right," she told him with a tired smile.

"I don't think I'll ever get tired of hearing that. Unaccustomed to it as I am."

It took another fifteen minutes before Buckwell rowed up in his boat to take them ashore. She watched as several Edgers under Buckwell's direction dumped gasoline into the lake. When the first spark blossomed into orange flame above the water, she felt a great sense of satisfaction.

It lasted until Declan came to stand next to her. Her throat closed in. It was time for him to go after Casshorn, and there was nothing she could do to help him now.

She turned to him. Declan's face was cold like a block of ice. He had locked himself into a rigid stance. Behind him, William waited, a dark shadow. Now wasn't the time to break down and start crying. It was all or nothing. Either he came back and they had everything, or he would never return and they had nothing. She wanted desperately to run and throw her arms around him, but if she did that, letting go would be that much harder for both of them, and she sensed he was fighting for control.

Rose looked into Declan's green eyes. "I love you," she said. "Come back to me alive."

He nodded, turned without a word, and walked away, William in tow.

Something broke inside her. It hurt, and she just stood there, trying her best not to crumble.

"He isn't dead yet," Tom Buckwell's gruff voice said behind her.

Rose turned.

The big man was looking at her. "Wait until he's stopped breathing before you have a funeral."

She simply nodded.

"Well, don't stand there all night. There is cleanup to be done."

Cleanup sounded good. Any work sounded good right about now. Anything but waiting.

She followed him next to the shore. Jennifer Barran handed her a pole with a hook on the end. Rose reached into the water, hooked a charred carcass, and dragged it to shore. She hadn't realized how tired she was. Flashing had worn her out, and the hound's body might as well have been made of cement. She was on her third when Tom Buckwell dropped his hook next to her and swore. "What the devil . . . ?"

A man was running up the road toward them, his face so pale, it took Rose a moment to recognize him. Thad, sprinting so fast he had to be running for his life. She dropped her pole and ran toward him, a step behind Buckwell. The others joined.

Thad crashed into Buckwell, gulped air, and bent over gasping. "Hounds."

It couldn't be. They'd killed all the hounds.

"How many?" Buckwell asked.

"A shitload of them." Thad spat on the ground, blinking. "They've busted our trucks. We're cut off."

Only one road led out of East Laporte. With the vehicles gone, getting into the Broken would be nearly impossible. They were a full four miles from the boundary. Rose surveyed the people around her: six in all, including Buckwell and Thad.

"We go to Wood House," Buckwell said calmly. "Keep your machetes ready, and stay together."

They followed him, circling the lake to the right.

Two shapes tore out of the woods, running at full power. Declan and William, heading straight for them.

"Change of plans," Declan ground out when they neared. "Casshorn's outsmarted us. His reserves are coming up."

"We can't fight them in the open. Too many." William's eyes glowed amber.

"We need a defensible position," Declan said. "Do you have a jail?"

Buckwell stared at him like he was crazy.

"A town hall?" Declan asked.

"No," she shook her head.

"Gods, what do you have?" William growled.

"A church!" Rose said. "We have a church!"

William glanced at Declan, who shrugged. "I've seen it. It's not much, but it will have to do. Lead the way."

They dashed down the street past the tiny convenience store owned by Thad's uncle, past the meth heads' mansion, down to the hill, and into the church. They rammed the doors open and burst inside. George Farrel appeared from behind the pulpit, his shotgun at the ready. His gaze fixed on Declan. His eyes sparked with crazy light.

"Get ye from the house of God, defiler!" Farrel jerked his shotgun up.

William leaped past them and punched him off his feet. Farrel hit the floor and didn't rise.

"Bolt the door. Stack the pews at the sides!" Declan ordered. "We need a narrow path so they can only come to us a few at a time."

Rose grasped the nearest pew. At the other end, Leanne strained, and together they flipped it on to the next pew. In minutes the nine of them piled the benches in two heaps at the sides of the church, leaving a narrow strip of open space between themselves and the entrance.

A thud shook the door. Rose jerked. Leanne backed away, past her, to the pulpit and Buckwell. Declan and William took a step forward in unison. Declan had his two swords out. William held a knife.

"Rose, step back," Declan said.

She remained where she was, directly behind the two of them.

Another thud crashed against the door.

"You have no flash left," Declan said.

"I have more than they do," she said quietly.

He glanced over her to the six people at the pulpit gathered into a tight clump, and turned away.

The doors flew open with a sound of thunder. Beyond

them a gory sunset splashed across the sky, yellow and red, the sun a molten coin of gold on the horizon. Hounds slunk into the church, moving one by one, hesitantly, slowly. A man in a dark robe followed them, nearly black against the setting sun, as if cut out of darkness. He advanced at an odd gait, bobbing up and down, as if unsure how to walk upright. The hood of his robe hid his face. He stopped in the doorway and spoke, his voice carrying with unnatural clarity through the building.

Casshorn surveyed the church. "Such a humble, quaint building, this house of the murdered god. I find it oddly fitting that our struggle comes to its end here. It is said that gods inhabit the churches built in their name. So once you have nourished me, I shall raze this structure to the ground, and from the ashes I shall forge the house of a new god. A house befitting me. For you see, I have come to know what I am. I have become a god." He craned his neck. "Perhaps I shall even hear his cries as he flees from the wreck of his house. After all, he is a god of pity and compassion. He should know how to mourn."

"You finally lost what pitiful grip you had on this reality, I see," Declan said, his voice dripping contempt. "You're not a god. You're a spoiled child, just as you always have been. You simply stopped all pretenses at adulthood."

"A child that had seen clear through your trap. It was a good plan for a small mind like yours, Declan. It had only one small flaw. For you see, they had sent a man to me, and before I dined on his magic and body, he told me everything I wanted to know and so much more. I knew their capabilities, and I anticipated their curse, and I had given them the means to cast it, delivered by you. The Universe is clear to me. It has unfurled like a flower before the brightness of my being. You've done well, but you cannot kill a god, Declan."

"We'll see," Declan said.

Casshorn turned to William. "My son. Have you finally chosen your side, then?"

"There was never any choice about it." William shook, snarling. Sweat broke out on his forehead. His eyes had gone deranged.

Casshorn's voice gained a kindly tone. "I will grant you

this one boon, my son, for you are my only heir. Kill Declan, and I will let you run."

William grinned. His face set into a pale mask, his grin an ugly baring of teeth. He barely looked human. "I served seven years with him in the unit where you lasted a mere fifteen minutes. Had you managed to stay in instead of pissing on yourself and running like a dog with your tail between your legs, you'd understand. If I owe anyone a crumb of loyalty, it would be him. Not you. It's good that you decided to be a god, because I'm about to go to a place that suffers none."

"Then it is decided." Casshorn raised his arms. "You have no priest to give you your last rites, but do not fear. For I give you your absolution and my communion. I forgive you your past sins, and I shall welcome you into my fold by partaking of your body and power."

"Get on with it," Declan said.

Casshorn tore off his cloak. His body was no longer human. His limbs were long and tightly muscled, his digits grotesquely large and clawed. His skin had become purple and yellow hide. Spikes thrust through his spine, rising in a crest above his hunched shoulders. His face had lost all humanity. His eyes glowed gray. A second pair of eye slits, narrow and shunted, shone on his cheeks. He opened his mouth and showed them a forest of bloodred fangs.

Behind Rose, someone retched.

Declan spun his sword in his hand.

Casshorn reared back and emitted a sharp hoarse screech.

Hounds streamed from behind him in twin currents.

With an inhuman snarl, William ripped into them. His face turned demonic. Bodies flew, and silver sprayed. They piled on him, and he cut them down faster than she could see. A psychotic high-strung sound full of mad joy rang through the carnage, and Rose realized William was laughing.

Tendrils of dark magic rose from Casshorn: black veined with polluting streaks of purple and yellow. He clawed at the air. The dark magic streamed to Declan. Declan's eyes turned white. A wave of flash erupted from him. The two crashed together: the brilliant white against the diseased purplish glow. Immense pressure slapped Rose, nearly taking her off her feet.

The church shuddered.

A support beam split behind Casshorn.

Cuts on Declan's face bled. She saw a line of red swell across his back.

Casshorn's face shook with strain. His magic gained a foot. And another. They were too evenly matched, and Declan was tired. If only she'd kept him from that dock . . .

Streaks of silver poured from Casshorn's eyes. He snarled. His magic gained another foot. If Declan's flash collapsed, all of them would be wiped out.

Rose stood, untouched, unhurt, in the middle of chaos, listening to the sounds of the church breaking around them and hounds dying under William's knife, and realized that she would have to watch Declan die. His death would begin the chain reaction. One by one everyone she knew would die as well, and the Edge itself would follow. She couldn't let it happen.

Rose gathered her power. She had to reach deep, very deep, and drag it out, as if pulling her heart out of her chest. She focused it all into a single point, condensing her magic so tight, she shook with the strain of trying to contain it.

The dark magic advanced. Blood dripped from Declan's leather.

She wished she could have said good bye to the boys. She wished she had told them how much she loved them and not to worry and to listen to Grandma. She wished she and Declan had just a little more time.

Rose took a deep breath. It hurt so much she shut her eyes. Then she opened them and let her magic go. She held nothing back. Everything that she was, everything that made her alive, she gave all of it, so Declan and the boys would live. She would have given more, if she could have.

It tore from her in a blinding beam of light, straight as a needle. The beam pierced Declan's flash and the darkness beyond it. She saw Casshorn's face, a horrified mask, eyes wide open, mouth dropping downward in slack bewilderment and terror. She heard Declan scream.

The white beam sliced through Casshorn. The two halves of his horrible body stood still for a moment and then fell apart.

Blackness pounced on her and swallowed her whole.

DARKNESS.

Darkness all around, empty, blocking the world like a wall. If only she could break through it . . .

She didn't want to die. She flailed, willing her hands to rise and tear up the darkness, but her arms were missing and she could do nothing as the blackness dragged her off, deeper and deeper into its depths.

A bolt of lightning tore through the dark wall. For a moment she felt Declan's arms cradling her, she saw his eyes, heard his lips whispering over and over, "Don't leave me!"

The darkness pounced, and he vanished.

A dozen narrow streaks shattered the darkness, and she screamed, because she was clenched in his arms, and he was flashing again and again, siphoning his life into her, his magic a dozen white currents binding their bodies into one.

TWENTY-SIX

ROSE opened her eyes. Daylight.

A ceiling stretched above her with an all-too-familiar yellow stain. It had appeared two years ago, right after Jack in his lynx shape chased a feral tomcat up into the attic. She had long suspected it was cat pee.

"Here you are," Grandma's voice said softly.

Rose looked at her, wide-eyed. A terrible fear clamped her. "Declan?"

"Alive. Barely, but he's eaten some chicken soup this morning, so I do believe he'll make it."

"The boys?"

"Fine. They're fine. Thad died. Tom Buckwell's leg had to be cut off. Jennifer and Ru didn't make it, but other than that, we've survived the storm."

Rose breathed.

Tears swelled in Grandma's blue eyes. "Never again, you hear me? Never again. Next time something like this happens, you go into the Broken and let somebody else fight it out!"

"Okay." Rose reached and touched her hand. "It's okay."

"You were almost dead, baby. Your blueblood dragged you back from the dead, kicking and screaming."

"What happened to William?"

"He's gone. Didn't say a word. Just vanished after everything was over."

Declan loomed in the doorway. He saw her and swallowed. Quietly Grandma rose and stepped aside. Rose held out her arms. He staggered in, slowly, and lowered himself on the floor near her. She took his hand in hers and fell asleep.

* * *

ROSE awoke in her bed. The light coming through the window meant late morning. She had woken up several times during the night, terrified that she had only dreamed being alive and having Declan near. He'd slept by her bed on the floor, on a stack of blankets, and every time she panicked, he was there, until finally she crawled off the bed and lay on the floor next to him, drifting off in his arms. The next time she had shrugged off sleep, she found Jack curled up on their feet and George out cold in her bed.

Declan and the boys were gone now, and she was back in her bed. She didn't worry. She knew he wouldn't leave without her.

It didn't seem real. She lay for a long time feeling the texture of the sheets under her fingers and trying to convince herself that this was real, that it wasn't some hallucination flashing before her mind as she lay dying on the church floor. She failed and finally pushed herself upright. If it was a hallucination, she might as well enjoy it while it lasted.

The muscles in her legs felt soft, like wet cotton, but she managed to make it to the bathroom and then to the kitchen before her legs gave out.

"Rose!" Grandma dropped the steaming kettle back on the stove and caught her, sliding her into the chair.

"Where are they?"

"Outside. He went walking. He can't run yet, but he wouldn't stay in bed. I sent the hooligans with him in case he topples over. Here." Grandma put a bowl of Cocoa Puffs in front of her.

Rose put a spoonful into her mouth. "Oh, my God. Thish ish the besht thing I ever tashted."

"That's because you haven't eaten in four days."

The cereal crunched in her mouth. She emptied the bowl and instantly felt sick.

"More?" Grandma's eyes twinkled.

"I'd better not. It's trying to come back up."

"Drink some tea, it will help."

She sipped the hot, fragrant brew. "What happened to the device?"

"Jeremiah and the rest dragged it out into the Broken,

chainsawing whatever came out of it. The damn thing stopped right away past the boundary. They poured concrete on it, drove it to the coast, and dumped it off into the ocean. I saw it with my own eyes. Your blueblood wouldn't shut up until I went with them. Would you stop staring out the window? He will be back soon enough."

Rose looked into her tea.

"Where does this leave the two of you?" Grandma asked softly.

"I'm not sure," Rose said.

"He's been making plans to leave for the Weird as soon as he can. He's determined to take you with him."

"Do you think I should go?"

A troubled expression flickered over Grandma's face. "This is one of those times age's wisdom meets youth's passion. Do you know what usually happens?"

Rose sighed. "I'm about to find out?"

"Wisdom dashes passion's hopes and you stop speaking to your grandmother."

Grandma Éléonore clenched her hands. "You know I love you, Rose. I have to tell you this, even if you shall hate me for it. I was not lucky in love. I loved madly. Passionately. Mine was the kind of love that burned so brightly, it made me blind. When the fire finally dimmed enough for me to see clearly, I found out that what I wanted most of all was a man I could depend on. A man who would be by my side, come hell or high water. And that was the only thing Cletus denied me. He loved me. He yearned for me. He set our bed on fire. But when I needed him, I'd turn around and he'd be gone, chasing off after some swamp light. So when I say this, you must take into account that I speak from a lifetime of bitter disappointment."

Rose blinked.

"Your Declan, he's a dream. Courageous, assertive, strong, kind. Let's not forget rich and of noble blood."

"Also arrogant, condescending, high-handed, and snooty." Rose smiled.

"Shush. You wanted my opinion, now you're getting it. Declan is everything a woman could want. And he looks . . ." Grandma sighed in resignation. "You know the way he looks.

I'm over a century old, and my heart hammers faster when he walks by. You must ask yourself, what would a man like this want with a woman like you?"

"I think he wants to marry me. I made it plain that being his girl toy was out of the question."

"You asked for my honesty." Éléonore twisted her hands again. "You're my granddaughter, Rose. There is no girl brighter or prettier. You deserve all the best in the world, and if it was in my power, I'd give it to you. But you and Declan aren't on the same footing. I think you love him. And I think he loves you very much. Right now. But does he love you deeply enough to spend a lifetime with you? So much has happened. Both of you got caught up in this life-and-death excitement. But eventually he has to go home, where he's a noble and you are what? Even if he thinks he'll marry you right now, what will happen when he returns to his life and his friends and family see you? They're nobles, Rose. They're born into the life of privilege, and they don't know what it's like to scrape and scrounge for change so you can buy bread for the kids. He might understand it now, but what about his parents? What if he's determined enough to marry you against all odds, and they shun him for it? It could make him a bitter, hard man. He might always blame you for it. He won't ever let you forget that he threw away everything for you."

Rose looked into her cup.

"If you go with him, you must go knowing that you might end up a rich man's mistress or that you could cost him everything," Grandma said. "I don't think that's what you want. I think you love him too much. I'm afraid he'll break your heart. There, I said it. Think about it, Rose. Think long and hard before you let him shatter you to pieces."

ROSE sat on the porch. She supposed she should have stood, but she felt queasy. Declan waited on the grass before her. She was aware of Grandmother behind her and the kids perched on the rail to the left.

It had taken her three days to finally recover to the point that she could travel. Three days of Declan by her side showing her how it could be. This was going to be a very difficult conversation.

"So the third challenge," she said.

Declan smiled, and her heart jumped. "You could give me something easy. Ask me to pick you some flowers."

"I can't do that."

The smile slid off his face. "Very well."

Rose took a deep breath. "I want you to trust me."

She was hot and cold at the same time. Anxiety prickled her skin, as if she were a kid who had just broken some prized trinket and expected her parents to yell at her.

"Winning the challenges gives you the right to own me. I would belong to you completely. I'd be your possession."

"I simply phrased the oath in a way most advantageous to me at the time," he said. "I don't want to own you, Rose. I want you to want me. And I think you do."

She couldn't let him derail her. "I understand why you've done it that way. But the fact remains that I have to trust you completely to let you win."

He raised his arms. His tone grew cold. "Do you want me to marry you right now, is that it? If that's the only way I'll have you, I'll do it."

She winced. "That's exactly what I don't want."

"What do you want?"

She held herself straight. "I want you to sign three writs of citizenship for myself and the kids. I'll go with you into the Weird. You'll introduce me to your family and friends. If in one month's time you still want to go through with the wedding, I'll marry you."

He stared at her. "What would be the purpose of that?"

"You're giving me the power to take the writs and vanish once we reach the Weird."

"Are you afraid I'll mistreat you?"

"It's about trust, Declan. I will trust you to take me to the Weird, to not kill the children, to not sell me to the highest bidder, to not turn me into your mistress only to be abandoned when some noblewoman catches your eye. And you will trust me to come with you and marry you of my own free will, not because of some dumb challenge."

His face snapped into glacial calm. "Is that what you

think of me? You think me the kind of man who would murder children and take advantage of you?"

"No," she said. "I don't. I want to be with you, Declan. I
love you very much. But your family might hate me, and you
might change your mind. If you do it my way, you'll have an
out. You'll lose nothing."

"So you want me to trust you, but you don't trust me," he
said.

"This is the challenge," she said. "Three writs, thirty days.
I won't back away from it."

His expression didn't change. "George, there is a wooden
box in my room. Fetch it. You'll have your writs," he said.
"Start packing."

IT took them the whole day to pack what little belongings
they had. They had to travel light, no more than they could
carry. Rose packed a couple of changes of clothes for everyone.
The kids took their toys and the three volumes of *InuYasha*.
The Broken money would be useless in the Weird, and Rose
handed it all over to her grandmother. She would go into the
Weird without a single cent to her name.

Declan had transformed back into the Weird blueblood.
The gray leather armor, the sword, the pack, and the wolf
mantle were back. So was the haughty expression. He hadn't
said more than two words to her.

They said their tear-soaked good-byes to Grandma.

"Come with me," Rose asked. "Please."

Éléonore just hugged her. "I couldn't have left Cletus
even if I wanted to. I had no place to go and no means to
cross the ocean. But you will have a choice. If it doesn't
work out, you can always come back here. Always, Rose. No
matter what, no questions asked. Let me do this thing for
you. I'll sleep better at night."

"We'll come back to visit next summer," Rose promised.

As they headed down the path into the Wood, Rose looked
back and saw Grandma on the porch, a lost expression on her
face.

George sniffled.

"Next summer we'll talk her into coming back with us," she told him.

They walked for the better part of the day. The Wood grew darker and stranger with each step, the trees becoming thicker, branches more twisted. Odd creatures skittered among the canopy and bizarre flowers bloomed among the roots, like beacons of white and orange.

Finally Declan stopped. "The boundary," he said.

The moment of truth. Either they had enough magic to cross or they didn't. Rose held the boys by the hand and took a step. Pressure clutched her. She gasped at the sudden weight and took another step, then another and another, and then they were through.

An incredible lightness filled her. The magic pulsed within her, vibrant, strong, and she laughed softly at the simple happiness of it.

Declan reached into his leather and produced a small whistle. A shrill sound sliced through the Wood. Magic pulsed from the whistle. A rapid thudding of a horse answered, and a large animal pushed through the underbrush. Thick, stocky across the shoulders, with a deep chest and powerful legs, it looked like a cross between a Budweiser stallion and a wild ram. It dipped its head, crowned with two steel-capped horns, and nuzzled at Declan.

"His name is Grunt," Declan said.

The mount grunted in reply. They packed their belongings into saddlebags, loaded Jack and George onto Grunt's back, and set off.

Two days later, they finally made it out of the woods and onto the road. Declan pushed them, and by nightfall, they came upon a settlement.

It was a small town, poised about a paved road running up a hill. Two- and three-story houses climbed up the slope, cushioned in greenery. Some were whitewashed, some built of pink and yellow stone, most roofed with reddish orange shingles. Here and there streetlamps sparked with magic. Some buildings showed odd cupolas; others had peculiar hieroglyphs scrawled on their walls in flowing script.

A small carriage slid by them, heading up the hill. It had no horse.

Declan led them up the road to a wide blocky building, marked by a tall post with a glowing green lantern atop it.

A dark-haired boy ran out to take Grunt's reins and bowed deeply. "My lord!"

"Quiet," Declan told him, pointing at the two boys passed out on Grunt's back. He tossed a coin to the boy. It looked a lot smaller than the doubloons with which he'd paid her. "Family suite, top floor. And a dinner for four."

They had two adjoining rooms connected with a door and situated on the end of the second-floor hallway. The rooms were clean and beautiful. For some reason she had expected a smoky medieval tavern, but instead the rooms were almost modern, except for the absence of electric outlets, TVs, or anything else that was meant to plug in. The walls were a gentle peach, the floors golden hardwood. Each bedroom came equipped with a canopied bed and soft dark red chairs. Clusters of elegant glass bellflowers mounted on the walls spilled soothing light.

The innkeeper deposited Jack onto the bed in the right room and withdrew. Declan placed George next to Jack.

Rose went into the bathroom and saw a toilet, a double sink, and a shower with a huge bathtub sunken deep into the floor. A robe hung on the hook, so ordinary she nearly laughed. Suddenly she realized she stank. She stripped and climbed in, wanting nothing more than to wash off three days in the forest. It took her a little while to figure out the contents of the twisted green and blue glass bottles, but in the end, she emerged, clean, smelling like tangerines, and wrapped in a fluffy cream-colored towel.

They didn't appear to have electricity, but the water pressure was excellent and the water was hot. She'd have to ask Declan about it.

She tiptoed past the sleeping children into the second room and gasped when Declan pounced on her, sweeping her off her feet. His lips touched hers, and she melted. She missed him so much, she almost cried.

His voice was a husky growl knitted with need. "I missed you."

She put her fingers on his lips. "Quiet, the kids . . ."

He glanced at the door and roared at the top of his lungs, "Kids?"

She gasped, expecting Jack or George to fly through the door. Declan reached over, swung the door open, and showed her the boys asleep in their room.

"Soundproof sigil," he said, shutting the door. "We can hear them, but they can't hear us. You can scream all you want."

"So I'm completely at your mercy?" Rose laughed.

He carried her to the bed. "You will be . . ."

MUCH later, warm and ridiculously happy, she lay on her side, her head on his arm, his body pressed against her. "So this is your idea of slow and sensuous?"

"Pretty much," he said. "Explain the thirty days to me."

"It's your chance to change your mind," she told him. "I'm scared you'll fall out of love with me. I'm scared your family will hate me, and then you'll marry me anyway to rescue me, but you'll become a pariah and blame me for the rest of your life for being disowned."

His chest shook, and she realized he was trying to hold in laughter. She stared at him, indignant. "I want to give you a choice, you idiot. I don't want to make you feel like you have to do it."

He broke into laughter. She groaned and curled into a ball.

"I've made my choice," he said. "In fact, I've done everything in my power to get you right here into my bed, and I had to work very hard for it. I gave you no reason to believe that I'll abandon you. Or murder the children and leave them on the side of the road. Really, that was priceless. I was a bit put out."

She glared at him. "A bit put out" apparently meant three days of the silent treatment.

He pulled her close. "I'm not doing this to rescue you. I'm doing this for entirely selfish reasons—I love you, and I don't want to be without you."

"I love you, too," she told him.

"Let's get married now," he offered. "We'll go down to the magistrate in the morning . . ."

"Thirty days," she said firmly. "After your parents meet me."

"You're an impossible woman," he said mournfully.

"You wouldn't love me if I wasn't," she said.

"True."

She kissed him. He wrapped his arms around her, and she smiled. Tomorrow would bring new troubles, but for now she was perfectly and completely happy.

THE castle was enormous. It spread atop a hill like a crouching dragon: at the front, heavily fortified entrance, like a mouth, followed by the stretch of the wall—the beast's neck. Next a round tall tower stabbed the sky—the dragon's leg, followed by a cluster of fortified buildings surrounded by a high wall with a spiked parapet curling on the edge of a cliff, like a massive ridged tail around hindquarters. The brown stone, darkened with age, intensified the illusion. Rose gaped at it.

"It only looks severe," Declan informed her. "Inside, it's very open. The Duchess of the Southern Provinces has a fondness for natural light and gauzy curtains. It will be quick, I promise. We go in, I report to the Duke, and then we depart for Camarine Keep. We'll be home by tomorrow night."

Rose shrugged, trying to get rid of the tension sitting between her shoulder blades. Her horse, a smaller version of Declan's Grunt, immediately reacted by dancing in place. He had bought it for her in that first town. The kids each got a mount of their own. George rode like a natural, with almost Declan-like elegance, while Jack mostly clung to the horse, clawing at it at every bump, until both he and his horse dashed about in blind panic.

The trip across Adrianglia had taken almost a week. Both she and the kids had ended up with raw thighs after the first day of riding, and after that, they'd taken it slow and easy. It was an odd place, clean and beautiful in some areas, stark in others. Ruins dotted the countryside here and there, scars of old wars. She had tried to prepare herself for the possibility that she might dislike the Weird, but it grew on her, with its patches of forest and horseless carriages, and children playing with magic on the sides of the roads.

She had been completely blindsided by Declan's status. She had known he was a Marshal, but she'd never quite realized what it entailed. People bowed. When he passed through a town, a report was brought, usually by a commander of the local militia. Every stop was a working stop. The first time someone called her "my lady," it zoomed right over her head. She had tried her best not to embarrass him. Unfortunately, she knew this would last only until she came into contact with other nobles.

Now she had to face the Duke of the Southern Provinces. He was the man to whom Declan answered. The man she desperately needed to impress, even more so than Declan's parents. She still wore her jeans and a T-shirt. Her hair was still a short mess. She was still unrefined. She was Rose. And Declan was determined to drag her into the castle.

They rode up the road. This was so not going to end well.

They passed under the portcullis. Declan merely nodded at the guards, dressed in gray and blue. Everybody bowed. He jumped off Grunt and helped her down off her mount. The kids dismounted, and Declan started toward the doors.

"I was thinking, we might just stay here," Rose said. "We can wait for you."

" 'Dear Declan, where is your bride?' 'Oh, I left her outside, Your Grace.' " Declan shook his head. "I don't think so."

He took her by the hand, gently, but she knew with absolute certainty that she wouldn't be able to get away, and guided her inside into the lobby. A wide room stretched before her, terminating in a staircase leading up. On both sides of the staircase she saw arched entrances opening into a vast hall. The floor was old worn stone. Tapestries decorated the walls. Small trees and bright flowers grew in huge pots along the walls. Bathed in the light of numerous windows, the hall looked surprisingly cheery.

A man appeared. His hair was silver, his clothes black leather, his face grim. He looked like he could kill people with his stare alone. "He's waiting for you, my lord," he said.

Declan nodded and glanced at her. "Wait for me, please," he said, "I'll be right back."

He ran up the stairway. The man followed him. They were alone.

George looked at his shoes. Jack reached over, plucked a small leaf from the nearest tree, and nervously chewed on it.

"Jack, don't do that," she murmured.

A woman emerged from one of the entrances on the right. Jack swallowed the leaf.

She was older, tall, dark-haired, very beautiful, and dressed in a ragged shirt smeared with cream-colored paint. They looked at each other.

"Who are you?" the woman asked. A frosty sheen crossed her eyes and melted into their dark depths.

Oh God. A blueblood.

"I'm here with Declan," Rose said. "These are my brothers. We're just here for a minute."

The woman pursed her lips. "Are you from the Broken?"

"Actually, I'm from the Edge," Rose said carefully.

"Can you paint walls?"

Rose blinked. "Yes."

"Would you mind helping me? I've been painting non-stop, and my back really hurts."

There was only one answer to that. "Not at all."

The woman smiled. She had a very warm smile, and Rose relaxed a little. "Come with me!"

They followed her into a side hallway, up a window stairway to the second floor and into a room layered with cloth. Half of one wall was cream. The rest was steel gray.

"I think it looks better with cream, don't you?" the woman said.

"It looks brighter."

The woman handed her a roller. In a few minutes all three of them were painting.

"When I become worried, I paint the walls," the woman said. "I've done four rooms so far. Well, six, actually, since I changed my mind several times on the color. Your brothers are adorable."

"Thank you. Why were you worried?" Rose asked.

"Because of Declan, of course. The whole mess with Casshorn nearly brought me to an early grave. I realize we won, but would you mind filling in the details?"

Rose bit her lip. "I'm not sure I should tell you."

The woman smiled. "I know most of the story: Casshorn

had stolen a device from the Duke of the Southern Provinces that feeds on magic and makes hounds. He took it across the country into the Edge. Declan left to retrieve it and save William, who managed to entangle himself in this mess. So how did it end?"

"Declan was flashing and Rose almost died, because she flashed to kill Casshorn and she had no flash left, and then Declan flashed at Rose to save her," Jack said.

"Jack!" Rose snapped.

The woman's eyes widened. "Really?"

Jack nodded. "Grandma said Rose's mouth and her eyes were bleeding."

George dug his elbow into Jack's side. "Shut up."

"I have to know the whole story now," the woman said

"I'd rather not," Rose said.

"Please, I insist."

Twenty minutes and two walls later, she had the whole story, and Rose wasn't quite sure how she'd gotten it.

"You really intend to make him wait a month to marry you?" The woman laughed softly.

"I want him to be sure."

"Do you know how long the Duchess has been trying to marry him off? If she discovers he found a bride, you won't escape."

"I'm hoping to avoid the Duchess. I don't know anything about manners, haircuts, or proper clothes, and I hope to learn a bit before we meet." Rose hesitated. "Why would the Duchess care whether or not Declan is married? I mean, he's a courtesy earl. I know the Duke seems to rely on him and he's the Marshal, but I was hoping the Duchess wouldn't take an interest."

The woman stopped her roller. "Oh, dear."

"I'm sorry?"

"Declan has this annoying habit. He doesn't quite lie. Instead he allows people to arrive at the wrong conclusions and doesn't bother to correct them."

"You know him very well." Rose smiled.

"Dear, in Adrianglia, nobles—they are called peers here—peers carry several titles. A duke might also be an earl or a baron. An heir can assume the rank of his sire only when his sire retires or dies. Until then, if the heir has completed his service and passed his examinations, he assumes the next best title in his bloodline. Declan is a courtesy peer, because although he completed his service, his sire is still alive. He is the son of the Duke and Duchess of the Southern Provinces."

"Oh God." Rose dropped the roller.

"Look on the bright side: you don't have to worry about clothes, haircuts, or manners. If you marry Earl Camarine, you could prance into society in a potato sack and it would become the latest fashion."

"So Casshorn was his uncle?" Rose asked. Maybe she misunderstood . . .

"Indeed. And he always hated Declan and Maud, his sister. You see, the mother of the current Duchess was born in the Broken. That's why Declan can travel back and forth between the worlds. He is what you might call a mix. Casshorn never could stand the Duchess. Nobody quite knows why, and so he—"

Footsteps echoed in the hallway. Declan's voice called, "Mother?" He ducked into the doorway. "Mother, have you seen—"

He saw Rose and clamped his mouth shut.

"I've seen, and I approve!" the woman said brightly.

"Mother?" Rose stared at her.

The woman frowned. "I probably should have mentioned: that annoying habit of letting people come to the wrong conclusions and not correcting them? He got it from me."

Declan's face turned icy. "You just couldn't leave well enough alone."

"No, I couldn't. But I absolutely love her," the Duchess answered. "Don't worry about the one-month requirement— it will take me that long to organize the wedding."

Rose simply stared. An older version of Declan appeared in the doorway. "We've misplaced the bride . . . Oh, here you are." He shouldered his way into the room.

An even older man followed. Gaunt and dressed in dark purple, he saw Rose and said, "Why, she is lovely." He glanced at the boys. "Which of you is the necromancer?"

A young female voice yelled at the door, "Let me into the room! I'm his sister, damn it!"

Rose backed away, pressing against the freshly painted wall. They were too big, too loud, too full of magic. Jack hissed.

Declan stepped forward, pushed the double doors open, took her hand, and pulled her through onto a wide balcony.

"Did you see that?" the Duchess yelled. "He rescued her from us. This wedding is on!"

"Sorry. They're just excited," Declan told her, leading her to the end of the balcony.

"You lied to me again."

"No, I just didn't tell you the whole truth."

She shook her head. "A duke'?"

"Not for another twenty years or so."

"God, your mother probably thinks I'm an idiot."

"She likes you. She likes the kids, too. Rose, I'm still me. Does it really matter if I'm a duke or not? If I didn't have a title, you would've married me already. Forget the castle. Forget my family."

One of the older men leaned out of the doors. "I just want to see the triple arch," he called. "Then I'll leave you two alone!"

"I love you. Marry me," Declan said.

His eyes were green like grass blades.

She put her arms around his neck and kissed him as the triple arch of her flash spun about them. In the doorway, the older man swore.

Declan grinned at her. She grinned back.

"Say yes," he said.

"Yes," she said. "But not before the month is over."

Read on for an exciting excerpt from
the Kate Daniels novel

MAGIC BLEEDS

by Ilona Andrews

Available now
from Ace Books!

NO matter how carefully I patted the chopped apples into place, the top crust of my apple pie always looked like I'd tried to bury a dismembered body under it. My pies turned out ugly, but they tasted good. This particular pie was rapidly losing the last of its heat.

I surveyed the spread in my kitchen. Venison steaks, marinated in beer, lightly seasoned, sitting in a pan ready to be popped into the oven. I'd saved them for last—they wouldn't take but ten minutes under the broiler. Homemade rolls, now cold. Corn on the cob, also cold. Baked potatoes, yep, very cold. I'd added some sautéed mushrooms and a salad just in case what I had wasn't enough. The butter on the mushrooms was doing its best to congeal into a solid state. At least the salad was supposed to be cold.

I plucked a creased note from the table. Eight weeks ago, Curran, the Beast Lord of Atlanta, the lord and master of fifteen hundred shapeshifters, and my personal psycho, had sat in the kitchen of my apartment in Atlanta and written out a menu on this piece of paper. I'd lost a bet to him, and according to the terms of our wager, I owed him one naked dinner. He'd added a disclaimer explaining that he'd settle for my wearing a bra and panties, since he wasn't a complete beast—an assertion very open to debate.

He'd set a date, November 15, which was today. I knew this because I had checked the calendar three times already. I'd called him that evening and set the place, my house near Savannah, and the time, five p.m. It was eight thirty now.

Food—check. My most flattering set of bra and panties—check. *Makeup*—check. Curran—blank. I drew my finger along the pale blade of my saber, feeling the cold metal under my skin. Where exactly was His Majesty?

Did he get cold feet? Mr. "You'll sleep with me and say please before and thank you after"?

He'd chased a flying palace through an enchanted jungle and carved his way through dozens of rakshasa demons to save me. Dinner was a huge deal to shapeshifters. They never took food for granted, but making a dinner for someone you were romantically interested in took a simple meal to a whole new level. When a shapeshifter made you dinner, either he was pledging to take care of you or he was trying to get into your pants. Most of the time, both. Curran had fed me soup once, when I was half-dead, and the fact that I had eaten it, even without knowing what that meant, amused him to no end. He wouldn't miss this dinner.

Something must've held him up.

I picked up the phone. Then again, he enjoyed screwing with me. I wouldn't put it past him to hide outside in the bushes, watching me squirm. Curran treated women like wonderful toys: he wined them, dined them, took care of their problems, and once they grew completely dependent on him, he became bored. Maybe whatever I perceived to be between us was only in my head. He'd realized he won and had lost interest. Calling him would just give him an opportunity to gloat.

I hung up the phone and looked at my pie some more.

If you opened a dictionary and looked up "control freak," you'd find Curran's picture. He ruled with steel claws, and when he said, "Jump," there was hell to pay if you didn't start hopping. Curran and I mixed like bleach and vinegar—the moment we made contact, everyone wanted to be somewhere else. He infuriated me, and I drove him out of his skin. Even if he wasn't truly interested, he wouldn't miss a chance to see me present this dinner in my underwear. His ego was too big. Something must have happened.

Eight forty-four. Curran served as the Pack's first and last line of defense. Any hint of a significant threat, and he'd be out there, roaring and ripping bodies in half. He could be hurt.

The thought stopped me cold. It would take a bloody army to bring down Curran. Of the fifteen hundred homicidal mani-

acs under his command, he was the toughest and most dangerous sonovabitch. If something did happen, it had to be bad. He
would've called if he'd been delayed by something minor.

Eight forty-nine.

Screw pride. I took the phone, cleared my throat, and di-
aled the Keep, the Pack's stronghold on the outskirts of Atlanta. Just keep it professional. Less pathetic that way.

"You've reached the Pack. What do you want?" a female
voice said into the phone.

Friendly people, the shapeshifters. "This is Agent Daniels.
Can I speak to Curran, please?"

"He isn't taking calls right now. Do you want to leave a
message?"

"Is he in the Keep?"

"Yes, he is."

A heavy rock materialized in my chest and made it hard
to breathe.

"Message?" the female shapeshifter prompted.

"Just tell him I called, please. As soon as possible."

"Is this urgent?"

Fuck it. "Yes. Yes, it is."

"Hold on."

Silence reigned. Moments dripped by, slowly, stretching
thinner and thinner . . .

"He says he's too busy to talk to you right now. In the fu
ture, please direct all your concerns to Jim, our security
chief. His number is—"

I heard my voice, oddly flat. "I have the number. Thanks."

"Anytime."

I lowered the phone into the cradle very carefully. A tiny
sound popped in my ears, and I had the absurd idea that it
was my heart forming hairline cracks.

He stood me up.

He stood me up. I cooked a huge meal. I sat by the phone
for the last four hours. I put on makeup, my second time in
the past year. I bought a box of condoms. Just in case.

I love you, Kate. I'll always come for you, Kate.

You sonovabitch. Didn't even have the balls to speak to me.

I surged off the chair. If he was going to dump me after all
that shit, I'd force him to do it in person.

It took me less than a minute to get dressed and load my wrist guards with silver needles. My saber, Slayer, had enough silver in it to hurt even Curran, and right now I very much wanted to hurt him. I stalked through the house looking for my boots in a fury-steeped daze, found them in the bathroom of all places, and sat down on the floor to put them on. I pulled the left boot on, tapped my heel into place, and stopped.

Suppose I did get to the Keep. And then what? If he decided he didn't want to see me, I'd have to cut my way through his people to get to him. No matter how much it hurt, I couldn't do that. Curran knew me well enough to recognize that and use it against me. A vision of me sitting in the lobby of the Keep for hours popped into my head. Hell no.

If the asshole did condescend to make an appearance, what would I say? *How dare you dump me before the relationship even started*? *I've traveled six hours to tell you how much I hate you because you meant that much to me*? He'd laugh in my face, then I'd slice him to ribbons, and then he'd break my neck.

I forced myself to grope for reason in the fog of my rage. I worked for the Order of Knights of Merciful Aid, which together with the Paranormal Activity Division, or PAD, and the Military Supernatural Defense Unit, or MSDU, formed the law enforcement defense against magical hazmat of all kinds. I wasn't a knight, but I was a representative of the Order. Worse, I was the only representative of the Order with Friend of the Pack status, meaning that when I attempted to muscle my way into Pack-related issues, the shapeshifters didn't tear me apart right away. Any issues the Pack had with the law usually found their way to me.

The shapeshifters fell into two categories: Free People of the Code, who maintained strict control over Lyc-V, the virus raging in their bodies; and loups, who surrendered to it. Loups murdered indiscriminately, bouncing from atrocity to atrocity until someone did the world a favor and murdered their cannibalistic asses. The Atlanta PAD viewed each shapeshifter as a loup-in-waiting, and the Pack responded by ratcheting up their paranoia and mistrust of outsiders to new and dizzying heights. Their position with the authorities was precarious at best, saved from open hostility by their record of cooperation with the Order. If Curran and I got into it, our fight wouldn't be seen as a conflict between two individuals, but as the Beast Lord's assault on an Order representative. Nobody would believe that I was dumb enough to start it.

The shapeshifters' standing would plummet. I had only a few friends, but most of them grew fur and claws. I'd make their lives hell to soothe my hurt.

For once in my life, I had to do the responsible thing.

I pulled the boot off and threw it across the room. It thudded into the wood panel in the hallway.

For years, first my father and then my guardian, Greg, had warned me to stay away from human relationships. Friends and lovers only brought you trouble. My existence had a purpose, and that purpose and my blood left no room for anything else. I had ignored the warnings of the two dead men. It was time to suck it up and pay for my carelessness.

I'd believed him. He was supposed to be different, to be more. He'd made me hope for things I didn't think I'd ever get. When hope broke, it hurt. Mine was a very big, very desperate hope, and it hurt like a sonovabitch.

Magic flooded the world in a silent wave. The electric lamps blinked and died a quiet death, giving way to the blue radiance of the feylanterns on my walls. The enchanted air in the twisted glass tubes luminesced brighter and brighter until an eerie blue light filled the entire house. It was called post-Shift resonance: magic came in waves, negating technology, and then vanished as abruptly and unpredictably as it had appeared. Somewhere, gasoline engines failed and guns choked midbullet. The defensive spells around my house surged up, forming a dome over my roof and hammering home the point: I needed protection, and I had neglected it.

I forced myself up off the floor. I'd lived guarding myself against human interaction before. I'd do it again. I could shut myself off until it stopped hurting, and when I encountered the Beast Lord, as my job frequently required, the only thing he'd get from me would be painfully polite courtesy. I'd rather slit my throat than let him know what his stunt had cost me.

I marched into the kitchen, trashed the dinner, and strode out. I had a date with a heavy punching bag, and I had no trouble imagining Curran's face on it.

I rode through the streets of Atlanta, rocking with the hoof-beats of my favorite mule, Marigold, who didn't care for the birdcage attached to her saddle and really didn't care for the globs of lizard spit dripping from my jeans. The birdcage contained a fist-sized clump of gray fuzz, which I'd had a devil of a time catching and which might or might not have been a living dust bunny. The jeans contained about a half gallon of saliva deposited on me by a pair of Trimble County lizards, which I'd managed to chase back into their enclosure in the Atlanta Center for Mythological Research. I was four-teen hours and thirteen minutes into my shift, I hadn't eaten since that morning, and I wanted a doughnut.

Three weeks had passed since Curran had stood me up. For the first week, I was so angry I couldn't see straight. The anger had died down now, but the dense, heavy stone remained in my chest, weighing me down. Strangely, dough-nuts helped. Especially ones drizzled with chocolate. As expensive as chocolate was in our day and age, I couldn't afford a chocolate bar, but the drizzle of chocolate syrup on the doughnuts did the job just fine.

"Hello, dear."

After almost a year of working for the Order, hearing Maxine's voice in my head no longer made me jump. "Hello, Maxine."

She called everyone "dear," including Richter, a new addi-tion to the Atlanta chapter who was as psychotic as a knight of the Order could get without being stripped of his knight-hood. Her "dear"s fooled no one. I'd rather run ten miles with a rucksack full of rocks than face a chewing-out from Maxine. Perhaps it was the way she looked: tall, thin, ramrod

straight, with a halo of tightly curled silver hair and the man-
nerisms of a veteran middle school teacher who had seen it
all before and would not suffer fools gladly . . .

*"Richter is quite sane, dear. And is there any particular
reason you keep picturing a dragon with my hair on its head
and a chocolate doughnut in its mouth?"*

Maxine never read thoughts on purpose, but if you concentrated hard enough while "on call," she couldn't help but
pick up simple mental images.

I cleared my throat. "Sorry."

*"No problem. I always thought of myself as a Chinese
dragon, actually. We're out of doughnuts, but I have cookies."*

Mmm, cookies. "What do I have to do for a cookie?"

*"I know your shift is done, but I have an emergency peti-
tion and nobody to handle it."*

Argh. "What's the petition?"

"Someone attacked the Steel Horse."

"The Steel Horse? The border bar?"

"Yes."

Post-Shift Atlanta was ruled by factions, each with its
own territory. Of all the factions in Atlanta, the People and
the Pack were the largest and the two I really wanted to
avoid. The Steel Horse sat right on the invisible border between their territories. A neutral spot, it catered to both the
People and the shapeshifters, as long as they could keep it
civil. For the most part, they did.

"Kate?" Maxine prompted.

"Do you have any details?"

*"Someone started a fight and departed. They have some-
thing cornered in the cellar, and they're afraid to let it out.
They're hysterical. At least one fatality."*

A bar full of hysterical necromancers and shapeshifters.
Why me?

Because it was my job. Anything Pack related was my job.
And I'd be damned if I let that arrogant bastard keep me
from doing it.

"Will you take it?"

"What kind of cookies?"

*"Chocolate chip with bits of walnuts in them. I'll even
give you two."*

I sighed and turned Marigold to the west. "I'll be there in twenty."

The mule chugged through the night-drenched streets. The Pack members drank little. Staying human required iron discipline, and the shapeshifters avoided substances that altered their grip on reality. A glass of wine with dinner or a beer after work was pretty much their limit.

The People also drank little, mostly because of the presence of shapeshifters. A bizarre hybrid of a cult, a corporation, and a research institute, they concerned themselves with the study of the undead, primarily vampires. Vampirus Immortuus, the pathogen responsible for vampirism, eradicated all traces of ego from its victims, turning them into bloodlust-crazed monsters and leaving their minds nice and blank. Masters of the Dead, the People's premier necromancers, took advantage of this occurrence by navigating vampires by riding their minds and controlling their every move.

Masters of the Dead weren't brawlers. Well-educated, lavishly compensated intellectuals, they were ruthless and opportunistic. Masters of the Dead wouldn't be visiting the Steel Horse either. Too lowbrow. The Steel Horse catered to the journeymen, navigators in training, and since the Red Stalker murders, the People had tightened their grip on their personnel. A couple of drunk and disorderlies, and your study of the undead would come to an untimely end. The journeymen still got drunk—most were too young and made too much money for their own good—but they didn't do it where they'd get caught and they definitely didn't do it with shapeshifters watching.

The People were led by a mysterious figure known as Roland. To most people, he was a myth. To me, he was a target. I had the unique misfortune of being the only person on the planet who could call him Father. He knew I existed—he murdered my mother because of it—but he didn't know who I was. When he found out, he'd move Heaven and Earth to murder me. That's why I'd spent my entire life hiding and training to kill him. I wasn't strong enough to fight him. Not yet. Contact with the People meant the risk of discovery by Roland, and so I avoided them like a plague.

Contact with the Pack meant the risk of contact with Curran, and that was infinitely worse.

If the Steel Horse had been attacked, I'd likely have to deal with both. Who the hell would attack the Steel Horse anyway? What was the thinking behind that? *Here is a bar full of psychotic killers who grow giant claws and people who pilot the undead for a living. I think I'll go wreck the place.* Sound reasoning there. Not.

I couldn't avoid the Pack forever just because their lord and master made my sword arm ache. Get in. Do my job. Get out. Simple enough.

THE Steel Horse occupied an ugly bunker of a building: squat, brick, and reinforced with steel bars over the windows and a metal door about two and a quarter inches thick. I knew how thick the door was because Marigold had just trotted past it. Someone had ripped the door off its hinges and tossed it across the street.

Between the door and the entrance stretched potholed asphalt covered with random patches of blood, liquor, and broken glass, and a few moaning bodies in various stages of inebriation and battle damage.

Damn, I'd missed all the fun.

A clump of tough guys stood by the tavern's doorway. They didn't exactly look hysterical, since the term was conveniently absent from their vocabulary, but the way they gripped makeshift weapons of broken furniture made one want to approach them slowly, speaking in soothing tones. Judging by the battle scene, they had just gotten beat up in their own bar. You can never lose a fight in your own bar, because if you do, it's not your bar anymore.

I slowed my mule to a walk. The temperature had plummeted in the past week, and the night was bitterly, unseasonably cold. The wind cut at my face. Faint clouds of breath fluttered from the guys at the bar. A couple of the larger guys sported some hardware: a big, rough-hewn man on the right carried a mace, and his pal on the left wielded a machete. Bouncers. Only bouncers would be allowed to have real weapons in the bar.

I scanned the crowd for telltale glowing eyes. Nothing. Just the normal human irises. If there had been shapeshifters in the bar tonight, they'd either cleared off or kept their human skins securely on. I didn't sense any vampires nearby either. No familiar faces in the crowd. The journeymen must've taken off, too. Something bad went down, and nobody wanted to be tarred by it. And now it was all mine. Oh, goodie.

Marigold carried me past the human wreckage and to the doorway. I pulled out the clear-plastic wallet I carried on a cord around my neck, and held it up so they could see the small rectangle of the Order ID.

"Kate Daniels. I work for the Order. Where is the owner?"

A tall man stepped from the inside of the bar and leveled a crossbow at me. It was a decent modern recurve crossbow, with close to two hundred pounds of draw weight. It came equipped with a fiber-optic sight and a scope. I doubted he'd need either to hit me at ten feet. At this distance the bolt wouldn't just penetrate; it would go through me, taking my guts for a ride on its fletch.

Of course, at this distance I might kill him before he got off a shot.

The man fixed me with grim eyes. Middle-aged and thin, he looked as if he'd spent too much time outdoors doing hard labor and it had melted all the flesh off his bones, leaving only leathery skin, gunpowder, and gristle. A short dark beard hugged his jaw. He nodded to the smaller bouncer. "Vik, check the ID."

Vik sauntered over and looked at my wallet. "It says what she said it did."

I was too tired for this. "You're looking at the wrong thing." I took the card out of the wallet and offered it to him. "See the square in the bottom left corner?"

His gaze flicked to the square of enchanted silver.

"Put your thumb over it and say, 'ID.'"

Vik hesitated, glanced at his boss, and touched the square. "ID."

A burst of light punched his thumb, and the square turned black.

"The card knows you're not its owner. No matter how

many of you mess with it, it will stay black until I touch it." I placed my finger over the silver. "ID."

The black vanished, revealing the pale surface.

"That's how you tell a real Order agent from a fake one." I dismounted and tied Marigold to the rail. "Now, where is the corpse?"

The bar owner introduced himself as Cash. Cash didn't strike me as the trusting kind, but at least he kept his crossbow pointed at the ground as he led me behind the building and to the left. Since his choice of Order representatives was limited to me and Marigold, he decided to take his chances with me. Always nice to be judged more competent than a mule.

The crowd of onlookers tagged along as we circled the building. I could've done without an audience, but I didn't feel like arguing. I'd wasted enough time playing magic tricks with my ID.

"We run a tight ship here," Cash said. "Quiet. Our regulars don't want trouble."

The night wind flung the sour stench of decomposing vomit in my face, and a touch of an entirely different scent, syrupy thick, harsh, and cloying. Not good. There was no reason for the body to smell yet. "Tell me what happened."

"A man started trouble with Joshua. Joshua lost," Cash said.

He'd missed his calling. He should've been a saga poet.

We reached the back of the building and stopped. A huge, ragged hole gaped in the side of the bar where someone had busted out through the wall. Bricks lay scattered across the asphalt. Whoever the creature was, he could punch through solid walls like a wrecking ball.

"Did one of your shapeshifter regulars do that?"

"No. They all cleared off once the fight started."

"What about the People's journeymen?"

"Didn't have any tonight." Cash shook his head. "They usually come on Thursdays. We're here."

Cash pointed to the left, where the ground sloped down to a parking lot punctuated by a utility pole in its center. Joshua hung on the pole, pinned by a crowbar thrust through his open mouth. Parts of him were covered by tanned leather and jeans. Everything uncovered no longer looked human. Hard bumps clustered on every inch of his exposed skin, dark red and interrupted by lesions and wet, gaping ulcers, as if the man had become a human barnacle. The crust of sores was so thick on his face I couldn't even distinguish his features, except for the milky eyes, opened wide and staring at the sky.

My stomach sank. All traces of fatigue fled, burned in a flood of adrenaline.

"Did he look like that before the fight started?" *Please say yes.*

"No," Cash said. "It happened after."

A cluster of bumps over what might have been Joshua's nose shifted, bulged outward, and fell, giving space to a new ulcer. The fallen piece of Joshua rolled on the asphalt and stopped. The pavement around it sprouted a narrow ring of flesh-colored fuzz. The same fuzz coated the pole below and slightly above the body. I concentrated on the lower edge of the fuzz line and saw it creep very slowly down the wood.

Fuck.

I kept my voice low. "Did anybody touch the body?"

Cash shook his head. "No."

"Anybody go near it?"

"No."

I looked into his eyes. "I need you to get everyone back into the bar and keep them there. Nobody leaves."

"Why?" he asked.

I had to level with him, or he wouldn't work with me. "Joshua's diseased."

"He's dead."

"His body's dead, but the disease is alive and magic. It's growing. It's possible that everyone's infected."

Cash became very still. His eyes widened, and he glanced through the hole and into the bar. I followed his gaze. A dark-haired woman, slight and bird-boned, wiped up the spills on the counter, sliding broken glass into a wastebasket with her rag. I looked back at Cash and saw fear.

I kept my voice quiet. "If you want her to live, you have to herd everyone back into the bar and keep them from leaving. Tie them up if you have to, because if they take off, we'll have an epidemic. Once the people are secure, call Biohazard. Tell them Kate Daniels says we have a Mary. Give them the address. I know it's hard, but you have to be calm. Don't panic."

"What will you do?"

"I'll try to contain it. I'll need salt, as much as you've got. Wood, kerosene, alcohol, whatever you have that might burn. I have to build a flame barrier. You've got pool tables?"

He stared at me, uncomprehending.

"Do you have pool tables, Cash?" I asked again.

"Yes."

I dropped my cloak on the slope. "Please bring me your pool chalk. All of it."

He swallowed. If he panicked, the crowd would scatter and infect half the city.

"I need your help. Work with me."

Cash walked away from me and spoke to the bouncers. "Alright," the bigger bouncer bellowed. "Everybody back into the bar. One round on the house."

The crowd headed into the bar through the hole in the wall. One man hesitated. The bouncers moved in on him. "Into the bar," Vik said.

The guy thrust his chin into the air. "Fuck off."

Vik sank a quick, hard punch into his gut. The man folded in half, and the bigger bouncer slung him over his shoulder and headed back into the Steel Horse.

Two minutes later, I dumped a three-inch-wide ring of salt around the pole. Cash emerged from the hole in the tavern carrying some broken crates, followed by the dark-haired woman with a large box. Cash dropped the crates. The woman handed me the box, filled with blue squares of pool chalk, and caught a glimpse of Joshua on the pole. The blood drained from her face.

"Did you call Biohazard?" I asked.

"Phone's out," Cash said softly.

Can something go right for me today?

"Does that change things?" Cash asked.

It changed a short-term fix into a long-term defense. "I'll just have to work harder to keep it put."

We didn't speak as I arranged the wood into a circle around the pole. The fire wouldn't hold it indefinitely, but it would buy me some time.

The flesh-colored fuzz tested the salt and found it delicious. Figured. I didn't feel any different, and I was closest to the body, so I'd be the first one to go. A comforting thought.

Cash had brought down some bottles, and I dumped their contents onto the crates, soaking the wood in hard liquor and kerosene. One flick of a match, and the wooden ring flared into flames.

"Is that it?" Cash asked.

"No. The fire will delay it, but not for long."

The two of them looked as though they were at a funeral.

"It will be okay." *Kate Daniels, agent of the Order. We take care of your magic problems, and when we can't, we lie through our teeth.* "It will all turn out. You two go inside now. Keep the peace and keep trying the phone."

The woman brushed Cash's sleeve with her fingers. He pivoted to her, patted her hand, and together they went back into the tavern.

The fuzz crawled halfway across the salt. I began to chant, going through the roster of purifying incantations. Magic built around me slowly, like cotton candy winding on the spire of my body and flowing outward, around the flame circle.

The fuzz reached the fire. The first flesh-colored tendrils licked the boards and melted into black goo with a weak hiss. The flames popped with the sickening stench of burning fat. *That's right, you sonovabitch. Stay the hell behind my fire.* Now I just had to keep it still until I finished the first ward circle.

Chanting, I grabbed the pool chalk and drew the first glyph.